Operation Bluebird

<u>**1:**</u>

<u>**04 January 2018**</u>

Nobody knew.

\-

"Listen to me," David commanded. "Telling them now won't do anyone any good; it'll just get us both in trouble."

"But why?" she questioned desperately. "This is all my fault, not yours."

"Because I promised I'd look after you," he answered. "And because if you deny it enough you might forget it was ever true."

"It isn't true," she insisted.

He smiled at her with a bittersweet fondness. "Don't bullshit."

\-

Carrie opened her eyes. The room was bright – too bright. It hurt her head. It hurt her whole body. She ached all over and felt physically sick. Something was incredibly wrong, but she couldn't remember what it was. She couldn't remember much at all. She had been in a room – a different room – with David Watts and Wendy Pullman. He meant a lot to her. There were others who did too, but she couldn't see their faces. Something told her she wanted red wine.

"Carolyn?" a voice sounded beside her. She knew that voice well. "Carrie?"

"Fiona?"

She turned her head to see her sister sitting in a chair at her bedside. That was right; she had a sister. She looked older than she had the last time she saw her. The skin under her eyes was dark as if she hadn't slept, her hair pulled back into a rough ponytail. She wore a loose, plain shirt and there was no make-up on her face. She didn't look much like Fiona.

"I'm here," the older woman took her hand. "Mum and Dad are on their way; they caught the first flight they could."

Yes, she recalled, their parents lived in Australia. She had parents. That wasn't the sort of thing a person should forget, even for a moment.

"Fi," she squinted against the brightness. "Have you got any wine? My head hurts."

"You can't have that anymore," Fiona shuffled uncomfortably.

"Right," Carrie shut her eyes again. The light was making her want to heave.

They sat in awkward silence for a while.

"Carrie," Fiona said eventually. "Where have you been?"

Carrie tried to remember.

"What happened to you?" she continued. "All I know is you went undercover, then I'm getting a call from Wendy…Palmer or something, saying you posted something weird on your Instagram and they were fishing you from the Thames. I didn't know you even had an Instagram."

"Wendy Pullman," she corrected her.

Wendy Pullman was important. But the case was over. Wendy Pullman had resigned the day after – the day after what? She remembered but she didn't. There was light streaming through the window. There was blood on the carpet. She remembered screaming and running and the feeling that there was nothing left. She just ran and ran and ran and then there was blackness. There was blackness for a very long time.

"Yes, Pullman, that's it," Fiona swallowed hard. "What happened? You disappeared for years, then you turn up pumped full of drugs in a river."

Operation Bluebird happened. David had told her not to tell anyone, but she couldn't remember what it was she was supposed to not be telling. She could see his lips moving but couldn't hear the sound, like she was only half there.

"Did you do that?" Fiona sniffed. That was strange; Fiona didn't cry. "Did someone do it to you? Why didn't you ever call me… if you were in trouble-"

"Are you sure there's no wine?" Carrie groaned. She felt like death.

"There's no wine," Fiona said firmly, wiping her eyes. "Carrie, can you please tell me what's going on? Wendy wouldn't say a thing."

"I can't remember," she told her, almost honestly.

What she could remember didn't make any sense. It was like a highly confidential case file with most of the information blotted out. It was like a movie she had only half been paying attention to while she had her nose down in her work – a movie where herself and David Watts were the stars. She saw the main occurrences as played out on a screen; glitz and glam and somebody else's emotions that you see but don't feel. They had been good cops – at least that was what Brian Hole had said. Her information had saved people's lives.

But David had done something – or was it her? She had done something and he had told her never to tell. She was the only one who knew, and even she saw it through a veil, from a great distance away.

It hurt.

She didn't want to think about Operation Bluebird.

2: Welcome to Paradise

It was a chilly morning in early May when Cara Parry first stepped through the gilded doors of Paradise Casino. Her black Doc Martens trod apprehensively from the polished stone threshold onto a rich red carpet that ran through the centre of a parqueted lobby. She shrank beneath the high embellished ceiling, well aware that she did not belong here. The tinted glass doors were decorated in gold, a neatly suited porter positioned to hold them for anybody arriving or leaving. They opened up into an even grander hall that centred around golden bannistered stairs to the first floor, behind which lay the entrance to the main casino. The place oozed class and decadence; a Dorian Gray of a building that hid its twisted heart behind a glamorous façade.

She faltered, unsure what to do with herself. If only she had worn something a little more sophisticated than a short skirt over leggings and boots. They were new, like her black hair dye, and she had been sort of proud of herself for splashing out on something trendy. Now they felt very cheap and common beneath the light of the magnificent chandelier. She zipped her jacket up higher, making absolutely certain that nobody could tell there was a sporty crop-top beneath it. It had seemed sensible for a dance audition. Not so much for the lobby of one of the swankiest establishments in London.

She took a deep breath. She could do this. It was just dancing and she loved dancing. As soon as the music started and she got her legs around a pole she would forget all about her surroundings, who she was auditioning for and everything that was hanging on her success.

She just had to get there first. She could do this. She was Cara Parry and Cara Parry had no reason to be nervous. She tucked her hair behind her ears and approached the front desk.

"Can I help you?" a woman with a bob and a smart black uniform greeted her.

"Yes," she pulled the printed interview confirmation and her proof of ID from her bag. "Yes please. I'm here for a dance audition with Robert Bricklee."

"Lovely," the concierge smiled, reviewed the paper and her passport, then extended a hand. "Welcome to Paradise. I'm Bea; pleased to meet you."

"Cara," she shook her hand. "You too."

"Right," Bea picked up a telephone. "Just one second, I'll give him a call."

She tapped in a number and held it to her ear, calling through a partially opened door behind the desk as the dial tone rang: "Jerome! Would you mind asking Patty to cover the desk for me please?"

Cara stepped back politely and continued to admire the décor. She had never been anywhere so posh in her life.

"Okay," the concierge put down the phone and picked up a key card. "Follow me."

She left the front desk to somebody who Cara assumed was Patty and led her past the stairs, through doors with frosted glass windows.

"Usually you would go round the back; there's a courtyard that leads straight to the changing rooms," Bea explained. "But I'll take you this way today so you can see a bit of the casino. Meeting rooms and executive floors can be accessed directly from the lobby, but for everything else we send customers through the slots. You'd be surprised how much revenue comes from simple temptation."

Cara nodded and made a noise of agreement. They walked along what seemed like a never-ending path between row upon row of slot machines and other mechanical games. Lights flashed and buttons buzzed and beeped, creating the illusion of a gambler's metropolis. Scarlet uniformed waiters and waitresses deftly navigated the model streets, delivering snacks and beverages to red eyed punters unwilling to leave their stations. It was all glamour and shine that got into a person's mind like alcohol, turning everything else on its head and making the irrational seem flawless. She could see how people could be trapped here forever.

"Tables are just ahead," her guide pointed forwards as they reached a crossroad in the scarlet carpet. "But the show hall's this way. This is where the real fun happens." She flashed a friendly smile. "Now, I don't want you to worry but I should warn you that it's not just Brick and Lisa in there; apparently the boss has some free time."

"The boss?" Cara's stomach did a somersault. "You mean Mr Park?"

"Mr Yoonho Park," Bea clarified. "There are quite a few Mr Parks, but it's Yoonho who runs Paradise."

Well, Yoonho was slightly less intimidating than *the* Mr Park, as a gangster's son is slightly less intimidating than the gangster himself. But only slightly. Yoonho Park was the whole reason she was here: to impress, to gain his confidence and ultimately to get her brother a job with the biggest crime family in London. She hadn't been expecting to meet him before she was even hired.

"Don't worry," the concierge noticed the apprehension on her face. "He's a good guy. Just dance like you would for anyone else."

She gulped.

"Good luck."

<u>13 May 2012</u>

"Lucy," Carrie held out a hand to the trembling teenager.

She felt the sweat sticking to her shirt – she was shaking almost as much as the girl.

"Look at me. You're safe now."

She extended her hand a little further. Lucy drew back, teetering at the edge of the building.

"No, no, no!"

Carrie withdrew, holding up her palms to show she wouldn't touch her without consent.

"You don't need to do that. We've got you now. We'll hide you, give you a new identity; you'll be able to live a normal life."

Lucy gave her a hopeless look. She was only fifteen, but her eyes carried the weight of someone five times her age.

"They'll get me," she choked.

"No they won't. I've seen it before; witness protection is nothing like you see on TV," Carrie lied. She was a rookie; she had never been involved in a case that required witness protection.

Lucy shook her head. "They'll find me. Everyone's scared of them – all the bosses. We're not supposed to know they exist, but I heard Big Mo talking and now they're gonna get me!"

"Who's they?" Carrie asked softly.

"The Parks," Lucy whispered. "You can nick Big Mo, but you'll never get them."

It had been Carrie herself who had gained the girl's trust and convinced her to give evidence against the prostitution ring run by the man known as Big Mo. She had come to rely on the young police constable almost as a big sister figure, despite

Carrie being totally unqualified for the job. And now she was terrified enough to want to end her own life. Carrie had initially seen their connection as a personal success. Now it felt more like the biggest mistake of her short career.

She smiled at her with a look of determined optimism; aware that it was up to her to save a teenager but afraid she wasn't up to the task.

"We'll get them," she promised. "I'll make sure of it. And in the meantime, you can have a new start. We can relocate you wherever you like, get you out of London and away from all this. You won't be Lucy Flynn anymore; you'll have no criminal record, you can finish your GCSEs, go to college or uni or get a job in a nice café or something. You have so many options, you just have to come downstairs."

"Where would I live?" Lucy asked sceptically, but shifted slightly away from the edge. "I'm fifteen. I can't rent."

"We'll sort that," Carrie promised. "We'll find you a lovely family."

Lucy's expression darkened. "That's what the social workers said. Three times."

Shit. Carrie flinched. Maybe she should have saved that part for later.

"This isn't the standard foster system," she assured her, hoping like hell that was true. "They'll be properly vetted by the police force. No domestic problems, no money issues, no connections down here."

"I do wanna be a florist," Lucy said quietly, the bittersweet shadow of a dream passing across her tear-stained face. "I don't wanna fucking die."

She hugged her knees and buried her head between them. Carrie shuffled forward cautiously and the girl let her put an arm around her, her head moving to press into Carrie's chest.

"You don't have to die," she kissed her forehead. She wasn't entirely sure she was allowed to do that, but it felt right. "You go to school, finish your exams, get whatever training florists need. You don't have to do any of this ever again."

Lucy smiled weakly and wiped her eyes. "And Big Mo? And the Parks?"

"They will never find you."

-

Carrie was absolutely exhausted – both emotionally from talking Lucy back to the ground and physically from having been up all night researching – but she refused her colleagues' kind suggestions that she take the rest of the day off. She had been doing her job just like anybody else and she couldn't let personal fatigue have a negative impact on her work. She had reports to write and wanted as much out of the way today as possible, so she could be fresh and ready for whatever fell onto her desk tomorrow.

"Carrie?"

She turned to see her superior standing behind her with a concerned expression on her face.

"Oh, hi Rosemary," she greeted her. "Is everything okay?"

"What are you doing here?" she asked.

Not Rosemary too. Carrie smiled sheepishly. "I just want to get this written up."

Rosemary frowned. "Well I've just had your sister on the phone. Check your voicemail, and check your annual leave roster."

"Shit," Carrie's stomach plummeted. "Fiona's wedding."

She hurriedly scraped her things together and rammed them into her bag, almost forgetting her car keys on her way out the door. She would have to change when she got there. She punched in her sister's number as she entered the motorway and switched her phone to speaker.

"Fiona?"

"Carolyn."

She flinched at her sister's tone.

"I am so sorry," Carrie squirmed. "I had to-"

"One day," her sister interrupted. "You had to pretend to be happy for me for one day."

"What?" Carrie faltered. "No, this isn't about Mark. It was work, there-"

"It's always work," Fiona snapped. "Ever since school. Who needs a bloody family? I'm Carolyn Hart, I have to study, I have to work overtime, I have to miss my sister's bloody wedding!"

"No, Fi, it's not like that!" Carrie pleaded.

"Mum and Dad came all the way from Australia – *Australia*!" her sister continued. "And you can't make it from London? You were meant to be here last night!"

"Something came up," she said, guilt tugging painfully at her insides. That was what she got for ignoring all but work calls. "I'm on the way now; I won't be long."

"I'm getting married in half an hour!" Carrie could hear the sobs catching in her throat. "And you've ruined it! Nothing is more important than that! You know what, don't bother. You don't like Mark, you don't like me, just go home. I don't want to see you, just don't bother."

"Fiona," she tried to explain. "I just stopped a girl from killing herself."

"I don't care." The line went dead.

Carrie pulled a little too sharply into the next layby and dropped her head onto the steering wheel. She couldn't even tell if she had messed up. She had a special rapport with Lucy and she wasn't sure if anybody else would have been able to talk her down. But she had crossed a line with Fiona that she doubted could ever be un-crossed. Her sister had always made known her irritation at Carrie's prioritisation of work, not understanding the amount of effort it took to even half measure up to their parents' golden child, or the fact that police work often affected innocent people's lives a lot more than dinner parties where women with superiority complexes sold organic soap and Mark droned on about nonsense. But this was her wedding.

Carrie groaned and hit the wheel. She had always tried her best to be a practical person rather than an emotional one and she rarely had the energy to cry, but this was one of those times where she came close.

Her phone bleeped and a text message illuminated the screen. She was tempted to ignore it.

Neil: *"Call me when you're not driving."*

She sighed, tucked her hair back behind her ear and cleared her head.

"Hello?" she picked up the phone.

"Caz?" there was something else hidden behind the surprise in her colleague's voice. "That was quick – aren't you on the M25?"

"What's up?" she got straight to the point. Neil wasn't bad but she didn't need his flirting right now.

"I'm really sorry," he hesitated. "Lucy's dead."

Carrie cried.

10 January 2014

The TV flashed in the break room, barking an American documentary through the evening's silence. DC Carolyn Hart tapped her foot in irritation as her train of thought was interrupted again and again. Even coffee and biscuits weren't helping.

"Neil?" she spoke as politely as she could.

DS Neil Gammon was also supposed to be working – in fact he was supposed to be the one supervising her – but the folder on his lap wasn't even open.

"I think there's more we could get from Roget's ex. If you let me go with you to interview-"

"Did you know," he interrupted. "At least six death row inmates killed themselves last year?"

"That's sad," she took another glug of coffee and continued to underline things. "N-"

"It is though, isn't it," Neil agreed. "America's meant to be 'leader of the free world' but their justice system is fucked."

"Yeah," Carrie looked up momentarily.

She wasn't assertive enough to tell him straight-up that he needed to turn off the TV and let her focus, as much as she would like to. Neil was one of those irritating people who could concentrate on nothing then produce stellar results anyway, as if out of thin air. Sometimes it was easier to humour him so he could let it all out and let her get back to her job.

"When people are so scared of dying they kill themselves..."

"People don't kill themselves because they're scared of dying," Neil told her. "Everyone dies eventually. They do it cos they're scared of the living beforehand. I had a friend once, diagnosed bipolar. Spent half the time bawling his eyes out in his bedroom, the other half singlehandedly keeping British Airways in business. The places he would turn up when he was manic..." He shook his head in fond nostalgia. "Then one day he decided everything was too good to last. He wasn't worried about dying; he was just too damn scared of the lows that came after the high."

"Oh," Carrie said awkwardly. "I'm sorry."

"Yeah, me too," Neil mused. "Makes no logical sense to you and me, but there you go. People are scared of living through all sorts of things."

"Yeah," she tucked her hair nervously behind her ear and returned her attention to her notes. She wasn't very good at talking about emotional things.

"You know, I really think this woman knows more," she ventured after a while. "There are three girls somewhere on the run from a trafficking gang; they must be scared as hell. We should get on-"

Neil sighed and flicked off the television. "You still think about Lucy Flynn, don't you."

"Not really," she pulled her hair out from behind her ear then put it back again. "Only if she's relevant to a case."

"You're such a bad liar," Neil gave her a sympathetic look.

She didn't want his sympathy, she wanted to do her job right. Of course she still thought about her – how could she not? – but it wasn't something she wanted to talk about. She was a teenager who had lost her life. She was a wedge between Carrie and her sister. She was also potentially the reason why Carrie's career wasn't going as well as she hoped it would. Lucy's death was a personal failing and her insistence on following up on the lead of "Park" rather than closing the case with the charging of Big Mo had fallen on deaf or disapproving ears. She was sure it was because of one or both of these things that she seemed to have been overlooked ever since, though of course she would never breach the subject with her superiors. All she could do was keep working her hardest and not let any inner feelings stop her.

"How much do you know about Paradise Casino?" Neil asked.

"Just a bit," Carrie replied.

That was also a lie. She had done extensive research into DSI Brian Hole's longest running investigation when she had tried to connect its subjects to Lucy, though the vast majority of files were classified. She had been a little disappointed that the Superintendent himself hadn't paid her any attention, but he was very important and already had enough people saying he was crazy to waste so much effort on that particular case. She supposed his reputation wasn't worth risking further for such a shaky link as a statement from a dead teenaged prostitute.

"Why?" she questioned.

"I heard the Super talking to Rosemary this morning," he continued. "Your name came up. Didn't you think the Parks had something to do with Lucy?"

"They didn't though," Carrie's brow furrowed. "That's what the investigation concluded. Why would they be talking about it now?"

"I dunno," he shrugged. "I didn't hear everything, but the Sup' definitely mentioned you. Rosemary seemed a bit pissed off to be honest, or stressed at least. Did you say anything recently, about Lucy?"

"No," Carrie shook her head. "Why would I? DSI Hole has tonnes of other important cases; he wouldn't be worrying about that now."

"Well I can't say for sure," Neil leaned back on his chair. "But Partridge reckons he wants you for something and Rosemary's worried about letting you go."

That was unlikely, but she couldn't help but feel a little flattered at the thought that DI Darren Partridge might think it were true. Despite the jokes about his unorthodox methods and unrelenting desire to bring down the man known as Mr Park, DSI Brian Hole was a highly respected detective. If she could somehow impress him, her career was made.

"Hey," Neil gave her a wink. "If you get some big old promotion, you have to let me take you out to celebrate."

"I think I'd be too busy with 'big old promotion' work," she pointed out.

"Workaholic," he tutted. "Alright then, let's get on with this."

<u>02 May 2014</u>

Bea the concierge opened another frosted glass door and let Cara into the show hall. It was just as huge as the casino demanded. A bar ran along one wall, within easy reach of tables and chairs dotted about the floor; enough for a decent sized audience but with ample space for dancers to move between them. Cara had seen halls like this before, but on a much smaller scale.

The centrepiece, of course, was the stage. It ran along the width of the room, a catwalk jutting out from the centre and finishing close to the bar, poles set out at intervals along it. It was around a table at the end of this runway that three people sat; a blonde woman with a strong tan, a burly bald man and Yoonho Park.

"Cara Parry?" the man, who she assumed was Robert Bricklee, spoke.

"Yes," she tipped her head nervously. "Hello."

"Thank you for coming," he stood to roughly shake her hand. "You can call me Brick; everyone does."

"Nice to meet you," Cara nodded.

"Lisa," the blonde woman followed suit. "Lovely to meet you too, doll."

"Yoonho," he held her hand a lot more smoothly than the others; firm but gentle.

She gulped a hurried "pleasure to meet you, Sir" and followed Brick's directions to the changing room. She removed her jacket, boots and leggings and pulled her pleaser heels from her bag, then stepped up and placed her hands around the cool metal of the pole.

"Whenever you're ready, hon," Lisa smiled kindly.

Cara nodded and the older woman started the music they had agreed on previously. It was just the tonic she needed. Her mind flew out of her body and let her muscles take control. This was no different to a university performance, amateur competition or private practise in the gym. It was just dancing and dancing was fun. When she twirled around a pole she was her own person and she didn't care who was watching. The casino was intimidating, but she *was* the casino. She was the pole and the stage and the room and anything she wanted to be, because her mind wasn't there to stop her.

She had a beam on her face as the choreography came to an end, finishing with a perfect martini. Jesus, she had missed this.

"Bravo!" Lisa clapped enthusiastically.

To her delight, Yoonho and Brick also looked pleased.

"You can dance, hon," the blonde woman congratulated her. "And…" she looked down at her notes. "You do a bit of Latin and ballroom too?"

"Not professionally," she clarified bashfully. "But yeah, practically all I do is dance."

"Sounds like a good life to me," Lisa approved.

It was the second part of the audition that worried her more. The place claimed to be a respectable establishment and the dances the real choreographed shows of beauty and talent that she had enjoyed at uni, but punters were punters and audience interaction was often encouraged. It was only natural that she should be tested for her aptitude at closer quarters and she had spent a long time successfully steeling herself. But she had been expecting Robert Bricklee to be her subject, not Yoonho Park.

The CEO seemed just as duplicitous as the casino itself. He gave off the air of a perfect businessman; dressed in a full suit and tie with hair combed neatly back from his face, which bore a confident but amiable smile. His mannerisms were open and charming, inviting people to like him in a way that still commanded respect. And then there was the covetous look in his eye and the shape beneath his trousers that told her this was all a charismatic, sickening front.

He was a 'gentleman', Cara reminded herself as she forced back her discomfort. He looked but never touched; that was his reputation. She was Cara Parry, she was dancing, and she did not need to be afraid. Perhaps it was even nice to be admired.

The man quietly appreciated her then sat back and let Brick do most of the talking, ensuring that his face displayed interest in what she was saying, like a perfectly pleasant employer. She answered a few questions about customer service and bar work (thanks Durham Student Union) and the usual interview content of competencies and where she saw herself in five years. Then Yoonho leaned forward.

"I hope you don't mind," he said. "But I did a bit of looking into you."

"Oh, that's fine," Cara replied quickly. "That seems sensible."

"Your brother works in a specific industry, I believe," Yoonho continued. "Don't worry; I'm not judging you. I was just wondering – did you know?"

"Everyone knows," her hand slipped up to play with the ends of her hair, but she stopped it.

She wished she had some sort of idea what he was getting at; Lisa was looking at him very strangely.

"He went to prison," she said. "He's out now though, but you probably already know that."

"Before then," he specified. "Did you know of his affairs?"

She hesitated, then nodded. "Well, he is my brother."

"Indeed," Yoonho smiled. "So I take it you can keep a secret? Nothing below board, of course, but I have high profile clients here who would rather not have their gambling habits or any business secrets spread across London. I'm sure you understand."

"I can keep a secret," Cara confirmed. "Above or below board."

"Excellent," he sat back in his chair. "Thank you very much, Cara. We'll be in touch."

Lisa winked and raised her fingers in an 'OK' sign.

Cara swapped her heels for boots once more and followed Bea from the hall, catching Lisa's voice as she exited: "Keeping secrets? Ex-con brother? I know you and that ain't about no gambling habits. You want her for top team."

She stepped back onto the street with a fire in her chest, pretending she really was stepping glamorously from a place she was part of. She could do this; she really could. Dancing for an audience was something she hadn't done in years and she hadn't felt this confident in just as long. She had expected to join as the lowest novice and have to put in a lot of hard work before Yoonho Park even noticed her existence, but there he was, noticing her already and even asking about Drew.

She took a look back at the grand entrance of Paradise Casino as she turned right for the bus stop. It loomed over her; ominous and magnificent. Like the countless customers who graced the slots and tables, this place would make her or it would break her – of that she was certain.

Neil gave Carrie a knowing smile as DCI Rosemary Vane approached her the day after their chat in the break room. Her chest tightened in anticipation.

"You seem to know what I'm about to talk to you about," her superior said with intrigue.

"Not really," Carrie replied nervously. "I just saw you talking to DSI Hole yesterday."

Neil mouthed a "thank you" for not dobbing him in. He and Darren Partridge were often in casual trouble for being the biggest gossips in the office.

"Well I can't blame you for being curious," Rosemary perched on the edge of her desk. "As a matter of fact, you're right; the Superintendent wants to see you. I'll let him give you the details, but I will say one thing: no pressure either way. If you want to stay here, we're delighted to have you and if you choose to accept his offer, it's with my blessing and a high recommendation."

"He wants me to transfer?" Carrie asked in surprise.

Rosemary put a hand on her shoulder. "He'll explain when you get there."

Neil had been right to suspect that Rosemary and DSI Hole's conversation had been about the Parks and the newest venture in his war on their patriarch, but in a way that neither he nor Carrie had expected:

Operation Bluebird.

"I'm going undercover?" she had to stop herself from gaping.

She stood in the Detective Superintendent's office with Hole himself and another man called DS David Watts. Brian Hole was a well-built but greying man in his fifties, wearing a sharp suit and a serious demeanour. David Watts was very casually handsome, with short blonde hair, mild stubble and a blue polo shirt. According to Hole's introduction, this man was already experienced in undercover work, having successfully completed an operation with a gang in Birmingham. He was also going to be her brother.

"It's not as scary as it sounds," he chuckled good-naturedly.

"I…" Carrie breathed, fixing that bit of hair that always fell out of her ponytail. "I'm honoured, Sir… sorry, I don't know what to say."

"No need to feel honoured," DSI Hole replied. "I expect hard work and results – God knows I've waited long enough. You were highly recommended by your Chief Inspector; I hope you won't let either of us down. That is, if you accept the role."

"I do," she nodded a little too enthusiastically, hugging the case file to her chest like it was her most treasured possession. It was an amazing, amazing opportunity and she wanted to claim it before he realised she was far too young and inexperienced.

"Perhaps you might want to review the file before you commit," the Superintendent looked amused. "But your eagerness is commendable."

"Yes," Carrie winced. She was making herself look like an idiot already. "Sorry."

"Not a problem," he assured her. "Anyway, as I was saying, I've had my eye on Mr Park for the best part of ten years, since before his wife disappeared in 2006. No matter what I've found, he's clean as a whistle – or so his lawyers have proven every time – but that man is the most rotten I've met in thirty-one years with the force.

"A little background: he claimed political asylum with his family in March '94, on the premise that he was fleeing for his life from North Korea after falling out with the regime. Whether or not that's true, I would put a lot of money on bribery being involved in his speedy acceptance; he had a substantial pile of cash for a refugee, political or not. It would also explain why the home office is so reluctant to re-review his application; that and the fact his lawyers have us by the balls for racism, defamation and police harassment. He's made generous donations to the Tory party, not to mention countless charities and good causes that juries and the public love him for, but his fingerprints are all over the London underworld. I just can't seem to prove it."

He sighed heavily.

"It's an investigation a lot of my bosses and colleagues would rather we forget entirely. But if he is who I know him to be – which he is – if we bring him down then the whole crime ecosystem comes toppling down with him. He's something worth chasing, whatever the means, which I believe you already have an inkling of."

Carrie nodded. "A prostitute once mentioned the name Park…"

"But it wasn't followed up on," he finished for her. "I'm sorry for that; we have to pick our battles carefully, and even then we lose. However," he spread his knuckles on the table. "We have an opportunity now that it would be stupid not to take. We've tried undercover agents and CIs before, but they never make it far enough up the food chain to get any mud that sticks. That was with Mr Park in charge. Last month he retired as CEO of Paradise Casino – their flagship legitimate business – and as far as we can tell he's dropped control of everything else too. It'll fall to his sons to run the empire. They're smart and he'll have trained them well, but they'll be vulnerable, stressed, not wanting to let him down; more likely to make mistakes and more likely to need outside help. Which is where you two come in."

He paused to take a drink of water.

"We managed to keep it a secret that Dave was a cop in Birmingham; everyone there thinks he went to prison," he continued. "But he built up a reputation that he can call on. So as far as they're all concerned, Drew Parry from the Birmingham

Splitters is set to be released for good behaviour and start a new life of crime in London. But there are plenty of better criminals out there who would kill to be part of Park's crew, and nobody can get close without help or a long, long time of servitude, giving the old man a long, long time to be retired and clean off every last trace of himself.

"Now this," he pointed to a picture of a man in his late thirties. "Is Yoonho Park; Park's eldest son and the new CEO of Paradise. According to our sources, he likes the ladies; in fact his favourite dancers are deeper in his confidence than his own wife. I doubt he'd share anything that would get him in trouble unless he's absolutely stupid – which he's not – but it's them he'll take solace from when stressed and it's their advice he'll listen to. The brother of one of his harem with a reputation from Birmingham and by then, with any luck, some sort of foothold in the London trade, would seem very attractive when he's feeling overwhelmed and in need of trustworthy assistance. It could all come to nothing, but it's the best shot we've ever had."

"We're not asking you to be a prostitute," David clarified, noticing the concern on Carrie's face. "That's the best thing about Yoonho; his younger brothers are promiscuous little shits but he likes to think that he's respectable. He makes it known that he's never cheated on Margot and he has a strict 'look but don't touch' policy when it comes to his libido. Soju might be easier to get to – he's the third brother – but that's why we're aiming at Yoonho, not him."

"Right," Carrie said, relieved. Of course the police force would never ask such a thing, even crazy Brian Hole.

"There's a lot more detail in the file," DSI Hole finished up. "Past failed attempts, information on the family etcetera – all classified info and strictly confidential whether you're in or not. Wendy will go through everything in relation to your involvement. Dave, it would be great if you two could get together and come up with a name and identity that Carrie would be comfortable with, and get that and some old photos through to forensics A.S.A.P. – you know, the usual things."

David nodded. "No problem, boss."

"Good," he looked pleased. "You can both go. Report to Wendy first thing tomorrow morning."

Head a little faint, Carrie exited the office, then remembered she had no idea who Wendy was or where she was supposed to be meeting her.

"DI Wendy Pullman," David read her mind. "Been following the Parks almost as long as he has. She'll be our direct link back to civilisation. I'll check where she wants us and let you know."

"Thanks," Carrie smiled in relief. He was very easy to like, though his impressive experience still made him pretty intimidating. "Can you find me on Lync?"

"I'm a detective," he tapped his temple.

"Right," she laughed. "Obviously."

"Actually," he stopped her as she was about to go. "Have you got a moment?"

He gestured to an empty meeting room.

"Sure," she replied. "DCI Vane said to give DSI Hole's work priority."

"Great," he led her in and rested his briefcase on the table, retrieving a file significantly thinner than the one from DSI Hole. "Wendy and I pulled this together for you."

He handed it to her, Carrie having to set down the ring binders already in her arms to avoid dropping everything. She read the cover: *Dave's Guide to Bullshit.*

She chuckled and flipped it open, reading the first page aloud: "First rule of bullshit: don't bullshit."

Carrie was confused.

"Most important thing to know about going undercover," he said seriously. "Keep the lies to a minimum. You'll have enough to think about protecting your identity; no point in making things more complicated than they have to be. You're a lot less suspicious if you're being yourself and you've not got a web of fibs to keep up with. Which is also the point of me making this." He gestured at the file. "Brian's a great detective and knows this case inside out, but he's never been covert himself. He wants you clued up on ten years of data; I personally think that's a bad idea. You'd just have to pretend you didn't know it all and you might slip up and mention something nobody told you. Better to stick to the basics. Plus, it'll take you a lifetime to get through the whole case file."

She smiled sheepishly. "I had been prepping myself for an all-nighter."

"Don't do that," he instructed. "In fact, I'll take that file and remove the temptation – I've heard you're a workaholic." He flashed her a grin to show he meant that in jest. His teeth were very white. "If Brian ever decides to spring a pop quiz I'll cover for you."

She thanked him.

"No worries," he put his hands loosely into his pockets. "See you later, little sister."

Carrie checked the board beside the door; nobody seemed to have booked the room. She returned to the table and took her laptop from her bag, spreading David's file open beside it. She might as well get straight to it. She had a lot of reading and processing to do, as well as thinking of an identity that wasn't a cop but wasn't bullshit; such things were better done without Neil's chatter in her ear.

David's dossier was a lot more compact than DSI Hole's and she suspected a lot less formal. As well as his own advice on undercover work, he had grouped together Wendy and their boss's observations of the major players in an informative but chatty way, coupled with their business cards and a photo or two:

Mister Park (per immigration form – no way is that his real name, which makes me wonder if any of them are)

Born: 31.01.1953

Came to the UK March 1994 with his sons, apparently running from a North Korean death warrant. Opened the first Paradise Casino November 1994 – it's moved and grown a few times since then. Married 19 year old Emilia Young October 1994, who formally adopted all four sons, then the whole family applied for and was granted British citizenship.

He's a tough man. Shows no empathy in interrogation (on the rare occasion Brian managed to get him there), enjoys playing with investigators, knowing with his money and influence we can't touch him. Claims police harassment whenever approached these days. Sends Brian a Christmas card every year just to piss him off.

People around him tend to disappear when a threat or surplus to requirements, including his wife, who vanished sometime around February 2006. No missing persons report was filed and the family claims she left him. No body or evidence of suspicious circumstances to open a proper investigation.

We doubt you'll ever meet him but if you do, be careful. Let yourself be scared of him – it's a natural reaction and a good excuse not to say too much. He can smell bullshit a mile away, like he can read your mind. If you lie to him, he'll know, and you'll be dead.

She was a little disappointed to find that he looked surprisingly normal. Of course, she had been in the force long enough to know that bad guys didn't all have scars and fluffy cats, but she had sort of hoped that the leaders of a huge crime empire would look a bit more evil. Mr Park – the mastermind who had been eluding the police for a decade – just looked like someone's dad, which she supposed he was. Yes, he looked like a rich banker dad who probably owned ten Rolexes and a Ferrari, but there was nothing sinister about his face. If anything, he just looked tired. She supposed that was all part of how he managed to function overtly as an innocent man.

His first son, known as Yoonho, fitted the bill a little more – very business-like but with a greedy glint in his eye that implied a love for money prone to trump any moral concerns. But then she supposed that most top CEOs probably looked like that, gangster or not.

Yoonho Park

Born: 29.10.1975

Eldest son, was 18 when came to UK. Never registered for school or uni, presumably went straight into business with his father in the underground drugs trade before moving 'above board' as a director of the casino. Clearly the main focus of Park's interest – as the now CEO and heir to the family empire, we believe he's been groomed for this since a young age.

Typical businessman – great at loopholes, lavish & charming host, will woo you with a smile while his lackies work on destroying you. Smooth-talking and slippery, very good at networking, knows everybody who's everybody and doesn't waste time with anyone who isn't. Definitely his father's son in terms of business-mindedness, but without the same edge – his joy is clearly money and the life of a millionaire, he doesn't seem to enjoy playing with people like Park.

Married Margot Stuetz but still very fond of dancers. According to our sources, he's a watcher not a doer. Has his favourites and they attend on him a lot, sometimes in business meetings too as part of his 'lavish host' persona – where you come in.

-

Han Park

Born: 01.01.1979

Unbothered by women or money – unsure what his motivation is. Very quiet when questioned and only responds when told to by Park or Yoonho.

Smart, streetwise, merciless. Expert with firearms and knives, also a lot physically stronger than he looks. Has been in charge of security since officially joining the board on his 18th birthday, and we have a very strong suspicion he might be the instrument of Park's surplus 'disappearances'.

Watch out for him. He will not trust you. If you don't have Yoonho's protection, Han won't think twice about killing you.

-

Soju Park (registered on arrival as Taeju Park, changed name by deed poll 2007)

Born: 12.12.1988

Very smart – Yoonho's prodigy. Interestingly for a finance director, doesn't seem to be particularly bothered about money – perhaps that's the reason they trust him to manage it. His motivations are clearly more about power – he loves it even more than Park does. Enjoyed playing with people since school, where he was easily the most popular 'cool' guy, while maintaining stellar grades.

Previously a party animal, landed in jail for a year for drugs (apparently his own of course and unbeknownst to the family – just a maverick rich kid). Unsure why Park let his son go down on such a petty charge, potentially to sober him up or punish him for something.

He has an ego though. Submit to him, let him think he owns you, and he's not the one to worry about. He'll play with you, but killing you would stop his fun.

-

Jay Park (registered as Taehwan Park, ditto)

Born: 13.06.1990

Youngest brother – definitely the baby of the family and pretty useless as far as we can tell. Easy to rile and goes off in a tantrum at any opportunity, violent as Han and spiteful as Soju but with none of their self-control. Essentially just a spoilt brat.

Grades at school not great, not helped by the fact he never turned up. Enjoys showing off his money to anyone who cares, tends to spend his time intoxicated with people further down the social scale – presumably because they're easier to impress. Previously inseparable from Soju as his party sidekick, but since his spell in prison Soju doesn't have much time for him anymore – none of the brothers do. Supposed to be a director but seems to do bugger all.

-

Margot Stuetz-Lee, nee Stuetz (yeah, interesting, not sure what's going on there)

Born: 17.09.1976

Birthplace Dusseldorf, Germany. Self-made woman from a poor background, met Yoonho while working as a lawyer. Change of name apparently nothing to do with him, but interesting. Intelligent lady, but no evidence that she has any say in the running of the casino or any other business – she's there for her looks not her brains. Essentially a trophy wife, seems content to spend Yoonho's money and let him show her off at business dinners with little thought for him otherwise – they're clearly not the most loving of couples. Best case scenario: she enjoys the company of another intelligent woman and can help you get in. Worst case: she's not so keen on dancers, could try to get you in trouble. Most likely: she'll just ignore you.

It was simple information and even Google couldn't shed much light on the family's darker side, but she understood David's concerns about knowing too much. It was up to her to get to know them organically, which was a lot easier to get her head around.

The trickier part was going to be getting her character right.

Carrie was incredibly glad that her defining purpose was dancing. She enjoyed dancing a lot and she was good at it; she had been ever since Hannah Starr (her neighbour in first-year halls) had dragged her to a freshers taster session at Durham Pole Society. The two of them had even co-chaired the group in second and third year, before Hannah dropped out and the 'Star & Heart' duo was disbanded. She still practised fairly regularly in private, for simple enjoyment and fitness purposes, and had picked up a few extra classes too. Still, she wasn't quite confident that she was good enough to catch the eye of the CEO of a top London casino, especially when she suspected that any dancer with ambition would be aiming for the same.

"I thought you might still be here," David popped his head around the door many hours later. "Have you been studying all day?"

"I went out to get lunch and snacks," she gestured at a bag of empty food packaging, not wanting to show her need for so much preparation to this seemingly effortless man. "And I had to get a few things done on cases for DI Partridge and DCI Vane – my bosses. But I've had a good look through."

"Alright sis," he chuckled. "It's not an interrogation. I'm heading off if you fancied getting something to eat?"

"Sure," Carrie eagerly accepted.

"Great," David leaned casually against the table next to her. "I figured we should get to know each other properly; hang out so much we get sick of each other, like real siblings." He flashed her a teasing smile. "I've apparently been in prison for two years, which would explain any distance between us, but we want that family vibe as much as possible. Plus we don't want to catch each other out talking about hobbies you hate or ordering sushi when you're allergic to seafood."

"I'm not allergic to seafood," Carrie said quickly. Her stomach was starting to rumble at the thought of dinner.

"Sushi then?"

-

"So," he started, once they had settled down to a table in Wagamama. "What are you thinking so far? Ready to run for the hills?"

"No," Carrie laughed. "It's not that easy to scare me off."

"Not as easy as a family of gangsters, ey?"

"No," she chomped on a cucumber maki. "I've been thinking about what you said though, about not lying. Obviously I'm going to have to have a different story for what I've been up to since uni. I was thinking a bit of dancing and admin to live on – bar work might be better for my CV, but I haven't done that since uni so I might be suspiciously rusty. Does that sound about right?"

David nodded in approval.

"So I was thinking," she continued with more confidence. "I had a friend called Hannah; she's the one who got me into dancing in the first place. She dropped out of uni to try to go professional and we lost contact, but I thought that maybe I could be like her, use her stories if I need to. Then I'm not a cop but I'm not completely making it up."

"I like it," David looked pleased. "You're thinking it through; that's exactly the sort of thing you need to do. If you can't tell the truth: substitution, not fiction. It's a lot easier to remember something you know rather than something you plucked out of thin air."

Carrie allowed herself to feel proud of her intuition, but not too proud. She couldn't allow one small victory to affect her performance.

"I've got a name too," she said. "Cara. That's from Hannah as well. We decided that Anna Star and Cara Heart felt a bit more showbiz, so it's been a while but I've been Cara before. She was sort of my dancing persona. I think I'd answer to it pretty naturally with a bit of practise beforehand."

It seemed that Carrie and David were going to get along well as siblings. Over the course of their dinner she discovered that they shared a love of cheap takeaways and exercise (David's idea of a perfect evening was arms day followed by bargain bucket chicken wings) and neither could understand why anybody would want to do karaoke sober. David also couldn't stand cats – a creature that Carrie had longed for since childhood, when Fiona's allergies had denied her – which gave them a bone of contention for healthy sibling rivalry.

The idea of them worked together, almost like herself and Fiona but without the snobbery or wedding fiasco. There was the confident, clever, good-looking one set to both take care of and overshadow their awestruck little sister. She was glad to have him on her side, and glad also to have a second chance at impressing a family member, even a fake one. It was something she had thought she had given up on.

"I'm trying," Carrie blinked back tears. It was easier not to cry; she could see things objectively, scientifically, like a good detective. "I'm making progress, aren't I?"

"You are," Dr Burgess told her encouragingly. "You're free of toxins and you're holding up as well as I'd expect; you mustn't be disheartened if things feel slow at first. The thing is, substance dependence is never an isolated problem. There are underlying issues that need to be addressed."

"I know that," she nodded in earnest. "I've dealt with those things. I just want to get on with my life now and forget about it."

"That's what we need to address," he looked her steadily in the eye. "There are things you aren't dealing with. Now, I'm not sure if you're just keeping them from me or if you hide them even from yourself, but you seem to think that you've become two different people."

"Cara," Carrie sighed. "She was my undercover personality and she got carried away. But it's fine – she only really comes out if I'm drunk."

"You see," he continued. "I think that's why you get drunk. You can't split yourself in half, Carrie, it isn't a viable solution. Cara isn't a separate person; she's a defence mechanism. You're keeping these things at bay, but you're also missing parts of yourself that you can't function without. Do you ever feel numb, and that only alcohol or drugs can fix it?"

Yes. Yes, she did. But what was the alternative? Separating her feelings for the world of Paradise Casino and her feelings for the world of reality had always been her only option. Both herself and Cara knew the facts, but Cara cared about some things and she cared about others. To combine them, to know everything and feel everything, just wasn't possible. Their views were polar opposites and it hurt too much; if she were to try to connect them she would only tear herself apart again.

All she needed was to get back to work and sufficiently distract herself enough to put Cara back in her box forever. Carrie Hart was a detective, and a bloody good one. She had never been seduced by the place they called Paradise. Or, at least, she didn't have to remember that she had. That had been her Cara side's fault, so it was her Cara side's problem. Because every time she almost remembered, she just wanted to take every drug she could and vomit her guts up on the floor. Only Cara's delusions could save her. They were separate and that was how they had to stay.

"Numb is fine," she replied, forcing the feelings back down her throat. They weren't hers. "I don't want to fix it. My job requires numbness."

"Carrie," Dr Burgess said kindly. "You need to prioritise yourself, not your job. You have the right to feel your feelings."

No. No. No, no, no, no, no. She did not need to prioritise herself. Feeling feelings wasn't a right, it was a torture. Nobody deserved to be tortured. She had done the right thing. Taehwan, Han, David; everyone had said so in their own way. She had done the right thing. This man didn't know what he was saying. Her throat tightened and her breathing quickened. She had done the right thing. She had done the right thing. She had done the right thing.

She shot up from the sofa and pelted from the room, from the building, from the complex, from everything. She didn't need money or clothes or any possessions at all; she just needed to talk to him. She needed drugs, she needed red wine and she needed to talk to him. That was how she existed.

DSI Hole's bunker looked exactly how a case briefing room should look; like something straight out of a homicide thriller. Photographs and newspaper clippings were plastered across the walls, with tape, string and frustratedly scribbled marker pen connecting and disconnecting them. People hadn't been joking when they said that the Superintendent was obsessed. There were documents and reports dating back as far as the mid-90s, when Carrie herself would have been just into her first years of school. The pinboards were filled with drugs and violence and prostitution, but nothing official that mentioned the Parks – only Hole's own observations, circling similarities and anomalies.

"He's a genius, isn't he."

Carrie jumped. She hadn't heard David enter the room. Another article, again seemingly unrelated to the Parks, had caught her eye – the breaking up of a prostitution ring under the control of a man named Big Mo.

"DSI Hole or Mr Park?" she asked.

"Both," he put his hands in the pockets of his jeans and followed her gaze to the wall. "That's why I got involved; this stuff is fascinating."

"Yeah," Carrie agreed, sipping her coffee. "I still can't believe I'm here. I'm just a DC; it's crazy."

"Everyone does say Brian's crazy," David told her. "If the time had been right, he wouldn't have waited even this long to bring you on board. You're an attractive detective with a nose that looks like mine and a dancing history; I doubt your police experience means much to him. He's not exactly orthodox. Some of the stuff he had me doing on the Splitters op was dubious, and that wasn't his life's work.

"But don't worry," he smiled reassuringly. "I was a newbie once too."

DI Wendy Pullman was an imposing woman in a sharp blue suit; tall and dark with thick braided hair and a no-nonsense air. As well as having followed the Parks with DSI Hole, she had also been David's handler on his previous assignment, where both were highly commended. Carrie felt very small beside the two of them with their blatant confidence and experience.

"You two are early," she commented as she strode into the room. "That's not like you, Dave."

"Couldn't wait to see my pretty boss," David nudged her humorously.

"You watch this one," Wendy mimicked clipping him round the ear. "No respect for anyone."

David chuckled. "How could a sleazy drug salesman be anything else?"

"Right, you, focus," she dropped a collection of objects and papers on the table. "Passports, driving licenses, phones. Waterproof phones." She gave David a look; clearly there was some sort of inside joke going on there. "National insurance numbers, credit cards, CVs. If anyone calls the references on there, they'll be clean. Dave, you already know the deal. Carrie, the more you can memorise the easier life will be for you."

Carrie cast her eyes over the papers, trying to take everything in at the pace in which it was provided. It was all a bit overwhelming. She certainly wasn't stupid, but she hadn't sailed through school like Fiona. Her sister saw things and they clicked immediately. It took Carrie a little longer and a lot more hard work and concentration to keep up. She would definitely have to study these properly later.

"We've taken the liberty," Wendy laid out some glossy photographs. Carrie was surprised to recognise her own pictures;

the same she had submitted, but different. "Of merging some family photos. I doubt you'll need them, but better safe than sorry. You know Brian; no stone left unturned."

Carrie picked some up to examine them. There was her six year old self dressed as a policewoman, but a little boy wearing the armour of Saint George replaced Fiona's pink princess. There was David smiling with her and Hannah in a club, in the place of a boy called Jack Harvey who they had house-shared with. And there was her own face on the body of a girl in a yellow dress, clapping as a teenaged David looked incredibly pleased in a grubby football strip. She knew them all to be false, but the job had been so well done that even she almost believed them.

"These are amazing," she congratulated Wendy.

"Thank Tomasz in forensic arts," Wendy replied. "If you're the soppy sort you can frame them on your bedroom wall, or hashtag them to shit on social media. Otherwise, just have them locked away somewhere for realism, just in case."

Carrie wasn't the soppy sort – she had left the job of keeping family photos to Fiona and their parents – but the recreations were so impressive she sort of didn't want to waste them. And as Drew and Cara's parents were apparently dead, she supposed at least one of the siblings would have held onto such things.

Wendy took them through the rest of the details again, which swum erratically around Carrie's head as she tried desperately to keep them in order. She would get an ordinary job as soon as possible and find them somewhere to live in time for Drew's release date in March. Once their new existences were well enough established, one of the casino's dancers would be picked up on some unrelated charge, leaving a vacancy that would need to be filled – by Cara Parry. Then the main plan would come into play: she would find an opportunity for Drew to enter the business, then she would leave her brother to it and return to Durham (where she had apparently been living since university) and Carrie would return to normal life. It seemed like a lot of waiting around doing nothing to begin with, but she supposed the time would be needed to get her head around resetting her life and training like hell to perfect her dancing.

"If you need anything before I'm out," David assured her. "I'm just a phone call away."

"And I'll check in as much as I can," Wendy promised. "Though the more you can do on your own, the better."

"I'll be fine," Carrie said quickly. "I've found jobs and rented flats before."

She may be inexperienced, but she wasn't a child. If she couldn't do something as simple as set up a move to London, what use was she?

"She can be a bit intense, ey?" David smiled kindly when the briefing was over and Wendy had left the room. "But she's the best handler there is. You're in safe hands. But seriously, if you need anything at all, I'm here. There are things that come up when you start a second life that you wouldn't even consider now. There's a fine line between fitting in and losing yourself. Sometimes a chat with someone who knows who you really are is what you need to stop you going crazy."

He laughed and picked up a photo. Carrie wondered if it was realistic for a man apparently just out of prison to have such white teeth. "I miss these shorts."

"David?" she started.

"Yes, little sis?"

"I was wondering," she continued. "With all this stuff about not making things up, how are you going to talk about being in prison?"

"Good question," he praised her. "Luckily I have a handy Uncle Richard to draw on; he's actually the reason I joined the force. He did some crime and did some time, which he liked to tell me about when Mum wasn't listening. I used his stories getting in with the Splitters, and now I've got a few of my own.

Rich and I; together we're Drew Parry, past and present. Like you and your friend Hannah."

-

Wendy had recommended that, as a person who was supposed to be boosting her dancing career on coming to London, Cara Parry should have an Instagram account. Carrie flicked through the photos she had uploaded to *carara*'s page, triple checking there wasn't anything there that would give her away. She had debated with herself whether it was appropriate to include ones containing Hannah and concluded that she could do so if she blurred out her face. Her ex-best friend would be free from any gangster-related stalking, and she wouldn't have to worry about not having her permission. She liked the idea of her alter-ego appearing to have friends and it would surely make her more realistic. Their history could remain unchanged; they had been best friends and dance partners at uni, then Hannah had gone her own way, they argued, lost touch and now she was blurred out of photos. Perfectly believable, because that's what had happened.

She also liked the feeling that the girl was with her. In a way, Operation Bluebird was her chance to make peace with their split. When Hannah had dropped out to follow a career in professional dancing, Carrie had been too practical and too afraid to join her. Hannah had begged and pleaded for her to "grow a pair" but for once Carrie had put her foot down. There was a part of her that had always wondered what had happened to her and what kind of life she herself would be leading if she had taken the plunge. Well, now she could find out. The more she looked at the photos, the more she forgot to be scared of entering a den of gangsters and became simply excited by the prospect of following this tentative dream, safe in the knowledge that whatever happened she had an ordinary life to return to.

<u>8: The Family</u>

<u>15 May 2014</u>

It was obvious early on that Lisa was the mother figure to all the casino girls – dancers, bartenders, cleaners and waitresses alike. She was in her late thirties and had clearly had work done; her face was as smooth as a baby's despite the fact she smoked like a chimney. She looked and sounded like she was straight out of a country song; Texas drawl and bleached blonde hair permed to perfection above red lips and Daisy Dukes that she wore whatever the weather. If anyone wanted the definition of larger than life, Carrie would show them Lisa. She was a woman who knew what she wanted, and what most of the other girls wanted too. She was clearly in her element, going out of her way to give the newbie a full tour of her beloved casino.

To Carrie, it seemed more like its own autonomous small town. Lisa led the way through slot machines, public tables and private poker booths, the standard bars and restaurant and one reserved for VIPs, hotel rooms and meeting rooms, plus a basement gym and swimming pool (to which, as part of Yoonho's top team, Carrie would have access all hours).

She was introduced to anybody they came across – Lisa knew everyone, including a fair few of the regular punters. Her chat about the building and the job was interjected with comments such as: "he's a creep – avoid", "he gives good tips" and "watch out for her; she was outed from Grosvenor for counting cards".

"And of course there's the family," she continued, thoroughly enjoying helping Carrie apply her make-up in the changing room, where the other two girls in their group were donning their scanty costumes. "Soju belongs to Jennie. Not officially of course – everyone's entitled to a bit o' cash if he asks – but be sparing about it. Sisterhood, y'know."

"Oh," Carrie blanched. "I don't want money like that. No offence."

"None taken," Lisa smiled. "Yoonho looks after his girls. We dance, serve booze and deal cards; no-one can make us do nothing we don't wanna. Anyone tries, you take it to me or Brick, and we'll take it to him."

"Exactly," Jennie shook out her hair. "No means no, and if you actually understand that then I already like you better than those other whores." She glared at the other side of the changing room. "Except for Lali – I don't think no does mean no to her."

Lali was Sri-Lankan and spoke little English, but she looked and danced like a goddess. Thick black hair cascaded down a dark back, with perfectly shaped eyebrows defining deep, soulful eyes. She always looked graceful whatever she was doing, and on the rare occasion that she did speak, her voice was golden honey.

Jennie was pretty much the opposite. Her alabaster skin was mottled with freckles almost as orange as her hair and her face was sharp with a pointed nose. She was significantly younger too, looking below the eighteen years she insisted she was. She was the tallest of the group and wouldn't be out of place on a Parisian catwalk, if she could only tear herself away from her unhealthy obsession with Soju Park. Carrie wondered if the girl knew the extent of what her amore was involved in.

"Everyone else is fair game," Lisa informed her. "All the girls are welcome to earn what they like on the side, as long as we're tasteful and discreet about it and Paradise gets a cut o' the dolla'. Only if we wanna, of course. I haven't done in a while myself, but if Soju Park came knocking even I'd be tempted, and I'm practically his grandma."

"Hands off, old lady," Jennie scowled. "All these girls think they can have him any time they like because they're greedy whores and he's the sexiest man alive." She sighed deeply. "I would do him for free every night if I could."

"Dream on, chick," Lisa teased. "Even if he wanted to, that is not advised. You give free stuff to anyone, you're stealing good business and Brick'll have your head. You give free stuff to the family, you put Yoonho in a complicated situation. No-one wants to perv on their brother's girlfriend, and more importantly, lovers' tiffs ain't conducive to keeping family secrets. You really wanna boyfriend, I'd recommend you get one with nothing to do with no Parks."

Carrie nodded. Lisa had nothing to fret about on that score.

"That said, you won't have a hard time there," Lisa reassured her. "Soju aside, the family's pretty safe. Yoonho's married and a gentleman – he'll watch us enough but he don't go no further than that. Han… I don't think he's ever looked at a woman in his life."

"Or a man," Jennie added. "The only people he looks at are causing trouble and about to get a thumping."

"And Jay," Lisa continued. "I don't think even his mother loved him, though Mr Park's second wife spoiled him rotten."

"We leave him to the real whores," Jennie laughed. "Us Paradise girls are better than that. Honestly, that guy is *the* most pathetic person. Half the time he's too coked to get it up and the other half he's done in five seconds then runs off to cry. Plus he's got a tinier dick than my guinea pig." She pulled a face. "Can confirm."

"Ain't no comparison, huh?" Lisa winked.

"Soju *definitely* stole all the sexy," Jennie groaned. "I cringe just looking at him."

"But he does throw some sick parties," Lisa noted. "So I'd recommend being nice to his face."

"And he'll splash his cash whether you shag him or not," Jennie hung up her bag and started to apply her own visage. "Fucking show-off."

Paradise Casino was a 'respectable' establishment, or so Yoonho liked to say. The dimmed lights in the show hall illuminated the stage where they spun, somewhere between a dazzling exhibition of perfect choreography and a spectacle of skin for hungry punters with an appetite for more than just gambling. Carrie forced herself to remember the interuniversity finals: feeling sexier and more self-assured than she had ever been before. In reality, it was more than technique that was being appreciated from the tables in the dark. Lisa's outfit designs rarely left much to the imagination: gold trim on black retreating from the spotlight and exposing their bare flesh to the glare, careful shades of body paint enhancing cleavage and toned stomachs. It was what she had been expecting and what Cara was born for, but it didn't stop Carrie's heart from beating hard every time she stood in the wings, waiting for the music to switch off her nerves and let her escape for a while.

At least Han's security team were always close by to stop the audience from getting too friendly, though that was intimidating in itself. They seemed to lurk in every area of the casino, their eyes following her eerily, hands folded neatly behind their backs to hide the toughened and often broken skin of their knuckles. She couldn't help but wonder which of these pairs of hands had Lucy Flynn's blood on them.

As well as their shifts on the poles and the associated rehearsals, Lisa and the others were tasked with showing Carrie the ropes working the three bars (the show hall, the public bar and the more refined VIP area), manning the tables in the casino and attending on Yoonho in his private chambers.

The CEO's quarters were more like a throne room; a significant contrast to the contemporary office with its swivel-chair and mounds of paperwork. It was clear that the place had been designed by Mr Park rather than his neat, modern son, but Yoonho still managed to own it. He sat in a magnificently carved oak chair with blood red cushions that spilled down onto the floor where the girls gathered to hold his whiskey and flash their legs tauntingly at his guests. This was the place where he entertained the most important of his shady partners, whose ideas of a generous host somewhat differed to those of the legitimate businessmen with whom he endeavoured to gain favour. Not that he would admit in front of the girls that they were anything but investment associates, of course – Yoonho Park wasn't stupid.

In fact, Carrie sometimes wondered if he himself even willingly forgot on occasion. Yoonho clearly enjoyed the high life, mingling with esteemed peers at dinners and events as if he had always been one of them, and of course he would do anything to gain the money to do so - if anything was going on beneath the corporate jargon then he certainly knew the nature of it. But he also seemed to prefer pretending that he didn't, wherever possible. By his own declaration, he was respectable.

It was Soju who could be seen to relish the dark undertones of their lavish 'business appointments'. In fact, Lisa believed that Yoonho was personally training him to take complete charge of many areas (those areas, Carrie suspected, that the CEO deemed beneath himself, and more importantly, bore a higher risk). He already took on several engagements without his brother's supervision, as well as accompanying him to meetings with their most longstanding and valuable partners.

It was in one of these meetings that the CEO now sat above the world, watching as his prodigy played cards and spoke in codes with a group of men identified as Enrique, Ripley and the Dragon.

Soju Park really was the most suave man Carrie had ever seen and it was understandable that half the casino staff were in love with him. Dark hair swung seductively over a handsome face with chiselled cheekbones that the case photos really didn't do justice. He was as sharply dressed as his brother, but with a few less buttons fastened at the top of his shirt, revealing skin that Jennie's eyes were always drawn to. He lounged in his chair, casual but in total control, regarding everything with a look of indifference that verged on boredom. He was above these mere mortals, and they all seemed to agree.

"I'm done with the fucking Russians," Enrique threw his cards in in frustration.

"Likewise," Soju revealed his own, to groans from the others.

"You know they're still trying to say Knightsbridge is theirs?" Enrique continued. "Mr Park should never have let them have that; it's too close. They're diluting the toff market."

"Mr Park was still growing when he made that pact. Have you not noticed," Soju said slyly. "That every time they 'dilute the toff market', they get a bit of dilution of their own?"

Carrie had no idea what that was supposed to mean, but it didn't sound pleasant.

"Mr Donny asks too much," the man known as the Dragon glanced up from his hand. He was old and wrinkled, with leathery skin bearing scars from a lifetime in the industry, and owned a string of shops in Chinatown. "Did Mr Yoonho approve agent commission?"

"Mr Yoonho did not," Soju looked highly unimpressed, as he often did at mention of their agent.

The CEO had brought him on following Mr Park's retirement; himself and Soju being promoted and Jay not yet ready to take on his brother's previous responsibilities. Soju, however, saw no need to pass on his responsibilities to anyone and the man's existence did nothing but irk him.

"We'll talk about that," he told the Dragon. "Keep paying what you owe and tell him to speak to me if he disagrees."

"Forget Donny Logan," Enrique insisted. "It's the Russians you should be worried about. They've been unsettled ever since Mr Park retired and they're getting bored of giving me generous offers. You know if they cost me much more everything goes bang for your rents too, and your reputation. They think they can mess with me; they need to know I still have your backing. Even

Russians wouldn't dare to directly challenge the Parks – unless you let them think you've gone soft. People are already saying you're not your father."

"I'm not my father," Yoonho replied. "But I am his son and nothing has gone soft."

Lisa rubbed his shoulders soothingly while Carrie continued to grind slowly against Lali, feeling the Sri-Lankan's dark hand running its way uncomfortably up the lace that decorated her leg. They were in red today, with straps of black that criss-crossed around their hips and torsos, directing the wandering eye to the places it most wanted to go.

Carrie found it a lot harder to lose herself when the music was quieter and the performance required in these meetings significantly more unnerving than that of their public shows. It wasn't that she had never danced sluttily with Hannah, but that was on stage or drunk in clubs, not in an intimate room where she suspected the only thing keeping her troupe from violation was Yoonho's will.

"Of course," Enrique dropped his head at the man's tone. "And I for one am right there behind you. But a great CEO invests in his partners."

"And chases away their enemies," Soju played coolly with a card. "Trade wars are getting boring. Mr Park would send a more… professional gesture to ease the tension."

Yoonho sighed but nodded. "My brother is right; I should give them a present. Dragon, you know the type. Han will provide raw material."

Han tipped his head in acknowledgment but said nothing.

While Yoonho commanded respect through carefully placed smiles and clever words, Han needed none of that trickery. Per the accounts of both David's file and her fellow dancers, he had never shown any sort of fear or desire for anything, and to look at him was to easily believe it.

He shared Yoonho's straight nose and strong jaw, but while they made his brother look pleasantly tidy, on Han they were just intimidating. He wore a security officer's earpiece and a suit not as pristine and stylish as Yoonho's but fit for purpose – to show that he meant business. If anybody were to threaten the peace of Paradise Casino, they would have him to contend with, and both his reputation and his eyes said he didn't practise mercy. There was no malice or kindness visible on the surface of those dark pools; nothing to appeal to, just the perfect soldier. That was what made him deadly.

"I thought Mr Yoonho did not want this sort of gesture?" the Dragon asked curiously.

"I suppose sometimes it can't be helped," Yoonho replied. "With any luck this will settle things down and won't be necessary again until someone else sits in this chair and I'm sunning myself in Monaco." He chuckled amiably but extremely falsely. "Chance would be a fine thing. Five rings, please."

"Perhaps six?" Soju added darkly. "I'm sure you'd agree that our agent deserves a token of appreciation. He has a son."

"Five," Yoonho fixed him with a stern look.

"Five," the Dragon agreed. "It will be done."

-

"He pushes his luck, that Donny Logan," Lisa shook her curly head in disapproval once their guests had left.

"Precisely," Soju dropped his cards casually to the table and turned to Yoonho. "You should leave all this to me."

"You know you don't have the time," Yoonho rubbed his temples. "If your brother was less useless… Where the hell is he anyway?"

"Asleep?" Soju shrugged. "Dead? Who cares?"

Jay Park did not belong in his brothers' meetings. While Yoonho was the smiling face of capitalist success, Jay was the embodiment of its decadence. When the sun set and respectable guests retired to their hotel rooms, the moon rose on the bar in the show hall and the tab he kept behind it. It was Jay to whom flocked the opportunists, the gold diggers and the addicts; the underbelly of the casino that both embarrassed and sustained it.

And why wouldn't they? If Carrie had ever imagined the atmosphere at Gatsby's house, it would have been similar to this. Most nights were essentially a free-for-all of boozing, dancing and spending money that didn't belong to any of those who reaped its rewards. Temptation called even to those who sat perfectly sensibly at daylit poker tables and dined with sophistication in the restaurant. Gods became people became animals became monsters beneath the embellished ceiling and Jay's credit card. As Lisa had said, he knew how to throw a party.

And it wasn't like Lisa or any of the others to pass up on a party, whatever they thought of him in private.

Carrie's first sighting of the fourth Park brother was a young man in a leather jacket and studded belt, swinging from a pole and chugging a pint of liquor to onlookers' whoops and cheers. He saluted somebody in the crowd and sprung down from the stage, yelling at staff to turn up the music and throwing twenties in their faces like confetti.

"Sambuca please, Lydia," Jennie perched on a stool. "Times three. And a slim vodka tonic."

"Jay's tab?" the barwoman asked.

"Obviously," Jennie shook back her hair.

"Are you sure it's okay?" Carrie checked uncertainly with Lisa. "We can just use a Park's tab without asking?"

"Trust me, hon," Lisa gave her a knowing smile. "He loves it."

-

Fortunately, early morning library shifts alongside her Paradise work left Carrie little time for Jay's parties, as much as the girls would have loved to keep her. She knew that, in comparison to his brothers at least, Jay was nothing to be afraid of, but she took little pleasure in accepting the money, drinks and drugs of the youngest Park's ego trip.

Lali and Jennie had been at the casino for around two years – Lisa a lot longer – so they had had plenty of time to get used to wandering hands and shadows of secrecy. They knew what to ignore, how to keep themselves safe and how to have fun at the end of the day with no sense of guilt or fear. Carrie didn't feel safe at all, and didn't want to ignore anything.

16 May 2014

As well as adding to her persona as a dancer, Cara Parry's Instagram provided a useful communication channel with the police force. Wendy had her own fake teenaged girl account that she used to follow Carrie's posts and interact using a sort of code (and Carrie had a feeling that a rather crude fat man was Neil in disguise – God knows how he had found her).

Before auditioning for Paradise, Carrie had got a part time job at a library for the sake of Cara's sensible 'Plan B' income and a place to rendezvous with Wendy. The handler was provided with her shift patterns and any picture hashtagged *#London* was a request for her to show up at the next opportunity, in the guise of a technophobic customer photocopying knitting patterns. More importantly, any comment from Wendy warned Carrie of her own intention to visit or a further coded message, removing the risk of suspicious texts being received at awkward moments. There was no associate that she might have to explain, just an unknown teenaged girl who, along with many other accounts (both real and fake), treated the dancer as a role model.

"Caz?" she heard the call of her fellow library assistant as she finished showing a youngster where she could find books on trains.

Ashley was a bubbly girl of twenty who also worked part time while studying Engineering at Queen Mary's. Her sleek strawberry-blonde hair was kept off her face by a different coloured Alice-band each day, revealing an infectious smile that she wore often.

"There's a lady here for photocopying – can you take her?" she asked. "I've got a failing internet and a bunch of schoolkids."

"Sure," Carrie smiled at Wendy and led her upstairs to the print room.

"So," Wendy handed her the mound of papers to feed into the machine. "Sorry about the rainforest; I apparently have a very large knitting group with tastes varied enough to cover the time needed for a proper conversation."

"That's fine," Carrie chuckled, tucking her hair back behind her ear and starting the photocopier.

"How's it going?" the handler asked. "Settling in okay?"

Carrie wasn't entirely sure what the answer to that was. She was thrilled to have caught Yoonho's eye so early, she was honoured to be working and living with David, and the freeing distraction she felt on the stage allowed her to mostly disregard the crude looks and catcalls. But that distraction didn't carry into Yoonho's meeting rooms or Han's cold eyes, and as soon as she stepped off the stage it all became stiflingly overwhelming. She wanted to do well – she *was* doing well and she was excited about that – but at the same time, she was terrified.

"I think so," she said positively. "DSI Hole was right; Yoonho definitely loves his dancers, and he likes me already. He'd heard about Drew – I guess from Birmingham people – and I think he thinks that makes me trustworthy."

"Good," Wendy nodded approvingly.

"He was right about him needing outside help now too," she continued. "There's an agent called Donny Logan, who I'm pretty sure is working for that side of things, though when they talk it's like they pretend it's only normal investments and business things. Yoonho keeps as far away from everything as he can. I think Han and Soju are a bit more involved, but Yoonho makes it sound like he doesn't know anything except casino income, rents and dividends."

"The old man's even further," Wendy added. "His sons are his fall guys and they have fall guys whose fall guys have fall guys."

Carrie tried to keep up with the number of apparent fall guys.

"DSI Hole might be able to figure some of it out though," she said eagerly. "If I wore a wire, I could record conversations for him."

"Don't worry about wires," Wendy told her. "You just need to get Dave into the trade side."

Unsurprisingly, David was already getting his name out in the London scene, which she was delighted to report. Though he was nowhere near the level of Yoonho's fall guy's fall guy, he had been pleasantly surprised to run into an old Splitter acquaintance who had been quick to set up Drew "The Slippery Salesman" Parry with a few small-time distribution jobs. Bence himself was working in "the creation of money", as he had told David over a pint. Carrie wondered if any of those counterfeit notes might find their way into circulation through the winnings of Paradise Casino.

"Anything extra you overhear is great," Wendy continued. "But don't go blowing your cover by sniffing around. What we need you to do is fit in and be trusted."

She was a little disappointed – operations were all about wires and sniffing around – but she supposed that would be David's role. She would only be showing her inexperience by trying too hard for things beyond her remit. She wanted to be good at her job, not mediocre at someone else's.

<u>05 June 2014</u>

Soju Park was an exceptionally good poker player, and it had nothing to do with the cards. He could make people do things without even trying; slyly mimicking their behaviour to make them feel at ease then throwing them off completely when he needed to. A look here, a flick of the wrist there, a carefully placed nod and people were doubting themselves without realising why. Perfectly composed ladies touched their earrings in concentration as gentlemen wiped their brows, handing him their tells on a plate while he sat back, observing the show. He didn't play games; he played people. Which Carrie supposed was the way poker should be played.

His younger brother was not so refined. He scowled and grinned at cards with no restraint as he threw rash piles of chips into the centre. He talked a lot too, despite scattered requests for quiet and Soju's complete dismissal of his existence. People didn't seem to know what to do with this irritating bug whose name demanded respect and behaviour begged for reprimand. They gave him the same sort of looks that Carrie had seen many a time on the faces of her colleagues: a desire to strangle hidden beneath the simpers and fake smiles of politeness. She wondered if that had been what she looked like every time she had attended one of Fiona's awful dinner parties.

"Oh for fuck sake!" Jay hurled his cards across the table and threw back his chair with a bang. "Fine, just fucking keep it all; this game is bullshit anyway."

He stormed away from the group, turning back only to demand that Carrie bring him a whiskey and food.

"Irritating," Soju gave her a pitying look while lazily flipping a poker chip between his fingers. "I would love to advise you to let him starve, but he is family." He released the chip and let it spin like a top before falling. "It's the cocaine mostly, if I were to give him an excuse; does awful things to the temper. You should pity us who've had to deal with him his whole life."

"Are you fucking deaf?" Jay yelled from the walkway.

She gave Soju an apologetic smile, tucked her hair back and turned to go. Brick would not be pleased with her if she allowed any disturbance, even if it was from a Park.

"Wait," Soju stopped her calmly. "Watch this."

His eyes were fixed on a man sitting across from him, dressed in a grey suit and top hat, who was carefully examining his cards. His hand hovered over a pile of chips, leaning forwards in preparation to raise.

Soju surveyed him closely, his fingers stroking the hilt of an ornate ivory penknife that somebody had bet earlier. Suddenly his arm straightened. The penknife flew from his grasp, lodging itself deep into the top hat. Everybody jumped, Carrie included, several letting out alarmed squeals as the man's eyes widened.

Soju said something to him in a language that Carrie didn't understand (potentially Russian), dark malevolence dancing in his eyes. The man didn't respond.

"Jerome," he called languidly to the head of Han's security team. "Call Han please."

He cast his eyes around the stunned people at the table, landing finally on Carrie.

"This is a classy establishment," he explained simply. "It's rude to wear a hat indoors."

"Of course," she nodded in shock.

"For fuck sake!" Jay banged on an empty table. "Where's my fucking drink?"

Carrie hurried to fetch it, glad of the distraction. As much as she hated herself for thinking it, there was something dangerously attractive about Soju Park that was best avoided.

She had just set the tumbler down when Han entered the room, striding over to the poker table where the man had removed his hat and seemed to be trying to reason with Soju and appeal to the others, who were now very intentionally avoiding his gaze. He spotted the security director and tried to make a run for it, but was halted by Soju's leg stuck casually out across the walkway. Han pulled him roughly to his feet and spoke quietly to his brother before leading the man away.

Carrie had a strong feeling that he had done more than wear a hat indoors. She wondered if this was the usual treatment for cheating at poker or if there was something darker afoot, but that was the sort of thing that Lisa and the others didn't ever want to talk about. The look on this man's face, Soju's air when he talked about seemingly innocent things like rings, and the dancers' silence were more than unnerving. She hovered uneasily near Jay's table, reluctant to leave a relative comfort zone. Rudeness was just a thing that happened when working in hospitality. Soju Park was not.

"Don't smoke inside," Han ordered as he passed.

"What the fuck?" Jay complained. "You just tackled a customer, but I can't smoke?"

Han gave him a withering look. He scowled but put the cigarette out on the table, leaving a nice burn that somebody else would have to fix later.

"And keep your voice down."

"You keep your voice down," Jay grumbled when Han was safely out of earshot, pulling out another cigarette and drawing a disapproving look from the security chief. "Oh, fuck off Jerome."

The man backed away obediently but Jay returned it to his pocket anyway and filled his mouth with whiskey instead.

"You can fuck off too," he said moodily to Carrie. "Have a drink and don't look so judgy."

She hadn't realised she had been looking "judgy" – she must be more unsettled than she thought.

She did her best to hold herself together for the rest of her shift, watching Soju win the poker game then refund his haul graciously in return for silence. Not that such a payoff was necessary – every person at that table clearly admired him just as much as the dancers did and he didn't look at all concerned.

Carrie herself ran about the floor like a madwoman, trying to keep multiple punters fed and watered while obeying Soju's requests for her to observe the game and keeping up her own poker face of the perfect smiling employee. At least the uniforms in the main casino were modest enough and the gamblers more interested in winning or losing than the shape of her arse, but the incident with the top hat had made her jumpy and she couldn't help but see things that probably (or hopefully) weren't there. What was it that man was looking so beadily at? What did that woman keep touching beneath her collar? What was going on in Jerome's mind as his eyes darted about the room, the only part of him that moved? The buzzing in her head made it difficult to concentrate, and difficult not to snap at each person who blamed her for an incorrect order or demanded she clean up a spillage.

By the time Brick had signed her out and she was able to remove her uniform she was utterly exhausted. She opened the door that led from the changing room to the sheltered courtyard outside, dropped her head back wearily against the wall and closed her eyes, dreading the thought of having to catch a bus.

"You look like shit," a voice sounded beside her.

She jumped; she hadn't even noticed Jay was there. The last time she had seen him he had been having a very noisy lucky streak on the roulette wheel, collecting a gaggle of spectators but continuing to fail at gaining his brother's attention. Now he leant coolly a little way away, one leg bent so his posh trainers scuffed the brickwork as he puffed on a cigarette.

Although his features were essentially those of his brothers, each one seemed to have something not quite right about it. His studded ears stuck out further than the others' and his chin was somewhat weaker. While Soju's lips were full, Jay's were too full, giving the look of a constant pout. His nose was softer and less defined, with nostrils that flared out beneath a rounded tip, and endless nights of partying had given his eyes bags far beyond their years. He was a haphazard person and it showed.

"I'm fine," Carrie said automatically. It wasn't like he actually cared.

"Bullshit," he raised an eyebrow. "You look like you need a fag."

"I'm really fine," she insisted, managing to keep the exhausted frustration from her voice. "Sorry, I don't smoke anyway."

"You should start then," he said.

"Yeah, maybe," she sighed. "Not now though."

"Yes now," he pulled a fresh one from its pack and waved it irritatingly in her face. "Just one. You'll feel better."

She looked at him wearily. "Y'know what, go for it."

She didn't want to argue and she had been meaning to use this job as an opportunity to try out things she'd never done. Surely one cigarette wouldn't hurt Cara Parry, even if it was from a Park.

"You can do it properly, right?" he asked.

"Probably not," she took a deep breath then coughed a lot. "Jesus!"

"Yeah, that happens," he laughed. "Not so fast to start with."

She inhaled slower, trying to take less of the tainted air into her lungs. She was sure she was still doing it wrong, but just the act of letting go a little helped to ease the tension in her chest.

"You need to man up," he blew a stream of smoke across the courtyard. "You can't just jump every time someone tells you to if you wanna last here."

"I'm fine," she repeated. "It's my job; sometimes it's tiring. C'est la vie."

"Woah," he seemed suddenly impressed by something. "You speak Russian?"

"What?" an involuntary laugh burst from Carrie's throat.

She waited for him to shout at her for it, but he just looked confused.

"Sorry," she winced. "It's French. It means 'that's life'."

"Well I'm not fucking French am I," he pouted and flicked ash to the floor. "Why would I know that shit?"

"I dunno," Carrie apologised. "Sorry."

"Fucking hell, you say sorry a lot," he pulled a face. "You really do need to man up."

Carrie stopped herself before she instinctively said it again. He was annoying; he didn't deserve so many apologies. She got to the end of her cigarette and looked about for somewhere to put the butt.

"Just drop it," Jay threw his to the floor, where it lay releasing a trail of smoke into the air. "No-one cares."

She dropped nothing. "I don't wanna make a mess."

"Why?" he shrugged. "The cleaners'll get it. I'm basically helping them keep their jobs."

Carrie was unconvinced.

"It's true," he said casually. "Bad shit is underestimated. Casinos make people rich, drugs make people happy, loads of people would starve if they weren't trading stuff. And cleaners would have no job if there was nothing to clean."

"I dunno if they'd see it like that."

Carrie had never met someone with such a warped understanding of the world. She supposed that was what happened when a person grew up getting everything they ever wanted and taking responsibility for nothing.

He looked at her very curiously. She doubted he was used to simple casino staff questioning his logic. She certainly wasn't used to questioning people like him, or anyone at all. Cara Parry could do things like that.

"It's just a fag end," he frowned. "I'm not saying to chuck a whole tub of shit on the floor. Drop it – that's an order. Or I'll fire you."

"What?" she looked at him incredulously but let it fall from her fingers and onto the concrete.

"Now doesn't that feel better?" he grinned in triumph, winked and disappeared back through the door – the door to the ladies changing room.

Carrie kicked the cigarette butt, still smouldering on the floor. There was a sort of sheepish satisfaction in pointless rule breaking. She was certain that David wouldn't have thought twice about things much worse than littering when he was in the Splitters. Neil didn't think twice about littering as a law-abiding detective, and she was sure she had smelled weed on him more than once.

But it really was pointless. She bent down, picked up their mess and continued her search for a bin.

<u>25 June 2014</u>

The VIP room was supposed to be reserved for VIPs; particularly wealthy punters and legitimate business partners, some of whom Carrie was told were actual celebrities. It had a much smoother, more exclusive feel than the show hall or even the chic Paradise bar and restaurant. Padded booths bathed in deep indigo and purple lighting, where sophisticated people sipped spirits from crystal tumblers. The bar itself was obsidian black, illuminated by an electric blue that shone from behind the collection of shapely bottles along the back wall. It refracted through Curacao and Bombay Sapphire, giving the impression of lightning halos around Carrie and Lali's heads.

However, family counted as VIP and Brick could do nothing to stop Jay from bringing in a few of his less-than-sophisticated friends – not unless he wanted him to start throwing a strop and reminding him he could fire him. Whether he actually could without Yoonho's say-so, Carrie wasn't sure, but her manager certainly would get in trouble for disturbing the ambience if he kicked up a fuss.

Lali rolled her eyes and smoothed back her hair as he strutted over from his booth, tipsy already. He plopped onto a stool, pulled a small bag from his pocket and started to tip the contents onto the bar. Lali looked at it disapprovingly but said nothing.

"Whiskey," he waved a hand.

Lali obliged.

"Are you allowed drugs in the bar?" Carrie asked tentatively, knowing full well that he was not.

"I own the bar," he looked at her incredulously. "Want some?"

"What? No," Carrie pulled back. "I don't think Brick-"

"I own Brick," Jay banged on the bar. "Oi! Brick!"

"Shh!" Carrie put a hasty finger to her mouth, very aware of the looks several unhappy customers were giving her. "You'll get us all in trouble."

He laughed and snorted his powder through a fifty pound note. "I'm good at trouble."

Lali set down a tumbler and he immediately downed it.

"What?" he raised an eyebrow at the disapproval Carrie had failed to keep from her face, spreading his arms to show off his expensive-looking clothes. "I'm the family shit. Might as well be shit in style."

Carrie had nothing to say to that.

Jay leaned back to count the people in his booth.

"I need nine more," he told Lali. "No, ten. And get her one too."

"No, no, no," Carrie said quickly. "Don't do that; I'm working."

"Stop working then," he ordered. "You have to do what I tell you, and I'm telling you to loosen up. Why bother with anything if you can't have fun?"

Because some people actually had to earn their own money, not that he had ever considered that.

He grinned and swung himself off the stool, leaving the note on the bar.

"Bring them over," he called back at Lali. "And get her drunk."

"Cocky prick," the Sri-Lankan muttered, tucking the money into her bra.

Carrie laughed; that sounded very funny in her beautiful, smooth voice. The woman definitely knew a lot more English than she let on.

"Truth," Lali shrugged.

It certainly was. Trying to keep the VIP room respectable with his hundred decibel voice singing in the corner, coupled with the whooping of his alpha-male lad friend Ieuan, was near impossible. As Lisa had said, the guy lived for attention and he certainly got it. Jay seemed to have no qualms about saying and doing whatever was in his head; he knew full well that people like Ieuan didn't care as long as he kept supplying them with cash and drugs, and as long as he had his gaggle of followers, pissing everyone else off was just entertaining. Carrie spent half the night apologising to disgruntled VIPs and trying to minimise any embarrassment to Yoonho's good name, while his brother continued in his campaign to get the whole world looking at him.

Admittedly, they were sort of amusing. Ieuan was a carbon copy of the tools she used to serve in the student union, and though Jay was a pain in the arse, he was very easy to laugh at, which the dancers did frequently. Still, she did want to smother them all by the time her shift ended and it was time to shut the bar.

A collective groan went up from the booth as they finally realised they had to leave.

"Hey gorgeous," Ieuan leant over the bar. "We need Jay's card back. Going M.O.S, if you're up for it?"

Carrie hesitated but Lali reached immediately for the credit card beside the till.

"Normality," she reassured Carrie, then coolly turned to Ieuan. "No thank you."

"Suit yourself," he saluted.

Carrie watched the group as they staggered out, each in varying stages of intoxication.

"Wait," she called after them, but they had already squashed themselves into the lift. "Where's Jay? They've got his card; shouldn't he be with them?"

"Normality," Lali shrugged again and continued tidying behind the bar.

Carrie wasn't entirely sure if Lali had understood her, but normality or not, she wasn't comfortable with it. He might like to splash his cash but if Yoonho found out they'd just given away his brother's credit card she doubted he'd be pleased.

"There," Lali pointed elegantly at the booth.

Carrie almost couldn't see him. Jay was sprawled unceremoniously on the floor, head lolling onto the seat, dead to the world.

"Jesus," Carrie slid out from behind the bar.

"Not problem," Lali proceeded to clean up around him as if he were just another piece of furniture. "Clean, go home. Not problem of you."

"We can't just leave him here," Carrie frowned. "We're shutting up the bar."

"Not problem," Lali told her. "Normality."

Carrie headed to the booth anyway. Yes, he was a Park and by definition an arsehole, but nobody deserved to be so carelessly abandoned while their so-called friends spent their money. She should at least get him off the floor and back to his room.

"Get up," she knelt down and roughly threw his arm over her shoulder.

It instantly fell off again.

"Oh, wake up," she slapped his cheeks.

He groaned and opened his eyes.

"Right, come on, get up."

She heaved him to his feet, being nearly pulled over in the process.

"Piss off," he tried to shove her away. "I'm a Park; I can walk."

"Yeah right," she picked him back up.

He was the one who had suggested she "loosen up" and not jump every time she was told to – well, pissing off was going to be one of those orders that she ignored. He was hardly in any state to tell her what to do or to expect her to take his shit, especially when nobody else was showing him any sympathy.

"Yeah right," he repeated and gave up, drooling on her shoulder.

"Thank you," she said sarcastically.

"I'll buy you a new one," he slurred.

"A new shoulder?" she questioned. "I don't think even you can buy that."

"I can buy what the fuck I like," he retorted. "I'm a Park."

"You're a pain in the arse, is what you are," she told him, very tempted to leave him after all.

He scowled. "You can't say that to me."

Cara Parry could, though she definitely shouldn't. She wouldn't dare with anybody else in the family, and he was part of that family; her employer and one of the most influential gangsters in London. But he was also a slobbering drunk who was too dysfunctional to be frightening and probably wouldn't remember in the morning anyway. Maybe Yoonho would even thank her for putting up with him long enough to get him off the VIP room floor. Plus, if more people actually told him the truth he might not be such a brat.

She practically dragged him over to the lift, praying that he wouldn't vomit in the finely carpeted corridor.

"You're gonna have to help me here," she held his face close to the keypad. "Your floor has a code."

"Get in."

She almost dropped him in shock. The lift doors had opened as soon as they drew near enough to activate the sensors, but she hadn't noticed Han standing quietly in the corner. Carrie obeyed, avoiding the man's black eyes as he typed in the access number and they rose to the floor that contained the living quarters of the two youngest brothers. She thanked Han, bowed like an idiot and helped Jay out of the lift. That man really was the scariest person she had ever met. She stared at the closed lift door for a while, then felt Jay nuzzling into her neck and remembered what she was here for.

Luckily, her charge had not given away his room card and she could finally get through the door and deposit him on the bouncy leather sofa. She flexed her shoulder then went in search of water. It was more a studio apartment than a hotel room, which she supposed made sense for someone who lived here permanently. She could make out a sort of living room, bedroom and en-suite bathroom, and curtains covering glass doors that opened onto a balcony. The carpet and drapes were rich shades of red, the sofa and surfaces black. They gave the impression of having been very chic and polished once, but now bore the scars of cigarette burns and all sorts of knocks and scrapes. It wasn't exactly dirty or untidy – the long-suffering cleaning staff clearly serviced the place regularly – but she could tell that the room wanted to be much grander than it was allowed.

"Beer's in the fridge," Jay flopped his hand in the vague direction of a minibar.

"I'm not looking for beer," she said, to no response.

Fortunately, there was also mineral water in the fridge. She plonked a bottle onto the coffee table in front of him.

"Drink it," she ordered, feeling oddly powerful.

"Don't fucking tell me what to do," he scowled, but obeyed. "Ugh, what the hell? This isn't beer."

"It's water," she told him. "It's good for you. Now drink it and go to bed."

"I'm not sleepy," he complained.

Carrie sighed. "You're like a child."

"Fuck off," he glared suspiciously at the water like it was about to stab him when his back was turned. "I'm not going to sleep. Last time I went to sleep I woke up on the roof with sunburn and a condom on my face."

Carrie snorted. That was funny.

"I promise I don't have any condoms or the access code to the roof," she chuckled.

"What then? Why are you even here?"

Now it was her turn to be looked at like she was going to stab someone. He definitely was sleepy, whatever he said – his eyelids were drooping even as he stared at her.

"Do I owe you money?"

"What?" she was confused. "No."

"Did I mess up again?" he squinted. "Did Han make you get me?"

"No?"

She was starting to feel bad for laughing as she began to understand the bewildered look on his face. It really was normality for him to be left passed out on the floor. To his brothers he was an irritation that if ignored would go away. To everyone else he was connections and a credit card. Neither camp saw any point in looking after him at the end of the day.

"Did no-one ever just give you a water and put you to bed?" she asked sympathetically.

"I don't need that shit," he poured the rest of the bottle over his head and shook himself like a dog. "I'm a Park."

"You're a drunk and a cokehead," she corrected him. "You need to look after yourself, or someone does."

"What?" he tried to throw the bottle at her but gloriously missed. "Don't be a wanker."

"I'm not being a wanker, I'm being honest." She guessed people didn't really do that either. "You don't need another one of them; sucking up to your face and taking your money."

"They can have money," he puckered his lips. "They're nice to me."

"Do condoms on your face count as nice?" she asked dubiously.

"Obviously," he dabbed his nose on the back of his hand – it had started to bleed. "It's funny. They love me; I buy them drugs."

Carrie looked around for a tissue.

"Don't be gross," she handed it to him.

He held it against his face and let his head droop onto the arm of the sofa.

She peered at him. "Are you actually just gonna sleep on the sofa?"

"Mm," he hugged a cushion. "I'm not tired."

"Right."

She sighed and went to fetch a duvet from the bed, putting the bottle in the bin on the way. He was already asleep by the time she returned, bleeding all over his fancy velvet cushion. He didn't look much like a gangster, just a bit pathetic. At least she had spied the floor code beneath Han's fingers. That might come in useful.

10: Never Indulge a Narcissist

<u>**26 June 2014**</u>

The casino was busier than usual. Well, perhaps that wasn't quite the way to describe it. Carrie had started to notice a pattern that Wendy was keen to get a deeper understanding of. It wasn't regular enough to cause suspicion unless you were specifically looking for cracks, but certain repeat customers were incredibly bad at gambling. At first she had thought they were simply addicts – there were certainly plenty of those about – but as, with Lisa's help, she had begun to get to know the loyal clientele, it had come to her attention that these particular people never seemed to mind. Perhaps time spent with Yoonho was making her snobby, but they didn't seem rich enough not to care if they recurrently lost thousands of pounds. They wore suits and shiny shoes, but not to the standard of the CEO and his favourite millionaire acquaintances, and they never paid for access to the executive floors. Plus any apparent anxiety was only skin deep, or so it seemed; they showed none of the distressed frenzy or depression she saw in the others whom Lisa had marked as people who couldn't quit.

"Can someone please tell him it's not okay to sleep on tables?" Jennie approached where Lisa and Carrie were working side by side, jabbing her thumb at Jay who was face down on a blackjack table.

Carrie had been distracted by the sight of the man with the top hat, who had returned to the casino a few times in the last week – minus his hat and a number of fingers. Rumour had it he had lost them in a boating accident.

Lisa gave Jennie a look. "You ain't got no mouth, girl?"

"Ugh, he's annoying though," she scowled. "He'll just be a prick."

They were rather similar in that aspect; Jennie and Jay. They both possessed a good deal of self-importance and unwillingness to do anything they deemed beneath them. Perhaps that was why the girl disliked him so much.

"Language on the floor," Lisa warned her.

"I'll sort it," Carrie offered. "Just take over for me here."

"Is that a good idea, hon?" Lisa raised her pencilled eyebrows. "You should never indulge a narcissist. Jennie, doll, go do your job."

Last night had already been brought up in their changing room chatter and everyone seemed to agree that her reaction had been entertainingly naïve and unnecessary, although it may result in her receiving a lot of cash. She wasn't sure she would ever get used to that mindset – using people purely for the sake of money – but Paradise was overflowing with it. She supposed that was to be expected.

"I don't think I indulged him," Carrie frowned. "I just took him upstairs and told him his friends are rubbish."

"You actually said that?" Jennie asked in amusement. "I've never heard you say anything bad to anyone."

"You're coming outta your shell, girlie," Lisa clapped her on the back. "Congratulations. But probably best not to take it out on a Park, even if it is Jay. You don't know chaos 'til you seen one o' his temper tantrums. It ain't pretty."

Carrie promised to bear that in mind. She liked that she was beginning to learn how to speak her mind, but she doubted it was worth being on the wrong end of a Jay temper tantrum.

"Are we going to play or what?" a gambler interrupted impatiently.

Jennie seized Carrie's deck before Lisa could object any further and elbowed her out from her table. Carrie took a breath and headed over to Jay, where another worker was tentatively trying to wake him.

"Morning," she sat down next to him. "You do have a bed, y'know."

Her colleague stared at her in alarm. Nobody spoke to Parks like that.

Jay raised his head and opened his puffy eyes.

"I can sleep where the fuck I like," he yawned loudly, ruining any pretext of aggression.

"Well it's five o'clock and people are trying to use the table," she pointed out.

"They can use the table," he pulled a face. "No-one's stopping them."

She shook her head in disbelief. "You sort of are."

She was already forgetting Lisa's advice, but there was something so petty about him that she couldn't make herself be scared. Even David's briefing had ridiculed him and marked him as useless, and she had seen nothing to suggest otherwise. Besides, his snoring was definitely costing Yoonho revenue and Yoonho was actually important.

"I'm your fucking boss, staff lady," he scowled at her. "Who the hell tells their boss what to do?"

"Someone who wants their boss to make more money by moving off the blackjack table and letting people use it," she answered. "I'm just doing my job."

"Blah blah job," he wrinkled his nose like he was smelling something disgusting. "Jobs are boring; take the day off."

"I don't think I can do that," Carrie chuckled despite herself.

"Yes you can," he replied and banged his fist on the table. "Oi! Brick!"

"Will you please stop doing that," Carrie winced. "You'll get me in trouble."

"Brick!" he ignored her. "Get the fuck over here!"

The supervisor bustled over, clearly displeased. "What is it?"

"Her shift's over," Jay told him.

"No it's not," Carrie said, puzzled.

"No," Brick echoed. "It's not."

"I'll pay you," he pulled a wad of cash from his pocket.

"Stop joking around, Jay," Brick said grumpily. "We're busy."

"I'm not joking," Jay waved the money in his face.

Brick's eyes followed it, looking tempted.

"Look here," he puffed out his chest and tore his gaze away. "I answer directly to Yoonho and Cara answers directly to me."

"And I'm Yoonho's brother so my orders are his orders and worth much more than you," Jay tried to stuff the notes into his hand. "Or do you want me to tell him you're being a shit?"

Brick huffed but took the money and instructed Carrie to obey him until her shift was actually over. The entire thing was utterly ridiculous, but if Brick commanded it then she didn't have much of a choice. Jay smirked triumphantly and finally vacated the table.

"You'd better not get me fired," Carrie looked uncertainly after her supervisor's retreating back.

"Nah," he replied with a confident smile. "Yoonho likes to be pissed off at me, not random workers. Now," he stretched and yawned. "I'm fucking starving. You been to the restaurant?"

She hadn't because it was horrendously expensive, but she did as she was told and he insisted that he would foot the bill. It was a sort of payment, he told her, to make them even for her helping him out last night. She also suspected it was a bandage for his ego and a way to make himself feel like the big man. She ordered the cheapest thing on the menu – a salmon fishcake, which was definitely not cheap – and he ordered something that wasn't on the menu at all. Parks didn't "need that shit" apparently.

For somebody who just wanted to pay her back for carrying him upstairs, and had only just re-emerged from sleep, he was incredibly keen on talking. She let him blabber on about anecdotes from parties (some of which were admittedly pretty entertaining) and how great he was at poker when everyone else wasn't apparently cheating. Maybe Lisa was right; she was sort of indulging him. It could be a good opportunity though, to get in with another brother as well as enjoying the feeling of actually being equal to (or perhaps even better than) someone. She hadn't realised how inferior other people made her feel until she found that he didn't.

She was just hearing about a time when he and Soju had broken into a zoo while high off their nut when the food arrived – apparently the only thing that could shut him up. He was already digging in before the plate had even touched the table, then realised it was piping hot and proceeded to make it known with a lot of flapping and loud noises. Carrie couldn't stop herself from chortling.

"Sorry," she said sheepishly when he had finished flapping and she had finished laughing. "I do that all the time too."

"Well you could've done it this time," he huffed, but continued to shovel boiling food into his mouth. "You think I'm a twat, don't you."

"What? No," Carrie answered automatically.

"Don't bullshit me," he scorned. "It's not like I care. Why should I? I'm rich."

"Is that all you think about?" she chomped on a piece of salmon. It was good. "Money and parties?"

"Obviously," he looked at her like she was from another planet. "What else is there to care about?"

"I dunno," she shrugged. "World hunger?"

He pulled a face. "You're so proper; live a little. I never see you out."

"I've been to your parties," she told him. "There's a lot of people there; you must not have noticed."

"Good point," he nodded conceitedly, still stuffing food into his mouth like it was about to disappear. "There are a fuck tonne of people. Pretty, right?"

"Yeah, I guess so," she thought about it as she chewed more salmon. It was really, really good. "It always reminds me of Gatsby parties."

He seemed very pleased by that thought.

"Really? I actually read *The Great Gatsby*," he said proudly, as if reading a book was a huge achievement to show off about. To be fair, she was surprised; David had said he hardly went to school. "It was Emilia's favourite, and the guy's fucking awesome."

"You think?" she sucked on her fork. "No-one really liked him though."

"Who cares?" Jay dismissed her. "He has epic parties and everyone knows who he is."

"I guess," she contemplated. He had definitely missed the point, but oh well. "If that's what's important to you then yeah, he's pretty cool."

"Exactly," he agreed. "Life's for having fun. You, though," he pointed his knife at her. "Are definitely a Nick. You don't do anything. You need a mate who can show you all the cool shit."

He flashed her a showy grin.

"Right," she laughed. "Just don't expect me to join your bootlegging business or set you up with my cousin."

She realised she should have jumped on the chance to do some digging at the mention of Emilia Young – David probably would have done so without even needing to think about it – but she had been too surprised to suddenly be discussing classic literature with the Park family delinquent. She would have to keep a better ear open in future and seize any opportunity to shed light on Mr Park's probably murdered visa-bride. It wasn't her actual job, but surely Wendy and Brian would appreciate that.

In the meantime, Jay was determined to be true to his promise of showing her "cool shit" as often as her schedule would allow. When she told him that Bea and Lisa had already given her the grand tour, he took great delight in pointing out that they couldn't possibly have shown her the exclusive family places, and she took great delight in seeing them. There could certainly be no harm in collecting an ever-growing list of lift codes and random information; for the case and for her reputation as a hardworking detective. Plus, rooftop pools were pretty damn cool. She was going to be as useful as possible before her stint on this job ended, and she might as well have a bit of fun while she was at it.

<u>**06 July 2014**</u>

"He really is the most ridiculous person," she told David. "It's like he actively wants to tell me everything I'm not supposed to know. I don't think anyone's actually talked to him before; the girls definitely haven't and Ieuan's not interested in anything except getting stoned and laid. We should've aimed for him all along."

"Unfortunately he doesn't know much," David leaned back on the sofa. "It's a shame, but understandable."

"I have found out *some* things," she popped a chip into her mouth to hide her mild indignance. "He knows a lot of pimps and dealers, and some of them are pretty nasty too."

"We will get them eventually," he promised. "You're getting us a nice backlog to clean up once the big fish are fried, but it would be too suspicious to suddenly round up everyone Jay knows. We've been down that track before; the small guys are too scared to take a plea deal and it's all water off Park's back."

He was right, of course. It was annoying but undeniable. Sneaking around with access codes was all well and good when not in a casino full of security cameras that Han probably monitored even in his sleep. If he did sleep. And now identifying drug dealers was apparently pointless too. She was just playing spy and showing her inexperience.

She did know more personal things about the family now though, such as Jay's suspicion that Margot and Yoonho couldn't have children and that, while they had never disobeyed Mr Park, it was Han to whom the security team really belonged. Jay would have one line of coke or a spliff (or both) and not shut up about how great or awful his brothers were, depending on his mood. Or how cool his car was.

The latter aside, David had to admit that being aware of topics to approach and to avoid would be handy for both of them to bear in mind when navigating the path to Yoonho's trust. She wasn't completely useless.

"You're doing great," he reassured her. "There's definitely no harm in fitting in if you're careful. It's like Bence and me; you can make friends as long as you're cool with it and don't come across as a fake."

"I know," she ate another chip. "I don't think I'll come across as fake. He's actually sort of funny; I don't mind hanging out with him when I'm not working and my big bro's occupied."

She held up her thumb and finger in an 'OK' sign. "No bullshit."

It was true; he was sort of funny. He said things without thinking, seemingly safe in the knowledge that everyone knew he was a mess so he could proudly own it. To her, who had been socially acceptable all her life, the concept was completely alien and almost inspiring. The Hannah-ish confidence that she had secretly longed for started to raise its head when she spoke to somebody who just didn't give a shit. She was sarcastic and made jokes and it was fun. It wasn't that she particularly liked him as a person, but she liked herself when she was with him.

David laughed. "No bullshit."

The agent, Donny Logan, wasn't quite respected enough to be entertained in Yoonho's throne room, but he did get a full spread of food and a full team of ladies to watch more seedily than the eldest Park did. He looked to be perhaps in his fifties, with badly dyed hair gelled back in a quiff like he thought he was living in the '60s, and he chewed a lot on a toothpick, giving the impression of somebody who wanted so badly to be cool that he missed the mark by a mile.

Yoonho and his brothers hosted him in a blue meeting room below ground, beside the parking lot and away from the eyes of any curious casino-goers. Carrie was surprised to see that Jay was actually in attendance this time, though apparently only as a gesture to persuade Yoonho to stop boxing in his car – a cherry red Mustang convertible that he showed off at any opportunity. When asked why he was boxed in in the first place, he simply flashed Carrie a grin and told her "I'm irresponsible", like that was a thing to be proud of.

Donny Logan finished with his fish, picked the specks of flesh from between his teeth and finally began to talk business.

"There are a lot of new people in town," he informed them. "A few dealers from Birmingham and a Scottish man sniffing about in the shadows for something he won't let on about."

"Yes, it's called social mobility," Soju said uninterestedly. "People move house these days. What's your point?"

"It's causing problems," Donny replied coarsely. "I'm already up to my ears in people pushing their luck since Mr Park retired. Chinatown still won't pay up."

Soju glanced darkly at Yoonho.

"We're not increasing rent in Chinatown," the CEO said firmly. "The Dragon is one of our oldest allies and we have a mutual respect."

"Well he wants too much, if you ask me," Donny told him.

"We don't," Soju narrowed his eyes coldly.

"What other problems?" Yoonho changed the subject, speaking a lot more cordially than his brother.

"There are skirmishes in Brixton," he continued. "It's getting crowded in there with all the new blood and people being kicked off Russian turf. Lots of small-time stuff going bad. With all the extra work I'm getting my son involved, so I'll need a higher cut."

"Oi," Jay stopped stuffing his face to speak. "What about me?"

"What about you?" Soju gave him an incredibly disinterested look.

"I'm supposed to be the one helping this prick," he protested.

"Yes, you can get your son on board," Yoonho said quickly. Carrie could feel the exasperation radiating from him. "Just please sort these things out and stop bringing them to me. Skirmishes in Brixton are hardly the problem of a property shareholder. Anything that can't be fixed, publicly disinvest; make it known that we don't stand for less than perfect."

"Small-time stuff going bad": she wondered if anybody had ever said that about Big Mo, when it was Mr Park sitting in that chair. He would have dismissed it just as easily as his son did now, like these lives were nothing more than an irritation to be dealt with lower down the food chain. They were despicable; the both of them.

The agent eventually left and Yoonho exhaled heavily, closing his eyes and intentionally avoiding the requirement to acknowledge his youngest brother's continued existence. As the weeks went on, Carrie had noticed more and more how tired he seemed behind the composed exterior. Brian Hole had been correct in his assumption; running both a legitimate business and a crime empire in his father's shadow must be tough.

"When can we remove him?" Soju questioned. "I can make the finances say we need a restructure; voluntary redundancies and the like. Or involuntary ones."

His mouth twitched in a dark smile.

"To make a person redundant they should actually be redundant," Yoonho reminded him.

"That's not what Dad thought," Soju replied. "If he isn't loyal, he should go."

"Donny is loyal and important," Yoonho said finally. "That's the end of it. We're not restructuring anything."

"Shame," Soju yawned and stretched out his arms along the back of the sofa. "I have never met anyone more useless." He turned his head to Jay. "Well, maybe I have, hey Wanwan?"

"Fuck you," he scowled.

"I suppose you did show up this time at least," Soju drawled. "Should I congratulate you?"

"You should fuck off," Jay glared at him. "You can all fuck off. Why am I here if you're just gonna chat shit about me all the time?"

He stormed from the room and slammed the door, causing Yoonho to sigh deeply and rub the bridge of his nose.

"Why is he here?" Soju asked. "We already tried getting him involved, and all he did was get high and punch a Chinaman."

"I ask myself the same question every day," Yoonho told him wearily and got to his feet. "Cara, please accompany me. I need you to explain my brother."

Carrie wasn't sure exactly what light she could shed on the subject, but she obliged as best she could. Being asked personal questions could never be a bad thing when it came to working her way into his confidence.

Soju watched her with interest as they left the room, Han with something darker and less discernible. She glanced back at them before Yoonho closed the door.

"I don't trust her," Han was saying in a low voice. "I can't work out what she wants from him."

Carrie got the feeling he was talking about her.

"Who cares?" Soju swilled his martini indifferently. "Let Wanwan pretend he has friends. No-one else loves him."

Her chest tightened. Han didn't trust anyone and David's file had correctly predicted that she would be no different, but that didn't stop her pulse from quickening. David's file also suspected that Han made people disappear.

Soju and Yoonho liked her, she tried to reassure herself. Han listened to them and wouldn't hurt anyone without the CEO's approval. That was what David said anyway – did he really have any proof? Jay had also mentioned Han's devotion to his older brother, she remembered with a calming breath, and he actually did have proof. She picked up her pace and hurried after Yoonho. He liked her, and that seemed to be keeping her safe from a lot of things.

"Where did I go wrong with him?" he asked as they took the lift up to his rooms.

"Jay?" Carrie thought hard. Letting him run wild and throwing money at him to make him shut up probably counted as going wrong, but that would not be the right thing to say. "I don't think anything's your fault. He just likes having fun."

"I suppose," he concurred. "But it's highly impractical. We have a reputation to uphold and there's a big difference between the odd night out and scrapping with business associates. I really can't trust him at all."

He skipped the throne room and led her into his private quarters. They were significantly larger than Jay's and very modern; none of the rebellious reds and blacks and bins overflowing with empty bottles and cigarette packets. Everything was very bright and clean and reminiscent of the fancy apartments in American city dramas. He even had his own full kitchenette, complete with hanging LEDs and an island where Carrie could imagine Fiona chopping fruit for smoothies. She couldn't decide what was more pretentious; Jay's bad boy gangster pad or Yoonho's banker penthouse. It wasn't even a real penthouse – that luxury belonged to Mr Park alone.

"Must you really bring them in here?" Margot spoke coolly from a large armchair, legs crossed elegantly and delicate nose in a magazine. "I'm getting rather sick of this."

"Don't overreact, darling," Yoonho said with empty affection. "Cara and I simply need to speak about a few things."

Carrie gave the woman an apologetic half-smile. Yoonho was more fake with his own wife than Carrie was with a crime syndicate, and as much as she wished she would stop glaring at her so judgmentally, Margot could hardly be described as overreacting.

"Of course you do," she folded the magazine neatly and got to her feet. "I'm supping with Beatrice anyway and I need to get ready. Enjoy your chat."

"Have a good evening," Yoonho called after her.

She ignored him, gave Carrie a haughty look of distaste and exited the room.

"Wives," Yoonho shook his head in plastic fondness. "Be glad you'll never have one."

"Brothers are just as bad," Carrie ventured. "And I do have one of those."

"Ah yes," he smiled – still a model Yoonho smile, but noticeably truer than that which he gave his wife. "Please, have a drink."

He motioned to a jug of water, prettified by the bright yellows and greens of sliced lemons and mint leaves that floated within it.

"Would you like one?" she asked and poured herself a glass, more out of politeness than real thirst.

"Perhaps something stronger," he gestured towards a bottle of whiskey sitting neatly on a shelf and sat deeply into a pristine armchair. "And a dance. My head is heavy."

"Of course," Carrie nodded and obeyed.

Dancing in meetings was strange and sleazy enough, but a one-on-one performance without even Lisa, Lali or Jennie's presence was something she was definitely not yet used to. Yoonho had, thus far, continued to be what he considered a gentleman, but the bulge in his trousers still made Carrie wary. At least talking was less awkward when she had something else to focus on, even if that something was how best to relax her misogynistic employer.

"All I've ever wanted is money and beauty," he sighed. "What I get is brothers. They come at me from both sides. Soju wants to fire all the staff and do everything himself, and Wanwan is incapable of anything. I already have a business to run; is a little peace from them really too much to ask?"

He gratefully sipped his whiskey while taking in the movement of her hips.

"Don't misunderstand; Soju has a brilliant mind," he continued. "Perhaps a little too brilliant. He picks things up faster than I can teach them and is therefore easily bored. Sometimes I am very tempted to give him what he wants and let him run it all – at least it would keep him busy and allow less time for more unpleasant pastimes. He plays too many games. I'm sure you know of the scandal we had a few years ago because of his need to amuse himself. At least Wan only takes drugs – Soju had his own mini enterprise."

Okay, Yoonho Park, two could play at that exasperated innocence charade.

"I know the feeling," she told him, running her hands seductively up her stomach. "My brother's clever too and everyone loves him. If he isn't occupied he likes to talk his way into more 'exciting' jobs and be far too good at them, and he's already getting bored. It isn't so easy getting work after prison… I wish I could give him something to do."

She left it there. That should be sufficient praise and notice of Drew's availability for now; she didn't want to cross a line and seem too keen. Yoonho wanted trustworthy support, not overambitious drug dealers and their sisters.

He chuckled. "It seems we're both the long-suffering sensible sibling."

Carrie agreed. Empathy was good and she did sort of know what he meant. She had no maverick sibling, but perhaps too much being sensible had made her as frustrated as he was. Jay certainly thought so.

She got changed as usual after her shift was over, then returned to the lift and exited on Jay's floor. Yoonho had asked her to check on him and she had a few curiosities of her own that she wanted to settle. She rapped on the door a few times before it was opened and he led her through to the balcony. She sat down against the wall, glad of the opportunity to rest her feet, while he picked up an unfinished cigarette.

"You want one?" he asked, not sounding in the best of moods.

"No thanks," she replied.

She rested her chin on her knees and looked out on London through the decorative pillars of the concrete balustrade.

"Yoonho was just talking to me about you," she told him. "What's Wanwan?"

"Not my fucking name," he scowled.

She laughed at the immensely sulky glare on his face.

"Fuck off," he flicked ash irritably onto his shoes. "My brothers are just twats who think I'm five. It's bad enough they won't call me Jay, but I don't need fucking Wanwan."

"What do you mean, they won't call you Jay?" Carrie said cautiously. She was certainly intrigued by the change of names in his and Soju's case profiles, but couldn't let on that she knew about that. "I've heard them."

"Yeah, they let me get away with it in front of staff," he took the cigarette from his lips and glowered at it. "Most of the time. They don't think I'm good enough for business names. They call Taeju Soju these days, and they've been Yoonho and Han forever, but I don't even get fucking Taehwan anymore. Taeju started it, obviously."

"Wait, what?" Carrie stopped him. "I'm confused."

"Ah, fuck," he dropped his head back against the wall a little harder than intended. "I'm not meant to talk about this shit."

"What shit?" she pressed.

He huffed grumpily. He wasn't in the mood for keeping family secrets.

"Our names aren't really our names," he tried to explain. "Dad likes to fuck with our heads. We had proper names in Korea – Yoonho was Taeyoon, Han was Taejong, and me and Taeju were me and Taeju. I guess Dad must've had another name too, but I dunno what – he's always just been Mr Park or Dad to us."

That, Carrie thought with curiosity, was something that Wendy would surely be interested in. She supposed it did make sense for political refugees to create a new identity, but there must be something that Brian could do with this information and she wanted so desperately to be valuable to the case. She had already managed to mention Drew to Yoonho, she was pleased to remember – she was on a roll today.

"Why did they change?" she probed.

"I dunno," he shrugged. "Respect or some shit like that. It's like we're a different family; Yoonho and Han got business names that everyone has to call them except each other, and me and Taeju were just the kids that no-one gave a shit about."

"Oh," she gave him a sympathetic look. "So your real name's Taehwan Park?"

"Lee," he corrected her. "Taehwan Lee. We were all Lee before. Well, in Korea it's just 'Ee' but we say it 'Lee' in English; Taeju told me that. The others never talk about surnames, or anything else from before – not with us anyway – but it always pissed him off that Dad kept us out, so he never forgot what we were supposed to forget and he learned Russian so he could secretly re-learn Korean at the same time. It's fucking hard, by the way – Taeju's a genius."

"Why did he go to prison?" she dared to query while Soju remained the topic of conversation.

It was expressly against Wendy's orders to ask too many questions, but Jay was in such an obliging mood and Yoonho's mention of it had really made her wonder. Besides, he was incredibly easy to talk to and it hardly even felt like questioning.

"He was selling stuff," he said simply.

"Yeah, but why *really*?" she pressed. "Don't rich guys normally make more of an effort to get their kids a dodgy judge or something?"

"Well, yeah," he snorted. "He was definitely pissing Dad off. He didn't wanna follow orders, just be clever and fuck with people for the hell of it. Nothing else worked on him, so Dad got him put away to sort him out and 'realise his potential'." He shuddered. "It worked I guess; he's all businessy now and it's just me he fucks with for the hell of it. Everyone else he fucks with for a reason."

A dark shadow passed across his eyes. "I should be glad I'm too stupid for Dad to give a shit; at least he'll never do that to me."

Carrie wasn't sure what to say to that.

"Anyway," he kicked the floor moodily and changed the subject back again. "No-one calls me Taehwan anymore. Not that I give a shit, obviously. Fuck them – everyone else respects me enough to call me Jay like a real fucking Park."

"What is Jay then?" she asked.

"Parties and money," he blew a steady stream of smoke across the balcony.

"Right," she smiled with amusement and watched it twist and dissipate. "Parties and money. Gotcha, Wanwan."

"David?" she called. "Do you think I should go clubbing tonight?"

He popped his head up the stairs from the kitchen. The little terraced house they rented was the skinniest dwelling Carrie had ever seen. It felt like there had once been an alleyway between the rows either side and somebody had squeezed it in as an afterthought. The rooms were packed in over three storeys: the shower shared the top floor with Carrie's long, thin single bedroom and David's marginally shorter, wider one; the living room took up the middle one; and a set of steps led down below the pavement level to the kitchen. It was the living room, with its single sofa and surprisingly large TV, into which the front door opened and Carrie entered their humble home.

"Do you want to go clubbing?" David smiled in amusement. "I'm not actually your brother; you don't have to ask my permission."

"I know, I wanna know what you think though," Carrie replied. "Jay wants me to go."

"Why not?" he asked. "That sounds like a good opportunity to me; get him drunk, butter him up. Unless you're worried you might slip up?"

"I don't think he needs my help to get drunk, or any more buttering up," Carrie chuckled. "And I don't think I'd slip up; I've been fine when I've gone out with the girls and that's a *lot* of drinking."

"That's sorted then," he shrugged. "You have no reason not to. This pasta's almost finished, then you can head out."

"Wanna come with me?" she asked sheepishly.

"Are you scared to party with a Park?" David teased.

"No," she said quickly. "I just thought it might be a good chance to introduce you."

And yes, maybe she was a little scared of venturing out beyond the safety of the casino walls and into disputed territory with an alcoholic gangster brat – not that she was going to admit that.

"Sorry, little sis," he scratched the back of his head. "I'm on a job for Bence tonight and if there's anything that won't impress Yoonho Park, it's unreliability."

Carrie couldn't argue with that.

"Go out," he encouraged her. "Have some fun, live a little. This is your life for now – might as well enjoy it, get to know how the other side live."

Carrie could have fun when she wanted to. She had had her fair share of parties at uni. Of course, she had always been up in time for lectures the next day, as she would be up in time for the library tomorrow, but she had still enjoyed herself. With Hannah as her best friend, it would have been impossible not to dance on a few tables and snog a few dickheads.

"Yeah," she said decidedly. "Fuck it, why not?"

"That's my girl," he raised a hand to high five her through the stair rail. "Don't do anything I wouldn't."

Carrie didn't actually know what David wouldn't do, but being an undercover cop who infiltrated drug gangs, she assumed not a lot. She would follow his advice, she wouldn't slip up and she would show her brother that his faith in her was justified. She was pleasantly surprised by how easy it was becoming to slot into this life and it only made sense to turn on the Cara-courage and widen her experiences – she was on a roll today, after all.

Of course the great Jay Park couldn't hit the town without a full entourage, though he seemed to give as few shits about them as they did about him. Good, Carrie thought; they deserved that. He seemed a lot more excited about the fact that she was present and had cheered up immensely since their chat on the balcony a few hours ago. Carrie was also in a good mood, her progress with Yoonho and the family's real names still making her feel rather smug.

"Right," Jay pulled out a fifty from his pocket and turned it into a straw. "I am gonna show you how to do stuff."

"Are you?" Carrie snickered.

"Yes. Because you," he tapped his rolled up note on her nose. "Need to have more fun."

"And you," she pulled a face. "Have a problem."

"I have style," Jay corrected her with a grin. "Family shit, remember. Gotta own it."

He winked and turned in his seat to see where Ieuan and the others had taken over the bar, not bothering to hide the lines they drew out with his credit card – Fever paid Park rents so any companion of Jay's wasn't going to get evicted without his agreement.

"Why do you let them do that?" Carrie asked in disapproval. "And don't just tell me you can do what the fuck you like."

"Can't I?" his eyes glinted mischievously as he pulled out an identical card from his pocket. "The Dragon has some fucking awesome forgers. They're gonna get a surprise when they try to pay for shit."

Carrie burst out laughing.

"That's more like it," he smirked. "You're proper laughing."

"What is 'proper' laughing?" she chuckled.

"That is," he rapped on their little table. "Oi! Wankers! Gimme my stuff back!"

Ieuan chucked over the bag of powder. Jay caught it and turned back to Carrie.

"You having some?"

She considered it. It was tempting; now was her time to try everything once, after all, and David had said to experience the lifestyle. All the top London bankers did coke once in a while and they were fine – or so Hannah had insisted one intoxicated night at uni.

She leant forward. "Persuade me."

He was very happy to.

Snorting cocaine through a fifty pound note in a swanky club was not exactly what she had envisaged when she laid in bed wondering about her ex-best friend, but she was Cara now and she could suddenly understand the appeal. She didn't feel particularly drunk, just immensely, inexplicably joyful. There was no reason not to dance like a hooker with Lali or Jennie or some random guy she'd never met before, or to run after Jay screaming with hilarity and flicking the middle finger when Ieuan discovered he'd been duped into paying his own tab. They fled from the bar and into the rain with him hot on their heels, finding refuge in a 24 hour Tesco. Jay frowned snootily; this was far too common a place for him to be seen.

"You're such a cock," Carrie giggled.

"You think they've never done stuff like that to me?" he raised an eyebrow. "They're fucking wankers."

"Fucking wanky arsehole pricky cocky arsehole dickheads," she agreed, much to his amusement.

"Exactly," he chuckled. "You should talk like that more often."

"No," she refused. "I'm a nice polite nice person."

"Bullshit," he pulled a face. "You're not polite to me."

"That's why I like you," she said, then spotted a sale on Shiraz. "Ooh, cheap wine!"

The storm continued outside and they settled down in the cereal aisle, hiding sheepishly behind a shelf trolley as they inhaled more 'stuff' from the back of his hand and listened to the thunder.

"Tell me something," he commanded.

"You're snotting," she laughed.

"Not that," he scowled and wiped his nose on his hand. "I'm always telling you stuff; you must have things you wanna say too. 'Wanwan you're a brat' doesn't count."

She snorted. "Fine, umm, things… cats are really cute."

Why was that the first thing that came into her head?

Jay guffawed. "Okay, I guess that's a start."

"But I never got one cos Fi-Drew…" Yes, Drew, not Fiona, she reminded herself – don't fuck it. "Doesn't like them."

"Twat."

"Yes, twat," she sniggered. "He *is* a twat. She… he… he's so… blonde! He can just smile at people and they love him and I can't compete. Sh-he's the pretty, clever, social butterfly one, I'm just the shit one. I never even did anything wrong – I could've flunked school and been a meth head, but all I did was be boring and I still manage to fuck up. Stop working too hard Cara, your grades aren't good enough Cara, stop embarrassing us, blah blah smile for the neighbours, don't have emotions cos emotions aren't pretty. I was like five when she told me off for crying in a school play. And then I'm boring and a workaholic because he always *told* me to be boring.

"And I don't say anything and I don't get angry cos it's not his fault, he's just *better*. And he knows he is and he doesn't know what it's like not to be and I love her to bits and I know he was only ever trying to be nice, but he was a patronising prick sometimes, like he always thought I couldn't do it and he needed to look after me twenty-four-seven, and then I fucked up and she didn't talk to me for years."

She took a deep breath and tried to stop accidentally referring to David as a girl. Come to think of it, a lot of those things she thought about Fiona were things she feared might come to pass with him if she ever messed up. Her two lives were mixing in her head.

"He's here now though, right?" Jay reminded her.

"Yeah he is," she nodded. "And I'm paying the rent and helping him find a job, so I'm actually important, and I just want him to know that I can do it. He's so fucking cool and I wanna be him so bad. He's just the best person and I'm so, *so* happy right now, like, I have a real brother and he's too cool for me but it's just so fucking *nice*. Like really, really nice, and I don't wanna screw up and lose it again and I don't want it all to go away when this shit ends.

"What if I can't do it? What if Yoonho doesn't like me enough and I get fired or something? It's scary sometimes – the way people look at me – and I know Han doesn't like anyone and it's not just me, but he's still always there and… Jesus. I need Drew to think I'm good at this shit, and I *am*, I'm sure I am, but what if I'm not? He'll think I'm a twat and I'll be useless and I'll just go back to being nothing. I just wanna be good at things, Jay, and I don't think anyone gets it."

She sniffed and wiped her eyes. Jesus, where had that come from?

"You okay?" Jay asked in concern.

"Whew," she breathed. "I think I've wanted to say that all my life. Sorry. That was a bit too much telling you things."

She hadn't realised just how much any of that had been bothering her. It wasn't the sort of thing she had ever said to anyone before; she wasn't good at emotions.

"What are you sorrying for?" Jay crawled closer to her. "I definitely get it, trust me, so stop thinking you shouldn't talk about things. And don't get sad." He gave her shoulders a squeeze. "That line'll hit soon and you'll be singing into a banana."

"No I won't," she gave him a sideways smile. "People don't sing in supermarkets; we'll get chucked out."

"You look like you want to," he gave her a knowing wink.

She hadn't noticed that her foot had been circling along in time to Idina Menzel on the shop radio. It was a good song.

"Come on," he goaded and started humming himself.

"Shh you," she put a finger to her lips.

He stood up and sang louder.

"Sit down!"

She tried to pull him back down but he just converted to a really bad operatic version, then grabbed the trolley and wheeled it away from her, jumped on it and peddled down the aisle.

"Stop it!" she ordered, trying not to laugh.

He backtracked and returned the trolley to its place.

"I might shut up," he grinned. "If you join in."

She could join in. It was a damn good song, and he wasn't going to stop getting louder or swinging on displays until she did. She opened her mouth, intending to sing quietly but finding it burst passionately from her lungs.

"Yesss!" he slapped her a high five and jumped back on the trolley, chasing her down the aisle with it.

She shrieked and crashed into a pile of cornflakes packets, drawing the attention of the store manager.

"Uh-oh, go time."

Jay sprang from the trolley, seized a couple of the bargain Shiraz bottles and pulled her back out into the street just as a flash of lightning lit up the sky.

"Shit!" she threw her arms over her head; it was raining hard.

He just laughed at her.

"Does this happen every time I tell you something?" she demanded.

"Maybe," he smirked. "You should do it more."

"No," she pouted. "I'm Wanwan Park; you can't tell me what to do."

"Fuck you," he tackled her. "I'm not calling a taxi 'til you've said more things."

"Said what?" she tried to elbow him away. "I've already done that."

"Anything," he dodged her, blinked back rain and shook the drops from his hair, only to continue getting drenched. "What are you thinking right now?"

"I'm fucking soaked and I hate you," she replied.

"Say it louder," he gave her a prod. "Stop squishing yourself."

She squinted up into the clouds, heavy drops splashing onto her skin. She wasn't going to get dry until she did it.

"I'm fucking soaked and I hate you!" she yelled, her voice ricocheting off the raindrops and the sleeping buildings.

"Better?" Jay smiled triumphantly.

"Better!" she yelled again. It sounded funny in the storm. "Wooooooooooo!!!"

She didn't mind the rain anymore. She felt the coolness of it saturate her hair and spread her arms wide, opening her chest to the world as the lightning struck again. It felt so light now that the heavy weight had been lifted and she had given up caring about store managers and angry people trying to sleep. It was the most liberating thing.

"I'm Cara Parry and I can do what the fuck I like!" she hollered gleefully at the sky. "Fuck the world!!!"

She was Cara Parry. And she could do what the fuck she liked.

"Fuck the world!!!" he agreed.

"Aaaaaaaaaaaaaahhhh!!!"

She finished whooping and collapsed in hysterics. The two of them held each other up, laughing at the thunder.

"You," Carrie threw her inebriated arms around him. "Are the best person that ever happened."

He looked surprised, but pleasantly so.

"See," he grinned. "I do care about things that aren't parties and money."

"Oh yeah?" she teased. "Like what?"

"World hunger?"

They both burst into fits of giggles.

"Why is world hunger funny?" Carrie wheezed. "That isn't funny!"

She had never laughed so much in her life, at the stupidest things that shouldn't be remotely amusing. Being Cara, the drugs, the alcohol, the storm and Jay's bad influence – all these things made her feel so free.

<u>18 July 2014</u>

The high was starting to wear off by the time they eventually fell into a taxi in the early hours of the morning. Jay threw cash at the driver to make up for the fact that they had created a puddle on the seat, and started fumbling around for his bag of powder as soon as they entered his bedroom. Carrie collapsed gratefully onto the coffee table as he started to panic.

"Fuck!" he got down on his knees, scrabbling desperately about on the carpet trying to find anything he might have dropped earlier. "How did I run out? I never run out!"

"That was probably my fault," she watched him from her slump.

He didn't answer, just crawled beneath the table, blotted the floor with the fifty pound note and smacked his head hard against the wood as he tried to lick any residue from it.

"Ouch," she winced. "Are you okay?"

"No," he rubbed his head, eyes watering. "I can't find more stuff."

"You're an addict," she frowned. "You need help."

"I'm not a fucking addict," he scowled, still running his hands over the floor. "I can stop any time I want; I just don't want to yet."

"Right," Carrie forced her head off the coffee table and dragged herself over to the minibar. Her head was starting to hurt and everything was getting a lot less bright and funny. "I'm gonna get you some ice."

"There's no ice in there," he told her groggily. "It's a fucking fridge."

"Oh."

She glanced about, her eyes falling on the wine they had brought back from the supermarket. That was needed. She spun the top off as quickly as possible and glugged heartily, then held it out to Jay.

"You need wine."

"Han says red wine's for girls," he pouted, eyed the bottle suspiciously, then snatched it.

Carrie pulled a face. "Who cares? Since when did you do what you're told?"

"Han thinks I'm soft," he said sulkily, but it didn't carry quite his usual brattiness. He didn't seem to be vying for attention; he was just sad. "They all think I'm an idiot."

"You are a bit of an idiot," Carrie teased, taking the bottle back for more.

"Why wouldn't I be?" he scowled. "At least then they remember I exist."

She gave him a sympathetic smile. "Older siblings suck."

"Tell me about it," he kicked a bottle on the floor. "I have three. Taeju was my friend once, then prison turned him into a psychopath."

"Fuck Taeju," she told him. "What do you even want to be his friend for?"

"We used to have fun," he sighed, his aura getting steadily more unhappy. "He was always a bit… I dunno… but it was both of us together once. Now he just fucking hates me."

"You don't need that shitbag," Carrie rested her cheek on his shoulder. "We can have fun now."

"Yeah," he dropped his head onto hers. "Thanks. Y'know, you should call me Taehwan… if you like."

"You don't want me to respect you?"

"Nah," he replied quietly, in a very un-Jay way. "You're different. I just want you to talk to me."

-

At some point they must have fallen asleep because Carrie woke hanging upside down over the back of Taehwan's sofa, him still snoring on the floor nearby. She stifled a laugh and realised how much her head was throbbing. Hanging upside down probably wasn't helping.

She righted herself, found her phone on the coffee table and checked the time: 11:09. Shit. She was supposed to be at the library at twelve. She grabbed her card, abandoning anything else to be retrieved later. The dial tone was already ringing for a taxi as she hurried through the door, into the lift and out to the lobby. Straight into Han.

"Jesus!" she shrieked. Why did he always seem to pop up like this?

"Cara Parry," he spoke quietly. "You should stay out of my family."

Carrie gulped. She forced herself to look into his eyes, but couldn't think of anything to say. Her head hurt, she was late and feeling like death, and he was Han Park. He stared her down for what felt like hours, neither saying anything. Then he turned to go, satisfied that she had got the message.

"I don't want his money," she called without thinking.

Han turned back to look at her. She half expected him to be angry, but his face was still as calm and emotionless as ever. Only his eyes betrayed the faintest hint of surprise. He couldn't have been half as surprised as she was. Talking back to Taehwan was one thing, but Han? Her Cara side was getting far too bold.

"You all think no-one would bother with him unless they're after something," she continued. She was already in trouble now and this comedown was making her cranky as hell. "You don't see him. He's not as stupid as you think he is; he's just lonely. Y'know, I actually like talking to him. We're friends."

Her pulse raced as he strode slowly back to her. The soles of his shoes tapped dully on the polished floor; calm but deadly. This was a bad, bad, bad mistake. She had gone too far. Cara or not, "don't bullshit" was not synonymous with "get yourself killed".

Han came so close that she could feel his breath on her face. He put two fingers against her temple, imitating a gun.

"If you hurt my family," he said darkly. "I won't hesitate."

He pulled the trigger. Then he left, leaving her whole body shaking as she tried to comprehend what had just happened.

She took a few deep breaths and attempted to pull herself together. She didn't have the time or energy to comprehend right now. She was late for work and she still had to go home to shower and change (she figured that Mary, the head librarian, would prefer her to be delayed than stink of rain, sweat and booze). She ran from the taxi to the sliding door, skidding up to the front desk.

"I am so sorry I'm late," she panted. "I don't have a good excuse."

Mary took one look at her and smiled kindly. "I used to be a youngster too, you know. Just don't make it a habit."

Carrie breathed a thank-you and set about trying to be as useful as possible, while her eyes kept trying to close and a blackness in her head kept trying to tell her that life wasn't worth living. She didn't know why Taehwan put himself through this every morning – it was no wonder he slept so much.

Megan (a plump trainee-librarian and Ashley's best friend) picked up on her mood immediately when she arrived to relieve Mary half an hour later.

"Big night?" she gave her a knowing look.

"You could say that," she winced. "Got chased out of a nightclub, shouted in the rain, sang in a supermarket and woke up upside down on my friend's sofa."

Megan laughed. "Standard."

Forgetting her random outburst at Han, she was sort of proud of her ridiculous night out. In fact, now that she was out of immediate danger, she was proud of her random outburst too.

Even when chasing down bad guys on the beat she had never felt so brave.

She definitely wasn't very productive though. Luckily there weren't many customers and not a lot to do, so she got away with spending the next two hours sitting at a table by the window and reading the first line of a book over fifty times.

"Welcome to Victoria Library," Megan's cheerful voice sounded in the back of her head as she tried to move on to the second sentence. "Can I help you?"

"Is Cara here?"

"Jay?" she looked up. "I mean Taehwan. What are you doing here?"

He looked as ill as she felt, and nowhere near as pleased with himself. His usual studded leather jacket was very out of place in the tidy, modest library and his hair looked like he hadn't brushed it in years.

She chuckled despite the nausea that still slumped in her stomach. "Did you just wake up?"

"Did Han talk to you?" he asked, a panic in his bloodshot eyes.

"Oh, yeah," she flinched. "That was… interesting."

"What did he say?" Taehwan pressed anxiously.

"He basically told me to piss off," she squinted up at him.

"Shit," his face fell further than it was already. "Are you gonna piss off then?"

"No," she said sheepishly. "Actually, I think I sort of shouted at him."

She really, really should be more bothered by that, but she was Cara now. She had Yoonho, she had Taehwan, and most importantly, she had herself.

"What?" he looked at her in disbelief. "What did you say?"

"That we're friends and he needs to stop thinking you're an idiot," she gave him a sideways smile. "Should I be running?"

He gaped, eyes boggling.

"I know," she winced. "I didn't know I had balls either."

"There is something seriously wrong with you," he grinned with relief and sank into the chair opposite.

"Says the guy who just found out where I work to come ask me that," she joked, feeling pretty relieved herself that he didn't seem to think she should go into hiding.

"You weren't picking up your phone," he told her. "I should get you a new one."

"Don't get me a phone," she scoffed.

"I mean it," he said sincerely. "I need to get you something better than drugs and food. No-one talks to me like you do, and no-one's *ever* stood up to Han, no matter how much stuff I bought. Fuck Ieuan; you're the best friend I've ever had."

Carrie shook her head incredulously. "I'm not after your money, stupid."

"You're weird," Taehwan smiled and dropped his head onto her book. "Can I sleep here for a bit?"

She couldn't decide what was stranger; that he would say such a thing when he hardly knew her, or that he felt the need to thank her with presents. But then, she had just talked back to a suspected murderer on his behalf because one night of intoxication had made her feel good about herself, so perhaps she was just as strange. She hadn't ever thought she felt particularly bad about herself, but she hadn't felt particularly alive either; not like how she felt last night or standing up to Han. She supposed, in a drunk and peculiar way, she owed that to Taehwan, and in an even more peculiar way, that did make them friends.

"Sofa friend?" Megan asked in amusement.

"How did you guess?" Carrie replied, trying to poke him awake so she could retrieve the book.

"He looks worse than you," she laughed.

<u>26 July 2014</u>

The abnormally hot summer days saw the rooftop pool receiving a lot of family presence, enjoying a cool dip in the water or bathing in the sunshine from the comfort of shaded deckchairs and electric fans. It wasn't unusual for the casino's CEO to also request the attendance of his favourites, much to Margot's disgust and their delight; soaking up the rays was preferable by far to dealing cards with punters made irritable by the extremities outside.

"Lisa," Yoonho called her over, rearranging the laptop on the table beside him so he could work but also balance her on his legs. "Do you think I need to diversify my portfolio?"

Margot shot her a dirty look but was far too composed and ladylike to say anything. It was understandable; a highly intelligent former lawyer seemed like a much better person to ask about stocks and shares than a casino dancer.

"Oh, and Soju," he addressed his brother.

He was sitting on a deckchair and squinting in concentration at the tablet in his hands. It was a side to him that Carrie found strange to observe, though it shouldn't have come as a surprise that the notably astute finance director actually did work.

"Have you fixed that hiccough? The auditors are asking for our quarterlies and I can't deny them much longer."

"Oh, don't worry about that," Soju said lazily. "I've sent them over. Not that their manager will have much chance to review in detail; he thinks his wife's having an affair and it's leaving him rather distracted."

Yoonho studied him incredulously. "How did you manage to wangle an audit manager with domestic issues?"

"They're not difficult to find," Soju replied with a snide smile. "Especially with a little encouragement in the suspicion department. I'm on top of auditors; they think I'm their friend. Juniors will tick anything for a smile and a decent home time, and the signing partner's still as wet for Dad as ever. It's a shame about Matheson's accident; he was the only real challenge."

The enjoyment dancing in his eyes said that he did not consider it at all a shame or an accident. Carrie's gaze flicked to Han but he gave nothing away.

"Excellent," Yoonho dismissed it. "I've taught you well."

Soju returned to his tablet, a look of uncharacteristic intrigue growing on his face.

"Actually, Yoonho," he called to him. "There's something strange in the Sixtus account."

"Why are you looking at that one?" Yoonho frowned. "It's ten times removed and has been dormant for years."

"That's my point," Soju flicked his gaze to him. "It hasn't."

"That isn't possible," his brother maintained. "Mr Park closed it; he told me himself. We shouldn't even have access – how did you get in there?"

"I have my ways," Soju narrowed his eyes at the screen. "And I know what's in front of me. If Dad's the only one with access, he's not retired."

"Nonsense," Yoonho shook his head. "You've misnamed something, or the heat's frying your brain. If the audit's under control, you should take a break."

Soju continued scrolling through the figures, certain that he had not misnamed anything or had his brain fried. Carrie was inclined to believe him; Soju didn't make mistakes. But then, she supposed, Yoonho didn't either.

Han leaned across and whispered something to Yoonho in Korean, which Soju clearly understood but gave no reaction. Carrie had only ever heard Yoonho and Han speak the language, and then only sparingly. It was an intriguing dynamic; the eldest brothers with their hidden identities and private communication, so naturally elevated from the younger two. It had taken a lot for Soju to gain their respect; a lot that Taehwan seemed incapable of giving.

"You really should," Jennie raised her sunglasses to peer at her favourite Park. "Take a break. Who would want to work on a day like this?" She sighed. "There are certain people who are so much more hardworking and respectable than others in this world. And there are those who aren't."

The girl shot a disapproving glance at the youngest brother. Soju gave a sideways smile but didn't look up.

"Don't be so hard on yourself," Carrie said innocently, knowing full well that Jennie's own self was not who the comment was aimed at. To tell the truth, the girl's bitchy streak was starting to get on her nerves. Trying to catch Soju's attention brought out the worst in her. "You work hard; you deserve a break too."

Jennie gave her a funny look, but Carrie had left her towel and iced lemonade and slipped into the pool before she could reply. She swum a few strokes to the end, where Taehwan was floating with his sunburnt head resting on the side, still wearing his t-shirt and shades, as far from the rest of the family as the space would allow.

"Bad hangover?" she stopped beside him.

He winced at the sound of her voice. "Always."

"You really don't help yourself," she commented.

"Yeah blah blah blah," she could tell he was suffering beneath his sunglasses. "Thanks Mum."

Carrie chuckled, prodding at the soaking shirt. "Why are you wearing clothes?"

He did that in the underground gym pool too – when he was well enough to use it – and even in bed, if the casino girls were to be believed.

"I can wear what the fuck I like," he grumbled.

"True," she conceded. "But it is boiling and you're in a swimming pool. People think you've got some epic scar or mafia tattoo or something."

He scowled, then stopped as it hurt his head.

"I haven't got some epic scar, there's just no point," he tilted his head ever so slightly at the men on their deckchairs. "I'm the ugly brother, remember – they'll just pick on me."

"The point is it's boiling and you're in a swimming pool," she squinted against the sun.

Carrie wouldn't say he was ugly, just less conventional - and conventionality wouldn't suit him. She supposed it was just his bad luck that he was related to Soju, who made anyone look pretty terrible in comparison and seemed keen to ensure that Taehwan didn't forgot it.

"Since when did you care what other people think?"

"I don't," he snapped. "My head fucking hurts, please shut up. You're gonna kill me."

"Alright grumpy," she shrugged.

"Sorry," he groaned, sinking further into the water so only his face was visible. "I don't mean to be a dick."

Wow, Taehwan apologising. His hangover really must be bad.

"It's just stupid to think about that shit," he continued. "I'm good at parties and fun stuff – that's what makes me a person. Everything else can fuck off."

"Drugs don't make you a person," she frowned.

"What does then?" he mumbled. "A sack of skin and bones that's just a crap version of my brothers? No thanks, I don't wanna be that."

"You're an idiot; you shouldn't compare yourself like that," she told him, knowing that was pretty hypocritical coming from her; she compared herself to people all the time. "You're fine."

"Fine, great," he screwed up his face in pain. "Fuck that. Chuck me a fag."

"Say please," she nudged his shoulder. "Or you can get your own fags."

"I'm ill," he whined. "You can have one."

She gave him a look.

"Okay, please," he yielded.

She grinned triumphantly and returned to her towel, beside which sat her handbag. It also contained sunscreen, so she brought that too – he needed it.

"Why do *you* have fags?" he looked at her curiously. "Mine are over there."

"Because I saw them and I felt like it," she said, rather pleased with herself. It felt good doing pointless things just because she had fancied it in the moment. "I'm not even gonna use them all; take as many as you like.

"And I got a second piercing," she showed him her ear, unable to resist the urge to show off. Showing off felt good too. "I sort of wanted more ever since Jennifer Lawrence did, but I didn't feel cool enough."

Taehwan looked less ill already.

"I am such a good influence," he beamed smugly.

A good influence was definitely not what he was, but whether it was down to him or not, she certainly felt good. She leant her head contentedly against the side and tickled the surface of the pool with her toes. The sun was warm on her skin and the water lapped coolly at her shoulders. It wasn't a bad life, if she could ignore where it all came from.

She thought of Neil, Darren and Rosemary sitting writing reports in their badly ventilated office. They would be insanely jealous if they knew her job now entailed lounging in a bikini in a rooftop pool. The thought of Neil's face made her grin with amusement. No matter how hungover he was, he would certainly not be floating there moaning at her to shut up and she wouldn't be calling him an idiot or forcing him to say please. She also wouldn't have told Brick on her way downstairs that she couldn't cover a shift on Sunday evening, for no particular reason other than she didn't want to. Being Cara was fun.

It was easy to get used to; heading out from the library or the changing rooms to find Taehwan leaning up against the wall, cigarette in hand, waiting simply to chill with a spliff and a few beers on his balcony and chat about inconsequential nothings. Whereas it had initially been him always gushing at Carrie, now it was her turn. That night in the rain and the relaxant in her lungs had flung open the floodgates and now she never wanted to stop talking.

It was like she had aged backwards ten years. Everything was funnier these days and nothing seemed half as intimidating when she knew she could rant about it at the end of the day to somebody who actively wanted her to. It was getting easier and easier, too, to ignore the eyes in the show hall and simply kick back and perform like she had always wanted to. There were times when she even forgot that her real purpose for being here was to get David into the fold; she was just enjoying her time as Cara the dancer.

Much to Lisa and Jennie's delight, she was also developing more of a fondness for parties, following Taehwan's lead as she lost and found herself in the sparkling bowels of Paradise Casino. He became synonymous with the place and her ever-increasing confidence within it.

And aside from all that, she also seemed to be making significant progress with the family. Though Han watched her like a hawk, Yoonho now desired her company almost as much as Lisa's, forcing Brick to have to start putting his foot down when Taehwan tried to buy her out of shifts. He sank into relaxation as she twirled about, and asked her things that he deemed female like what he should buy Margot for her birthday when she was already so free with his bank account. Soju, too, was paying her a good deal of attention; something that Jennie noticed with poorly masked jealousy. It all made her feel very confident and very wanted.

"Cara," the third Park brother's drawling voice made her jump.

He flicked a lighter, illuminating where he leant casually in the corridor that lead from the show hall to the changing rooms.

"Jesus," she fumbled for the actual light switch. "Don't do that."

He gave her a haughty look. "Going home already? I thought you might be entertaining my stoner of a brother."

"Sorry," she shook her head. "If you're looking for him, I don't know where he is."

"I don't care where he is," he left the wall and approached her slowly, studying her face with a cold indifference that made her wonder why he was even here. "I was looking for you. I have a business proposition, if we could go somewhere private."

Carrie looked about the dark, deserted corridor.

"This looks pretty private," she hesitated.

Although David's case file insisted that Soju enjoyed playing with people far too much to kill them, she didn't trust those icy eyes. There could be anything going on behind them.

He said nothing, simply giving her a look that plainly stated he knew she would go anywhere he told her to. She did. She had no legitimate reason not to. He put an arm nonchalantly around her neck as they took a quick detour to the VIP bar area, making it very obvious that she was with him. She prayed that Jennie wasn't anywhere nearby.

"Where is my brother?" he surveyed the room with bored disappointment. "Shame. This was his idea."

Her chest loosened a little at the thought of that; for some reason she trusted him. Soju steered her into the lift, disembarking at the floor of his and Taehwan's bedrooms. Carrie went to stop at the first door, but he continued to lead her past it to his own.

"We don't need him," he instructed as he opened the door. "He'll find out later."

They proceeded into a space far grander than that of its neighbour. The sofa that Soju settled onto, arms spread casually across the back like he owned the world (which he practically did), was draped with a red chenille throw, the cushions patterned with black vines rather than cigarette burns. The air was still and hot, despite the balcony doors being open to the night.

Soju fixed her with that look of powerful apathy that made everyone go weak at the knees.

"If you have sex with me, I'll give your brother a job."

"What?" Carrie balked.

This wasn't part of the job description. Everyone had specifically stated that Yoonho played look but don't touch, and Lisa had assured her that no Paradise belle was obligated to do anything unsavoury.

"If you have sex with me," he repeated. "I'll give your brother a job. A good one."

She hesitated. "Was this really Taehwan's idea?"

"What do you think?" he looked at her seductively.

Carrie didn't know what to do. Soju had a terrifying but enticing way of getting people to do what he wanted, and making them think they wanted it too. His eyes stuck her in place, reminding her that he was evil and sexy and could do anything he liked with her. Yoonho might disapprove of coercion, but Yoonho wasn't here and refusing his brother was unlikely to gain anyone's favour when the other girls were so obliging.

She took an anxious breath and tried to ignore the dark way in which he observed her. Even if she hadn't seen him lodge a knife in a top hat, that haughty gaze made it clear that it was his place to command and hers to obey.

He smirked knowingly, like he could tell what was going on in her head, and brushed a finger against his lips. "Shh. The window's open."

Everything was very slow and deliberate, from the way he touched her cheek to how his lips caressed her stomach. He knew exactly what he was doing, but none of it was for her pleasure; it was in its entirety a display of power. Soju Park didn't make people happy; he owned them. He didn't want to make her moan, he wanted to know that he could. Perhaps she really did need to loosen up more, but the purposeful manipulation just made her uncomfortable.

Still, she could see why those who wanted to found him irresistible. And she could see why Jennie would be incredibly displeased when she found out that her so-called friend had trespassed on her territory.

17 November 2014

"He said he'd get my brother a good job," she quickly explained in the changing room after rehearsal, getting ready for her first shift since the Soju incident. "It's hard for him with a criminal record; he really needs the help."

"You ain't gotta justify yourself to no-one, hon," Lisa said firmly. Carrie had been afraid that she, too, would resent her decision, but the matriarch had picked up on her discomfort straight away. "Jennie girl, wipe that sour look off your face. It ain't attractive."

Carrie felt strange as she removed her bra, shifting around to hide her naked chest from view. Maybe she was misinterpreting, but this definitely didn't feel like just a random one night stand. She had thought it was for better reasons, but maybe it was that objectivity that made it feel so dirty.

"What the hell are you so awkward about?" Jennie prickled.

"Well ain't you a cactus today," Lisa raised her eyebrows. "Ignore her, sweetie. Everyone feels weird after their first time paid."

"I'm fine," she lied.

Carrie did her best to avoid conversation as they finished changing and headed to open up the VIP lounge. She just wanted Taehwan to stop being elusive so she could talk to someone properly about it, rather than worry David or risk offending the girls. According to Jennie, nobody had seen him since Saturday night, so he was probably still on a bender or dead in an alley somewhere. It bothered her that nobody seemed to care. Surely Han should have gone to find him by now, if only to stop him from doing something embarrassing. She hoped that he was just passed out in his room, too hungover to check his phone or hear a knock on the door. Or at Ieuan's perhaps, wherever Ieuan lived. She had just decided that she would have to ask Soju or Yoonho, when the door smashed open and Taehwan staggered in.

"Hey there, pisshead," she greeted him with relief. "Back from the dead?"

He said nothing, just sat down moodily at the bar and didn't look at her. His eyes were bloodshot and surrounded by dark rings, pupils huge, and a few specks of powder stuck in the dried blood caked around his nostrils. Lisa, Lali and Jennie shared disapproving looks. Carrie pre-emptively poured him a whiskey.

"Are you okay?" she asked. "You look like shit."

"Did you fuck him?" he glared at her.

Uh-oh.

"Soju?" she said hesitantly, quailing at the fury in his eyes. "Did you tell him Drew needed a job?"

"Did. You. Fuck. Him?"

Well she couldn't deny it. She didn't even know why it mattered so much; Soju slept with everyone.

"He's getting him the job," she ventured.

"Fuck!"

He swept the whiskey tumbler violently off the bar, glass shattering on the polished floor.

"What?" her shock turned to irritation. "You know that's the whole reason I'm in London."

"Fuck off!" he seized another glass and threw it hard at the spirits lined up along the wall. "You know he only did that to get at me! He doesn't give a shit about you or your brother, he just can't stand me being fucking happy! I get *one* fucking thing that isn't his and he has to go and fucking take it!"

"Oh grow up Taehwan," she retorted. "Not everything's about you, and I'm not your 'fucking thing'."

"No, you're his! You're just like everyone else!"

Whatever. Soju's influence was a lot more important than Taehwan's and Taehwan was being a dick.

He started screaming, picking up anything he could find and hurling it at the wall. Jennie yelped, cowering in the corner with Lali. Lisa ducked behind the bar and pulled Carrie down with her, covering their heads with her arms. When there was nothing more within reach, he whipped a pistol from his jacket and emptied the cartridge. Glass and spirits rained down on Carrie and Lisa where they crouched on the floor in alarm.

"What's going on?" Han's voice boomed through the bullets, followed by the sounds of a scuffle.

The gun skidded across the bar and clattered down beside them. Carrie resurfaced slowly, her heart in her mouth. Taehwan was insane, and Soju was insane too. He was probably right. His brother had no interest in her or Drew; this was a very deliberate set-up and purely for his amusement.

"Taeju's a fucking psychopath!" Taehwan struggled as Jerome held his arms behind his back.

"Taeju," Han grabbed him roughly by the collar. "Is not my concern right now."

Taehwan stopped struggling. Although there was no rage discernible in his face or voice, he knew full well that his brother was not one to suffer his outbursts.

"Take him to Yoonho in the yellow room," he instructed Jerome, before turning to the girls. "What happened?"

None of them said anything. He stood silently, staring them down until Lali finally spoke. Lisa gave her a warning look; Paradise girls didn't rat out Paradise girls.

"Soju…" she said hesitantly. "And Cara."

Han's eyes bore into Carrie and she instinctively shrunk back behind Lisa.

"It weren't her fault," the blonde woman stepped in quickly. "Everything was legit; she did nothing wrong. Jay just flew off the handle."

"With me," Han beckoned and Carrie followed.

The other girls began to clean up the mess as Han led a shaken Carrie from the room. He stopped her as soon as they reached the privacy of the corridor, bending so his eyes were level with hers.

"Do you understand now?" he said darkly. "Why you should stay out of this family?"

She did. She had been enjoying her success and newfound confidence so much she had forgotten where she was. Neither Jay Park nor Taehwan Lee was her friend. He was a criminal, and no matter how pathetic he was, he was just as dangerous as the rest of the family. If Soju was true to his word then David would be in soon enough and her work here would be done. She had no further reason or desire not to follow Han's advice wholeheartedly.

They walked briskly to catch up with Taehwan and Jerome and entered the family living room together; a disturbingly yellow collection of sofas that made Carrie feel queasy.

"You did what?" Yoonho snapped his laptop shut.

"It was him!" Taehwan angrily threw a finger in the direction of Soju, who was sitting calmly on a sofa, reading a book.

"Really?" he didn't bother looking up. "I didn't know my aim was so bad."

"He fucking started it!" Taehwan yelled, forcing Han to restrain him again.

"He wasn't there," Yoonho glowered. "Cara, my dear, could you please explain what the hell is going on?"

Carrie winced. It wasn't something she wanted to be talking about with her employer, especially given her reasons.

"I slept with Soju," she said quietly. "It was business, I didn't think I was doing anything wrong."

"Yes, Wanwan," Yoonho said sharply. "What exactly did she do wrong?"

"She's supposed to be my friend and he did this deliberately!" he continued to glare at Soju.

"Sex does tend to be deliberate," Soju said lazily, turning a page. "Otherwise it's called rape."

"Shut the fuck up!" Taehwan tried to wrench himself from Han's grip. "Yoonho, he-"

"For God's sake!" Yoonho shouted. "I don't care about your stupid sibling rivalry! Soju is actually contributing to this family; he can screw the queen if he likes, but don't you *ever* shoot up my bar or threaten my staff!"

"I didn't threaten anyone!" Taehwan protested.

"Did you feel threatened?" Yoonho asked. Carrie squirmed. "She felt threatened. Jesus fucking Christ." He massaged his temples in exasperation. "We have Donny coming in later. Are you going to behave then? Or do I need to lock you in your bedroom like a child?"

Taehwan's body stiffened and any strength fell from his voice. "I can behave."

"Unlikely," Soju shut his book with a definitive clap. "He'll be high. Unfortunately, Donny will notice his absence and Donny doesn't need to know our business, so I'd advise we have to keep him."

"Don't you fucking protect me!" Taehwan turned on him.

"I'm not," Soju finally raised his eyes. "I'm being practical."

"Y-"

"Enough!" Yoonho bellowed. "If you say one more word I'll give you to Mr Park and you'll be locked up for longer than a meeting."

Taehwan shut up.

"Thank you," Yoonho said through gritted teeth. "Now get out and sober up. Take a very cold shower."

Taehwan stormed from the room and slammed the door, but said nothing more.

"Cara," Yoonho took a calming breath and addressed her. "Are you alright? If you want to go home and skip the meeting, I'll let Brick know not to dock your pay."

Soju gave her a look that clearly stated she had better not skip that meeting.

"I'm fine," she told him. "I can work; the others are just as shaken as me."

"You're a good girl," Yoonho smiled gratefully. "Go and lie down; I'll see you later."

Han didn't look anywhere near as pleased with her. He didn't move as she squeezed past him into the safety of the corridor, his eyes boring into her as she tried to walk away calmly.

"Cara," Soju followed her out. "Get your brother here. Tell him to wait at the blackjack tables. I have a feeling he might be needed very soon."

He smiled ominously. As much as she wanted to get David the job, there was something sinister about that smile that made Carrie wish she had taken the offer of an early home time.

The meeting was held in one of the blue rooms below ground; the one with squishy chairs and heavy sound-proofing. Yoonho, as the perfect host, had laid on a lavish spread as usual, and as usual for Donny Logan, that had to include lavish ladies. Lisa arranged herself attractively on the sofa beside him while Jennie leant on the arm nearest to Soju, her long legs neatly crossed at the ankles. Lali massaged the shoulders of Donny's son, Jeb, and Carrie waited as far from everyone as politely possible with a crystal bottle of whiskey. It was Yoonho who had positioned her there, and she appreciated that.

He chatted charmingly to their visitors, covering all the necessary small talk while Han looked on, still as a statue. Taehwan seemed just as unkeen on being there as Carrie was, focusing determinedly on canapes as his brothers and their agent discussed business. She wouldn't have been surprised if they had sedated him to get him so quiet.

Jeb didn't seem to be too interested in his father's conversation; he was far more interested in Jennie's legs and Lali's hands on his shoulders.

"Sit on me," he instructed the dark beauty. "I can make you happy."

He leant around the back of the chair and ran his hand up her thigh. She withdrew quickly, still jumpy from earlier. Taehwan's puffy eyes snapped up from his food and Han shifted in his seat.

"Apologies," Yoonho flashed a charismatic smile. "The girls are only for decoration."

"Is decoration for sale?" Donny winked crudely.

"Is your son?" Soju gave him a superior look and placed a pistol very deliberately on the table beside him. "Our possessions are our own."

Taehwan's fork clattered loudly onto its plate.

"Whether or not the girls are for sale is up to the girls," Yoonho said, amiably but firmly. "You can ask them later, but first we have to discuss the situation with the Russians; I still don't trust them."

"How much do you want?" Jeb ignored him. "I'm not stingey. Whatcha think?"

He looked directly at Carrie, legs spread wide and patting his thigh.

CRACK.

Suddenly Jeb was screaming, blood spurting from his crotch. Yoonho recoiled in horror, the corners of Soju's mouth turning upwards in a look of genuine amusement as Donny froze.

"They're dancers, not fucking whores!" Taehwan yelled, shaking with rage.

His plate lay smashed on the floor where he had sprung to his feet, pointing Soju's pistol at the young man bleeding all over Yoonho's armchair.

Han finished the job with a clean shot to the head, without even rising from his seat.

"Don't play with your food," he gave his brother a disgusted look.

"W-" Donny started, but Han had already blown his brains out before his bottom could leave the chair.

Carrie was too shocked even to squeal. She had seen dead bodies, but never the actual act of murder. One look at Jennie's ashen face told her neither had she, and Lisa stared still and wide-eyed at the practically headless man beside her as if she had been turned to stone. Lali stood back from Jeb, breathing hard and splattered with his blood. She was certainly shaken, but there was something thicker about her skin – or she had seen such things before.

"Wanwan," Yoonho's face was pure thunder. "Why did you do that?"

Taehwan said nothing and Soju regarded him with relish. They both knew he was in big trouble.

"You're a headcase," Yoonho said through clenched teeth. "Donny was an ally; we were building something. I need a person who can handle the shit that you can't, without messing up or selling us out. Are you going to pick up one of those from the table and start waving it around?"

Taehwan shrank into his jacket as Yoonho glared at him and Han gave him a look of hard disappointment.

"I might have something," Soju said slyly. "Where's your brother, Cara?"

"Drew Parry?" Yoonho asked, surprised intrigue somewhat interrupting his anger. "You know him?"

"I know Splitters," he replied.

Soju was king of the underworld; Soju knew everyone.

"Did you look into him?" Yoonho questioned.

"Would I have suggested him otherwise?" he raised an eyebrow. "He was close to Carrick Litt, who would apparently recommend. Not to mention, he has a very good reason to be loyal." He tipped his head to Carrie.

Yoonho glanced at Han.

"What is it?" he asked. "You don't look keen."

"It's not my job to be keen," Han said calmly. "It's my job to trust nobody, and remove anyone who proves me right."

"Good," Yoonho gave him a thin smile. "Thanks. Fine, Soju, find him."

"I know where he is," Soju smirked. "Come on Cara, let's go."

Carrie's legs didn't want to move. He had to physically take her hand and lead her from the room, and even then it was a struggle. She stopped as soon as he let her go, her head in a daze.

"You planned that," she stammered.

"Did I?" he flashed her a sadistic smile. "I must be a genius."

<u>**15: Drunk People Crash**</u>

<u>**23 November 2014**</u>

"What do you mean it isn't enough?" Carrie whispered furiously. "Two people got shot right in front of me!"

They were back in the library printing room, photocopying yet more useless knitting patterns. Wendy could open a shop at this rate.

"The problem is," the handler said calmly. "Donny Logan isn't dead."

"What?" Carrie was taken aback. That made no sense. "Yes he is; I saw Han blow his head open! He did not survive that, trust me."

"Donny Logan isn't dead because Donny Logan wasn't there," Wendy explained. "We've been tracing him ever since you gave us the name. Yep, there's a guy called Don Logan who manages an investment portfolio for Yoonho Park, but he's at a conference in France and we haven't found any mention of a Donny Logan in the underworld. Your guys were fake names. My guess is it's another degree of separation for the family. Yoonho apparently meets with his investment guy, which I guess the big partners do too, while someone with another name runs around organising drug gangs unbeknownst to any of them."

"Fuck," Carrie swore. "So we have no idea who they are? Can you show me missing persons? I'd recognise their faces."

"Give me a description and I'll bring over any that match," she promised. "But I doubt they'd leave that end loose. I'm sorry Carrie, but we'd have a hard time getting a murder charge with no bodies and no victims."

"Fuck."

Carrie dug her fingertips into her scalp. She had been through all that for nothing. Well, maybe not nothing – David was now Yoonho's provisional agent and she supposed in a weird way she could claim credit for that – but it felt like an empty victory.

"You should let me wear a wire," she told her for what felt like the hundredth time. "If something like that happens again-"

"You'd be shot before it did," Wendy shook her head. "There's a reason you all get changed at the casino and it isn't because they think you'll lose the costumes. Your job is to be practically naked; concealed recording is an absolute no-no. Besides, Yoonho and Soju didn't do anything and Park wasn't even there. I don't think Brian would be happy outing you and Dave to put away the least important two."

"Least important?" Carrie couldn't believe her ears. "Jay's insane and Han's the one who kills everyone!"

"Han kills who Han's told to kill," Wendy said firmly. "And Jay's so dim he'd walk into us himself without their protection. Yoonho and the old man are the brains, and if what you say is true then Soju's getting there too. Add that to the history Brian has with Park; if we don't get him, we've failed." She sighed. "But it's not your job to worry about that. You're there to get Dave in, remember. He'll get the evidence we need. Don't put yourself in unnecessary danger."

"Right," Carried nodded and showed her out, publicly taking her payment and thanking her for using their photocopying service.

David was the experienced one; let him take the risks and get the evidence. It wasn't like she wasn't already taking risks, sleeping with psychopaths and getting shot at. It would have been nice to be thanked instead of patronised. It was like Fiona all over again and she didn't blame Taehwan for just giving up trying. That was essentially what she was being told to do; keep getting drunk, keep taking drugs and keep doing nothing. Let the grown-ups talk.

David arrived home that evening to find Carrie intently playing a game of Mario Kart, a few empty Corona bottles chucked carelessly on the floor.

"Hey bro," she greeted him.

"Are you drunk?" he asked in amusement.

David had been in and out of meetings with Yoonho and other accomplices all week, and Soju was making a point of taking particular care of him. As a result, he had become insufferably pleased with himself, although it had been Carrie's hard work that got him there in the first place.

"No," she jerked her head at the screen. "I'm winning. Drunk people crash."

"You're drunk," David laughed.

"I'm doing my job," she shrugged. "Being the un-useful one while you catch drug lords."

Her indignance at the underappreciation of everything she had witnessed – and probably Taehwan's influence – was making her rather bratty. Or it might just be the beer; Taehwan's influence was noticeably lacking these days. It was easy to avoid him while he was avoiding her, which was great for not getting a bullet through the brain, but it wasn't fair. He had no right to be such a childish prick; she had done nothing wrong. She didn't want to see him in case he flew off the rails again, but at the same time he didn't deserve the privilege of ignoring her. She had become kind of used to talking to him about everything. Of course in this instance the library girls could not be confided in, her fellow dancers seemed to want (or had been told) to forget anything had ever happened and David had hardly been home. Even if he had been, she would feel a bit pathetic complaining to him.

She missed the useful distraction of weed and *You've Been Framed* and the ability to get things off her chest; Paradise wasn't the same without it. For better and for worse, dancing was still the ultimate diversion, but when she wasn't on the stage she didn't have a lot to turn to. Except beer and Mario Kart. Maybe Wendy was right after all. She had no purpose here and it was time to go home.

"You've done great," David told her sincerely. "Wendy and Brian agree."

"Do they?" Carrie smashed her kart into a Donkey Kong. "When do I get out of here? I'm sick of this shit."

David flopped down beside her and pulled the other controller out from behind a cushion.

"Honestly, I'm not quite sure," he admitted. "It sounds like Brian's keen to keep you around until I'm further in with Yoonho. Everyone knows me as your brother so there's no chance of fake names like Logan – we need enough time to realistically make friends. And there's the risk that without Yoonho's protection, Soju sees me as pointless if you're not around."

"Soju can fuck off," Carrie glowered at the screen.

"You can forget about him soon," David promised. "I reckon you might be good to go after Christmas. Until then, Yoonho's promised that you're untouchable. It's official Park rules now – nobody gets to mess around with you, not even Soju. He seemed pretty keen on it actually; likes that I'm a family guy."

Carrie thanked him. It was a relief and very sweet of him, even if it did make her seem a little childish.

"No problem, sis," he nudged her playfully. "I'll miss you, you know. Except when you're throwing beer bottles all over my house."

"*My* house," Carrie corrected him. "I still pay for this shit."

He gave her a very brotherly smile.

16: Fuzzy Lines

<u>17 December 2014</u>

"You look distracted," Soju leant casually on the bar.

Carrie jumped. She had been staring into space and the wine she was pouring was getting dangerously full.

"Sorry," she winced, handed the drink to the woman who had ordered it and turned her attention to him. "What are you having?"

"Nothing for me," he said coolly. "I'm just checking you're alive. Our Wanwan really doesn't like you right now; I worry he might actually shoot you."

"I'm fine," she gave her best fake smile.

Talking to Soju about Taehwan was the last thing she wanted to be doing.

"Your brother's doing well," he commented.

"Good," she replied. "I'm glad… Thank you."

"Mine insists on having a month-long strop," he waited for her reaction. She didn't give him one. "He's currently upstairs drowning himself on the roof."

She busied herself with changing a Schnapps bottle that didn't need changing.

"I guess you don't care about that anymore," Soju sounded cruelly satisfied. "Very sensible of you."

She supposed that was what he was really doing here; finding out if he had succeeded in removing her from his brother's life for good. It made her want him to be wrong.

"You've been real quiet, sweetie," Lisa said kindly once he was gone. "You need to trust me. Jay throws tantrums sometimes and it can get ugly, but Yoonho and Han ain't never let him hurt no-one seriously."

Except Jeb and Donny Logan, Carrie wanted to say, but it wouldn't do anyone any good. Instead she just nodded and promised that she was fine. She had always been good at being fine. But she wasn't fine, whatever she told David or Wendy or Lisa. She didn't want to be fine. She shouldn't have to be; she had just as much right as anyone to not be fine.

She breathed fog onto the window of the night bus, watching how it distorted the lights outside. Steady streetlamps became fuzzy lines that blurred together into fireworks. What was light, really, but a slave to different perceptions? In its purest form, unfiltered by eyes or fog or windows, was it simply chaos that needed to be controlled? In which case, who got to decide what shape that control should take?

She took a deep breath and punched the stop button after the first traffic lights. She picked up her bag from the seat beside her and pulled on her hat, coat and scarf. Taehwan was a shit person and he didn't deserve her forgiveness, but unless she wanted to continue being not-fine on her own, she didn't have much of a choice.

She ran the few blocks back to Paradise Casino, entering through the main doors rather than wasting time with the courtyard. The grand staircase was decorated with ivy and tinsel, a huge Christmas tree standing guard over Bea at the front desk. With all the red and gold already embellishing the place, the seasonal spirit was almost sickening. She punched in the lift's access code a little too hard, still half trying to persuade herself to just go home. She didn't have long left here; what was the point in trying to fix something that had always been broken anyway?

The lift pinged and she made her way up the last few steps to the roof.

Taehwan was indeed in the pool, fully dressed, his head hooked onto the side while the rest of him floated in the moonlight. Carrie shivered, glad of her winter clothes.

"What are you doing?" she approached. Now that she saw him, she felt no need to be nervous. He was a mess; he wasn't able to hurt her. "You look freezing."

His eyes snapped open. "Why do you care?"

"Oh, fuck you then," she spun on her heel.

"No, that's not what I meant," he grabbed at the side but slipped back down again, his fingers blue. "Come back, I wanna talk to you."

"What do you think I'm here for?" she crossed her arms against the cold. "You're the one who disappeared for weeks."

"That's not my fault," he grimaced. There was a slur in his voice; he was probably drunk again. "You hate me, and Yoonho said if I bother you he'll tell Dad I shot Jeb."

"Right, cos nothing's ever your fault," she kicked her foot across the surface of the water. "You don't do things wrong; the world's just conspiring against you."

"It's *not* my fault though!" he yowled, wincing as it hurt his head. "This is all Taeju! He makes people do things and-"

"Yeah, Soju didn't make you do shit," Carrie said stonily. "You're not five; take responsibility."

"Sorry," he groaned and splashed his face. "I fucked up, but I'm sorry, okay? You don't know how hard it is being a piece of shit. Everyone fucking hates me and they just take my stuff and act like I did it to myself. Han's blocked my Amex-"

"I don't give a shit about your fucking credit card!" Carrie snapped. "I had sex with a guy I don't even like and I needed you to be nice about it but you just tried to kill me and shot a guy's dick off! How the fuck am I meant to cope with that!? You selfish, insensitive, entitled fucking prick!"

She kicked at the pool again, lost her balance and slipped painfully into the freezing water.

"Fuck!" she shrieked, gasping at the chill that hit her lungs. "It's fucking cold! And that's your fault too! Turn the fucking heater up! You fucking fuck!" She rammed her fists repeatedly against his chest, screaming and half drowning in the process. "I hate you! I wanna go home! I hate this stupid job and I can't do it cos you're a stupid fucking arsehole and you're the only person I can talk to and you're being a shit!"

She stopped punching him and broke down, crying into his shoulder as he tried to keep both their heads above water.

"Get me out of here," she sobbed, her teeth chattering. "It's fucking cold."

Shaking violently, he managed to heave her over the side then took a while scrambling out himself. Carrie reached over, her numb hands helping to pull him to dry land.

"Are you okay?" he rubbed her arms, trying to bring the warmth back into them.

"No," she told him, and felt instantly better.

Just being able to admit that without any feelings of guilt or weakness was a huge weight off her mind. She sank down gratefully into the hot bubbles of Taehwan's fancy bathtub then curled up on the sofa in a fluffy dressing gown and a pair of his silk pyjamas, emotionally and physically exhausted. The Dalmore on the coffee table looked very inviting.

"What were you doing up there?" she asked when he eventually emerged from the bathroom himself, looking rather ill.

"Waiting for the water to get cold," he mumbled, collapsing onto the sofa. "I was probably drunk."

She scoffed. "Probably?"

"Do I look drunk to you?" he picked up the whiskey and glugged it heartily, then coughed a lot of it back up again.

"You look like an idiot who's gonna get hypothermia," she took the bottle off him. "Give me some of that."

"Whatever," he said tiredly and wiped his chin on the sleeve of his clean pyjamas.

Carrie let her head fall onto the back of the sofa, feeling the fiery liquid burn its way down her throat and into her stomach.

"You're a shit, y'know," she sighed.

"I know. I'm really, really fucking sorry," he dropped his eyes to the floor. This time he sounded like he meant it. "I'm no good at dealing with shit; I just get high and freak out. I swear to fuck, I'm gonna stop all that. I already told Yoonho I would, but I actually will now. I'm done with fucking things up."

"Really?" she looked pointedly at the whiskey bottle that had found its way back into his hand.

"I'll start tomorrow," he said guiltily, his chin beginning to wobble. "Please… I dunno what else to do… I dunno what I'm doing."

He hugged the bottle and hunched forward, shoulders shaking.

Carrie hesitated, then reached out to put a hand on his back. She hadn't meant to make him cry, but perhaps he needed the release just as much as she did.

"Yeah, me too," she said softly. "I don't think anyone does really. Now Drew's sorted I don't even know why I'm still in London. I've just been floating around doing nothing."

"Shit, don't go," he hiccoughed a sob and slumped into the space beneath her armpit, spilling whiskey onto the floor. "I won't be a dick anymore, I promise! You're a really good dancer – Yoonho won't want you to go, he's got a pact with your brother!"

He really was pathetic and Carrie almost felt bad. In fact, she did feel bad, not that there was much she could – or should – do about it. It had been easy to forget, until that night with Soju, that she really would be leaving; Carrie was Carrie and Cara was Cara, and Cara lived in the moment, with no consequences for anyone. But Taehwan himself had encouraged that and she didn't regret it. He lived in the moment too and used her for attention as much as she used him for company. Cara and Taehwan were just two people passing the time with no responsibilities and no real thought for each other's feelings; he had shown that when he opened fire in the VIP lounge. He was just a brat who didn't like sharing his toys.

But she couldn't deny that she had missed him a lot more than she should have done and still wanted to spend as much of her time with him as possible before Wendy removed her for good.

"I dunno what I'm doing right now," she said honestly. "It's up to Drew really; if he's okay on his own. I can't say anything for sure."

It was true. She didn't know how settled David had to become before she received her withdrawal orders. He had guessed after Christmas, but that had been his own conjecture. Once upon a time she might have even been begging Wendy to let her stay and do some proper investigating, like a real detective.

"I'm sorry I'm such a fucking mess," Taehwan cried into her dressing gown. "I swear I didn't mean to freak out. I swear to fuck I'm not like that."

"You sort of are," she gave him a squeeze. "But it's okay I guess. Well, it's not, but I don't wanna waste however long I'm still here for and I'm bored of being mad at you. Can we just forget all this and have fun again?"

"Yeah," he sniffed hard and buried his face in her chest.

"Come on," she rubbed his shoulder. "You're gonna give yourself a headache."

She paused, waiting for him to pull himself together.

"I'm sorry too," she murmured eventually. "About Soju. I didn't know it would bother you so much."

"You should always expect me to be a twat," he half joked.

"I do," she hugged his head. "But you're my best friend and I'm sorry."

"Cara…" he mumbled something into the robe's fluffy lapel.

"Huh?"

He raised his head, looked at her for a second then pulled away hurriedly and began to stare wildly around the room.

"I'm hungry."

Carrie laughed with relief. This was the Taehwan she needed.

"What's the room service number?" she asked. "Your card's blocked, right?"

"Yeah," he confirmed sourly, still sniffing. "And they took my phone and my car keys and all my stuff, just cos I taught a prick a lesson."

"You're an idiot," Carrie smiled and he smiled back. "They should've done a lot worse."

"Whatever," he crawled to the edge of the sofa and picked up a sort of remote control. "I can still charge shitty food to the room, just not anything worth eating. And I've had to beg Taeju for booze and stuff."

Carrie sighed. Trust Soju to find any opportunity to hold something else over his little brother.

"Well I've got my own phone and debit card and the staff like me," she got up and made her way over to where her coat was drying on the radiator. "So I can order whatever I want, and I want Christmas cake and nice warm, red, girly mulled wine – after you just tried to freeze me to death."

"And chips?" he added sheepishly. "I can't remember the last time I ate something. I'll pay you back."

"Turkey roast then," she grinned. "And you're not paying me back; I probably owe you a house for that whiskey."

"It's not that expensive," he pulled a face.

"Which to you means a house," she elbowed him in the side. "Number please."

<u>**17: Red Wine**</u>

<u>**24 December 2014**</u>

Although his cigarette consumption had increased tenfold in the last week, Taehwan had kept his word not to get slobbering drunk or so high he was sniffing coke off the floor, and had been surviving by counting down the days to the staff Christmas party, where such behaviour would be legitimately excused. Carrie had started to count down too – she missed parties and she didn't have much longer to enjoy them.

True to his perfect businessman persona, Yoonho liked to ensure that Christmas was a big deal at Paradise, and not just for the punters. In fact, despite the huge dent it must be making in seasonal profitability, the entire show hall was shut to the public on Christmas Eve, with a significant reduction in all other casino, restaurant and hotel services in order to free up as many staff as possible for their annual celebrations. Those who volunteered to work received double pay and generous tips, while those who didn't received an all-you-can-eat banquet along with unlimited drinks and slots tokens. Given Yoonho's unconditional love for money, it was almost sweet, although Carrie was pretty sure it was mainly for securing staff loyalty and reducing the risk of betrayal. Lisa also said he was after some sort of 'Best London Employer' award.

Being hired for the underside rather than above board at the Paradise establishment, David wasn't invited, which was disappointing but unavoidable. Carrie promised that she would sneak him some mince pies and he promised that he would be there at midnight to pick her up – no funny business. She laughed and vowed she would be waiting, having not photocopied any body parts or snogged Jerome.

Yoonho had hired a live band to play a variety of classic dance songs, recent hits and cheesy Christmas belters. Carrie bounced about with Jennie at the front of the crowd, thoroughly enjoying herself and waving Taehwan over to join them.

"Happy Christmas!" she hugged him tipsily. "Dance with us!"

She essentially stole him for the night, recruiting Lisa in an attempt to teach him the rumba while Jennie and Lali cackled at his incompetence.

"I'm impressed," she congratulated him.

"By my sick moves?" he joked. Well, Carrie hoped he was joking – she hadn't seen any sick moves, unless sick meant severely unwell.

"By the fact you haven't thwacked Jennie yet," she corrected him.

"Oi," he scowled. "I haven't had any stuff; I'm being good." He looked longingly at nothing in particular. "Can we go have some stuff? It's Christmas."

"Sure," Carrie laughed.

She didn't see why not. This could be her last time, and it made no difference to her if Taehwan was clean or not; she would be gone soon. She swiped a bottle of red wine and two glasses from the table that had been set up along the wall and let him take her upstairs.

"Do you really have to have the window open all the time?" Carrie shivered as they entered his room. "It's fucking cold."

"Leave it," he told her. "I don't like getting trapped. You have wine; that warms you up."

"You're such a drunk," Carrie laughed, pouring herself a glass and necking it.

"Says you," he gave her an indignant look and took the bottle from her hand.

Her eyes met his and suddenly they weren't laughing anymore. Unsure what she was doing, she let the wine pull her head closer. Then she was kissing him. It was like fireworks had exploded in her chest. A second ago he had been the delinquent son of a murderous family, who kept her company but was first and foremost a suspect. Now she wanted him. She wanted him hard. Her whole body was screaming for him even before they fell backwards onto the sofa, her legs throwing themselves around him and pushing her tiny excuse for a skirt up above her hips. Damn red wine.

His fingers snaked into her hair, massaging her scalp as his tongue fought with hers in some sort of desperate war. She grasped the back of his neck, encouraging him to continue. The world was upside down but she loved it. Needed it. Nothing else mattered.

She popped a button on her blouse as she ripped it off, his lips caressing her collarbones as one hand struggled with her bra and the other rose up her thigh. Her breath caught in her throat and she clung to him, momentarily forgetting her battle with his belt.

He wrapped his arms around her and lifted her from the sofa, her tights in shreds and her skirt and top crumpled in a heap with his trousers. They tripped unceremoniously onto the messy bed, stealing clumsy kisses as they frantically wrestled with each other's pants.

The casino girls didn't know what they were talking about. There was something wild about the way he clutched at her that made her feel desired, needed, more sexy than she had ever been in her life. They had no need for calculated, empty techniques; just the two of them and how much they wanted each other. She seized the small of his back beneath his shirt, thrusting him forcibly into her with an intensity like nothing she had felt before.

"Tae…"

Her voice sunk into a moan. There was no point in trying to silence herself. As for that other rumour that went around the changing rooms; nothing could be less important. Whatever its goddamn size, it was ecstasy. She gasped for air, wanting to kiss him but unable to breathe. It felt like she was going to burst. Her fingers dug into his back, pulling him further, harder. She could feel it coming, tensing around him in anticipation. He knew it too. He pushed himself faster in a final effort, until she was screaming with bliss. It washed over her in powerful waves, consuming her whole body as her back arched away from the bed and into his chest.

Holy shit.

She felt like she was going to pass out. Her head swum as she tried to focus on him. He was panting hard and tears were welling in his eyes. She hadn't even noticed that he had finished already; he had continued for her sake.

"I better clean up," he jerked away awkwardly, attempting to hide his face.

She watched him leave for the en-suite, still trying and failing to steady her breathing. Then she reluctantly pushed herself up onto her elbows and swung her feet off the bed. Nuh-uh. She knew from the changing room gossip why he had left, and it wasn't fair to let him go cry on his own. He was just as vulnerable now as he had been when she dragged him up off the VIP room floor.

Her legs felt like jelly but she forced them across the carpet to the bathroom, where he had closed the door but left it unlocked. Taehwan stood hunched over the sink, sobbing quietly. The mirror showed that he had splashed his face, but she could tell that half of that water came from his eyes. She tiptoed up behind him and wrapped her arms around his torso, resting her head between his shoulder blades.

"Sorry," he sniffed.

"Don't you dare apologise," she barely managed a whisper. "You're fucking awesome."

"I'm fucking pathetic," he croaked.

"You're a whiny little shit, is what you are," she kissed his neck. It smelled of fags and booze.

He gave a small laugh.

"Come on," she snuck her hands beneath his shirt and went to remove it. "Let's have a shower."

He flinched and pulled it back down. "Don't. I'm ugly."

He wasn't. She supposed she might once have agreed with Jennie that he didn't match up to his brothers, but she didn't know why. Sure, they were more typically attractive and certainly took better care of their health, but who wanted typical? He did things they never could, so tonight that face that stared back at her in the mirror was the most beautiful thing she had ever seen.

"You're so stupid," she hugged him tighter. "You think I give a shit if you're not as ripped as Soju? Soju's a prick."

He laughed through sobs and finally turned to face her, looking at her like she couldn't really exist.

"There is something wrong with you," he hiccoughed.

Her mouth spread into an amused smile and she returned the sentiment, while she ran her fingers through his hair and he cried on her shoulder.

Maybe it was just her Cara side. Carrie sucked in her cheeks, laying on her bed and staring at the ceiling. The lack of inhibitions, lack of morals, doing and saying whatever she wanted; that had to be the reason.

She frowned. Why was she analysing it? Why was she even thinking about it? It was just a drunken fling; she had had those before.

None like that though. She could probably count on her fingers the number of times a previous lover had managed to get her to peak. It was downright embarrassing, which in turn put on more pressure and made her even less likely to. She had pretended with Soju, as was habit, but this time she hadn't even thought about it. There hadn't been the usual awkwardness or fear of not being good enough that she had thought came as standard. She was just comfortable with him. Because she was Cara and did whatever she wanted.

Whatever *she* wanted. Could she really blame Cara? She was Cara. Cara was her. That was David's first rule of bullshit: don't bullshit. Cara was Carrie's own self, before the application of pretences for the sake of social norms and career progression.

Maybe it didn't matter so much. From a practical viewpoint, sleeping with the guy could be a useful way to step further into the Parks' circle of trust. She had already done similar with Soju, to get David into the fold. Now she could use Taehwan to dig in further for some of that concrete evidence that had evaded Brian for a decade. Cara Parry didn't have to go back to Durham. She didn't have to leave all the hard work and glory to David. She could get Lucy's justice herself.

Her brow creased further. Now she was just finding excuses. She did want to put the family away and she did want a promotion, but she should stop lying to herself. She wanted to have sex with him again. She wanted it a lot. Nobody had ever done her like that before. Why did it have to be him? He wasn't even supposed to be the sexy one. He was a drunk and an addict and the whole point of him was being useless enough to be stupid with. She enjoyed his company because of that, right? – no other reason.

Cara Parry definitely did have to go back to Durham. Then Carrie Hart would never have the opportunity to repeat last night, so she could forget about wanting to.

She glared at the peeling paint on the ceiling. She didn't want to go back to not doing whatever she wanted. Not yet. And was it really harming anyone? Lots of people enjoyed their jobs.

It must have been because she was drunk. That was the only explanation. She was remembering it as better than it was. If she did it again, stone cold sober, she would realise he was nothing special and that would be that.

And there was yet another excuse.

She sighed and dragged herself upright. She was getting ahead of herself. He hadn't messaged her at all since. Maybe the decision wasn't even there to be made and all this thinking was for nothing. She shouldn't waste her efforts.

She finally got out of bed. Laying here ruminating all day was not going to help anything. She scrubbed at her teeth, ignoring his face in the mirror, and stepped into the shower, trying not to imagine what it would be like to fuck him in it.

"Happy Easter," David greeted her as she finally made it downstairs.

"Oh, shh you," she sniffed the enticing aroma floating up from the kitchen. "What's cooking?"

"Well somebody's got to make Christmas dinner around here," he smiled cheekily.

Carrie now noticed his rolled up sleeves and the apron that covered the Rudolph on his jumper. She laughed. Good food and a goofy brother would be a welcome distraction.

She left her phone decisively in her bedroom, under her pillow, power off. She didn't need or want to think about Taehwan and his tantalisingly oversized lips; she needed and wanted to think about how silly David looked in a Christmas hat while somehow maintaining his aura of cool. They sat at the creaky table that took up the majority of the space beside the kitchen appliances, pulling crackers, reading the stupid jokes and tucking into an almost complete roast dinner.

"I can't believe you don't like sprouts," Carrie shook her head in humorous disbelief.

David chuckled. "Is there any food you're not in love with?"

"Hmm," she considered the question as he got up from the table to check the mulled wine heating on the hob. "Tripe."

"I'm with you on that," he agreed. "Wine?"

"Han says red wine's for girls," she giggled, then remembered who had told her that and stopped.

"Last time I checked, you were a girl," he ladled them out a glass each. "And I'd say I'm comfortable enough in my masculinity."

She took the drink and he sat back down.

"There's plenty more where that came from," he raised his glass for a toast. "건배!"

"Yeah, what he said," Carrie clinked their drinks together with a satisfying little ding.

"Soju's been teaching me a bit of Korean," David informed her.

"You're such a suck-up," Carrie teased. "He's got you eating out of his hand."

"Which means I'm winning," he pointed out. "I can bite the hand that feeds me."

"Wow, nice pun," she snorted. "You should be in a cracker."

"Hey," he said in mock offense. "When did you get so cheeky?"

"Blame Taehwan."

"Oh yeah," David remembered. "Are you two friends again? I heard you disappeared at the party."

Carrie reached again for her glass and almost spilled it all over the table. In neither of her lives was she ready to tell her brother or her colleague about that. She wasn't even thinking about it. She let him believe that they had just been smoking weed and hastily changed the subject.

"I'm surprised Soju's teaching you," she remarked. "He must like you a lot more than Donny Logan."

She wasn't even sure that anyone but Taehwan knew that Soju was fluent (other than herself, David and Wendy). According to his youngest son, Mr Park had been so keen to integrate the family into British society that he had forbidden any of them to speak their native tongue. Eighteen year old Yoonho had spent a lot of time locked in solitary confinement by his own father for the crime of not learning English fast enough, and the youngest brothers had grown up entirely monolingual. Carrie supposed it was yet another way that he erased their identities and exercised control.

It was a thing that Taehwan greatly admired about Han that he had disobeyed and continued to use the language with his older brother when the old man wasn't around – it had seemed to give Yoonho comfort, especially in their younger years. Soju had re-taught himself secretly as a teenager, in order to understand what his brothers thought were private conversations, and Taehwan had tried to keep up with him, but his dislike of things he wasn't good at had stopped him pretty sharpish.

She almost giggled out loud. Taehwan was definitely not good at languages; he had thought "c'est la vie" was Russian.

Ugh. She was thinking about him again.

"Sorry," she realised David had been talking to her. "What was that?"

"I was just saying it isn't a lot; just a few simple phrases," he replied. "I've got one for you."

"Alright then," Carrie leaned forward on the table. "Teach me."

"내 오빠를," David said slowly.

"Nay opparule," she repeated.

"사랑하고"

"Saranghago."

"설거지를 할거야."

"Sulgojirule halgoya. What does it mean?"

"I love my brother and I'll wash the dishes," he flashed a mischievous smile.

"Oh ha ha," she said sarcastically. "Je suis David Watts et je suis un derrière."

He gave her a look that said very clearly he wasn't going to fall for that.

She laughed. "I guess you know GCSE French too."

David confirmed that he did and they continued their light-hearted sibling banter as the saucepan of wine steadily emptied.

"Happy Christmas, little sis," he hovered in the doorway to her bedroom as they turned in for the night. "Sorry we couldn't get you out in time to spend it with your real family."

Carrie thought about that. She hadn't spent Christmas with anybody at all for years; humouring Mark and Fiona's pretentious neighbours had been too much even before the wedding fiasco. Today had been incredibly nice.

"Nah," she snuggled into her pillow. "You're my real family."

"If you say so," he smiled.

She watched him turn out the light and close the door, leaving only the glow from the lamp on her bedside table.

"David."

He popped his head back around the door. She looked up at him curiously.

"Have you ever wondered what's real and what's bullshit?" she mused. "Carrie or Cara? David or Drew?"

David's brow furrowed. "I know what's real."

"You never thought, here or in Birmingham, that you might be more you now than you were before?"

"Maybe," he sat on the edge of the bed. "I might've had that for a moment. It's normal; undercover displacement. You get to know a situation and the people in it, and no matter how good you are at keeping yourself real, all people act differently in different situations. You live a lie for long enough then you start to believe it, but that doesn't make it true. You just need to concentrate on what's in here." He patted his chest. "That's who you are; not drugs or parties or anything external, even if it is a lot of fun. I won't let you forget that."

"Yeah," she said softly. "I'm just being stupid. Sorry."

"It's not stupid," he assured her. "Everyone gets confused at first; don't let it scare you. You're doing great, little sis."

She left it at that. She didn't really know how to tell him that it wasn't external things that were bothering her. She wasn't feeling displaced, or that she was buying into a lie, but that maybe whatever it was in her chest was better reflected now than it had ever been before – that she identified more with Cara than herself and that maybe she was enjoying that a little too much.

But Wendy, Brian and David all seemed to be pleased with her, so she must be doing something right. Nothing had changed, she reminded herself. She liked being Cara, and for now at least, that was what she was supposed to be doing. She could stop any time she wanted; she just didn't want to yet.

19: Firehouse

<u>27 December 2014</u>

It was chilly but clear as Carrie waited for the bus to the library. She shivered and pulled her scarf further up her chin as she boarded, had to remove it when she sat beside the heater, then shivered again for the short walk from the stop to the doors.

Megan and Ashley were already there, making a start on the huge boxes of new books that they had to accommodate. Although the library was closed to the public over the Christmas period, they had turned on the fairy lights that decorated the shelves and the large tree beside the entrance and Ashley was blaring tunes on her phone.

It was a tiring but pleasant morning rearranging shelves and removing dog-eared volumes for the charity box, while chatting about presents and Ashley's silly family anecdotes. Mary was still on leave, spending the holiday season with her wife's family in Newcastle, so the girls had the place to themselves.

Carrie was just reading out a list of ISBN numbers for Megan to check against the Classical Languages section when Ashley returned from downstairs, dumping another heavy box at their feet.

"Meg, can we let people in?" she asked. In the absence of Mary, Megan was in charge. "Cazzie's boyfriend's here and if you leave that car waiting for one more second I am going to steal it."

The blood rushed to Carrie's face and she lost track of the ISBNs. She felt suddenly nervous. She still wasn't sure what she wanted him to say. It didn't matter, she tried to tell herself; she would be gone soon anyway.

"Yeah, sure," Megan started, but Carrie cut in.

"Can I take my break now?"

She had already dropped the iPad onto Ashley's box and started towards the stairs. Ashley and Megan shared a dumbfounded look. With their naïve penchant for seeing romance where it wasn't (or maybe it was), the two girls had become increasingly interested in Taehwan's existence since July, especially as he liked to show up unannounced to drive her home in a car that Ashley would have killed for.

"You didn't deny it," Ashley's jaw hung open. "You didn't say he's not your boyfriend."

"I'm taking my break!" she shouted back, ignoring their shrieks of excitement.

She sprinted to the front door, realised she'd forgotten her coat and had to run back, entering the street a lot more flushed than she had wanted to be.

He was waiting outside, hunched over against the cold in an oversized puffer jacket as he leant on the door of the convertible.

"Taehwan!" she half walked, half ran from the library, trying to decide what she wanted to say.

He looked up apprehensively. Nerves didn't suit his face. She was used to him being stroppy and hungover, but never so uncertain or scared, not even in the library after she had spoken to Han.

"I'm sorry I didn't text or anything," he gulped. "I only got my phone and my keys back this morning and I tried to find you before but it's fucking hard wandering round looking for a house with no money or Google Maps. And I thought you might come to the casino so I should stay there, but you didn't and… shit, I'm sorry if you don't wanna talk to me. I just-"

"It's okay," Carrie said quickly. "I do wanna talk to you. I thought *you* might not wanna talk to *me*."

"I always wanna talk to you," the fog of his breath came sharp and fast. "Just talking, that's – I never meant to push anything – I never expected – I never even thought-"

"Me neither," she agreed. "I dunno what's going on, I've been going crazy, I dunno what I'm doing – you know I'm meant to be going home soon."

"Shit, I'm sorry," he winced. "I didn't mean to – I swear to fuck I wasn't trying anything, you just kissed me and I didn't think. Why did you do that? You know what everyone says – I'm crap, I'm shit, I cry, I'm just too – fuck, I'm sorry. You're still my friend, right?"

"Why wouldn't I be?" Carrie frowned in confusion, her thoughts in overdrive. "I'm the one who left. I forgot Han had your phone; I should've woken you up, I should've gone back to the casino. I was just confused, I needed time to think. I didn't – I wasn't… I had a really good night."

"Really?"

"Really," she nodded. "Really really. I dunno what I've been doing just sitting in my house for – are you okay?"

"Sorry," he wiped his eyes in his sleeve and sniffed hard. "Fuck, I'm a mess. I'm hanging bad, but I couldn't come see you coked off my face – it didn't feel right. Sorry, I'm chatting shit. I'll go now, I just had to check you're okay and tell you I'm not avoiding you."

"I'm okay."

She was pretty sure she was okay. He certainly was a mess and he wasn't making much sense, but it seemed like he was just as confused as she was and had not been ignoring her. That made her okay, right?

"Don't go. I just…" she fumbled for words. "Stop saying sorry and tell me what to do."

"What do you *want* to do?"

"I wanna kiss you," she spoke before her brain could catch up. "Can I kiss you?"

Surprise and relief flooded his face as he put a hand tentatively against her neck. She leaned closer and brought their lips together. Those explosions she had felt on Christmas Eve erupted in her head, warming up the winter air and sending everything else into blissful oblivion. The world was just his tongue and how it twisted with hers and how she wished that coat was on his bedroom floor.

"What are you doing tonight?" she spoke between kisses. "I can tell Drew I'm at Ashley's… sack off work tomorrow… get pissed in your bedroom… like Christmas Eve…"

She stopped and pulled back a little. "If you want me to."

"Of course I fucking want you to," he said incredulously. "I just don't understand what's going on."

"What is there to understand?" she smiled, her chest lighter than it had been in days. "We do what we like, right?"

Carrie's colleagues could not contain their excitement. They pounced on her as soon as she returned inside, Taehwan heading back to Paradise for a much needed sleep before he picked her up later. Of course, Ashley and Megan had been watching everything through the window and insisted that it had been just like a movie scene. The poor girl with the ex-con brother and dancing dreams had finally found her Prince Charming on his noble steed (aka bright red Mustang). She laughed at them. If they only knew just how far from a Prince Charming he actually was.

"RUMmikub," Ashley ordered. "Tonight. You are getting drunk and spilling all the beans."

RUMmikub nights were Ashley's favourite pastime: rum, boardgames and movies that she hosted for her housemates and any library colleagues she could recruit.

"Actually I'm going to dinner," Carrie said sheepishly.

"Ooh, where?" Megan asked.

"Some place called Firehouse?" she replied.

Ashley's jaw dropped. Ashley seemed to know everything.

"Chiltern Firehouse? Who the hell is this guy? There's no way he can get a reservation – people book months in advance!"

"It's that posh?" Carrie cringed. "Am I gonna look like an idiot? The best clothes I've got are still in the wash from Christmas Eve."

Ashley groaned. "Can you *please* set me up with a brother?"

"His brothers are arseholes," Carrie told her for what felt like the thousandth time.

"Arseholes who could pay off my student loan and buy me an E-Type," she said wistfully. "I am *so* jealous of your perfect life."

Taehwan looked a lot more alive when he returned at the end of the day, pulling the Mustang up to the kerb outside the library; roof down, elbow resting on the door and grinning like he owned the world. His ears were studded with black diamonds set in silver, which also embellished the lapels of his jacket and the rings on his fingers, forbidding the world to forget that he was definitely a millionaire. That entitled arrogance she used to see – well, it was still entitled arrogance but it did things to her that it hadn't done before.

"Hey there, show off," Carrie greeted him and hopped into the passenger seat.

"You look after her, okay," Ashley instructed as they waited for Megan to lock up. "If anything bad happens to this lady, I'm coming for your ass."

"And she does taekwondo," Carrie added.

"Exactly," Ashley winked and waved cheerfully as the two girls made their way to the bus stop together. "Have a good dinner, Caz! Don't do anything I wouldn't!"

"I like her," Taehwan commented, waving cheerfully back.

"Yeah, well, she's gonna steal your car," Carrie teased.

The restaurant was absolutely packed; every table taken by people who had more class in their big toe than Carrie had had in her entire life. Balls of light hung from the woven jute ceiling, creating an ambience that was both rustic and sophisticated, with a light spattering of tasteful Christmas decorations. It was the sort of place Mark might take Fiona for a very special occasion, but he would have to plan well in advance and would dress incredibly grey and boringly.

"How the hell did you get a booking?" she whispered in awe. "Ashley said it should take months."

"The Park name is very useful," Taehwan replied smugly.

"And you're rich," she gave him a knowing look. "I know your game. How much did you have to bribe them?"

"You don't wanna know," he winked, smugger still. "And you can't complain or pay me back because this is a date."

"Wanwan, you shh," she kicked him under the table. "If you're gonna be like that you won't get another one."

She ordered the cheapest thing on the menu, then giggled sheepishly and let Taehwan change it – he knew what she liked by now and it was sort of nice to permit him, just this once.

"What did you tell Drew?" he asked as the food arrived. "When you went in to get changed?"

"He wasn't there," Carrie shrugged. "I think he's out with Bence all night, but I've texted him I'm at Ashley's just in case."

"I guess that makes sense," he loaded his fork but didn't lift it, looking a little disappointed. "If Yoonho finds out we broke his pact, you're fired as fuck."

"And if I go back home and break your heart then Han will break my face," she said, only half joking.

"Yeah, he might do that," Taehwan chewed on his lip. "I don't wanna make you stay just cos you're scared, I wanna make you want to stay. I'm gonna get a you Paradise key card with cats on it and take you to our private island and we can take the Gulfstream to Vegas and LA and see the sets of all those movies you like and the stars on the Broadway, and Disneyland, obviously." He started getting excited. "Do you want a car? I could get your friend a car. I could get you a dance studio! You could make your own choreos like you wanted at uni, and when you get famous and realise you're way too good for me I'll buy up all your crappy fast food places until you have to take me back. I'll buy Durham; I've always wanted a castle."

"Stop it," she laughed. "You can't buy Durham."

"Yes I can," he pouted.

"Well don't," she said in amusement. "You know I don't need all that. I wanna do things like watch New Years fireworks in the roof pool and have sex at midnight like a semi-normal couple." His face glowed at the word. "Stop trying to buy me everything."

"Why?" he asked happily. "I'm rich. Everyone else lets me buy things."

"You're stupid," she took a sip of wine (something red that she hadn't caught the name of). "I'm still the same me, remember. I like you, not your money. Although, a key card with cats would be cool."

She picked up his fork, still holding a piece of pigeon, and stuffed it into his mouth.

"Now shut up and eat your fancy food."

Perhaps they had a little too much expensive red wine, but it was a nice sort of too much that kept them warm as they walked the long way back to Paradise, Taehwan having called one of the casino valets to retrieve the Mustang earlier.

Carrie smiled at the lights of Hyde Park's Christmas market, the crowds of people filtering out as they prepared for closing time.

"I can make them let us in," he offered.

"Not now," she hugged his arm, snaking her fingers between his. Her head was pleasantly woozy and she wanted to get back to the open window and cigarette scarred cushions. "It's cold, and I'm a bit knackered from chucking books around all day. I need bed."

"I better take you home then," Taehwan said reluctantly. "I'm okay to drive."

"Drive? Wait, my home?" she asked in confusion. "Why?"

Nobody had a swanky dinner like that and then went home, especially when they'd been waiting for three days. Jesus, that didn't sound very long. Was she really that impatient?

"I'm doing things respectfully," he insisted, hopeful uncertainty flickering in his eyes.

"You are the least respectful person I've ever met," she touched her lips lightly beneath his ear. "And you're not okay to drive, unless you're gonna let me keep you in my shitty house all night."

"You really do wanna sleep with me," he stared at her, the realisation hitting for what seemed like the thousandth time.

"Yes," she laughed. "Stop not believing me. It doesn't matter if you wanna wear a shirt or need hugs. You're sexy, alright?"

She held his waist and kissed him.

"Does this mean you're gonna stay in London?" he asked.

"Who knows what happens later," she replied. "But we can have fun now."

"I'll take that as a maybe."

He kissed her again before she could contradict him, then grinned and took her hand, the two of them starting briskly back towards the park's entrance.

She thought about his question. It wasn't a decision that was at all in her control but it was one she had been considering since Christmas Eve. The more she considered it, and the faster they ran back to Paradise Casino, the more she wanted to.

Carrie's head dropped back onto the wall of the executive lift. She needed to stop having fun for just long enough to do some serious thinking. The longer she left it, the weirder it would be to tell David and get his advice on whether or not she should ask to stay on the operation – and she was running out of time. Wendy was already talking about withdrawal plans and Yoonho had told her multiple times how impressed he was with her brother. She wouldn't be needed as collateral for much longer, and she wasn't entirely sure if she had a legitimate reason to continue after that – or if she would even want to by that time. And if she was going to leave, she needed to find a safe way to break it to Taehwan. That was why she needed to talk to David about it, but also why she couldn't.

She exited the lift and decided it was a lot easier just to text Ashley; she still hadn't confirmed if she could make RUMmikub tomorrow night. She grinned sheepishly at the previous messages in their conversation. She hadn't been so open about such things since uni – actually, not even then.

"What are you smiling about?"

"Jesus!" she jumped.

Soju was leaning against the front desk, which she had almost walked into while being distracted by her phone.

"Going somewhere?" he asked slyly.

"Just home," she replied.

"You should come with me," he suggested, a mysterious glint in his eye. "There's something I'd like to show you and your brother."

That sounded ominous, and she was supposed to be at the library in a few hours, but she still hadn't quite mastered the art of refusing Soju Park; not when she didn't have Taehwan to back her up. She hitched her bag further up her shoulder and followed him down to the carpark, where David was waiting in his new silver BMW. Soju took the wheel, steering them out of Mayfair and into the suburbs, then stopped in some sort of industrial park.

"I know this place," the blonde man frowned. "It's Bence's money shop."

"Not anymore," Soju shook his head. "I'm surprised you didn't hear – it's Russian land now. Jim Benson is dead."

"What?" David's face fell.

Carrie wasn't sure if she should say something. David was a professional and didn't actually have friends in the Birmingham Splitters, but still… She wondered how it would be if someone were to tell her a rival gang had killed Lisa or Lali or Jennie. She doubted she would feel particularly good about it.

"Only last night," Soju tutted. "Enrique was in floods; they had good business here."

David composed himself, maintaining Carrie's consistent admiration. "Won't the cops be crawling all over it?"

"I doubt it," Soju said flippantly. "But Russians will. We're not getting out here, I just thought you might like to know what you're up against. The Russians don't like us very much; one day you might be fighting them too. Are you up for that, Drew Parry?"

"Sure," he nodded firmly.

"Good," Soju's mouth turned upwards at the corners. "Then I have something else to show you."

Apparently the man tied to a chair in a derelict basement had had something to do with the extermination of Bence's counterfeiting crew, and the Parks' longstanding partner, Enrique, was baying for his blood. It was like a scene from every gangster movie Carrie had ever watched; the gagged hostage begging for his life in muffles and moans, and the cool, collected man standing over him, gun in hand. A nauseous feeling rose in the pit of her stomach. She had a strong suspicion that Soju had very intentionally organised for her to witness the execution of Jeb and Donny Logan; with this nameless man there was no doubt at all.

"The thing is," Soju flipped the pistol deftly around his fingers, then handed it to David. "I want you to do it."

"What?" David took the gun, looking quickly between it, Soju and the squealing man in the chair. "Why me?"

"Why not?" Soju raised an eyebrow. "Jim Benson was your friend, wasn't he?"

"I've never killed someone before," David said uncomfortably, shifting the firearm between sweaty hands but keeping it aimed at the prisoner.

Soju watched him. Carrie's heart raced, her own palms clamming up in the cold basement. David Watts could not kill a man. Their lives depended on whether Soju would believe that Drew Parry couldn't either.

"Shame," he eventually held out a hand for the gun. "So what do you suppose we should do with him?"

"That's up to you," David replied.

"You're my agent," Soju reminded him. "I'm asking you."

David hesitated.

"What did he do?" he asked hoarsely.

"He wasn't very discreet," Soju drawled. "He has to be silenced somehow."

"Cut out his tongue."

The man squealed louder. Carrie recoiled. That was not the answer she had expected. Weren't police supposed to protect people? She understood that Brian Hole could be unconventional in his grapple with the Parks, and that undercover detectives would have to witness things and say nothing, but suggesting torture themselves? Surely that was just wrong.

"Ah yes," Soju looked pleased. "Once a Splitter, always a Splitter I imagine."

"Yeah," David confirmed. "That's what we did."

Soju strolled over to a set of drawers and produced a switchblade knife. "Go on then."

"Woah, hold up," David held up his hands. "I was just the sales guy."

"Well you're the agent now," he gave him a goading look. "And Parks get their hands dirty."

That was utter bollocks. The biggest problem for the Bluebird investigation had always been that they didn't get their hands dirty. Yes, Han at least had the decency to do his own killing and Taehwan was a wildcard, but Yoonho, Soju and their father were squeaky clean. They got other people to do the nasty bits for them, Yoonho choosing to ignore it and Soju choosing to watch. This time the fall guy was David.

Soju said nothing more, just observed him calmly. This was entertainment for him. Any one of their many lackies could have done the job and been an extra link away from the family in the chain of causality, but Soju wanted to psych out the new recruit; make sure he knew who was boss. And judging by the fact that she was there, to play mind games with Drew's little sister and Taehwan by association.

David took a few deep, steadying breaths. They were all acutely aware that the two of them could be locked down here forever, Soju waiting patiently until the deed was done. Carrie wondered if she should beg David not to do it. Taehwan wouldn't allow them to be left to starve. He would burst in guns blazing and rescue them, no matter what the others said. Only for Han to shoot them in the head. Taehwan could throw as many tantrums as he liked, but he didn't have enough power. David didn't have a choice.

The man screamed as soon as he removed the gag, rocking the chair with all his strength. Carrie screwed her eyes shut and turned away, but jamming her hands over her ears wasn't enough to block out the shrieks of pain.

After far too long, the basement went silent. Carrie didn't know if he was passed out or dead, and she didn't want to check. It was all she could do to force herself to look at David; covered in blood and holding a mangled tongue. For all his composure, he looked like he was going to be sick.

"Bravo," Soju clapped slowly, a sinister smirk turning up the corners of his mouth. "Probation is over. Welcome to Paradise Casino."

He put an arm around David's shoulders, who to his credit didn't flinch. Soju took the tongue and held it up to examine it. He patted David on the back and made his way slowly across to Carrie.

"Cara Parry," he pressed the limp thing against her cheek and drew it upwards, as if it were licking her.

She gulped and forced herself not to run. It was still warm.

"This is your fault, you know," he mused. "You got him this job after all." He dangled the tongue before her eyes. "Did you know your brother was capable of such a thing?"

Carrie swallowed, but her mouth was bone dry. She could feel the heat of the blood sticking to her face.

"Don't worry, I've seen a lot worse. Wanwan," he paused for effect. "Has done a lot worse. But you already know that."

He withdrew the tongue and gave her the most sadistic look she had ever seen.

"How does it feel; fucking a psychopath?" he lowered his voice and brushed her hair back from the smear on her cheek. "Fun, huh?"

She tried her best not to give him a reaction. Obviously she knew the sort of thing he did – she had seen Jeb Logan with her own eyes and it had terrified her – but Soju was too late. She had accepted that already as something she had to get over, for the sake of the operation. And she had got over it. What bothered her a lot more was the way that Soju was hurting David.

"Don't worry," he whispered. "Your secret's safe with me. I'd be embarrassed too."

"Are we done?" David spoke up.

"We are," Soju reached into his pocket and tossed David the basement keys. "Leave him there and lock up after yourselves; I'll make sure the Russians answer for this. Oh and by the way, that man did nothing wrong. I just wanted to see if you would."

He flashed them a tyrannical smile and left.

"Oh my God, are you okay?" Carrie ran to David and threw her arms around him, feeling his heart beating as fast as hers.

"I'm okay," he hugged her back.

"Don't bullshit," she ordered him. He had the right to not be fine; everyone did. "You're not okay, *this* is not okay."

"No bullshit," he held her tighter, his breathing stabilising. "You're doing so well keeping it together."

"I'm doing well? You cut someone's tongue out!" she exclaimed. "You shouldn't have to do that!"

"And you had sex with that arsehole," he reminded her. "We do what we have to for the greater good."

It wasn't only Soju she had sex with, not that David knew. And as inappropriate as it was, it was for more than just the greater good.

"Are we monsters?" she asked uncertainly.

"Sometimes only monsters can catch monsters," David stroked her hair. "And you have to be a bad person to have the balls to do the right thing. But I promise you won't ever have to be. You're my little sister and I'll protect you and you won't ever have to do anything you don't want to."

"I'll protect you too," she said resolutely.

If Soju had intended on bringing her here to scare her away, his plan had backfired. She had really made up her mind this time. Soju Park did not get to win everything and she was going to do everything she could to stop Cara Parry from having to return to Durham. She had a solid, legitimate reason now. David was the strongest person she had ever met, but he needed her here with him. She was brave now and she wasn't going to abandon the man who had become her brother, especially when she was so perfectly positioned to further their reach into the Park family's confidence.

Nevertheless, Carrie was very glad of Taehwan's balcony. While she was determined to be strong for David, she needed a safe space to let out the shock and feelings of nausea that came with it.

Whether it was Taehwan's presence or his infinite supply of weed, being able to admit that she was shaken and allow herself a cry was a great help. She felt a lot calmer sitting on the floor with her head on his shoulder, watching her breath escape into the air.

"You sure you don't want tonight off?" he asked. "I can pay Brick."

"Nah, I'm okay now," she exhaled heavily. "Well, sort of. But I'm okay enough not to bail last minute and drop the girls in the shit."

"Taeju licked you with a disembodied tongue," he persisted. "I think that's a fucking good reason to bail."

"That's cos you're an irresponsible brat," she flicked his nose. "But thanks."

"Well at least take some stuff, have a line before you go out," he told her. "You're a bit spaced right now."

She laughed and accepted; she could definitely do with some energy for dancing.

"I'm not gonna let him touch you again," Taehwan scowled determinedly, reluctantly letting her leave to get ready.

"Yeah," she gave him a sideways smile. "Thanks."

She correctly predicted that Soju would have a table in the crowd that evening, and that he would probably bring David. He would be wanting to see if she was rattled. Ha. She wasn't.

What was more unusual was that Taehwan also shared their table. Once upon a time he had spent many nights in the show hall, but he confessed that recently the other men's eyes made him jealous and he didn't want her feeling guilty. The thoughtfulness had touched her – she would have expected him to throw a hissy fit and be possessive – but his attendance tonight touched her even more. He watched her carefully, checking she was alright, positioning himself between Soju and the stage. He knew he was going to feel uncomfortable, but he wasn't going to let his brother intimidate her. He surprised her a lot with how sweet he could be lately and she couldn't help but appreciate the gesture.

She felt the powdered euphoria spreading through her body as Lali stepped up to the microphone, her honey voice crooning Garbage's *The World Is Not Enough* as Lisa twirled elegantly behind her. Carrie and Jennie slowly stalked their way down from the stage and prowled amongst the audience. They were supposed to dance with various people before returning to the stage, but she (and drugs) had decided that she could be sweet too. Taehwan had made the effort; she wasn't going to rub it in his face by shaking her butt at anybody else.

She set a course for his table, brushing her fingertips seductively along the shoulders of the punters in her path but looking only at him. She beckoned him to his feet and put her hands on his chest, running them up to his neck. Cocaine made everything clear. It was time that people knew Cara Parry wasn't going anywhere. She would force their hand. She needed to stay for David, and she needed to show Soju that his games weren't going to work.

And there was the fact that those eyes that stared intensely into hers were as intoxicating as any drug on the market and she was addicted. Well, not addicted. She could stop any time she wanted; she just didn't want to yet.

"What are you doing?" he whispered.

"Whatever the fuck I like." It was a very attractive philosophy.

She held his gaze, drawing her fingers through his hair and circling her hips against him. She could feel Soju and David's eyes on her as she danced far closer than was technically allowed. She didn't care. Let them watch. Let everyone watch. That was the point. It was reckless, but Taehwan and everybody else needed to know that he had nothing to be jealous of.

"Interesting," she heard Soju say snidely to David. "Were you aware that your sister is having sex with my brother? It seems she actually likes it."

She draped her arms around Taehwan's neck and pressed her lips to his, her tongue diving deep into his mouth. She was vaguely aware of David making some sort of comment and leaving the table, but Taehwan's hands on her waist were too distracting. Woops. She had only intended on dancing.

"Naughty naughty," Soju mouthed at her.

She smirked at him, traced a finger down Taehwan's front and gave him a saucy wave as she backed away. Some men in the crowd started to whoop and whistle, requesting that it be their turn next.

Lali moved on to *La Lambada*, which Carrie spun into with gusto, feeling gloriously pleased with herself and more than a little hot. The girls continued to give her shocked and baffled looks until they left the stage and returned to the changing room for an interval.

"What the fuck Cara!?" Jennie exploded. "I know you're high, but you can't go around practically screwing people in the show hall! And Jay – seriously? How much did he pay you!?"

"Jesus, chick," Lisa shook her curly head. "You got some explaining to do."

"Sorry," she blushed. "I got carried away. Jennie, you know what I mean."

Jennie of all people shouldn't be cross, considering the amount of times she and Brick had altercations over her clear bias towards a certain Park.

"Yeah, with *Soju*!" she exclaimed in disbelief. "Who's actually *sexy*! What is wrong with you?"

"Is he the guy you've been smiling about all month?" Lisa asked in fascination. "Are you dating family, girl?"

Carrie grinned sheepishly.

"I thought Yoonho and your brother had an agreement?" she questioned. "Have you told him?"

"No," Carrie admitted.

"Guess he knows now," Lisa chuckled. "Girl, you are in trouble."

"But *Jay*?" Jennie still couldn't accept it. "You're all missing the point! *Jay* is your mystery guy? Have you been high your whole life?"

"Okay Jennie, drop it," Lisa laughed at the dumbfounded look on her face. "It's not the apocalypse."

"But he's shit!" Jennie was dropping nothing. "Everyone knows that!"

"Did Soju tell you to start that rumour?" Carrie interrupted.

"Rumour?" she replied. "I have personal experience!"

Carrie tried to ignore the small twinge of envy in her gut – it was childish and made no sense.

"Well so do I and I honestly don't know what the fuck you're talking about," she said pointedly. "I guess there are certain things that just put him off."

"Yeah I know coke can wreck your shit, but still," Jennie pulled a disgusted face. "Did he suddenly get clean in five seconds?"

"I wasn't talking about drugs," Carrie rolled her eyes, feeling far too powerful for her own good. Taehwan and cocaine were good things. "I'm talking about people."

"Oh burrrrn!" Lisa gasped with amusement. "She just said you ain't sexy."

"If that's how you wanna put it," Carrie said bluntly. "I'm just saying it's pretty difficult to do anything right when the other person's not properly into it. You give what you get – and he knows what you all say, by the way. You'd be shit if you had to deal with that pressure every time."

"Cara," Jennie looked at her incredulously. "It's a job. We're never 'properly into it'."

"Well there you go then," Carrie shrugged coolly. "You want extra cash from people you don't like, sure, I can't judge, but you don't have to be a bitch about it. You didn't see me telling everyone I had to fake one with Soju."

"What!?" Jennie burst. "That is the biggest bullshit I ever heard! What the fuck is wrong with you?"

"Okay girlies, shush your mouths, both of you," Lisa stepped in. "Jennie, be glad she ain't never gonna steal your man. Cara, we're very happy for your great sex, sweetie, just try to keep it outta work time."

"Cara?" Taehwan appeared in the doorway.

"Oi," Jennie put one hand on her hip, the other pointing at the corridor. "You. Out. This is a ladies changing room."

He ignored her, staring boggle-eyed at Carrie. "What the hell was that?"

"That," she told him. "Was your probation period being over. I'm done with keeping quiet just so I have the option to ditch you without Han shooting me. I don't wanna go anywhere, I wanna be with you properly."

He beamed and shook his head in disbelief. "You're crazy."

"Your fault," she said impishly.

"Is it true?" David burst into the room. "Are you-"

"Oh for fuck sake!" Jennie cried in exasperation. "You. Are. Not. Allowed. In. Here."

She was ignored again.

"Cara, show me your eyes," he grabbed her roughly and held back her eyelids. "We're going home."

She winced. She should have seen that coming. Lisa was right; she had a lot of explaining to do. She still wasn't sure what to tell David about why she hadn't said anything already, because she wasn't sure why herself.

"Get your hands off her," Taehwan snarled.

"You get your fucking hands off her," David replied angrily, seizing his collar and fuming into his face. "What, you think it's okay to shoot at my sister then get her hooked on drugs so she'll sleep with you?"

Carrie opened her mouth to protest that she was not hooked on anything, but Taehwan was already swinging for him.

"You piece of shit," David rubbed his jaw then struck back.

"Stop it!" Carrie yelled.

She had been right; David was definitely not fine. But taking it out on a Park brother who he knew to have anger issues was not the best way of dealing with it.

Taehwan snapped and David followed, flinging each other into lockers and clothes hooks, Carrie shouting at them both to "grow the fuck up" as she tried to pull them apart. She managed to grab David's arms while Lisa, Lali and Jennie wrestled Taehwan back against the mirror. They glared, panting at each other. David's lip was bleeding and an angry bruise was already forming on Taehwan's forehead as he jerked an arm away to wipe his bloodied nose.

"You better watch out, punk," David growled, straightening his shirt. "You fuck with her again…"

"He won't," Soju leant against the wall of the corridor outside, enjoying the show, that look of haughty amusement turning up the corners of his mouth. "You're in big trouble, Wanwan. Breaking a pact, punching an agent; there's only one way to deal with people like you."

"Fucking psycho!" Taehwan broke free from Lisa's grip and flew at him.

Carrie had never been so happy to see Han. He and his security team thundered down the corridor, burly arms wrenching the bodies apart. Soju held up his hands in calm surrender, brushed himself off and stepped back with dignity. Taehwan continued to lunge at him, kicking and lashing out at the officers holding him, despite his clear inability to escape.

Han seized the back of his collar, practically lifting him off the ground, and he stopped struggling. He seemed to be the only one who could ever get his brother to behave.

"Yoonho's office," he ordered. "Now."

They were all marched into the lift, like a troupe of naughty schoolchildren being taken to the headteacher. Han knocked on Yoonho's door and shoved his brother roughly over the threshold, the rest of them being encouraged to follow by the security team.

"What is going on?" Yoonho glared at Taehwan.

"Taeju made Drew cut a guy's tongue out," he said quickly.

"What?" Yoonho's expression hardened further. "Drew Parry is an agent, not a thug – why on earth did you do that? I thought you had grown up."

"Isn't it obvious?" Soju looked unconcerned. "We have to know we can trust him. Simple mathematics: if he was an infiltrator he would have shot him immediately; if he was police he would have tried for mercy."

"That is not for you to decide," Yoonho rubbed the bridge of his nose in frustration. "You're finance, not security; stick to your own simple mathematics. You do nothing of the sort again, do you hear me? Your responsibilities are elsewhere."

Soju opened his mouth, but Yoonho cut him off.

"Unless you want me to tell Mr Park you're still a maverick?"

"I hear you," he bowed his head stiffly, not looking quite so cool and Soju-ish.

"Fine," Yoonho waved a hand. "Get out."

"Wait," Han's attention was still on Taehwan. "Why do you care?"

The evil grin returned to Soju's face. "Because our Wanwan has his tiny prick hilt deep in Drew Parry's sister."

She felt David tense beside her and Yoonho's gaze moved to them.

"You two should probably leave," he addressed them darkly. "I have to speak with my brother."

Carrie hesitated, her feet putting her between him and Taehwan without her telling them to. Han's black eyes followed her.

"He didn't do anything," she said quietly. "It was all me."

"Drew," Yoonho persisted. "Please take her home."

David led her down to the carpark in stony silence, slamming the door as they got into the BMW.

"Are you fucking stupid?" he hit the steering wheel. "I'm just getting in with Yoonho and my sister decides to get high and humiliate him. Genius plan, Carrie, real brilliant."

"I didn't humiliate anyone," she objected. "It's me and Taehwan who are in trouble."

"Yeah, right, he's Taehwan now," he glared at her. "I thought you weren't even supposed to be friends."

"We're not friends," she insisted. "He's just useful. I'm not done yet; I can still help this case. I want to get justice for Lucy and I don't want to leave you here on your own – he's a good way of doing that."

"But you're fucking him," David stated. "That wasn't part of the plan."

"I'm getting his trust," she said in exasperation. "I can enjoy my job and still do it well; you told me that."

He sighed. "I should send you back to Durham right now. I should send you to Canada."

"No, don't do that," she pleaded. "I'm sorry, I messed up; I should've run it past you and Wendy first, but it's a good idea!

And I can hardly leave now without him doing something about it."

"That's up to Wendy and Brian," he said shortly. "But I'll be giving a recommendation."

"Please, David," she begged. "You know everything I've done for this case! I wouldn't do anything that didn't help it!"

"Carrie, you already have," he inhaled deeply. "Your conviction is great, but you don't think. I've done all this before and Wendy's co-ordinated for years. You're an amateur; if you don't stop doing things without consulting us you're gonna slip up and get us killed."

Carrie didn't know what else to say. She couldn't really argue with him. She did think – she thought very hard – but she thought after the fact. She decided her reasons for doing things once they were already done, and one day something would crop up that she couldn't justify.

David exhaled heavily. "Why are you suddenly so desperate to stay undercover? I thought you wanted out of here."

She thought about it. She knew that there was a lot more she could give and she knew she wanted to bring down the people who had killed Lucy Flynn, but that wasn't the question. She could probably do that just as well from an office, without being in danger every day.

"I don't wanna leave you," she said carefully. "You said about how important it is having someone to remind you who are you. I wanna learn from you and really be valuable – I could do more operations in the future, like you did with the Splitters. I know I've made mistakes, but I got you in way faster than anyone thought I could and it would be stupid to waste how far I am with Jay."

And she wasn't ready to stop being Cara. She had friends in this life and a brother and whatever the hell Taehwan was. She wanted to contribute more to the case, she wanted to keep playing at Hannah's dream and she wanted more of the feeling that she was doing something right. She didn't want to leave, especially on such a negative note.

"Look," David scratched the back of his neck uncomfortably. "Jay was a great way to get them to notice you, and I mean it when I say you were amazing, but this is different now. He's a drunk and the family disappointment, and I'm already in; there's nothing to gain from you being close to him that's worth risking our lives for."

"He doesn't have to be," Carrie said quietly. "He says he's gonna sober up. Soju was ignored once too, remember; what if Jay could go the same way if he stops messing around? Who knows: if I'm with him long enough and you're my brother, you might even start being family too. Agents collect rents and arrange deals that Yoonho doesn't want to know the details of; family handles the big fish, and if anything's gonna stick to Park it'll be that. Wendy already told me there's no point in getting anyone if we can't get him."

Now that she said it, it made a lot of sense. She must have subconsciously known that all along, her thoughts had just taken a while to catch up. With Taehwan, as with Soju, she hadn't really had the time to think things through before the moment passed. Soju had worked out perfectly (or as perfectly as such a thing could), which surely meant her instincts were correct. She just needed the chance to prove they were right this time too.

"David, please. We're a good team. You said so yourself that you'll miss me."

"This isn't about me," David frowned. "It's about survival. You can not afford to fuck up like that." He sighed. "Look, I'll tell Wendy what you just said, but I'm also telling her the truth; you're in over your head. If you think you're gonna clean up Jay, you've got to clean yourself up first and take this seriously. I'm not kidding, Carrie; this isn't just a job. One wrong move and we're dead."

"I know," she nodded determinedly. "I was stressed about Soju, I went overboard on the drugs, but it won't happen again. I guess you were stressed too, it just came out in different ways. At least no-one expects undercover cops to start falling out and punching people."

She gave a hesitant smile.

"And you're really okay with this?" he asked, avoiding her attempt at humour and the mention of his own distress. "It's a big sacrifice to make; one night is bad enough, but you're committing to a lot."

"Honestly, I'm fine," she reassured him. For once it wasn't a lie. "I meant what I said about enjoying my job; if I was faking it that would be breaking the first rule of bullshit. Just physically," she added quickly. "I'm not about to do a Brian O'Connor."

"Good," he finally put the keys in the ignition and swung the car around and up the ramp to the street outside. "I'll call Wendy tonight, and she'll need time to talk to Brian. You're not leaving your room 'til we've heard back; I don't care how many shifts you have to call in sick for. And don't get your hopes up."

19 January 2015

To Carrie's relief, eccentric Brian Hole was delighted that his rising star wished to extend her involvement, despite David and Wendy's reservations. Of course, her progress was to be constantly monitored and the team kept on red alert to remove her the instant it was deemed necessary, but she couldn't have hoped for anything else. It made perfect sense and she didn't actually want to be putting anyone in danger – she just knew that her use here wasn't done.

Now she just had one more boss to convince of her worth, and that he shouldn't let Han's gun make the decision for him.

"You're okay, hon," Lisa nudged her towards the door of the CEO's office. "You know Yoonho's reasonable. And whatever he says, I'll be waiting right here to give you the biggest hug."

Carrie gulped and knocked on the door, obeying the "Come in" that sounded from the other side. She hadn't slept at all last night and her head was still struggling with the usual comedown depression.

"Cara," Yoonho looked up tiredly from a mound of paperwork. "You're not on shift today."

"I know," she hovered in the doorway. "I thought I should probably talk to you as soon as I could."

Yoonho sighed. "You probably thought right. Come in, sit down. Do you want a coffee?"

"Oh," Carrie shut the door and remained standing. "No, thanks. I'm fine."

"Cara," he said firmly. "Sit down. I'm not going to eat you, we just have things to discuss."

"Yeah, right, sorry," she pulled back the chair opposite his desk then sat there, not knowing what to say.

"So," Yoonho put his fingers together. "My brother seems to think that you two are an item. Is that correct?"

"Yes," she nodded. "I started it though – you don't have to take his phone and stuff or tell Mr Park anything. He just did what I wanted him to."

It was the truth after all. It had been her who got carried away on Christmas Eve, when she had thought it would have no repercussions.

"So you said last night," he recalled. "Which makes me wonder why, when Drew so specifically asked us not to touch you."

"Well, when he said that Soju had just made Taehwan shoot Jeb," she reminded him. "I was scared."

"Soju didn't make anybody do anything," he gave her a look. "Taehwan can't control his temper – that should still scare you. He's already shot at you and punched your brother."

"I know," she said. "I just…"

She just what? Decided to forgive him because she wanted to not be fine, then got drunk and found out she really wanted to have sex with him all the time? How the hell was she meant to phrase that to Yoonho Park?

"Sorry," she shook her head. "I don't know what to tell you. I like him. I guess I just… I swear I never meant to hide anything from you, things just happened. I just wanna be able to see him properly now, no secrets. And… please don't punish him for me getting high yesterday. I wasn't thinking straight, cos of, y'know… the tongue thing. Please, Yoonho, Sir."

"Hmm," he contemplated. "Han thinks you're dangerous. He would rather remove you entirely, before anyone else gets hurt. As much as I like you, he may have a point."

Carrie swallowed hard. "Please don't remove me. I love my life here."

Plus she wanted to be there for David and impress Brian and Wendy, and regardless of any of that, Han's idea of removal probably resulted in her head looking a lot like Donny Logan's.

"What happens the next time my brother gets jealous of somebody looking at you?" Yoonho asked. "I have a business to run; I can't keep indulging his tantrums."

"I'll make sure he doesn't," she promised. "I wasn't with him back then. I know he's insecure, but he knows I'm here now so he doesn't need to get jealous – and he's been taking less cocaine. He wants to do things right, he just doesn't know how. Please, give him a chance to prove himself… and… give me a chance too."

"Fine," he rubbed his temples. "On your head be it. Just for God's sake clean him up. And you're fired; if you're going to date a Park, I won't have you flashing your legs about. We're respectable."

14 February 2015

Valentine's Day was an excellent time for casino profits; from both gambling and alcohol. Depressed loners needed something to take their minds off things, and a few consolation drinks between strangers at the bar led to a fair few last minute bookings for hotel rooms. People were even more keen than usual to part with their money and their senses and this particular crowd made Carrie incredibly glad not to be dancing anymore.

Valentine's Day was also an excellent excuse for the CEO to pretend to be a philanthropist. Loved up couples and people with public images to uphold were suckers for special occasion themed donations. While the majority of the public were drowning their sorrows or charming their beaus, he was putting the finishing touches to the guest list for next week's charity gala; some of the biggest show-offs (and biggest people with ill-gotten gains to launder) in London. While the casino and restaurant were enticing more people through the doors with Valentine's offers that appeared festive and friendly but also reminded them that spending money made them feel less alone, Soju was already allocating where all that extra income was really going to go. Han, of course, was monitoring security with Jerome – unhappy drunk people were liable to cause a fuss – and Taehwan was staring in disbelief at his own gala invitation.

"Yoonho never invites me to things," he gaped. "What the hell did you say to him?"

"Did I have to say something?" Carrie asked. "Why shouldn't he invite you? You haven't made a scene for what… four weeks?"

"Fuck off," he instinctively reached for a whiskey in some sort of attempt to make himself believe this was actually real. "This is serious; I'm gonna be playing golf with some rich guys like I'm an actual Park."

"You are an actual Park," she nudged him. "They're the ones who forget to notice."

"You gotta help me practise," he realised with a panic. "I haven't played in fucking ages!"

"In a week?" Carrie laughed. "I don't know shit about golf!"

"Bollocks," they shared a sheepish grin. "We're screwed."

"We?" she queried.

"Well obviously you're coming to the party bit," he told her. "I bet you're the only reason I'm even invited; Yoonho always said women make us look good. That's why he married Margot."

"Or because you've made a massive effort ever since December," she reminded him. "He might actually want you there. You're way more fun than normal stuffy rich people."

"Well you're coming either way," he said decisively. "I need you. But you're gonna have to deal with people dissing my golf swing without getting stroppy."

"You're the one who gets stroppy," she teased. "Wait, hang on, I can't go to a fancy party; I don't know how to be fancy."

Taehwan thought, then his eyes flashed triumphantly. "Lucky I've got a fancy sister-in-law then. You're gonna have to let me buy you a Valentine's present."

<u>20 February 2015</u>

Margot was waiting in the restaurant, sipping very elegantly on a lime and soda. She wore a tailored white suit with a sweeping neckline, diamonds glistening around her neck and on her heels. Carrie felt very underdressed. She had thought that jeans would be fine for a simple shopping trip. She should have remembered that nothing was simple for the Parks.

"We have a lot of work to do," Margot smiled dryly and uncrossed her slender legs.

"Don't worry about cost," Taehwan handed her his credit card. "Get everything she wants."

Carrie looked at him uncomfortably. He gave her a squeeze.

"Do not let her use her own money," he instructed Margot with a knowing grin.

He seemed to be greatly enjoying forcing her to be pampered. She guessed that sending her with Margot wasn't just for the sake of fashion advice; he knew she would find it a lot harder to refuse the intimidatingly glamorous older woman.

"I don't need that, really."

He kissed her to shut her up. Margot looked entirely unimpressed.

"Remember to be back and ready by six," he said pompously. "We'll be done golfing by then."

Carrie couldn't help but smile. After a week of non-stop practise Taehwan still couldn't play golf to save his life and he looked incredibly strange in his preppy attire, but he was just so happy that Yoonho had allowed him to come along. It was sort of cute.

"Come on then," Margot said sharply, standing and donning a pair of chic jewelled sunglasses despite it being the middle of February. Carrie supposed they let people know that she was one of the elite – if her clothes and general demeanour weren't enough for that.

"Alright, piss off then, you posh bastard," Carrie addressed Taehwan with a cheeky whisper. "Have fun."

She gave him a quick peck on the lips then ran out of the restaurant and down the hall after her guardian for the day.

They rounded the corner to New Bond Street, Carrie trying to emulate just a smidgen of Margot's poise and grace. The woman would get on well with pretentious Fiona, she thought, if her sister had a little (or a lot) more money.

"We really don't have to use Taehwan's card," Carrie looked apprehensively about as Margot led her into Fenwick's huge department store. "I have my own money."

"Your own money won't buy anything here, I can assure you," Margot replied, thumbing the fabric of a skirt.

Carrie picked up a dress she thought looked plain enough to be affordable and eyed the price tag. She hastily put it back. Margot was right; that was more expensive than a month's rent.

"I really don't need anything this fancy," she stammered. "There are really nice things in M&S. I don't wanna waste his money."

"You don't date a millionaire's brat and not want to spend money," Margot said cynically. "Look, I'm not here because I'm your friend, or because your boyfriend can tell me what to do. I'm here because I don't like to be embarrassed. You're a Park girl now; us ladies have to look the part. It is our purpose in this world to be absolutely gorgeous, and the entirety of that hall tonight will see you as my fault if you don't. People donate tens of thousands of pounds at these events; you can't show up in a dress from M&S. Here, try this on."

She handed her a shimmering gold frock. Carrie did as she was told. Had Taehwan been her companion she would have told him that was stupid and donating the money to a charity would be much more productive than spending it on a dress worth more than her house. Besides, what was wrong with M&S?

Margot, however, made her feel more guilty for not looking right than for spending somebody else's money. She didn't want to be one of those people who lived off others' means – especially when the funds were sourced through things like drugs and violence – but when she thought of how excited Taehwan was to be acting like a respectable member of the family, she couldn't let him down. It would not be conducive to her role in the operation. So, as per his instruction, she was at Margot's mercy.

As much as the older woman didn't want to be friends, she did seem to relish having a doll to play with. Carrie was sure she must have tried on all the clothes in London by the time they decided on a red cocktail dress; slim-lined and backless, with material that shimmered tastefully when she turned to the light. Margot had selected for herself a looser, flapper-esque silver number and a corresponding sequined headband. Then of course they needed jewellery, shoes and handbags, and Carrie's usual make-up brand needed to be replaced. She avoided looking at prices as Margot handed over the card again and again.

"Perfect," she held up a set of diamond earrings to check them against Carrie's complexion. "Now one more thing, then we can finish at the spa."

She gave Carrie a look that was almost cheeky, in a royal sort of way.

"The spa?" Carrie asked uncertainly. "I wouldn't know what to do in a spa. Are you sure we have time?"

"Why do you think we left so early?" Margot raised a perfectly sculpted eyebrow. "Don't cause a fuss; Taehwan insisted. I am to get you ready as I see fit, and tonight our skin is going to be glowing."

But first she led her around the corner to Rigby & Peller.

"What's the matter?" she laughed at the look on Carrie's face as she took in the proud displays of fancy lingerie. "Ladies are allowed to be decadent. In fact, I would say it's privately encouraged."

"Guests won't see my underwear!" Carrie protested. "Did Taehwan put you up to this?"

"He did not," Margot gave her a racy smile. "I don't think he'll mind though, do you?"

Carrie blushed. He certainly wouldn't.

She had to admit that it was shaping up to be a very enjoyable day. Margot loosened up considerably as the hours passed and by the time they were laying in an incensed room with cucumbers on their eyes, she seemed almost warm. It wasn't the warmth of equals – Carrie was clearly like a pet to her, or a clueless child – but it was warmth all the same.

"Now, they can't see us until we're ready," Margot stopped her in the lobby before she had a chance to run off and tell Taehwan how surprisingly nice she had been. "Come with me."

Despite being married to Yoonho and presumably sharing his quarters, the woman also had rooms of her own. The space wasn't quite as large as Taehwan's, but it was much more luxurious. It was very gold, with white fluffy throws adorning the bed and chaise longue. The side of the main room opened up into a spectacular walk-in wardrobe and an ornately framed mirror sat atop a grand dresser that took up a lot of the opposite wall. Carrie stared. This would all be too much even for Fiona. She felt a twinge of sheepish pride at being the sister who got to experience such glamour. It was like she was on holiday in another world, and it was the trip of a lifetime.

"Okay, Cara Parry," Margot invited her to sit at the dresser. "Let's blow them away."

Carrie had half expected her to have her own stylist for hair and make-up, but she preferred to do it all herself. It was something to take personal pride in, she told her; there were enough things for everybody else to claim credit for. Carrie wondered if she detected a hint of bitterness in her voice. The defence lawyer Margot Stuetz had been a rising star of the German courts; a self-made woman who clawed her way out of poverty on her own merit. It was sad, then, that the only thing Margot Stuetz-Lee had left to be proud of was her appearance.

"Do you ever miss being a lawyer?" Carrie asked.

"That isn't relevant," Margot held her head straight to stop her from moving. "Why would I need to work? I have everything I ever dreamed of."

"Is that why you quit?"

Margot sighed. "You have a lot to learn. A rich man has no use for a working wife. An intelligent one, yes; to introduce her at business dinners as a former lawyer is a huge boost to his credibility. To introduce her as a current lawyer is to admit he hasn't the money to keep her. Our Wanwan may indulge you for now, but don't expect to be a librarian forever."

"Taehwan wouldn't stop me working at the library," Carrie frowned. "I like the library."

She smiled bittersweetly. "All men are eventually the same. Enjoy him while you can – if you really find that possible – but learn to enjoy yourself."

Carrie felt oddly indignant. If Margot thought that Taehwan was anything like the men she met at Yoonho's dinners, then she didn't know him at all. Which wasn't shocking; nobody did. Nobody but herself. Plus, even if her warning was true, he would be in prison long before he had the chance to squash her – which he wouldn't do, being the one who raised her in the first place. Still, she had to appreciate the woman's attempt at solidarity. It must be very lonely, she realised, being Margot.

Carrie's mentor looked incredibly pleased with herself as she stepped back to admire her handiwork.

"My dear," she put her hands on her shoulders. "You look stunning. He'll hardly recognise you."

Carrie wasn't sure if that was exactly a compliment, but she had to agree; she barely recognised herself. Her face was contoured to perfection beneath a stylish up-do, a few sculpted curls falling to frame it. The diamond necklace showed off her collarbones and the dress hugged her curves in all the right places. As impressed as she had been by Lisa's human artwork, Margot had blown her out of the water.

"Wow," she breathed. "You're amazing."

"I know," she kissed her lightly on the cheek. In a day, Carrie seemed to have gained another mother.

Margot checked the delicate little clock on the mantelpiece then led her from the room, meeting the men at the top of the main stairwell. It felt like a scene from *Titanic* as she stood before the sweeping staircase, a gloved hand on the golden carved bannister.

She blushed as she caught Taehwan's eye. He was gawping at her, mouth open, all pretence of dignity momentarily forgotten.

"Perfect," Margot whispered and nudged her in his direction.

It was all she could do not to mirror his reaction. He had changed out of his ridiculous golf outfit and was wearing a tailored black suit, one button fastened over a crisp white shirt and chequered monochrome tie. A thick golden brooch on his lapel matched the rings on his fingers and studs in his ears and he had moussed his fringe to be ever so slightly messy. He looked high class, but incredibly Taehwan-y.

She beamed shyly at him as their hands met. They looked like they belonged here. Her Saint Laurent heels fell into step with his Oxfords as they descended the stairs, the picture of casino royalty.

"You look lovely," Yoonho gave Margot a quick peck.

"Thank you, darling," she smiled sweetly, but it was clearly Carrie whom she deemed her true success tonight.

They left the stairs and began their pretentious mingling with guests – something that was far too fake and refined for either Taehwan or Carrie to be particularly skilled at.

"You are so fucking beautiful," he whispered, pulling her to the side.

"Margot did well," she replied bashfully.

"No, you're just fit," he continued to stare at her.

She laughed. "You're not too bad yourself."

She grabbed his hand again, guiding him towards the pre-appetiser bread and olives already on the tables. The second most attractive thing in this room was food.

They passed a waiter with a tray of champagne flutes, which Taehwan instinctively reached for. He brought one to his mouth, but Carrie stopped him before he could drink it. His eyes told her he had already had a line for bravery; he should probably keep off the alcohol, at least until everyone else had had a few.

"You said you didn't want to," she reminded him softly.

He hesitated then handed her the glass. She glugged it, removing the temptation for both of them.

"Gone."

"Thanks," he smiled sheepishly. "I don't wanna fuck this."

"Then stop saying fuck in public," she teased, patting his tie.

Carrie hadn't known what to expect from a charity gala, but it was a lot of talking. Yoonho made a speech, Margot made a speech, charity representatives made speeches and so did some special donors. It was all a sham really; all this false philanthropy when half the people present were only there to launder their dirty money. She found herself playing footsie with Taehwan under the table as they agreed with glances that this whole thing was ridiculous.

The champagne continued to flow and he couldn't help himself, his usual rowdy self coming back to life with each glass as he gratefully drowned the gnawing gloom of a cocaine comedown. Dressing up and playing 'real Park' was exciting and watching Yoonho pretend to be a good person was downright hilarious, but talking about hedge funds with so-called respectable people verged on terrifying. This was not the sort of party that Taehwan was used to and Carrie could tell he was out of his depth, in danger of drowning himself in flutes of bubbly.

She spotted Yoonho looking their way as people continued to float between tables after dinner, discussing fake nothings. He tutted and whispered something to Margot.

"Shit," Taehwan winced. "I think Yoonho's pissed at me."

If the man had seen how fast the liquid was disappearing down his brother's throat then he was probably right, and if Carrie couldn't keep up her end of the bargain to push him higher up the food chain then it would be game over for both of them.

"Hey," she squeezed his hand. "You haven't done anything yet. You just need some air."

They could both do with a break and a cigarette. She knew where Lisa kept an emergency stash, and the matriarch didn't mind sharing with her Paradise daughters. Carrie would replace them at her first opportunity.

She pulled Taehwan away from Yoonho and Margot near the main door and escaped through the side entrance to the changing rooms.

"You okay?" she stepped gratefully into the courtyard and held out the pack of Marlboroughs.

Taehwan snatched one, lit it with fumbling fingers and inhaled deeply like he was about to die without it. He breathed heavily, relief flooding his face as his head fell back against the wall.

"Thanks," he blew smoke into the chill air. "I nearly fucked it, didn't I?"

"Well, maybe," she lit her own. "But you didn't, and that's the important bit."

"We haven't finished yet," he half joked. "I dunno how to talk to these people. I didn't mean to have any stuff earlier, but I was fucking tired from golf and I didn't think I looked right and if I just had pot then I'd stink of it."

"You definitely look right," she assured him. "And that doesn't matter now; it happened."

"But it does matter," he groaned. "It's making me feel like shit and I can't stop fucking drinking. Should I go get more? I can concentrate then at least. I dunno how to be a proper person; I need to concentrate."

"You don't need that," she took a deep breath herself, trying to chase the wooziness from her own head. "Just remember they're all acting too, and they're the ones trying to impress us. Isn't it you lot who clean up all their money? They should be scared of you, not the other way round."

"I'm not scared of shit," he scowled.

She gave him a look.

"Okay, maybe I am," he dropped his head onto hers. "I'm knackered and I feel sick."

"Well that's unsurprising," Soju's voice sounded from the entrance to the courtyard.

"Oh piss off," Taehwan tried to shut the door in his face.

"Charming," Soju caught it with a polished shoe. "There's a woman upstairs trying to talk to us. For some reason Yoonho wants you there. If you can handle it without your drugs?"

"Of course I fucking can," he snapped.

Well, if Soju's taunting was what it took to wake him up then so be it; Carrie would just have to be careful not to let him get too riled to the point of punching or shooting at things.

"You're dribbling," Soju informed him, patting his jacket before returning inside.

"Fuck sake."

Carrie caught him before he could wipe his nose on the back of his hand, fetching a tissue from the dressing table instead. She turned back to see Taehwan looking conflictedly at the little flask that his brother seemed to have inserted into his suit pocket. Carrie glared at it. She was going to make sure that Soju Park got a life sentence in the worst prison imaginable.

"Not now," she told him, and to her surprise he obeyed without question.

She took the flask and placed it in a locker along with Lisa's cigarettes, then returned to give him an encouraging squeeze.

"It's okay," she kissed him lightly. "We can get as pissed as you like after this, and I have posh lingerie. Just remember that and smile at people."

He snorted a laugh. "Is that how Yoonho does it?"

"Yeah," she sniggered. "Naked Margot – let's go with that."

She attempted to obscure their smell of smoke with a handy deodorant left in the locker – presumably by Lisa – and went to shut the door to the courtyard. Then something caught her eye. A mumbling of voices came from the far corner where two people headed down the darkened alley that lead away from the street, one stooped slightly over a walking stick. Her curiosity was piqued – they were acting like they didn't want to be seen.

"Who's that?" she whispered.

Taehwan gave a quick glance. "Oh, that's just Dad. Come on, we'd better go or Yoonho'll hate us."

They jogged back along the corridor, Carrie fixing their hair before pushing open the door back into the hall.

"Ah, there you are," Yoonho said cordially, flashing Taehwan a suspicious look. He straightened up immediately. "My youngest brother."

"Jay Park," he held out a hand in his best impression of a respectable businessman who was definitely not drunk.

"Heather Ballantine."

The woman who shook it was older than Yoonho and spoke with a strong Glaswegian accent. Her dark hair was cut and styled into a short pixie bob and the muscles in her limbs were poorly concealed beneath a red dress that bore a brooch with a family crest. She had the air of a person who knew how to look after herself, and a person who was certainly not here to make any kind of donation to any kind of charity.

"Ms Ballantine has been a very generous donor," Yoonho informed them. "And she's requested an audience with the whole family."

"The whole family?" Taehwan frowned, unable to keep his mouth shut. "What about Dad?"

Yoonho sighed and turned to explain to Ms Ballantine. "Unfortunately he's away. I'm unsure where; he's retired, you see."

"No he's not," Taehwan said in confusion. "We just saw him outside."

Yoonho's brow creased. "That isn't possible."

"Apologies," Soju came to his rescue, flashing their guest a charming smile. "You know how these galas go. My brother is a little drunk and probably mistaken. Why don't we go and talk somewhere more private?"

"Gladly," the woman agreed. "And don't worry, Mr Park, I understand." She gave Yoonho a knowing look. "We all want to improve on our father's empires. I like to know who I do business with, but I won't miss the presence of a retired old man."

Han stiffened a little at the slight against their father, but as usual said nothing.

The party migrated into one of the higher tier meeting rooms; modern but elegant with a retractable screen on one wall and the other a full window onto London. They seated themselves around the table, beneath a miniature chandelier.

"So," Yoonho touched his fingers lightly together. "How can we help you?"

"I'd like to start a mining company," she got straight to the point.

"Mining?" Yoonho said in interest.

Margot raised a hand very deliberately to her cheek, bringing attention to the hefty diamond on her engagement ring.

"Exactly," Ballantine acknowledged her. "I've heard a lot of business flows through your casino, Mr Park. You have significant influence and contacts. I was wondering if you'd like to be my partner."

Carrie and Taehwan shared a look. She doubted that this woman wouldn't have influence and contacts of her own, and if her donation was anything to go by, she had plenty of money. She just wanted an added layer of protection; an organisation otherwise unrelated to herself to handle the negotiations and take the risk. Even her donation had been made in the name of a foundation in which she shared only a minor, indirect interest.

"Why us?" Yoonho regarded her warily. "Why don't you go through Antwerp?"

"My father," Ballantine replied, again giving him that knowing look. "He had some… trouble in Antwerp; I want my name nowhere near it. But I want to finish what he barely started and I'll pay you handsomely for it. I believe we might be two peas in a pod, Mr Park. We could help each other."

"I'm interested," he leaned forward. "What are the terms?"

"Of course our agents can discuss particulars," Ballantine told him. "You'll understand we don't want competitive secrets escaping our lips."

"Absolutely," Yoonho agreed and looked to Soju, who nodded with cool pleasure.

It was how he did business with all his partners, after all; speaking in riddles and codes, uttering nothing from their own mouths that couldn't be claimed as squeaky clean should either party defect. Even to David he didn't yet talk plainly, giving vague instructions such as "Knightsbridge is due" and "by any means necessary". As far as anybody could prove, Drew Parry extracting drug money from a shady bar manager had nothing to do with Yoonho Park requiring a return on his investment in Enrique Ortego's chain of top end clubs and bars. And as far as anybody could prove, Heather Ballantine had mentioned nothing to do with blood diamonds.

"But my general proposal is this," she continued. "I'm not in the habit of throwing money away, so I would need a partner who could test the waters. I propose that you identify a suitable location and deliver an example of product before anything is committed. Once I've examined the quality, we can determine value, agree on future investment and set up officially."

"We would need a down payment," Yoonho said quickly. "Costs will be high, even just for testing the water, and you're aware that it would be us and our people taking all the risk."

"Of course," Ballantine confirmed. "Consider my donation tonight a non-refundable deposit. The remainder of the value of the prototype will be paid on delivery and examination, along with my first investment in the venture."

"Ah," Yoonho's eyes shone greedily. Yoonho liked money. "I'm afraid the donation has already been promised. I would imagine you're a lady who doesn't like to be seen as going back on a promise."

Bullshit was that money promised and she knew it, but Yoonho was a seasoned pro.

"Of course," the woman conceded. "The donation goes to the refugees. My agent can discuss a further deposit. I trust you have the facilities to receive it."

"Of course," Yoonho responded immediately. "Plus any remaining product value on delivery, valued independently."

"And you handle everything yourselves," Ballantine said sternly. "You speak to my agent directly and you deliver me the prototype with your own hands. Nobody else can know that myself or my agent exist – nobody you wouldn't trust with your own family. Any acquaintances you work with will believe the supply chain stops with you."

"Absolutely," Yoonho held out his hand, as did Soju. "Please have your agent visit at first convenience; my brother will speak for me."

Not David yet then, understandably.

"Agreed," Ballantine shook it firmly. "A pleasure doing business with you, Mr Park. Until next time."

She swept from the room.

"Fucking hell," Taehwan remarked. "What was all that about?"

"Diamonds," Soju replied, making it clear how bored he was of his incompetence.

"Of course we'll need to look into places where the trade is perfectly legal," Yoonho said, glancing at Carrie and Margot.

"Really, Taeyoon," Margot pursed her lips. "I know what a diamond is."

"Yes, darling, and I know you're discreet about it," he yielded and turned to his brothers. "Okay, listen up boys. This could be the biggest deal we've ever done – definitely the biggest without Mr Park – and we all need to pull together. Han, I'll need you on top of every aspect of security. Vet Ballantine, her agents, her dog if she has one. Any suppliers, import, cleaning; I want their history so shiny I can see my face in it. Soju, likewise for finance. I want accounts looked at, credit checks, solvency of supply chains – and I want you with me to oversee negotiations and put the feelers out. Talk to Chinatown about documents; don't give anything away but test their proficiency and availability. Jay, pick up the handling of some of our regulars – Soju will be busy."

Taehwan's eyes boggled.

"I can handle accounts?" he asked ecstatically.

"Welcome to responsibility," Yoonho said seriously. "Step up."

Taehwan nodded in delight.

"Thanks for almost behaving," Yoonho stopped him as they all left to return to the party. "But next time go easy on the champagne."

He patted him on the shoulder. Soju looked incredibly disappointed.

-

Carrie and Taehwan practically flew into his bedroom at the end of the evening, tipsy with elation and a celebratory Cristal in Yoonho's kitchen.

Everything was perfect. Wendy and Brian would be over the moon, she was definitely still on the case and she was trusted enough to sit in on family meetings. She was successful and appreciated and had never been so excited. Trying out Hannah's life? She had surpassed Hannah a thousand times over. Cara

Parry was queen of the underworld and Carrie Hart was queen of Operation Bluebird. Everything was perfect.

"We fucking did it!" Taehwan swung her about with glee, then started rifling through the cupboards. "I'm gonna be better, I really mean it this time. I'll stop it with the stuff and the booze; I don't need that shit anymore."

He pulled out a bottle of Dalmore, unscrewed the lid and poured the contents onto the carpet.

"What are you doing?" Carrie asked in baffled amusement.

He checked the bottle was empty then threw it hard into the corner, where it smashed against the wall.

"Gone."

"What the hell?" Carrie chortled. "Most people just pour it down the toilet."

"I'm not most people," Taehwan replied, taking hold of a Belvedere. "And the cleaners need a job."

He fixed her with a mischievous grin and sent the liquid splashing over his shoes.

"Not on my dress!" she jumped back but he caught her hand and pulled her closer.

"I'll buy you another one," he declared, running his fingers through her hair. "I'll buy you ten other ones. I'll buy you the whole fucking shop."

He dropped her briefly to clumsily gulp the last of the vodka and open a bottle of chilled French vermouth.

"Jeez, this tastes good."

His tongue darted about his lips, catching drops of vodka that had missed his mouth. She kissed him to steal some for herself, and he emptied the cold vermouth over both of their heads.

"Fuck!" Carrie gasped.

She blinked furiously then grabbed at a beer, wrenched the top off against the corner of the minibar and splashed it into his face. Taehwan was delighted. He yanked open another with his teeth and returned fire, catching her as she tried to steal three to throw at him from behind the sofa and throwing her onto the sofa instead. Her calves trapped him for just long enough to soak him with Italian lager, before he escaped to call room service and order "un-popped" champagne. They attacked each other like grand prix victors, spraying it from the balcony and into each other's mouths, Taehwan throwing cocaine into the air like confetti. It settled like a layer of snow onto their hair and shoulders, their clothing drenched and chilling their skin in the winter air.

Taehwan shivered, then pulled the sodden shirt over his head and tossed it from the balustrade. Carrie stared. Droplets of champagne and vermouth dripped from his fringe, ran down his chin and trickled between his collarbones where his chest rose and fell with the exertion of their battle. Sure, he was too hungover to use the gym a lot of the time and a life of drugs and parties had left him thin and tired, but his brothers' abs could sod right off. He wasn't the family shit anymore and he knew it.

"It's all gone now," he brushed back her wet hair and kissed her. "No more fucking up. We are gonna run this shit and I'm gonna make you so glad you stayed."

22: All Jobs Pay

21 February 2015

Carrie sighed contentedly the next morning, knocking the bedside phone off the hook before it could wake him. She ran her fingers along his spine as he snored in her arms, still smelling strongly of beer where he had collapsed in even more emotional exhaustion than usual before having the chance to shower. She had decided not to disturb him, unlike Yoonho whose voice was now crackling through the receiver and calling on her to pay him a visit.

She stretched reluctantly, cleaned herself up and made her way to his office, where he thanked her profusely for helping Taehwan survive the gala and appearing as a perfect lady herself. Carrie almost laughed; he hadn't seen them having a beer fight as soon as their door was closed.

"Now," Yoonho said, moving some papers from his desk. "I won't treat you like a fool. You know our business. You saw what happened to the Logans and Soju's little sport with your brother – that's more than Margot ever had to witness – and I'm sure you have some notions about our potential new partner. It makes you vulnerable, especially with Drew's, ah… previous history. There are certain things that need to be considered."

"It's okay, you can say it," she told him. "Me and Drew both know how this works – isn't that how I'm useful? Nothing touches the Parks – Drew's an ex-con with a sister whose rich in-laws he can scam, so anything higher up the chain that could be pinned on you is just him taking advantage. We take the fall, just like Taehwan would take the fall for Soju and Soju would take the fall for you, and I guess everyone would for Mr Park. I don't mind; we both knew what we were getting into."

In-laws? That was a weird phrase to use.

"I'm glad you understand the situation," Yoonho nodded with relief. "You're a clever girl. But it isn't you I want taking the fall for anything – Drew can do that perfectly well on his own and I'm sure he would want to protect you. Women are innocents. Of course, Ballantine is an exception and wants to know the whole family for her own security, but as far as you're concerned, we're making an investment in a company that imports and sells ordinary diamonds perfectly legally, and preferably you don't even fully understand that part."

Any type of diamond being considered ordinary struck her as a very Park thing to think.

"Anything Jay works on, too," he continued. "You shouldn't get involved. Whatever you two might like to think, you're here to be beautiful not smart, for your own safety and ours. I know you can keep a secret, but the fewer you have to keep the easier it is."

She knew that already; it was like a second helping of David's "don't bullshit". Of course, this time she had no intention of complying and she was lucky that Taehwan didn't share his brother's sense of warped chivalry. She doubted she would have any trouble being involved in whatever issues of his she desired.

"Right," she nodded. "Most people probably think I'm too stupid to get any of that anyway; I'm only a dancer – or was. Actually," she plucked up the courage to suggest an idea that she and Lisa had been toying with for a couple of weeks. "Would it be okay for me to help Lisa with new choreographies? I'd sort of like something to do. I know I shouldn't dance anymore, but I've always wanted to do something like that... if it's okay with you?"

"You don't have to ask me things like that," Yoonho smiled, then rummaged in a drawer and pulled out a little gold card. "And you shouldn't have to ask any of us when you want something either."

"Oh, I don't need a credit card," Carrie said quickly. "I still have the library and Drew does half the rent now, and I already spent enough of Taehwan's money for the gala."

And then doused it in alcohol and dry cleaner fees.

"His money is Park money, and to all intents and purposes, you are a Park," he pushed it firmly into her hand and curled her fingers around it. "You know too much not to be. Being one of us is a job just as much as dancing is, and all jobs pay. This one happens to pay very well. We have a reputation to uphold; don't be cheap. My brother certainly isn't."

Well, when he put it that way... she didn't want to disobey Yoonho Park.

22 February 2015

It was with a huge amount of pride that Carrie reported her progress in the printing room and with great satisfaction that Wendy received it. Taehwan was gaining responsibilities that she, too, would be freely exposed to, while his brothers focussed on a potentially huge and damning deal for which she herself had witnessed discussions. The CEO considered her a Park, she was a choreographer (irrelevant but something she had dreamed of for a long time) and she had even caught a fleeting glimpse of the empire's ominous mastermind skulking about in the staff areas. She truly was Brian's golden girl.

She left the library with a beam plastered across her face, sprung onto the bus and swung happily from the support grip, humming Ellie Goulding and looking out for a suitable en-route detour. She had already decided that David was getting a special cooked meal tonight, just because. Megan had even given her some recipes.

A full-time Park girl with a credit card, she decided, should definitely shop in Waitrose, and considering which Park it was she was dating, she was absolutely allowed to sing in the aisles.

She picked up a pair of dark glasses and heeled boots in M&S too and perused the shelves for more fancy underwear, hanging her bag from her elbow as if she were Margot. She strutted along the remainder of the bus route, enjoying the fresh air and exercise far too much to ride the thing until she was utterly exhausted. She grinned, flushed, at the driver and gave him a generous tip. She could definitely get used to this.

04 March 2015

Brian Hole had been right to suspect that half the dodgy money in London ran through Paradise and its subsidiaries. Tens of thousands of pounds came up through the casino floor each day that had to be processed and redistributed through legitimate channels, and that was only the accounts that Taehwan was allowed to touch – the real money was Soju's. It had taken Taehwan and Carrie all night to figure out movements that the finance director probably would have finalised in an hour, but Yoonho never needed to know how much help his little brother was getting. The eldest Park may underestimate his woman, but Taehwan trusted his more than himself. He even had his password as her name – well, Cara's name.

They sat on his sofa, bundled up in jumpers (hers a very cute grey one with little black and white cats that Taehwan had refused to tell her the price of), Carrie's chin resting on his shoulder so she could see the papers scattered across his laptop keyboard. They had started out so eagerly, laughing at how shit they both were at maths and getting distracted by extravagant and unrealistic ideas they could suggest to Yoonho, but the ticking clock had taken its toll. The obsidian ashtray on the table overflowed as Taehwan tried to keep himself inhaling something other than cocaine, the crumpled note beside it betraying where he had failed.

He was doing so well, Carrie tried to tell him, but despite his stubborn determination, such things weren't quite as easy as "it's all gone now." He had scowled his way through a few days of insisting he needed absolutely nothing and was going to do it 'properly' – he was a Park after all, doing whatever the fuck he liked and stopping whenever he wanted – but had been forced to accept that he couldn't cope.

In a way, Carrie was glad. It had been too much for him, trying to cut everything at once, and she hadn't known what to do with herself. Their relationship having an actual purpose had thrown things somewhat out of kilter, drawing lines that hadn't been there before and blurring others that had. He wasn't her own separate, inconsequential thing anymore and they couldn't keep just having fun all the time; she had to be careful and make sure his elevation continued.

But she liked having fun and she didn't like watching him vomiting into the bath or curled up in a slump of intense depression with a raging headache. Perhaps she was still indulging him, but it was much less unpleasant to encourage him to take things slowly. Besides, Yoonho wouldn't appreciate it if he simply swapped incompetence via intoxication to incompetence via withdrawal, and Yoonho's disapproval wouldn't help either of them. He certainly was cutting down on both the drugs and the booze, and even then it was mostly behind closed doors, just winding down and having a laugh with his girlfriend. He told her he didn't need parties and excess anymore to be happy – only her company and to know she still wanted his – and she believed him. His body just needed time to adjust at its own pace.

For now, he was working hard and staying out of trouble, and that was enough.

"You okay?" she asked, the screen swimming a little in front of her own eyes.

"Yep," he insisted. "I've got it now. I just gotta check these receipts, take off tax, take off our cut and match it to some invoice for overpriced chairs and crap paint jobs that accounts have gotta pay the day after tomorrow. Piece of piss."

He took a deep drag from what must have been his twentieth cigarette.

"How the fuck do we check receipts?" he squinted at the mass of numbers they had been playing with for hours. "The money goes in through roulette and blackjack – I get that bit – but how the fuck do we prove it? I've checked this shit a hundred times and it all just looks like people losing at casino games."

"I think that's sort of the point," she reached around his waist to pick up a remittance advice. Wendy would know what to do with these, and she would require significantly less cocaine and nicotine.

"Yeah," he agreed. "You're right. Fuck, why can't I concentrate anymore?"

"Don't worry, I can't either," she reassured him. "I just had to use a calculator for 30 x 10."

"I'd need one for 1 + 1 right now," he rested his forehead tiredly against hers. It was wet with the sweat of a comedown he was trying his hardest to ignore. "Can we stop with numbers for now?"

"Jesus, yes please," she did not need any further persuading. "We've still got a day, right?"

"Right," he confirmed with relief. "And then I can go kick butt and do the actual fun bit. Though it's fucking confusing. This guy hasn't paid but I'm not allowed to just go and smack him cos I've gotta talk to this guy so he can talk to this guy cos it's this other guy's fault and he's not meant to know who we are. But then I get to smack the first guy if he doesn't get it done, and Han's coming with me."

He smiled proudly at the idea of going on missions with the brother he admired the most.

"Right," Carrie pulled a face. "Cos smacking people is the fun part."

"It's not really hurting them," he sniffed and wiped his nose in his sleeve, as was habit from so many years of cocaine and not caring. Carrie handed him a tissue. "Just showing them who's boss. Cos I'm the boss." He grinned. "And then I can take you somewhere cool."

"Can we go to a spa?"

Since her outing with Margot, Carrie had become a little obsessed with the idea. They were so tranquil and pretty and made her feel like a posh person without being too extreme – Fiona went to spas a lot and she didn't need drug money to afford it.

Taehwan drew a hesitant stream of smoke into his lungs. "A private one."

No matter how much of a 'real Park' he had become, he still wasn't keen on exposing himself in public, which she supposed was fair enough. Besides, she didn't mind having him to herself.

"Sure," she raised his chin and turned it so he was looking at her. "Private ones are more fun anyway."

She took the cigarette from his mouth and kissed him. He smiled sheepishly. Sometimes he still looked at her like she didn't exist and could disappear in a puff of his smoke.

"You're knackered," she stroked back the hair behind his ear. "And I've got work tomorrow – well, today. Let's just go to bed."

"Yeah," he sunk down gratefully into her lap, eyelids already drooping despite the overload of nicotine that had been keeping them open. "I just need to figure out how to stop those Brixton wankers fighting over a shitty street."

"Give that one to Drew," she brushed his fringe away from his sweaty forehead. "He's good at talking."

"Mmm," he murmured. "You're sensible."

"Sometimes."

She continued to caress his cheek as he drifted into sleep, until he was safely snoring, then carefully transferred his head from her legs to a pillow. She collected up the invoices and remittance advices, re-opened his laptop and started copying files onto a USB stick. While Carrie and Taehwan may find money movements and chains of fall guys a little confusing, Brian would see them as a goldmine just waiting to be tapped, and would see her as his most valuable prospector. She secretly hoped that he might even be able to trace them far back enough to find a solid link to the man known as Big Mo, though she had accepted that the passage of time made that unlikely. Getting them for something, anything, would have to do.

She opened the box of tampons in her bag, wrapped the USB in a similar pastel coloured plastic and slotted it in amongst the real items as neatly as possible, the papers folded carefully into the wrappings of sanitary towels. She had learned from Hannah that nobody at all looked too hard at a woman's feminine products. Perhaps it was a little paranoid, but she didn't want to take any chances tripping in front of Han (or any one of them) and spilling confidential documents all over the floor. As for Taehwan, he would happily assume that she had simply tidied them away somewhere until they had already been photocopied by Wendy, perused by David and returned to his room. Her boyfriend being a careless, trusting idiot came in very handy.

He was also a very comfortable idiot and there were still a few hours before Carrie had to go to the library. She set her alarm to vibrate, tucked the phone into her back pocket and fell asleep on him.

<u>**23: Emilia**</u>

It was a beautifully clear morning; something which Taehwan seemed incredibly pleased about. He was out of bed and dressed in record time, encouraging Carrie to do the same. She was still getting used to him semi-sober and energetic.

"Wanna see something cool?" he asked with an excited smirk.

He bundled her into the car, giving nothing away until they were speeding down the A roads, wind in their hair.

"Where are we going?!" she yelled over the noise of the engine, the top down as usual.

He flicked his eyes to her, unable to control himself. "Ever seen a private plane before?"

"No!" she exclaimed.

"I have a plane," he told her smugly. "Actually I have two planes. They're hidden away, obviously – blah blah secrecy – but they're *my* planes. And we're gonna go fly one."

"Are you serious?" her mouth split into an excited grin.

"Why else do you think I've been boringly sober since Monday?" he winked.

"You have to be sober to ride a plane?" she laughed, then gasped with realisation. "Wait, you can fly it?"

"Proper pilot's license," he glowed with pride. "I keep trying to tell you I'm not a useless cokehead."

"Fucking hell," she exclaimed.

It was the sort of thing rich people did in movies, not ordinary London detectives. Maybe she should be used to such things by now, but they still boggled her mind. Her life had gone absolutely crazy and she couldn't deny that she was loving it.

"It's not the poshest plane in the world," he admitted. "It's only a Cessna, but it's gotta be small enough to go VFR. And I'm not allowed to fly the Gulfstream." He added sulkily.

It certainly looked posh enough to Carrie. The inside of the plane was everything she had imagined and more. Eight padded cream leather seats sat on rotatable rollers, each coupled with a mahogany table that folded back into the sides. The passenger windows were trimmed with thick curtains which matched the fluffy carpet, held back by gold coloured rope ties. There was even a minibar, which he had ensured was well stocked with wine and champagne.

Taehwan seemed very pleased with the look on her face.

"Happy birthday," he put an arm around her shoulders and kissed her cheek. "Sorry I woke you up early, but I wanted to make sure we got here before everyone else."

"Everyone else?"

"I'm a show-off and it's your birthday," he reminded her cheekily. "You've already had enough Paradise parties; I needed to up my game."

Carrie would never in a million years have imagined that she would one day celebrate her birthday on an aeroplane with a gangster, three top casino dancers, three library workers and Mary's wife Carys. She hadn't even had a birthday party in years. People didn't do this sort of thing for her; she didn't even think to tell anyone her birth date. Taehwan had clearly been doing his research.

She gleefully helped herself to drinks and nibbles, waiting to wake up in her old apartment and realise it was all an elaborate dream. Of course, Lisa, Lali and Jennie were to some extent used to the high life (though even Jennie had to admit this was the next level of cool), but Ashley and the others – Carrie included – were utterly flabbergasted by the luxury of it all. The youngsters took great pleasure in playing at billionaires; sipping champagne with a finger held classily away from the flute as Lisa, Mary and

Carys looked on fondly, Ashley frequently disappearing into the cockpit to marvel at the controls and grill Taehwan about every detail.

They were all a little tipsy by the time he brought the plane in to land – not so much as to become undignified, but enough to fill their heads with a joyful fuzz of disbelief.

"Happy birthday, Caz," Ashley squeezed her gleefully before turning to file down the steps back to ground with the others. "Your dude is freaking awesome and I am jealous.com. You're bringing him to RUMmikub; I still have lots to ask him about planes, and you."

Carrie laughed. The girl had no idea who she had spent the past few months babbling to in the library about Mustangs and Astons, and who she had just invited to her house.

She waved as smartly dressed drivers led the party away to even smarter cars, then made her way into the cockpit, snaking her arms around the back of the pilot's seat.

"That was crazy," she hugged him. "Thank you. And thanks for bringing them, I've never had anything like it – none of us have! I didn't even know I had enough friends for a birthday party."

"Obviously I brought them," he kissed her arm. "I'm a showy twat."

He said that, but this didn't feel quite the same as the way he bragged and threw money at Ieuan and people like him. He wasn't trying to buy her attention – he knew he already had it – he simply wanted to share his world with her and give her a good time. She considered that a much better present than some expensive jewellery, and she got the feeling that he knew it.

Carrie chuckled. "Well I'm glad you held back on the loop-the-loops and didn't kill us all."

"Oh ha ha, maybe I still will," he patted the co-pilot's seat. "C'mon, I wanna show you something else. Buckle up."

To her confusion, the plane took off again, sat at a steady altitude for a short period of time, then began its descent into a much smaller airfield than the one they had departed from. A plot of farmland spread beneath them, dotted with hangars and a single runway that to Carrie, in her limited knowledge of aviation, seemed very short.

"I couldn't fly everyone from here," Taehwan explained. "No-one outside the family's meant to know this exists, except Wally – the guy who owns it. He's got a tonne of his own planes here. He's some big cheese with a gambling problem; owes Dad a shit tonne of money so he keeps ours off grid for us and pretends they're his. Everyone knows about the Gulfstream cos we keep that separate and file things properly, so they think that's our only one. Obviously you can't tell anyone; Dad would kill me if he found out I showed you."

"Okay Wanwan," she promised. "I won't rat you out to daddy."

It was the best she could do without lying. A secret airfield where Mr Park kept aeroplanes without anybody knowing was something she would feed back to Wendy as soon as she could. She snapped a quick selfie of the two of them in the cockpit (making sure not to include any background that might give them away to the old man) and coupled it with a few photos of the girls to post to the 'Gram. "*Where am I??? #birthday #plane #bestboyfriendever*" – essentially "*#oi, Wendy, check the phone's location tracker*". Finding a secret airfield would be pretty useless if they didn't know where it was.

They taxied into one of the domes, inside of which was a camo-grey biplane. Taehwan took her hand and led her proudly to it.

"This is my plane," he announced. "The Cessna is too, but Dad uses it a lot when he wants to go places in secret. I think he hides stuff in the seats sometimes, like they did with my car when we shipped it from America, or takes them out completely. But this plane is only mine."

"Hello plane," Carrie smiled at it. "Can I touch it?"

"Sure," he beamed. "You can get in if you like."

He gave her a leg-up and she clambered into the cockpit, surveying the world.

"She's a rare Sopwith," he told her. "There's only six others left in the world. She was fucking hard to find and expensive as hell."

"Why am I not surprised?" Carrie teased, running her fingers over the display. "Show-off."

"I am a show-off," he agreed. "But you're actually the first person who's seen her, except Dad and Wally. She's like my one thing that's just mine... Now she can be yours too." He smiled happily, then added quickly: "Except you can't fly her; you're shit at driving."

She chuckled. "That's fair enough."

"I'll take you for a ride soon," he promised, helping her back down.

"Not now?"

"Not if you don't want me to go overboard on loop-the-loops and kill us," he joked. "I'm fucking knackered and my head is killing me. I need a fucking whiskey."

Her chest felt funny as his hands curled around hers. Playing around on a private flight was all part of the crazy Park life, but this was something more. She knew by now how special it was to him to have something of his own, untouched by anyone, and he was showing it to her. She wrapped her arms around his waist and gazed fondly at the biplane. Suddenly it was special to her too.

"I'm proud of you," she said. "I've never seen you go this long – not without going nuts."

"Don't remind me," he pulled a face and dropped his forehead onto her shoulder. Now that the others were gone, he could be honest about the throbbing in his skull. "I feel like shit. Jeez, I wish you hadn't finished off the minibar."

"Hey," she nuzzled his head with hers. "Smile. You're winning."

They stood for a little while longer and something caught Carrie's eye; a word painted onto the side in a green barely distinguishable from the grey around it.

"Emilia," she breathed.

Emilia Young: Mr Park's dead teenaged bride, whose favourite book was *The Great Gatsby* and who apparently spoilt Taehwan rotten.

"Yeah," he shrunk into her a little. "She's called Emilia."

Carrie held him and said nothing, sensing that if she pushed the subject she would get nowhere. There was a gnawing sadness about his tone and the way in which the name existed on the aircraft but hid itself, like it wasn't sure if it wanted to be there.

"I dunno why I called her that," he spoke heavily. "Emilia pissed off."

"What happened?" Carrie gave him a sympathetic squeeze. "Who's Emilia?"

"Someone who pissed off," he sniffed hard. "She was Dad's second wife, after Mum died in Korea. Yoonho and Han never liked her much – she was only a few months older than Yoonho and they thought it was weird – but she's the only mum me and Taeju can really remember. She actually paid attention to us, even though he was a shit to her. She used to come to my room and hug me when we were sad, and she'd get me a load of toys and stuff and take me out places. I thought she actually gave a shit, but I guess not."

"She gave a shit," Carrie said softly. "Parents don't leave cos of the kids."

"Maybe," he murmured. "Taeju thinks Dad killed her."

"Did he?" she whispered.

"No," he said decisively, like he had already had this debate with himself many times before. "He's not so bad he'd kill his own wife. Han saw her get on a plane and then she disappeared."

"Han saw her?" Carrie pressed.

Brian had had no justification to investigate a broken marriage, so she doubted anyone had it on record that the family hitman was the last person to see her alive.

"Yeah," Taehwan replied. "Gatwick Airport, going to Spain; she had suitcases and everything. She just took a fuck tonne of money and pissed off. I got angry and hated her for years… but I guess I can't blame her really. I wouldn't wanna fuck Dad either."

"Eurgh, definitely not," Carrie agreed. "Was it a long time ago?"

He sighed. "14th of January 2006; that was the last time I saw her. To be honest, I still miss her sometimes. Y'know… Jay comes from Gatsby… and she's the one who got me to read it. No-one knows that; they'd think I'm soft."

"You don't mind me thinking you're soft?" she smiled at him, something like real affection stirring in her chest.

Private airfields and leads on Emilia – they could mean a lot to Brian and Wendy. The fact that he showed the private airfield to her and only her, and opened up about Emilia when he had never done so before… that could mean a lot to her, if she let it.

He was a Park, she reminded herself; she wasn't supposed to let it.

"I don't have to impress you," he replied.

It was half a joke, half an imploring look of immense gratitude.

"You impress me anyway," she said.

It wasn't something she had ever expected to be true.

-

"A private plane party, ey?" David commented. "You can see why people turn to a life of crime."

"It doesn't excuse it," Carrie said automatically.

"You think?" he gave her a look of amusement. "You can't keep your hands off a certain someone; I figured he might be excused."

"Fuck off," she kicked his foot. "You know I can enjoy my job."

"You keep telling yourself that," David teased. "You certainly swear a lot more since you started hanging out with him."

"Confident people swear more," she told him. "There was a study."

He laughed.

"Seriously though, you're doing amazing. I'm proud of you, little sis," he ruffled her hair light-heartedly. "I have to admit I wasn't sure how you'd cope at first; you were a kid scared of your own shadow."

"I was not," she scoffed, knowing full well it was true.

"It's like you were made for this though," he praised her. "You're more real than I am. Half the time I forget you're not actually my annoying little sister. And anyone who sees you eating that little shit with your eyes – they know that's not bullshit."

"Oi," Carrie kicked him again. "I do not do that."

"It's a good thing," he reassured her. "Fake relationships are undercover taboo. Real ones get you access I never would. Just don't go getting too attached; you've still got to put him in a cell."

"Why would I?" she pulled a face. "He's a Park and an idiot, just one that's very good in bed."

"No, no, no, I don't need to know that," David put his hands over his ears. "Not listening."

"Well-"

He grabbed her in a playful headlock and wrestled his hand over her mouth. "Nope, little sisters don't say those things."

"You started it!" Carrie protested.

She liked having a brother.

"I do wish you'd tell me stuff sometimes," she said after a while. "Your things are more hardcore than mine; it's interesting."

"More hardcore than sex with a crap gangster?" he joked.

"Yes," she gave him a look. "You come home with cuts and bruises, have a beer and go straight to the boxing gym. You're more battered than Taehwan and he's the one who throws hissy fits at thugs. I thought you were meant to be a salesman."

"I thought you were meant to be a dancer," he replied, avoiding the matter in question.

"Oi," she hit him. "I'm serious; I wanna know things."

"I'm pretty sure you don't," he said casually. "You saw what Soju's capable of; he makes the Splitters look tame. Dunno how well I'd be doing without you to be honest. You're a much needed reminder of reality."

Carrie smiled. There were many reasons why she had persuaded them to keep her on the case, and knowing that David really did appreciate her topped that list. It seemed that both her and Taehwan were going up in the world.

28 March 2015

"That was some damn useful info," Wendy congratulated her at the photocopier.

"The plane?" she replied delightedly. "You managed to find it?"

"Serial number 208B-1307, registered to Walter Durden," Wendy recited. "Kept at his private airfield, which we now have somebody watching around the clock in case Park decides to do something interesting. Filed a flight plan to Barcelona 15th January 2006."

She fixed Carrie with a purposeful look.

"Jay last saw Emilia on the 14th," Carrie remembered with a jolt.

"Park followed her," Wendy said certainly. "Return flight recorded on the 20th, but Rajeet contacted the Spanish airfield and they don't have it down as parked there between 17th and 19th. He did say their records were dodgy and there are no flight plans filed on those dates so we're still looking into it, but if that plane did go anywhere, like hell was it legal, and at some point it was probably carrying a corpse."

Carrie wasn't sure how she felt about that. Wendy was an experienced police handler; of course she was immune to the idea of innocent dead people and Carrie should be too. But there was something about Emilia that felt almost sacred; perhaps something to do with the faintly painted name on the side of the little biplane she had decided wasn't relevant enough to require reporting. She didn't know why she had decided that – she had reported a lot of irrelevant things – but it wasn't like she could go around overwhelming Wendy with absolutely everything she knew. A painted name didn't mean anything. It was only a toy, like the Mustang, and she wasn't about to tell her his shoe size or the colour of his toothbrush.

People were watching the airfield; if anything was awry it would be picked up by them. It was only Taehwan who flew that plane anyway and that was just for fun.

"If Han followed her, Park must have gone too," she realised. "Him and Jay are the only ones who can fly, and I'm guessing they didn't hire anyone if they were… y'know."

"Nobody we've been able to track down," Wendy confirmed. "The flight was filed only for Durden, and security at these small airfields is great at not checking rich pricks' passports."

"But this is useful, right?" Carrie pressed eagerly. "We can use this to get to Park – we can prove that Han was there, and Han can't fly a plane so he must have been there with him."

"It's a great lead," she assured her. "There's something else too. Now this really might be nothing – apparently it's a very common surname – but do you remember the names you gave me?"

"The Parks' real names?" Carrie asked.

"Bingo," Wendy nodded. "I've had a team scanning everything we can think of for months, but it's all been dead ends. Now, though, we've pulled up every flight Walter Durden has ever made and we might have found something. He likes to faff about with fancy friends from around the globe and we have a big long list of names who've apparently been in his planes. One of which is a South Korean gentleman named Taesuk Lee."

"South Korean?"

"It makes sense," she continued. "If Park wants to be travelling below the radar, he doesn't want his name on anything to do with Durden, but not every trip he makes is going to escape immigration checks. Think about it: a lot of shit went down with Seoul gangs in the nineties; guy gets into some sort of trouble – maybe a spat with a rival or the police – runs to London and gets a new identity as a refugee, who usefully has no papers. Keeps his South Korean passport to move about on a tourist visa, with no links to anything in the UK. It's a long shot and we can't poke around much without raising suspicion, but Brian likes it."

"Taesuk Lee," Carrie repeated. "Even Jay doesn't know Mr Park's real name."

"Nothing's proven just yet," Wendy reminded her. "Don't get too excited. But we've got a lot of things to look into, and Durden's testimony could flip a lot for us when he's safe to interview. You know Brian's keen on this diamond deal killing two birds with one stone so we can't move in on him until that's all done, but when we do…"

"We might find Emilia."

<u>**24: Serpentine Bridge**</u>

<u>**27 May 2015**</u>

Carrie had never felt so successful in her life. Her information was useful, her choreography was commended and she drank red wine in jacuzzies every time Taehwan did something he felt was worth celebrating – which was a lot.

She enjoyed strutting into the lobby from the executive lift, waving at Bea and Jerome as the heels of her boots tapped on the shining parquet. She enjoyed sitting on the bus in her Margot-esque sunglasses, flicking through Instagram comments that admired her dancing and couples photos as if she were a minor celebrity. She enjoyed the look on Wendy's face when she handed things over, and the praise she passed on from Brian to both David and herself.

She enjoyed waking up in Taehwan's bedroom, or in her own when she knew she would see him that night. She enjoyed talking to David about him, and Ashley and Megan and Lisa and anybody who would listen. She enjoyed his company, whether they were doing something fancy or just sitting with a spliff on the balcony, laughing at memes about politicians. She definitely still enjoyed his body on hers just as much as she had on Christmas Eve, perhaps even more so.

That was a good thing, David had said – it made her convincing and got her access – and she agreed with him wholeheartedly. She could enjoy her job. She was good at it and in complete control of everything; there was no reason to stop the carousel when the world was falling into place so effortlessly. She could do this forever. Of course, if required, she could stop it any time she wanted. She just didn't want to yet.

"You look dapper," Soju was waiting for them in the corridor of his and Taehwan's bedrooms, an arm casually draped over Jennie's shoulders.

Carrie wasn't surprised to see her; she had heard her all last night.

Taehwan had mostly swapped his leather jacket for suits these days (though he kept the studs in his ears, rings and belt, and his shirts black as opposed to Yoonho's crisp white ones – to prove he hadn't completely sold his soul to good behaviour) and his hair was cut shorter now, looking almost professional despite the fact it made his ears stick out even further than before.

"Well, as dapper as you can manage. Shame you smell of pot."

His eyes flashed with alarm.

"You don't," Carrie assured him.

"You don't," Soju agreed. "But if you're going to react like that to every accusation, people might think you have a guilty conscience."

"Fuck off," Taehwan scowled. "Pot doesn't count, and everyone can chill when they're not at work; even Yoonho does."

Yoonho relaxed with whiskey, not marijuana, but for Taehwan the Dalmore was a lot more dangerous. He was trying hard, and if cigarettes and weed were required to keep him off the hard stuff then that was fine. Carrie was sure that Soju knew that, which was why he tried to persuade him otherwise at any given opportunity.

"Don't think I'm judging," the third Park shrugged. "In fact, I think it would be a waste if you sold out. You are who you are, hey Wanwan?"

Taehwan's hands balled into fists but he kept them by his sides.

"Piss off," he shoved past him. "I've got shit to do."

"Not you, Cara," Soju stopped her as she made to follow him. "Yoonho wants us in the yellow room. You know, family things."

Carrie hesitated. She hated the yellow room and she had wanted to go home and talk to David before her library shift, but Yoonho's summons could hardly be ignored. She accepted, told Taehwan that she must only be needed in order to pass on the "family things" to him – part of the family – and the four of them entered the lift together.

"What is he doing?" Jennie asked curiously as the door pinged and Taehwan left. "I can't imagine him being good at anything."

"Important things," Carrie said smugly.

"Like getting plastic surgery?" Jennie quipped.

Soju gave a derogative laugh and the girl looked very pleased with herself.

Carrie pulled a face. "Oh, go to Specsavers."

Jennie shook her head in disbelief and Carrie grinned at her.

"I still think you're mad," she told her, reluctantly disentangling herself from Soju.

"Oh, she is," he confirmed.

Carrie chuckled. She was quite happy being mad.

"See you at rehearsal," she bid her friend farewell.

The yellow room was what it said on the tin: yellow. It was a sort of living room for the family; a comfortable space away from prying eyes but not so private as a bedroom or formal as an office. The dandelion carpet supported a collection of butterscotch sofas around an oak coffee table, with a long bookshelf running along the beige back wall. It was certainly an interesting choice of décor and very different from the spectacular elegance of the rest of the casino. Margot was incredibly unkeen on it and Carrie had to agree with her. Perhaps that was the point; to be inhospitable to anyone without a screw loose.

"Ah, Cara," Yoonho greeted her as Soju settled onto a sofa and pulled out his tablet to work – clearly he didn't consider these "family things" to be quite the big deal he had made out to Taehwan. "I wanted to talk to you. We've been invited to a very prestigious party by a very important politician – one of Mr Park's old friends who previously didn't recognise us at all. I'd like us all to attend if possible. Are you up for it? More importantly, is Jay?"

She nodded earnestly. Prestigious parties were bewitching, Mr Park's powerful friends were not a secret but of interest nonetheless, and she was still very pleased to hear Yoonho call Taehwan Jay.

"Excellent," he looked pleasantly relieved. "Now, there are certain protocol we have to follow; this is more than just a Paradise gala – "

He was interrupted by a crackling in Han's earpiece. The security director held up his hand to his ear, grunted a few acknowledgments then bent down to mutter something to Yoonho in Korean. Soju didn't look up from his tablet, but his expression hardened with intense interest and Margot stopped flipping through her magazine. The eldest brothers exchanged a few more words that Carrie didn't understand, then got up and left the room.

"Very intriguing," Soju raised his eyes.

"What?" Carrie asked.

Seeing Soju genuinely curious about things that weren't his doing was rare and slightly unsettling.

"Dad's been asking questions," he told her. "He knows details about Ballantine, and almost everything else we've been doing."

"Is that a problem?" Carrie was puzzled.

"He's retired," Margot spoke up. "He's not supposed to be knowing details; that's Taeyoon's job now."

"Do you really think that's why he retired – to let Yoonho play businessman?" Soju said cynically. "No. He's just getting old and doesn't want to die in prison. Ironic, as he doesn't seem to mind putting us there." His face filled with shadows beyond his usual cruel amusement. "We don't just get an inheritance for nothing; he isn't the freebies type. He's testing us, or worse.

Cara, you might want to let Wanwan get back to his parties before Dad notices he exists. Or he goes the same way I did and Margot here gets a ticket for a one way flight."

"I'm not frightened of him," the woman said sharply. "If he wanted to remove me, he would have done so years ago."

"You should be," Soju fixed her with a dark look. "If you're a fan of breathing."

Yes, he was smirking, but there was something different about it. As much as he loved playing with Margot and flexing his control, it was the old man's control that was absolute and this seemed to bother him – perhaps even scare him. Telling Mr Park was Yoonho's biggest threat, and though Carrie was sure that Soju continued to disobey his orders not to mess with David, he had quailed at the mention of his father.

"What do you mean Taehwan goes the same way you did?" she questioned, an uneasy feeling stirring in her stomach.

"Don't pretend you don't know," Soju replied. "Business involvement and a young, potentially useful woman." His eyes flicked coolly to Margot. "Dad might actually find him interesting. And when Dad finds you interesting... you can't mess up."

"He won't mess up," Carrie said firmly.

Taehwan being sent to prison early would be incredibly inconvenient, but not as inconvenient as dropping everything just to avoid the old man's attention. Both of them were doing far too well to go back now.

"I find that highly unlikely," Soju drawled, casual again now that the topic had returned to his brother's weaknesses. "He was born to mess up. He already has Drew annoyingly busy keeping the peace in Brixton – something that was supposed to be his job."

Woops. That might have been her fault.

"In fact," he said decisively. "I'm bored of trade wars. Tell me, Cara, how do we stop irritations from squabbling, for good?"

Carrie stared him down. She had no veteran Splitter reputation to uphold and she was not taking the blame for Soju's dirty work.

Cold mirth turned up the corners of his mouth as he answered for her. "You give one of them guns, and wait for him to win."

Margot shook her head in disapproval but said nothing, her nose back in her magazine. Petty business troubles were of no interest to her.

"I thought they both paid you protection money," Carrie said stiffly. "You'll lose profits."

"Really?" he raised his eyebrows. "I thought Wanwan wasn't supposed to be telling you these things."

Carrie shut up. Soju wouldn't tell, as long as she played his game.

"Give me your bag."

Her stomach clenched but she handed it over. He smiled crudely at the box of tampons but otherwise ignored them, opened her purse and removed a penny. Thank God for Hannah and her desire to smuggle Es into Loveshack.

"This will do," he flipped the coin between his fingers. "Let's say you're Kwame. Heads or tails?"

"Heads," she said warily.

Soju tossed the penny and caught it deftly on the back of his hand.

"Heads," he revealed. "Kwame it is then. Deary me, Cara, you do like causing fights. You'll probably see a man called Clive Goodrem in the paper soon; your 'heads' just killed him."

He stretched and got up from the sofa.

"Oh, and keep an eye out while you're helping our Wanwan pretend he has a brain. Anything that looks out of place, you're going to tell me. Dad's up to something and that affects us all."

He left the room.

"Han also mentioned you," Margot put down her magazine and regarded her as if she were an ignorant child. "Whatever Taeyoon might want, his hands are tied if the old man doesn't trust you. You need to grow up and get smart. Learn the language, unless you want all your news coming from him." She tipped her head towards the door through which Soju had disappeared. "And be quiet about it."

Carrie was intrigued. "You know Korean too?"

"I have a lot of time," she replied. "And a few things for which I'd like a warning."

Carrie tried not to allow herself to be shaken. She was used to danger, and if Soju gave someone called Kwame a crate of guns with which to fight his rival then that was nothing to do with her pick of a coin toss. In fact, it was perfect timing; she would see Wendy today, and if Brian didn't deem it too suspect, perhaps even be the reason for an increased Brixton police presence that could keep Clive Goodrem and his crew in the land of the living. Plus, being in the loop while Soju Park looked for dirt on his father could never be a bad thing. She was useful, useful, useful.

Taehwan picked her up from the library as usual, dressed very casually in faded jeans and a loose red chequered shirt over a white vest. Despite his new professionalism around the casino, he had decided that he greatly enjoyed pretending to be a normal person, messing up his fringe as much as he could and claiming the 'cute' boyfriend vibe Ashley and Megan insisted he had. Carrie found that amusing; sure, he wasn't flinging extravagance at the world anymore, but Taehwan would always be Taehwan and couldn't resist a bit of showing off.

They dropped off the car and strolled aimlessly through Hyde Park, taking the opportunity just to wander in the darkening quiet, away from drugs and money and business. The dusk cast a pleasant glow over the greenery and it seemed a waste to head inside when the night air was so refreshing. It was a nice reminder of how they had started, when they were innocently separate from the rest of this world and being with him was a choice, not a job.

"Do you wanna learn Korean with me?" she asked, slurping cheerfully at an ice cream. "It might be easier with two of us."

"Yeah," he smiled with surprise. "That'd be cool. I'll be shit though."

"I'm expecting that," she replied cheekily.

"Oi," he stole a bite of her ice cream in retaliation. "You're supposed to be nice to me now. Ashley'll thwack you if you're not."

"When have I ever been nice to you?" Carrie laughed. "You've got ice cream on your nose."

There was something about tonight. She was too happy; things were going too well.

"I'm not selling out, am I?" Taehwan asked her once they had finished their cones. "I'm still me; you're still having fun?"

It must have been weighing on his mind ever since their talk with Soju that morning. That guy really did know how to mess with people and she wanted to give him a good slap.

"You're still you," she assured him. "Would I still be here if you weren't?"

"I dunno if you've got much choice," he chewed his lip.

"I mean here here," she clarified. "I could be Margot and just take a credit card and never see you."

"Nah," he grinned. "You make me let you buy ice cream; you're never gonna nick my money."

They stopped on the Serpentine Bridge, gazing out across the body of water that cut through the park and watching the ripples caused by a few stray leaves. Taehwan leant thoughtfully on the stone railing.

"You're the only real thing I've ever had," he murmured. "I didn't know what a real person was before. Nobody gave a shit, and I didn't even realise cos I didn't know what giving a shit felt like."

Carrie swallowed guiltily. Was she real? She heard her own voice in her head, asking David if he had ever wondered which persona was truly bullshit.

Taehwan took a deep breath.

"I love you, y'know."

He turned his eyes to her and the breath caught in Carrie's chest. It wasn't a joke or a drunken slur. She didn't want to hear that coming from him so sincerely, like he actually meant it. They weren't supposed to be having feelings like that, they were supposed to be having fun.

"Your brothers love you," she tried to shift the focus, though she suspected that may be the biggest lie she had ever told. "They give a shit really."

"I don't care," he said. "I love you."

She started to panic. Love didn't come into it. She liked talking to him because she could be herself. She was fascinated by the crazy dream that was the Paradise high life and she wanted his body every second of the day, but it was nothing more than that. His family killed Lucy Flynn. She was going to lock him up and she was going to be happy about it.

"Taehwan... I..." she fumbled, trying to find some way of explaining. "Sex is one thing, but... I... we're having fun, aren't we? I don't..."

She stared desperately at him, silently begging him for help. She should just say it and continue the ruse, but she couldn't bring herself to do it. It wasn't the sort of thing she felt comfortable faking, not to him.

"It's okay," he dropped his eyes to the river, the moon betraying the water gathering in them.

She couldn't stand it. It hurt. He lived his life throwing blood money around, doing whatever he felt like and not caring how many people were wrecked in the process, but it hurt to see him cry.

"No it's not."

Tears glistened in her own eyes as she cupped his face, bringing her lips to his. There were no words to describe these feelings that even she didn't understand, but she had to show him somehow. She wrapped her arms tightly around him and kissed him as hard as she could. He let her do it, pulling back only when she did, looking hopelessly confused.

"I don't wanna lie to you," she said wretchedly, stroking his cheek with trembling fingers.

It hurt. Just looking at him hurt. This wasn't supposed to happen. She was supposed to betray him physically, not emotionally too. They were supposed to just be having a bit of fun. She shouldn't be here; Cara Parry should have returned to Durham when she had the chance. She had thought she could live another life with no consequences. She had thought she wouldn't get carried away. She had overestimated herself.

"I'll give up properly," he croaked. "I swear to fuck."

"It's not that…" she spoke through the suffocating lump in her throat. "I don't want us to get hurt. I don't wanna say something I don't mean… I can't mean… I dunno how to explain… I care about you too much."

He blinked furiously and pulled her into his chest.

"It's okay," he repeated softly. "That's enough. You don't have to say anything you don't want to. That's why I love you; I know anything you do say is real."

A sob escaped her mouth. That wasn't true. She tried – she tried so, *so* hard not to bullshit – but there was one thing she could never tell him and that one thing made all the difference. He deserved prison, he deserved fines, he probably deserved a punch in the face… but she wasn't sure he deserved this.

"Oh for fuck sake," he drew back and started dabbing his nose with his sleeve. "Nosebleed."

She laughed shakily and dug about in her pocket. "Here, tissue."

He took it and held it under his nose, scowling in irritation. "Bad fucking timing. I guess my nose wants to change the subject."

She chuckled weakly into his chest. He always managed to make her feel better, even accidentally, even when the problem was his fault in the first place.

28 May 2015

"Is everything okay?" David asked. "You look like you've seen a ghost."

"Taehwan said he loves me," she told him glumly.

David's brow furrowed. "Isn't that a good thing?"

"Well I can't exactly say it back, can I?" Carrie hugged her knees.

"Why not?"

"Because it would be bullshit," she replied in frustration. She thought that was pretty self-explanatory.

He laughed good-naturedly. "I think you're taking the no bullshit rule a bit too literally. You're already sleeping with the guy; might as well go the whole hog. It won't open up some crazy web of lies."

He smiled encouragingly at her. Carrie didn't feel very encouraged. She dropped her head between her knees.

"He'd know I'm lying and I'd suddenly be just another gold digger," she muttered. "Or undercover cop."

"He'll believe you," David said with certainty. "From what I know, he's good at believing what he wants."

He was right, but that was why she didn't want to do it. Other than the obvious, she didn't lie to him. That was the whole reason he liked her and it was the whole reason she liked herself; it would be ingenuine to change that now.

"That would make me feel worse," she spoke into her legs.

"Feel worse?" a hint of concern entered his voice. "Are you worried about the case or his feelings?"

"The case," she snapped. "Obviously."

"Cos you know that's a slippery slope," he frowned. "You have fun with him, great – that's believable and useful. You start worrying about his feelings – that could become a problem."

"I don't care about his fucking feelings," she said angrily. "I talked a terrified girl down from a roof and then she died anyway because of these pricks. Which is why I don't wanna stuff it up by saying something I can't make convincing. Jesus."

"Okay," David held his hands up. "You know best. Just be careful."

Carrie stared gloomily at the carpet. It was already immoral, knowing how much she enjoyed this life while being acutely aware of where it all came from; she didn't want to start lying to the person who had taught her how to be honest. God, that was stupid – she had *always* been lying to him. Well, Carrie had. Maybe Cara was different. There was too much Carrie in her for such a thing to be true, but too much Cara for her to pretend without feeling guilty.

Ugh. Everything was getting too complicated. What was love supposed to be anyway? Liking their company, being yourself, getting hot whenever they touched you – and not knowing that they were a terrible person who you were going to lock up. His family killed people and he didn't care. That was a pretty damn big deal-breaker. She wished he had never said that; he had broken up the fun and made things serious. She didn't want to be fretting about his feelings, she just wanted to exist and not think about anything. Caring about him was problematic.

What was more problematic was how easily she fooled herself. Everything *was* fun and she had allowed that to distract her, forgetting to notice things that should have been nipped in the bud before they became even the slightest complication. She was sure that David would have listened to Ashley and Megan when they picked up on her attraction months before she did. He would have caught himself at the first indignant thought about Ieuan using his money or Jennie's sharp tongue. He would have accepted he wasn't ready and let Wendy take him off the case when she was supposed to.

She scowled, picked up the thought and plonked it with a lot of effort back in its box. Okay, maybe she cared about him, maybe she cared about him a lot, but that wasn't going to affect the operation. She cared about animals but still ate meat. She cared about orphaned children but she wasn't about to adopt one. She cared about her sister but she had missed her wedding, for God's sake.

The Parks killed Lucy. In this house, with David, she didn't need to think of Taehwan as anything more than a scribbled fact in a case file. With him... well, Cara would be Cara and Operation Bluebird would thank her for it.

Lali seemed noticeably distracted at their impromptu rehearsal, which was incredibly unusual for her. Carrie was used to Jennie's Soju-related daydreaming and Lisa, by definition, often interrupted her own practise to check on the others, but the Sri-Lankan was always the picture of perfect composure and concentration. Tonight, however, she had brought her bag with her behind the stage curtain and pulled out her phone at any acceptable opportunity, spending the rest of the time staring towards the door. She answered Lisa's queries with a simple "okay" and none of them could get anything more from her until they stopped for a quick rest and toilet break. She went immediately to her phone, saw nothing then turned discreetly to Carrie.

"Have you heard from Jay?"

"No," Carrie frowned. "My phone's in the changing room. All I know is he's out 'kicking butt with Han'. Why?" She quailed at the deep concern on the woman's face. "Is he okay?"

Worry rose in her chest. She didn't want him to not be okay. Nobody had been in love with her before. No, that wasn't the reason. If he was hurt or had done something stupid, he was useless to Yoonho so she was useless to Brian and couldn't have fun in planes anymore. No, no, no. For God's sake, what was wrong with her? All that was incidental. He had to be okay because he had access that David didn't and would help them bring down the empire. That was all.

"Sorry," Lali shook herself – something Carrie had never seen her have reason to do before. "He fine. I worry. You okay."

Jennie returned from the toilet and Lali backed away, leaving Carrie to run to the changing room and feel a little sick at the lack of messages. Ugh. That was completely normal and she was being silly. What did Lali know about Han and Taehwan's whereabouts anyway?

"You okay?" she typed furiously. *"Text me when you can."*

She forced herself to leave it in her bag, hanging on a clothes hook. She was a professional and could talk to him when rehearsal was over. Plus, whatever Lali was so jumpy about was clearly a secret and she didn't want to break her trust. But it didn't stop her from also becoming incredibly distracted for the rest of the session, trying to catch Lali's eye every time she picked up her phone.

She jumped out of her skin when the side door opened perfectly calmly and Han beckoned Lali into the corridor. Carrie's stomach clenched. Han looked fine, which meant Taehwan was also fine, right? The two talked for a while, Jennie and Lisa sharing intrigued glances but continuing past to the changing rooms and home time; they would quiz her tomorrow. Carrie stayed behind, nervously swinging about a pole in the pretence of perfecting new choreo while she waited for them to finish their conversation, afraid to check her phone.

"Lali," she caught her, dragging her back into the wings.

"Don't worry," the woman reassured her with a look of intense relief. "Everything's fine. Jay and Drew are on their way back now."

"Jay and Drew?" Carrie questioned.

What was this important, secret thing that involved both her brother and her boyfriend as well as one of Yoonho's dancers, but had only been described to her as "kicking butt"? Taehwan talked about whatever he wanted to talk about – sometimes it was work and sometimes it wasn't. David had always tried to keep her distant from most of his own activities, but she had noticed that ever since she had spoken to him about that night on Serpentine Bridge he didn't tell her anything at all.

"Okay, seriously, what is going on?" she demanded. "Why is Han talking to you? Han doesn't talk to people. And why are you speaking English?"

"It's easier to keep secrets when people think you can't talk," she replied mysteriously, avoiding the first two questions. "I have a lot of secrets."

"What secrets?" Carrie pressed. "You know I can keep secrets. Is this why we suddenly had to rehearse tonight; to stay out of the way of something?"

"Yoonho wanted us safe," Lali hesitated. "And Drew wanted you distracted. He said it was better if you didn't know."

"What?" she frowned. That wasn't fair; David could keep his own business to himself if that was what he wanted, but he couldn't silence her friends too. "Drew can sod off. Paradise girls are like sisters; Lisa always says so. You can tell me things – you've had me worrying all night!"

Lali considered, checking about nervously for eavesdroppers. Nobody would be able to hear them over the din of the bar beyond the curtain, but she took her hand anyway and led her down the corridor to a linen cupboard.

"They removed some bad men today," she whispered.

"Bad men?" Carrie winced.

Han removing people didn't surprise her, but the idea of David being involved wasn't comfortable and Taehwan taking part reminded her exactly why she needed to disregard his feelings and send him down.

Lali took a deep breath. "There was a man called Big Mo."

Carrie's heart skipped a beat. She knew that name.

"He was a bad man," she continued. "He brought me to this country. He promised me a visa and a good job, but I didn't get those things. There were a few like me and two people who were English but had nothing. He treated us very badly."

Lucy, Carrie breathed. Lucy was one of those people.

"Big Mo had men, but they were on their own. They had no deal with Parks or Russians or anyone. So when police started looking at them, he asked Mr Park for protection. He sent me to dance for Yoonho, and Yoonho liked me and I liked him. I told him what had happened to me and he wouldn't send me back. He told Big Mo if he doesn't stop hurting the ladies he will be finished. He said he would stop, but then an English girl died."

Lucy.

"The man called Silas came to Paradise. He told me she died because she talked to police, and he thought because I talked to Yoonho I would also talk to police. He told me he would kill me too. So I killed him first."

She shuddered.

"Wait," Carrie's stomach had become a trampoline that her heart was doing somersaults on. "Big Mo didn't work for the Parks?"

"Never," Lali shook her head. "Yoonho hates traffickers. Han even argued with Mr Park about it for him when Big Mo asked for help – Yoonho told me. I think… he saw some things when they came here. Drugs, yes. Fighting, yes. Ladies, yes. Ladies being trapped and hurt, no. Big Mo was not Park. Yoonho saved me from him. I was scared that I killed that man, but Yoonho told me not to worry. He said that no-one would find out, and if they talked Han would kill more men. Yoonho gave me a real job and a real visa. That's why I dance for Yoonho. He is a good, good man."

Carrie gulped. It was all overwhelming her and she couldn't think straight. Lucy had misunderstood. Big Mo hadn't been talking about the Parks because he worked for them; he had been talking about them because they were trying to shut him down. But that still meant her death was indirectly their fault, right? Surely it had to; that was how this world worked. There was no reason for the guilty feeling in the pit of her stomach.

"So what happened tonight?" she asked through the lump in her throat. "Aren't they in prison?"

"It finished, I suppose," Lali said uneasily. "And Yoonho as king is less scary than Mr Park. They came back for me. But it's all okay now. Yoonho keeps us safe."

Carrie stopped only for her key card, hurrying to the carpark in her loose shorts and gym vest. She couldn't just wait in Taehwan's room; her head was buzzing too much for even a second's delay. He and David were on their way back, Lali had said, so she would catch them as they arrived.

She skidded from the lift to see that the BMW had already deposited its passenger and was heading for the exit ramp. She ran to block its path. That was another thing making the blood rush through her veins in double-time: David had said not to tell her. He would have recognised that name as readily as she had and he had specifically instructed Lali to keep her in the dark.

"What happened tonight?" she demanded as soon as he had rolled down the window.

"I didn't do anything," he replied, knowing full well that wasn't what she was asking. "I don't even know the details for sure; I just drove and kept a lookout."

"Big Mo, Drew!" she thundered. "Why didn't you tell me? Did you not think that was something I might want to know?"

"Alright, keep your voice down," David shushed her. "Yes, I didn't tell you. I didn't want you getting upset and going looking for them."

"I'm not five!" she retorted. "I'm not gonna run around having a tantrum!"

He gave her a look. Okay, she might be heading into tantrum territory right now. Perhaps it was better to keep emotional outbursts between her and Taehwan.

"You could have told me," she took a deep breath, not feeling any calmer. "I'm supposed to be your sister."

"That's exactly why I didn't," David sighed. "As my partner, sure, but you are more like a little sister these days."

"Oh my God, semantics."

"Look," he leaned his elbow out the window. "I can handle this side of things. I don't want you getting hurt and I don't think this story should change anything. Get in, I'll take you home."

It didn't change anything, she assured him, but she wasn't going home tonight. She flew up the fire stairs, her pulse racing far too fast for lifts. She fumbled for her key card and threw open the door to the bedroom.

"Taehwan?" she called.

He was standing on the balcony, leaning casually over London with a cigarette in his mouth and a sleeveless shirt baring his arms to the summer breeze. He turned as she rushed past the open curtains and stood in the doorway, panting from her sprint.

"Did you kill Big Mo's crew?"

"Is that bad?" his brow creased apprehensively.

There was a big purple bruise forming around his eye and a graze on his bottom lip, and as was usual when he was chain-smoking his way through a sober patch, he looked rather ill.

"It's not bad," she breathed.

It should be, it really should be. Killing people was killing people and killing people was bad. But, in this case, her heart didn't seem to think so.

He grinned with conceited relief. "You proud of me? Han is. Just one shot – no playing around."

"All of them?" she stepped out onto the balcony, her hands gripping his waist as she stared questioningly into his eyes.

"Well, I got the first one," he admitted. "Then the other two jumped me and Han got them. But that's a third of the ones who are out, right? Mo's still in prison, obviously, so he hasn't done anything to piss off Yoonho, but these guys were being shits. The deal was we left them alone if they said nothing to the cops and never came back to London, but these pricks were trying for their old turf as soon as they got out, and they got Russians on side."

"Right," she winced. "Of course Mo's still in prison."

"Is that a problem?" Taehwan asked. "We can get him too if you like; we've got people who can do that, no worries."

That was very tempting. David had cut someone's tongue out – would it really be so bad for her to order a hit on Big Mo? Yes, yes it would. Jesus. Besides, he deserved time to feel just as trapped as his girls had; he didn't get to simply die.

Her heart pounded against her chest and her blood ran hot as she resisted the urge and told him not to.

"How do you know him?" he looked at her seriously. "I swear to fuck, if he hurt you I'll kill him myself."

"I'll tell you later."

She pulled him closer and kissed him hard. Her emotions were in overdrive and fighting passionately to break free, and there he was with his bare arms and his bashed up face and his lack of Lucy's blood on his hands, telling her he'd kill for her. Her heart beat faster, mad with adrenaline.

"Just fuck me."

She seized his belt loop and dragged him back to where the edge of the balcony met the hotel wall, the cigarette dropping from his hand as she clambered onto the balustrade, one leg on the concrete and the other wrapped around his hips.

"You're a crazy sex addict," he laughed incredulously as he steadied her between his body and the wall. "You're gonna fall off."

"Stop me then."

He didn't. She wrestled the shirt over his head and kept kissing him, unzipping his jeans and helping him to push aside the gusset of her shorts.

"You're fucking insane," he breathed heavily into her neck.

"Mmhmm," she agreed, her fingers massaging his back. "I need Wanwan rehab, before I start getting nosebleeds and acting like a twa-"

She gasped as he buried himself between her thighs.

Maybe she did love him. If this was her reaction to something that should have horrified her… Addict was correct. That's what it was; she didn't love him, she *needed* him, or she would die and go back to being nothing. That's what he said about coke and booze, and if Taehwan could kick his vices then so could she.

Just not yet.

Definitely not yet.

Holy shit, not yet.

-

"Wanna know something sort of cool, but sort of gross?" he asked, having showered and ordered late night snacks to fight his usual post-coital vulnerability.

"Sure," Carrie chuckled contentedly.

She lay with her legs curled up on the sofa and her head in his lap, occasionally raising it to allow him to feed her a peanut. The night air that filtered through the curtains was warm and fuzzy, making her pleasantly drowsy and at ease with everything.

"You can't tell anyone you know," he instructed. "Margot definitely doesn't and I think Han deliberately didn't say it in front of Drew. I dunno if Yoonho even knows; he doesn't like details and stuff. Han told me today though, cos he had to go and drop them off."

He looked incredibly proud that he had been trusted with this information, especially by Han. She wondered if his brother knew that he had shown her the airfield. He would have found out about the Cessna, she was sure – they had taken the girls, after all – but Taehwan had dressed that up as just him hiring a plane to show off his pilot skills. If the security director knew just how liberal he was with his tongue, Carrie would probably be dead by now and Taehwan would be back to being trusted with nothing.

"So y'know Dad and the Dragon have been friends for ages, right?" he continued. "When they were first getting big, they killed a shit tonne of people – I guess that's just how people did things back then – and that's when the Dragon opened his shop. Did you know that bone china has real bones in it? It's meant to be animals but apparently, if you mash up humans in there too, bone ash is bone ash and no-one's gonna know. They used to burn the bodies and make jewellery out of the bones, and then they'd give it to people they wanted to scare and sell the rest in the shop like necklaces and shit, or crushed up with the normal cow bones in teapots and plates. Grim, right?

"Apparently the jewellery's all legit animals or plaster shit now, and we're more respectable than Dad anyway – we don't do random murders – but every now and then, if Han has to get rid of some shitbag, they end up in the bags of cow ash. So someone's out there drinking tea out of Donny Logan's ribs."

"Eurgh," Carrie pulled a face. "Thanks for that image."

Yes, thank you Taehwan. That was more like it; the potential for Brian to find Mo's crew in vats at the Dragon's warehouse, or older victims of Mr Park himself by tracing previous Dragonbone jewellery sales. Perhaps the rings that Yoonho had commissioned last year could also be hunted down and tested for human remains.

Plus, more immediately relevant was the reminder of death and coverups and the fact that Taehwan dismissed all of this as "sort of gross" and even thought of their current activities as respectable. David was right; tonight's news didn't change anything. Sure, the Parks hadn't killed Lucy, but they had killed plenty like her. They were absolutely still crime lords who killed people. Lots of people. Both directly and indirectly they killed hundreds, or thousands, of people.

She moved her fingertips in absent-minded circles around Taehwan's knee.

But not Lucy Flynn. That meant more than it should.

As Taehwan had told her previously, the family didn't take the Cessna on holiday; it was reserved for stealth and secrets (and the youngest Park messing around showing off, pretending he had chartered it from Walter Durden).

"We take it under the altitude limit at VFR so we don't have to file flight plans," he explained as he pulled the Mustang up to airport parking. "Or file them as Wally when we go international. The villa's a legitimate holiday so we don't want him on record there; he's not supposed to know us personally. Plus the Gulfstream is *way* more our style."

He winked and threw the keys to the valet.

It felt incredibly strange, heading through the expedited checks at Gatwick's private terminal with the most prominent crime family in England; millionaire gangsters in airport security really didn't seem to fit. They boarded the Gulfstream G650 jet – significantly larger and harder to manoeuvre below the radar than the turboprop, granting it the ability to also be significantly grander. Carrie hadn't thought that possible.

"Not too shabby," David raised his eyebrows in admiration.

Carrie was incredibly pleased that he had been invited along, for many reasons. Firstly, it meant that Yoonho really did consider him part of the fold; secondly, she enjoyed his company (when she wasn't overreacting at him); and thirdly, he had been working much harder than she had and he deserved a share in the unending leisure that had become her Operation Bluebird. Not many people in the police force could say they had vacationed on a private island while bringing down a drug empire.

He seemed genuinely happy about it too, which made a pleasant change. The discovery of Mr Park's morbid links to Dragonbone China (and the fact that tracing such links could possibly re-open several of Brian's old murder enquiries) had cheered him up significantly, as well as the prospect of two weeks far from London and anything unpleasant that Soju could ask him to do.

A woman dressed as a waitress came through the main body of the aircraft – more a lounge than anything else – and offered wine, whiskey and champagne. Taehwan's hand twitched and Carrie was certainly tempted by the thought of champagne on a private jet, but that wouldn't have been fair.

"No, thank you," she curled her fingers through his and kept them firmly on his lap.

Yoonho nodded in approval. She wished she wasn't starting to like him, but she supposed that was the whole point of him – Yoonho Park was likeable. It was all fake, of course. But he hadn't killed Lucy.

"Who needs wine anyway?" Soju said after the woman had disappeared back into her cupboard.

He winked and produced a small bag of white powder. Taehwan's eyes widened. Carrie scowled; Soju kept doing this. She did try frequently to convince Taehwan that he was not being a nice, friendly brother but was actually just trying to mess with him again, but Taehwan was good at believing what he wanted.

"How did you get that through so easy?" he stared.

His brother gave him a haughty look. "Nobody checks if I don't want them to."

"Soju Park, will you please fuck off," Carrie said coolly.

Han's black eyes moved to her but she didn't care; maybe Han would tell him off too and that would be extremely funny. Either way, Taehwan's hand was staying firmly in his lap. He had beaten the headaches and depression and taken nothing for over a month (not counting the odd spliff for relaxation and pain relief); he didn't need to go through all that again. And he hadn't killed Lucy.

"Your loss," Soju shrugged.

"Fuck off," Taehwan scowled at him, clutching tightly onto her fingers.

She smiled proudly at him and dropped her head onto his shoulder, while he began to excitedly detail all the things he could show her on the island.

David watched them with even more interest than Han, though she supposed Han just wasn't as good at showing emotions. It struck her that her brother had never really seen the two of them together before; not when they weren't discussing business or humping in the show hall. It felt weird, like she was introducing him to her parents. She blushed and squeezed his hand tighter.

All thoughts of champagne on private jets paled into insignificance at the sight of the Park family villa. It was situated atop the highest point of the most beautiful island Carrie had ever seen (not that she had seen many islands); large enough for a full day of walking but small enough for them to have it all to themselves. The walls were white – traditional yet modern – where they weren't made entirely of glass, welcoming the sunlight into the living and dining rooms and the separate breakfast area that opened up onto a crystal pool surrounded by sun loungers. It was large enough for a family twice their size to live comfortably, but of course anything less would not be excessive enough for the Parks.

Herself and Taehwan shared a bed that was larger than her entire room in London. It was set within a corner bedroom with two glass walls that looked out over the trees and onto the Mediterranean Sea, the option of privacy being provided by pretty blue curtains with a silvery pull-cord. Taehwan popped a key into the slot below the handle and opened one of them a fraction, letting in the salty sea breeze.

"Chuck your stuff wherever you like," he instructed her as she gaped open mouthed at the view. "The others'll be chilling outside by the pool."

"Awesome," Carrie beamed at everything.

Jesus, her life was crazy.

And they hadn't killed Lucy. As irrational as it was, everything had felt so much lighter since Lali's confession, and now it was bright and warm and Taehwan was clean and they were on a beautiful island far away from anything important. It meant a lot, a lot, a lot. She was running out of reasons for it not to.

"I wanna go swimming."

They had both always liked swimming, but the underground gym or the mini rooftop pool at the casino were nothing compared to this. It sat proudly overlooking the luscious greenery of the island, glistening in the sunlight like it was scattered with diamonds.

Carrie dropped her towel to the ground and dove gracefully into the cool water.

"Come on!" she waved.

Taehwan hesitated.

"It's not too cold," she promised. "I know everyone says that, but it isn't!"

He laughed, threw his own towel from his shoulders and leapt into the pool, sending a tidal wave over the edge of the rockery. Carrie cheered in delight and swum across to where he was shaking the wet hair out of his eyes.

"Hey there sexy," she ran her hands over his bare chest.

It made her very happy, seeing how much his confidence had grown. A year ago that would have sounded absurd; she hadn't thought there was anyone in the world who needed confidence less. But then, she had never realised just how much she needed it too.

"Get a room," Soju drawled, throwing a grape casually at Taehwan's head.

Carrie flashed the middle finger and kissed him, to Yoonho's apparent amusement.

She couldn't remember the last time she had been on holiday, and she had certainly never been anywhere like this. She felt like the giddy teenager she hadn't allowed her younger self to be; high off sunshine and swimming, splashing about with Taehwan like they were children while the adults watched from the poolside.

Margot lounged elegantly in a Monroe-esque white swimsuit, casting them disapproving looks while her husband's brows furrowed over the newspaper crossword. Soju lay in a deckchair, lazily popping grapes into his mouth and sunning his perfectly sculpted abs, David beside him reading a book and sipping a cold beer. Even Han was relaxed; his Hawaiian shirt unbuttoned and hanging loose from his shoulders to reveal the heavy metal cross he wore around his neck. They didn't look like a group of killers. They looked like a family.

"Really, you three," Margot snapped as Soju launched a few more grapes into the pool and Carrie and Taehwan started to return fire. "Are you five years old?"

"Leave them, Margot," Yoonho stretched contentedly. "They've been working hard."

Taehwan beamed. Carrie guessed this was probably the first trip where he had been judged as deserving of his rest. The Mediterranean heat had brought his brother back too; throwing fruit and laughing like an actual human being.

"Hey Yoonho, get in!" Taehwan beckoned.

"Why not?"

To everyone's surprise, Paradise Casino's CEO folded up the paper, donned a pair of sunglasses and lowered himself into the water.

"Park-Parry volleyball?" Carrie looked hopefully at David. "I think I saw a ball by the li-los."

David smiled and fetched it, launching it hard between Taehwan and Yoonho before bombing in himself.

"I'll referee," Soju offered, looking slyly at Carrie. "Losers have to sunbathe naked."

Taehwan threw the ball at his face.

A perfect day probably shouldn't involve gangsters, even ones who hadn't killed Lucy Flynn, but this certainly came close. Carrie lay happily with Taehwan in the hammock, sharing a spliff and watching the sun go down. A soft breeze dried the water droplets on their skin and passed a gentle hand of tranquillity across their faces. She felt as if they were actors in an old movie which somebody had paused on the picturesque calm before the storm. Their characters swung from sculpted trees in a studio against a painted backdrop, blissfully unaware of the scenes that had gone before and the filming yet to come.

"Hey Wanwan," Soju flipped the hammock and dumped them unceremoniously onto the ground. Taehwan scowled indignantly, sending Carrie into giggles. "I'm taking Drew to Blue Moon. You can tag along if you put some clothes on."

"Does he have to put clothes on?" Carrie asked cheekily.

"You disgust me," Soju gave Taehwan a superior look. "Your choice."

Blue Moon was a chic bar that dominated a micro island a short boat ride away. It was frequented by members of the richest families who vacationed at the properties nearby and had once been a favourite haunt of the youngest Park brothers. They used to sneak out in a rowboat while still underage, Soju's charm blagging their way onto the dock. That journey hadn't been made since his spell in prison and Taehwan was clearly ecstatic to be returning together, despite his brother's snide remarks, with Carrie being personally delighted that David was accompanying them and seemed to be actually enjoying himself.

She perched on the side of the boat (this one powered by a motor rather than oars), feeling very glamorous in a summery but expensive navy dress that Margot had selected for her. Once, she had felt a fraud in such fineries. Now they seemed an entirely natural choice.

David manned the rudder, his blue linen shirt rolled casually to the elbows atop smart white trousers. Soju was as smooth as ever in an embellished light jacket; a princely vibe that Taehwan had tried to emulate before giving up and going with his usual socialite renegade.

The bar's docks were teeming with similar small vessels slotted neatly along tastefully illuminated jetties. Others were left in a less orderly fashion along the beach, waiting for the valets to deliver them to a more fitting parking spot. Soju instructed David to follow suit and they hopped onto the warm sand with varying degrees of dignity. Carrie slipped off her shoes to feel the grains between her toes as they walked towards the building, guided by fairy lights strung between twisting olive trees. The slick tones of a saxophone floated through the open doors, calling to the people still making their way up from the beach. The whole atmosphere was enchantingly beautiful.

The bouncers at the door took one look at the brothers and waved their party straight through.

"It's exclusive," Taehwan said snobbishly. "They still know us."

"Apparently not so well, or you'd be banned," Carrie whispered.

He squeezed her waist in a mixture of jest and pride as a pair of well-dressed men made their way over. Whatever the situation, he was still an insufferable show-off.

It turned out that Taehwan had not been exaggerating; they really were known here, despite their years of absence. They were approached by many people whom he smugly explained as being very wealthy indeed. They all wanted to buy drinks for the brothers and their companions, who Taehwan introduced equally smugly. Carrie gathered that they had been a group of swashbuckling mavericks in their youth (with Soju of course as their ringleader), who were now very keen to brag about how respected they had become. Understandably, they were all stunned to find that their youngest and most notorious member had a serious girlfriend. They congratulated him profusely – and often rather crudely – and he lapped it up in ecstasy.

"Cocky prick," she grinned mischievously and kissed him on the cheek. "I could tell them stories."

"And we would love to hear them!" a devilishly handsome Swede exclaimed with enthusiasm.

"You would not," Soju assured him.

The world within Blue Moon seemed like an entirely different time, in an entirely different universe. They weren't the infamous Soju and Jay Park here. They were Taeju and Taehwan; the sons of an affluent London businessman without even a hint of suspicion regarding connections to the underworld. They were friends again – at least as friendly as Soju was capable of – laughing at the pompousness of their acquaintances and filling in Carrie and David with amusing anecdotes.

Despite a fair amount of cajoling from Soju and his followers, Taehwan managed to keep the same small glass of red wine in his hand, Carrie encouraging him with her eyes whenever he seemed to be gravitating towards a top-up. She couldn't help but feel exceptionally proud of him, and unwaveringly amazed at the life he was giving her. Neither of them were nothings anymore.

They did give in a little and drop a tab, as provided by one of Soju's suavely suited friends, but acid was fine – they were on holiday, it kept him away from the drink, and one-offs never hurt anyone, right? Plus, it made everything full and bright and pretty colours. The lights swayed and waved, snaking together in their perfect, unfiltered chaos. Everything was beautiful; the walls, the floor, Taehwan's stupid face – everything.

"Let's dance," she grabbed his hand as Soju slyly led David away to be introduced to the handsome Swede's sister.

The back of the bar opened up into a prettily fenced courtyard, where a live band played to twirling couples. Vintage lampposts cast a blue glow over the sand, joined by shooting stars that dazzled their way to earth and burst at their feet, unnoticed by anyone but her.

Carrie kicked off her heels and practically dragged him into the centre of the floor, losing herself in the music. The lights lost themselves with her, spinning and spinning, unchained to reality and free to do whatever they wanted – just like she was. The tempo increased and she matched it gleefully, laughing at Taehwan as he completely lost his timing and just stared at her in perplexed awe as she cha-cha-cha-d around him. Quite a few other people had also stopped to watch her by the end of the song and she gained a spattering of applause that Taehwan seemed to enjoy more than she did. She just wanted to dance forever.

The band played more jaunty numbers, before deciding to give people a rest. The lights became fireflies that settled on Taehwan's shoulders, bathing him in blue and white and colour – her eyes didn't seem to differentiate anymore. Carrie fell into his arms, her face flushed; acid, exhilaration or breathlessness making the stars swim in gentle circles around the slower, more sensual melody. Her eyes met his in an intoxicated daze. This person: she couldn't resist him. She ran her hands down his neck, her fingers beginning to unfasten the buttons of his shirt.

"Oi-"

She kissed him before he could protest, rolling her body against him in time with the tune. He took hold of her hips and she kissed him harder as the rest of the dance floor disappeared entirely.

"I've never had sex on the beach," she whispered in his ear.

He didn't need any further hint. He picked her up and whisked her from the courtyard, carrying her on his back to an emptier section of shore among the olive trees. The music and the lights continued to wash over them as he held her against the rough bark and she pulled him into her. This island was heaven. This man was heaven. This whole fucking world was heaven and she never wanted to go home.

"I love you," she clutched at his hair. "Fuck… Taehwan… I love you."

In that moment, in her pretty movie scene with the painted backdrop, she meant it.

-

She had never seen a happier person as he lead them back to the boat. His shirt hung open and there was a spring in his step that reflected the utter joy on his face. He hadn't even cried.

"You all look pleased," Soju smirked.

David smiled sheepishly and Carrie's grin almost split her jaw open.

They circled the little boat around the back of the island, partly to see the view and partly because David was drunk and headed the wrong way.

"It's beautiful," Carrie said contentedly from Taehwan's arms, listening to the sea hugging the shore.

"Yeah," David steered them closer to a small cove, cut into the side of a much larger island across the water from Blue Moon.

Taehwan barked a short laugh. "This place, we used to camp here and make – wait, who's that?"

"You're high," Soju reminded him. "It's a tree."

"No," David squinted. "I can see someone too."

Soju peered through the darkness. A sliver of moonlight bounced off a long cane-like object in the person's hand.

"Is that Dad?" Taehwan stood a little too quickly, rocking the boat.

It easily could be. Carrie couldn't recognise the two blobs seemingly talking to each other on the beach, but there was something about him that drew her mind back to the man she had seen sneaking around outside the gala.

"What the fuck's he doing here? I thought he wasn't meant to get here 'til tomorrow."

"He wasn't," Soju said with interest.

He pulled Taehwan brusquely back down, put a finger to his lips and motioned for David to take them in closer. The little boat snuck around the bottom of the cliff and to the edge of the cove, where David cut the engine, removed his shoes and slipped into the water to pull them quietly to land. Soft waves lapped lovingly around the hull as he found a safe looking rock to tie it to and held out a hand to help Carrie down.

She hesitated. Of course she wanted to see what Mr Park was up to, but the sea and the sky were so enchanting and she wanted to learn all the constellations by dawn. Mr Park would still exist in the morning; the stars would not.

"You coming?" David beckoned.

"Yes!" Taehwan said enthusiastically, jumping into the shallows with a splash loud enough to wake the islands for miles around.

David sighed in exasperation. Carrie watched the ripples spreading out around him. They were shiny. Maybe there were jellyfish in there. Jellyfish were pretty. Pretty and dangerous – just like him.

"Is that really wise?" Soju rolled his eyes at David. "I doubt stealthy is in their dictionary."

"Cara can be stealthy," he reassured him.

"Maybe," she said thoughtfully. "But there are jellyfish in the stars. We should find the jellyfish, or they might give us away."

David gave her a concerned, incredulous look.

"Really," Soju raised his eyebrows. "You two are the most useless things. Come on Drew, let's go. Leave the dribbling children."

"Go fuck yourself," Taehwan replied contentedly. "You'll be shit."

Carrie snorted. It wasn't the same as the desperately jealous, defensive way in which he used to speak to him; he wasn't about to get up and punch him to make himself feel like he could be top dog too. Soju had lost the stranglehold he had had on his brother. Taehwan was just as much part of the family as he was these days, and that made them equals. Judging by the look on his face, Soju did not like that one bit.

Carrie looked at him in wonder. He really was beautiful.

"Fine," Soju shrugged icily. "Get back in the boat before you drown yourself. We'll find out what's going on. Maybe we'll tell you."

"Cara," David continued to hold out his hand.

Carrie was too busy looking at Taehwan.

She wasn't ever going to sleep again, she was just going to look at him. He was so many pretty lights. She needed to know his every atom; all the things that made him him and her her. They were one and the same. David would do better without her and she couldn't focus on crime lords right now.

"I found a jellyfish," he said after a while.

She followed the path of his finger into the sky. It was a star, but it could be a jellyfish if it wanted to be. It could be anything it wanted. She watched it swimming about happily, unaware that it had been spotted.

"I think night time is bullshit," she mused. "And daytime. It's all the same thing, we're just facing the wrong way. People think stars are small and they just stay there, and the sun goes up and down cos that's how we see it. We separate things, like there's really good and bad and mornings and evenings. But the sun is a star and the stars are suns and it's all chaos. We just don't want it to be cos then we'll burn."

"We're all chaos," he told her. "And it's fucking beautiful."

"It is," she agreed.

She touched his face. It was chaos and it was the prettiest thing.

"I really do love you," she whispered. "I mean it."

She had thought she couldn't say it, but this island wasn't real and that made it the only real thing there was. It was the place where the stars met the sun and the night time met the day and everything was whatever it wanted to be.

She smiled. "I'm not facing the wrong way anymore."

<u>**27: Mr Park**</u>

<u>**05 July 2015**</u>

Carrie was exhausted and entirely unkeen on the sound of a chopper whirring through the open window. Having been up all night concluding that all rooms have either zero or infinite ninjas and trying to figure out what the hell actually happened in *Donnie Darko*, they were finally regaining the ability to sleep and the tiredness that came with it – and now a helicopter was ruining their chances.

"Wake up," Margot's voice echoed her sharp knocking at the door.

"No," Taehwan replied tetchily, throwing a pillow at nothing.

"Drop that tone," she warned. "Your father's here."

His chest stopped moving and Carrie's insides twisted with fear. Mr Park was only a man, but he was the most dangerous man in London – probably the whole country, or even the whole of Europe. He was smarter than Yoonho, deadlier than Han and had a mean streak that Soju would be proud of. Fooling the brothers was one thing. Mr Park had been said to be able to look into people's souls. He knew if you were lying or not fully committed to his cause and he would kill his own wife if she was found wanting.

"Get dressed; you're needed," Margot continued. "Cara, I suggest we make ourselves scarce."

Taehwan jumped out of bed and hastily pulled on the smartest clothes he had, tripping on socks and struggling with buttons. He was nervous – really nervous. It was Yoonho who was his father figure really, who chastised him himself and seemingly protected him from the old man's discipline. Mr Park had never shown him love, even in an irritated, exasperated sort of way; only indifference. To this person whose acknowledgement he desperately craved on instinct, he barely existed.

"He's an arsehole," Carrie said firmly as she straightened his tie, wondering how he wasn't going to boil in such a get-up. "You don't need to give a shit what he thinks."

Margot called a water taxi to take her shopping on the mainland, but Carrie and David took the opportunity to explore the island (or more like David took the opportunity and dragged his knackered little sister along with him). She filled a Camelbak with all the energy drink in the kitchen and trudged after him along stunning cliffside paths that she couldn't fully appreciate, determined not to let him see her flagging.

"Why this morning?" David pondered. "He was round here last night. If he's got his own chopper he doesn't need to wait for taxis; he could have come straight to the villa."

Carrie shielded her eyes from the sun, wishing the man had stayed away for longer and let her sleep.

"He really didn't want us to know he was here yesterday, ey?" David continued.

"He did not," Carrie concurred. "Did you and Soju get anything useful by the way?"

"We did," he fed back. "It's definitely suspicious."

"And?" Carrie pressed.

He looked at her strangely.

"Are you gonna tell me?"

"He was with someone," he said guardedly. He sounded like Yoonho in meetings; saying things but not. "Another old man; Soju recognised him as one of the rich guys who lives around here. They walked for a bit then went inside and we couldn't follow, but they were talking business and they're both meant to be retired. Soju's taking it to Yoonho and that's gonna grate." He took a deep breath. "We should push that. Divide and conquer."

"What business?"

Carrie squinted painfully. She really should have brought sunglasses.

"I'm surprised you didn't come," his steps paused. "I thought you'd be dying to find something on Park."

"I was high," she frowned – that had felt rather accusatory. "What if I made a noise and gave us away?"

"You're high a lot," he scrutinised her. "I thought you and Wanwan were giving up."

"We are," she said indignantly. "Well, he is – I had nothing to give up in the first place. That was only LSD; he doesn't even have that normally so it doesn't count. And don't call him that."

"You do," David pointed out.

"I'm different," she said irritably. She was tired – she didn't need this interrogation shit.

"Are you?" he asked. "Last time I checked, we were both undercover cops trying to bring down these arseholes."

"Why are you pissed at me?" she snapped.

"I'm not pissed at you," David rubbed the back of his neck. He was definitely pissed at her. "I'm looking out for you."

"You need to relax," she started walking again. "We're getting fucking awesome information and we deserve a holiday. Loosen up, have some fun; you're the one who told me I could do that."

"I'm trying," he said. "We had a good time yesterday. But I'm working."

"I'm working too," she pulled a face. "I got high cos I'm on holiday and I'm being realistic. How was I supposed to know we were gonna run into Mr Park? And you don't *try* to have fun; that's not the point. You just have it."

"Not at the expense of the case," he told her firmly. "Pull yourself together. Look, I'm gonna go and check for stockpiles in the caves. You stay here; I'm not having you climbing down hungover."

She was secretly glad – she didn't feel much like slipping to her death. Anyway, he needed some alone time to chill out. David was a lot less effortlessly cool these days.

She sat for a while, then decided that staying still on an uncomfortable rock wasn't really useful to anyone. She could do her own exploring; it wasn't only caves that may hold something of interest. She strayed from the track, drawn by a crop of little purple flowers. They took her upwards through the trees, to a place where they opened up again and a person stood with his back to her, overlooking the water.

She stopped before the clearing. It was Han. She thought at first, with a rush of concern, that he was watching David, but the undersides of the cliffs weren't visible from here. Instead, he seemed to be gazing intently at the ground beneath a solitary olive tree, where the purple flowers congregated. He held his cross in his hand and seemed very solemn. Carrie was intrigued. Han didn't do sentimental, but the whole place echoed his mood, despite the sunshine and colourful flora. It felt like a memorial… or a grave. A grave of somebody important.

The name came to mind, nestled on the side of a biplane: perhaps Emilia had never become ash in the Dragon's teapots.

But Taehwan had said that Han never cared much for Emilia and hadn't seen her as part of the family. Was it too much of a stretch to believe, that in this case at least, Han could have a conscience?

She backed away quietly, acutely aware that she was interrupting something private.

"What are you doing here?"

"Jesus!" she startled. "Shit, you made me jump. I thought you'd be with Mr Park."

"I was looking for you," he said darkly, returning the chain to its usual place beneath his shirt. "You didn't go with Margot to Athens."

He definitely didn't look like a person who was searching for anyone. If that was what he was supposed to be doing, he had taken a detour.

"Me and Drew wanted to explore," she told him nervously.

"You and Drew?"

"We wanted to explore different things…" she winced. "He told me off for getting high and went to the beach or something. Seriously, I was just wandering about; I didn't mean to walk in on anything."

"You didn't walk in on anything," he said firmly. "I just don't like you snooping around."

"I-"

"You're an anomaly, Cara Parry," he cut her off. "I can't make you out and it's my job not to believe anything I don't understand. I put up with you because Taeyoon trusts you and Taehwan loves you, but if you give me any reason to make up my mind…"

"I'm dead," she swallowed. "I know."

"You're dead," he confirmed. "Happy exploring."

It took her a while to re-find David, by which time she had decided to hold fire on telling him her curious suspicion about Han and the olive tree. He had his own secrets and she could feed back to Wendy herself once they got back. She didn't need to bother him when he was clearly good enough at bothering himself. She was on top of this operation and she wanted her brother to be able to relax and have a real holiday.

"Where have you been?" Soju was waiting when they returned, leaning casually against the villa gatepost.

"Checking out the island," David replied. "It's a sweet place you've got here."

Soju ignored him, giving Carrie the eye. "You're wanted at dinner."

"What?" her stomach did a somersault. "With everyone?"

"Including Dad, yes," his mouth twitched in amusement. "You don't have time to change; he doesn't like waiting."

"I'm in shorts!" she exclaimed.

"Lucky you have nice legs," he smiled malevolently. "Don't panic; he only kills his own wives. So far."

She felt like she was going to be sick as he led her into the villa and through the dining room doors. Everybody looked up as they entered, Margot haughtily displeased and Yoonho in clear dismay at her clothing, and Han as usual giving away nothing. Taehwan went to leave his seat and go to her, but his second eldest brother calmly put out a hand to stop him. He anxiously played with the tablecloth, wide eyes flicking wildly between her and his father.

Carrie's gaze went to the man at the end of the table. He was older than the photos in the case file, with more wrinkles around his eyes and a cane hanging from the arm of his chair. If she were to take a picture of him now it might even depict him as frail. But a photograph could never convey the sense of power that emanated from him, or the deep-seated greed in his beady eyes. They regarded Carrie with interest, standing there in her shorts, vest and trainers.

Soju very deliberately took the empty seat next to Taehwan. Taehwan glared at him, but said nothing.

"Come," Mr Park patted the place beside him. "Sit with me. I've been wanting to meet you, Cara Parry. In fact you're the very reason I'm here."

She obeyed, her heart in her mouth. She tried her hardest to remember that she was a grown adult – a detective at that – and she should not be this afraid of a man in his sixties with thinning hair and a rasp in his voice. She cast a nervous glance at Taehwan, who stretched out beneath the table to rest his foot reassuringly against hers. Soju kicked his leg away.

"You're very pretty," Mr Park commented. "I can see why Taeyoon liked you."

Margot stiffened, her eyes flashing daggers. Taehwan didn't look too pleased either. Carrie could see where Soju got it from; the delight in playing with other people.

"You were one of his favourites, I believe," he put a forkful of steak into his mouth. Carrie hadn't even noticed the food was there.

Margot cleared her throat icily and Yoonho shot her a warning look.

"Now, now, don't get jealous," he did his best impression of an innocent old man. "I'm only making conversation. You're still the queen, Margot; it's just nice to have a princess."

"Then please do remember that it is Taehwan who is the prince," Margot reminded him, doing her own best impression of sweet politeness.

Carrie had to admire her courage, speaking back to her father-in-law while her husband shrunk before him.

"Yes," he turned sharply back to Carrie. "What is it that you want?"

"What?" she tried to talk past the tightness in her throat. "I don't want anything… Sir."

"Sir," he chuckled. "You have manners. But you didn't answer my question."

"I…" Carrie faltered, trying to guess what answer he wanted. That wasn't what she was supposed to be doing. Guessing at answers would get her killed; she had to tell the truth. Though she wasn't sure exactly what the truth was. What did she want, other than Taehwan?

"Is it money?" he shovelled more food into his mouth. This must be where Taehwan got his appetite from. "Do you like the high life, Cara Parry? Or is it secrets that make you tick?"

"I don't want any money," she told him as he interrupted his eating to take a long glug from a tumbler. "I was a dancer, and then-"

"Do you mean to tell me," Mr Park waved a hand at Taehwan, who was gripping his chair so hard his hands shook. "That you actually like this ugly waste of space?"

"Yes," Carrie said stupidly.

"Bullshit."

Soju chuckled quietly.

"The only reason a pretty young thing like you would touch my son with a barge pole is because you want something; money, or secrets. Money," he took another mouthful and gestured at Margot. "I can tolerate. Secrets," his beady eyes stared into hers, scrutinising her every blink. "I could tell you secrets that would blow your mind."

He put the emphasis on the last three words. The image flashed into Carrie's head of Donny Logan after Han had shot his brains out.

"I don't bullshit," she croaked, drawing strength from Margot's proud defiance. "It's my brother's most important rule."

She could easily believe in that moment that he could see into people's souls. It felt like he was reading every thought she had ever had. Taehwan reached out his foot again and she hid hers beneath it, forcing herself to hold eye contact with the old man in front of her.

"You don't bullshit?" he said finally. "Prove it."

"What?" Carrie was caught off guard. "How?"

"Tell me," he suggested. "What has my son been working on?"

Carrie faltered. Taehwan wasn't supposed to be asking for her help; he was supposed to be proving himself to Yoonho and she was supposed to be being a good little trophy woman like Margot. But she also wasn't supposed to be lying. Her eyes jumped away from Mr Park's despite her resolve to keep them there, shooting a desperate look at Taehwan. He returned it.

"Okay, new question," the old man gave her a hard stare. "Who do you think I am? Am I a person to be trifled with?"

"No Sir."

"Then who am I? Your honest opinion; no bullshit."

Well that was a trap if ever there was one. How could a person respond? Nobody in her position, regardless of the undercover cop part, would have anything positive to say without lying through their teeth.

"I've only just met you," she wavered.

"Take a guess. I'm intrigued."

"Leave her alone," Taehwan stood and Han pulled him back down again. "How's she meant to know that?"

"Will you always be an insolent child?" Mr Park said irritably. "Your brother told me you had grown up."

Yoonho winced.

"Cara?" he turned back to her. "I'm waiting."

Taehwan opened his mouth to respond, but he was cut off.

"Shut up," the old man lifted his cane and waved it at Han. "Teach your brother his place."

Taehwan shrunk a little as Han went to raise himself from his seat.

"No," Carrie snapped.

Everyone stared at her, gobsmacked.

"You wanna know who you are?" she said, her voice surprisingly calm despite the quivers all through her body. "You're a crap parent."

Taehwan yelped and Margot dropped her fork with a clatter.

"What did you say?" Mr Park asked quietly.

Her breathing quickened but she forced herself to talk, repeating David's mantra over and over in her head and letting her mouth say what it wanted. She was tired, her nerves were shot and she was done with people picking on Taehwan all the time. The question was a test and she knew that if she lied she would be dead. He wanted honesty; he wanted to know she had nothing to hide. Well here it was.

"You're a crap parent," she spoke over Taehwan, who was desperately trying to smooth over the situation. "You're supposed to be his dad. He's your son and all he wants is for you to notice he exists, and all you do is ignore him or tell him he's crap. You treat him like shit – you treat them all like shit. They work their arses off and you need to show some fucking appreciation; that's my honest opinion. Sir."

Nobody said anything. She breathed heavily, aware she may have just signed her own death warrant. Well if so, at least she was going down in a blaze of glory. Cara was stupid, but Cara was brave.

"Please don't hurt her," Taehwan looked like he was about to cry.

"Why would I hurt her?" his father asked calmly. "She proved it. Now don't ever do that again."

He continued eating, gesturing for everyone else to do the same. They obeyed in silence, each one of them watching him continuously out of the corner of their eye, like he was an unexploded bomb that could blow at any moment. Eventually the old man stood, leaning heavily on his cane, and called for Yoonho to accompany him on a stroll. Carrie's concern could now turn to Han, whose eyes were burning into her with an intense interest far beyond any look he had given her at the olive tree.

"Holy fucking shit," Taehwan's voice cracked as he dove across the table to grab her hands. "What the fuck did you do that for?"

"I don't know," she replied shakily. "He asked for the truth."

"You're actually crazy," he told her, blinking back tears of relief.

"Congratulations," Margot also got up to leave, her usual superiority interjected with something like real admiration. "He isn't going to kill you."

"And Wanwan grew balls," Soju looked sideways at her. "I've never seen Yoonho stand up to him for you."

Margot's eyes narrowed.

"Taeju, enough," Han ordered, still examining Carrie like she was a rare and potentially dangerous specimen in a science lab.

Then he lifted his glass from the table, held it up to her and solemnly tipped his head.

-

"Why did Han bow at me?" she asked Taehwan when they were finally allowed to collapse into bed, utterly exhausted.

"Because he has to believe you now," his eyes studied her face as if he too thought her an impossible occurrence. "Now that Dad does, he's got no choice. You wouldn't be that stupid if you didn't really love me."

Carrie ducked sheepishly under the light blanket.

"You do, don't you?" he followed her beneath the covers. "You weren't just high?"

"I do," she confessed.

"Say it sober," he demanded, a triumphant grin spreading across his face.

"I love you," she looked fondly at that smile that nobody properly appreciated. "You egotistical twat."

Cara loved him – she had done for a long time – and her love for him had just allowed her to fool the great Mr Park. Loving him had saved her life, and what a life it was. Of course, Carrie could stop being Cara any time she wanted; she just didn't want to yet.

"Jay," Yoonho addressed him on the plane home. "Are you ready to deal with a real partner?"

"Yes!" Taehwan sat bolt upright in his seat.

"Ripley's setting up a new club," he explained. "He wants recommendations for a supply line and we need to arrange a rent price, of course, but I'm going to be away. Can you handle it? I'll give you my terms; you just need to deliver them."

Taehwan's eyes boggled with delight. Ripley was a big player, controlling a vast area below the river. Carrie felt incredibly proud.

"You know he's still on grass all the time and spent the first night here dribbling in a boat?" Soju raised his eyebrows.

"Grass doesn't count," Taehwan scowled. "And I wasn't fucking dribbling."

"Temper, temper," Soju tutted. "Don't worry, I can go."

"You know he likes it when I take Margot," Yoonho reminded him. "It makes him feel important."

"Ripley likes me," Soju shrugged. "I'll take Jennie."

Carrie almost felt bad for stealing what would have been the single greatest experience of the girl's life.

"You know that isn't the same," Yoonho said. "Besides, you're busy and he needs to learn eventually. You can't do everything."

Soju did not look pleased. As far as he was concerned, he could do everything, and he was probably right.

Yoonho fixed Taehwan with a stern look. "Can you do it?"

"Yes," he confirmed, his face full of determination.

"Soju," Yoonho turned back to him. "If you're worried, I'll send Drew along as backup."

As Taehwan rightly identified, Soju was unlikely to be worried as opposed to simply wanting to 'wreck his shit', but he accepted the condition of David's company with as much dignity as he could muster. It was better than his brother's, at least.

<u>20 July 2015</u>

Ripley was already aware of Drew Parry's existence as the Park family's agent and he welcomed him graciously onboard the small yacht he kept on his private Thames mooring. Carrie could see why the image appealed to him; dining on deck with his sophisticated business partner Yoonho Park, Margot gracefully sipping champagne as they passed Buckingham Palace. She hoped that if she just sat there in this nice dress and didn't say much then she would be an acceptable replacement for the elegant older woman.

Taehwan just scoffed that he could afford a much bigger boat. She knew it was his nerves coming out (he had been panicking in private for the past two days, while maintaining an outward show of smugness), but it was still funny. She thought back to that first shopping trip and how unprepared she had been for the life of a Park girl. Now she helped herself to a plate of lobster, feeling the breeze in her hair and watching the lights of the city with an important business partner on a yacht. A bit of Taehwan-y bratty humour was the last piece in the puzzle of perfect.

Margot must have felt a lot less at home below deck – in fact Carrie guessed that she probably stayed at the candlelit dinner table while the men went downstairs to talk business. Ripley's office reminded her of Yoonho's blue rooms but larger, darker and stocked with alcohol and cocaine, which four of his accomplices were busy preparing.

David took over the details of the negotiations, being a lot better at slippery talk and sticking to codes than Taehwan was. The youngest Park was supposed to be watching and learning, but his attention kept being stolen by the white lines on the table. Carrie rubbed his arm nervously. Fear of messing up had kept him awake all night, getting through a whole pack of Treasurer Aluminiums (apparently the most expensive cigarettes in the world) to avoid regressing back to his old go-to method of stress relief. David's growing rapport with the man he was supposed to be wooing himself didn't seem to be helping.

Carrie attempted to catch her brother's eye and somehow communicate this, but to no avail.

"Help yourself," Ripley offered, noticing Taehwan's wandering gaze. "Everything's free for a Park. In fact, Soju told me you're a fan; I stocked up especially."

"Much appreciated," David stepped in quickly. "But I don't think that's a good idea. He's recovering."

That was the wrong thing to say. Nobody could fault the effort he had made over the past six months, but Taehwan was still Taehwan and agents didn't tell him what to do or call him an addict in front of business partners.

"Fuck that shit," his nerves snapped. "Parks accept our partners' nice gestures."

"Jay…" Carrie said hesitantly.

"It's just one time," he told her, seizing the straw like his life depended on it.

It was just one time, and the relief on his face seemed almost worth it. At least he would be a lot more comfortable now, and therefore better at negotiating. They were gangsters; this was how business was done.

Ripley raised his eyes to David and Carrie. "You gonna let your boss do a rail on his own?"

Carrie snatched the straw and inhaled the next line before Taehwan could be tempted by more.

"Not my brother," she said firmly and handed it back to Ripley. "Agents need their wits."

She couldn't tell if David was pleased with her or not. She supposed perhaps that had been pretty condescending of her, especially being the younger sibling. He had been a Splitter and currently spent most of his time as an agent in the underworld; he had probably done a lot of cocaine before. Still, she had made sure that one of them was completely sober and she thought that had been rather clever of her.

Yoonho would be pissed though, and Taehwan would be pissed at himself. She slipped back out to the deck for a moment before the high took hold, taking a break from the stuffy room and the weird way in which David was looking at her. She leant forward over the railing, watching the sun set and gathering her thoughts together.

"Cara?"

She jumped. She had thought that Ripley was still in there with the others.

"You know," he came closer behind her and whispered in her ear, his crotch pushed a little too deliberately into her back. "I've been watching you all night."

Carrie froze and didn't say anything. She needed Margot; she would be able to tell her how to correctly react to advances from business partners. Perhaps neither she nor Taehwan were suited to Yoonho-type charming after all; perhaps his eldest brother had overestimated them. That made a change, she supposed – they had always underestimated him before.

"I could give your boyfriend a better price," his lips brushed her neck. "If you could give me some… private compensation."

"I don't think that would be appropriate," she said stiffly and tried to shuffle away.

"I thought you were a dancer," he continued. "It would be very appropriate."

"Yoonho doesn't trade his dancers," she said quickly, very glad that that was well known to be true. "And I don't do that anymore anyway."

To her relief, the man shrugged and backed away. "Have it your way. I was just giving you a chance at good business."

"What the fuck?"

They both turned to see Taehwan fuming in the doorway.

"It's okay," she reassured him. He didn't look very reassured.

"Don't fucking talk to her!" he snarled and thundered towards them. "You wanna know what happened to Donny Logan?"

"Hey Park," the four rough looking accomplices skirted the sides of the deck to stand between him and Ripley. "You got beef with our boss?"

"No," David spoke quickly, also emerging from below. Carrie was suddenly very glad that Yoonho had sent him to babysit. "He knew he was joking." He glared warningly at Taehwan. "Didn't you?"

"Fuck off," Taehwan tried to shove him away and whipped out his gun.

David knocked it out of his grip.

"Easy guys," he held up his hands to the thugs.

Everyone was still, staring each other down, each warily waiting for somebody to make a move.

Then one of Ripley's men turned to the others: "Get the Park."

They flicked switchblades from their sleeves and advanced in unison.

David had to react. In a split second he had thrown Taehwan back down the steps and landed a punch square in the forerunner's face. The man staggered backwards and he was onto the next, Taehwan flying back up to help. Carrie took a moment to admire David's superior training before she was kneeing Ripley in the balls and forcing her way into the brawl.

"No you don't."

David thrust her at Taehwan, dodging a blow but catching a knife to the tricep as he knocked an opponent through the door and slammed it shut.

"Get her out of here!" he yelled at the younger man who was still struggling to keep a blade from his face while David took on the other two. "You can both swim!"

Carrie seized the gun from the floor and whacked it hard against the skull of Taehwan's attacker, catching him off-guard so Taehwan could smash him back against the railing, where he slumped in a daze. Their eyes met – enlivened and dilated – and they shared a look of understanding. Taehwan wasn't going to patronise her and ask her to leave the fight. They pulled the first henchman away from David together, leaving him to incapacitate the last by wrestling him over to the railing where he could flip him with a splash into the river.

The three finally stood, panting, adversaries on the floor, below deck or in the Thames, and Ripley staring with shock and more than a little admiration at David. Taehwan started forwards again.

"Get out of here," David turned on him. "I'll fix this shit."

He scowled angrily.

"I'm a fucking Park!" he retorted. "You can't tell me what to do!"

"Go!" David bellowed. "Unless you want to be dead and start a gang war?"

Carrie knew he was right. "Get the Park" they had said. Drew Parry was in no immediate danger and could talk his way out of anything – if they weren't there to aggravate the situation. And Yoonho certainly would not be pleased if a supposed business meeting turned into Ripley going sour, defecting to the Russians and giving them more excuses to start trouble. As exhilarating as this was, it was time for them to go. At least they both liked swimming.

She left her bag on deck, hoping David could bring it back, and climbed onto the railings.

"I dare you," she grinned at Taehwan and dove into the water.

Their teeth were chattering as they staggered up Bermondsey Beach, clothes drenched and clinging to their skin. Carrie couldn't help but laugh at the thrill of it as she took his hand and pulled him back into the city, running across roads and through passageways with no particular direction. She could still get bad guys – in a much more base, animalistic, Cara sort of way. She felt alive.

Taehwan spun them around the corner into an alley where they stopped, breathing hard and dripping all over the concrete.

"Bollocks!" he threw his head back against the wall behind a skip. "I fucked it!"

"It's okay," she told him. "You were just protecting me, and Drew's good at this shit."

"I'm sorry," he groaned. "I really, really fucked it. It was the stuff; you know it makes me pissed. Shit! I keep getting you in trouble."

"Actually that was sort of exciting," she gave him a sheepish smile. "You did warn me you were good at trouble."

She should have stopped him from humouring Ripley and should now be telling him off for being weak and completely screwing everything up for himself. But what was done was done and his brothers would do enough of that later. Right now, she was Cara and she was high and she was converted. She loved this life.

She hadn't been detective Carrie since before the holiday and it was with a great deal of reluctance that she shut herself down in order to speak to Wendy in the library. She dutifully fed back her observations without the usual vigour; the happenings of last night, the suspicious sighting of Mr Park and her subsequent perfect fooling of him. In fact, she was so distracted that she had forgotten to mention Han and the potential grave site beneath the olive tree.

David's voice floated up from the living room, seemingly on the phone to their handler right now. She wondered why; she could have passed on any message for him that morning. Oh well, this was useful – she could simply tag on her own missing piece before he hung up, then head back over to Paradise to blissfully drop this 'real life' ruse again.

"I managed to fix the damage," David was saying. "Saved the little shit, kept the buyer. They've brought me right to the frontline of the Ballantine deal."

The faint fuzz of Wendy's voice came from the speaker.

"Hey, what did you expect from a sleazy salesman?" he replied.

He sounded very pleased with himself and that was fair enough; she doubted there were many people who could have talked Ripley around and she was very pleased to hear that he was fully in the loop for the main deal now.

"They trust me completely," he scratched the back of his head. "I can handle this on my own from here."

Carrie did a doubletake. It had been Taehwan who messed up, not her. She had been doing everything perfectly; Wendy had said many times how impressed Brian was with her. And now

David was asking for her to be withdrawn from the operation, like she had made a mistake or wasn't coping. Neither of those things were true. He was the one who was looking drained – she had been thriving!

"You told them to take me off the case!" she confronted him the moment he hung up.

He sighed. "You're in too deep; you're losing yourself. You're hooked on all sorts of drugs and the tiny pricked little twat clearly has you head over heels. It's my fault; I should've noticed earlier and got you out of here."

"How dare you!?" she exploded. "We have eyes on the Cessna because of me! I'm the only reason you're fucking here!"

Patronising prick. She had *found* herself, she was hooked on nothing and she was a professional. Whatever her feelings for Taehwan, they had never interrupted her work and David had no right to assume they ever would.

"I am doing a good job!" she thundered.

"No-one's saying you're not," he responded. "And I don't wanna see you wreck that. I saw you on that island and I've seen you since and I'm worried about you. You're in love with all this."

"Well *don't* worry about me," she spat. "I'm not in love with shit."

"Do you wanna explain the way you look at him then?" David demanded.

"Oh my God!" she exclaimed. "Do I really have to explain to you the concept of sexual attraction? Are you five?"

"I think you have to explain it to yourself," he said heatedly. "Because *that* is more than sexual attraction."

"Oh fuck off, David," she seized her bag from the rack. "I stuck around cos I didn't wanna leave you on your own, but you've always thought I'm just a rookie idiot. Go to hell."

She slammed the door and stormed around the corner to the bus stop.

"He's being such a prick," Carrie glowered into the whiskey sitting on the VIP bar. "He always thinks I'm gonna fuck something up."

"Older siblings suck," Taehwan said sympathetically.

"Exactly," she huffed. "Has Yoonho said anything?"

"The usual," he shrugged glumly. "They took my card and my phone again."

"Blah blah," she continued to glare at the drink. "I wanna get pissed tonight."

"Fuck yes," he agreed. "Fuck their rules. They hate us anyway."

"Hey Wanwan," Soju slid onto the stool beside him, a martini in his hand.

There was something chilling in his eyes as they fixed onto his brother's face. Gone was Taeju Lee who had thrown grapes into a swimming pool; he was Soju Park and he was pure evil.

"Dad knows you fucked up," he slowly swilled the cocktail. "I told him."

"Fuck you!" Taehwan shot to his feet, eyes widening with fear.

"Threatening Ripley, shooting Donny's boy," Soju's mouth twitched with cruel amusement. "He'll give you solitary for sure."

Taehwan looked about in panic, spotting the six security officers gathering at the door.

"What's going on?" Carrie demanded, her own stomach clenching with the feeling that something was very wrong.

"It's about time you learned a lesson," Soju coolly addressed his brother. "Relax. I survived it fine."

"You're a fucking psycho!" Taehwan screamed and flew at him.

The security team surged forwards, some ushering away the spattering of alarmed guests while the others turned on him. They jerked him roughly away from his brother and knocked him back over a table, two holding Carrie as she shrieked at them to leave him alone.

Yoonho wouldn't stand for this, she tried to tell them, but Yoonho was away on business and the controller on shift tonight was a lot less reasonable than Jerome. All she could do was shout herself hoarse and watch them throw him against the bar and hold him there until he was too exhausted to struggle.

The door burst open and Han and Margot entered, the latter wearing only a gold silk dressing gown over an ivory nightdress and slingback heels, having been rudely awakened from an early evening nap.

"What's going on?" she breathed, realisation hitting her face as she took in the scene.

The security team straightened at Han's approach, leaving Taehwan to cling panting to the bar. Carrie went to run to him but Margot caught her, pearly white nails digging painfully into her arms.

"Be quiet and don't move," she whispered sharply. "You'll only make it worse."

Carrie was stopped more by shock than obedience. She had never heard Margot sound so grave.

Everyone's attention was suddenly drawn to the door, where Mr Park stood leaning on his cane, a dark silhouette against the glare of the corridor lights. He walked slowly between the scattered tables, advancing on his son as he flattened himself against the tap. A squeak escaped from Carrie's throat. Margot drew a sharp breath between her teeth and Han shot her a warning look, edging closer.

"Why are you a consistent disappointment, Taehwan?" he lifted his chin with the tip of his cane.

Taehwan averted his eyes and said nothing.

"You're not a Park, are you?" he said in disgust, then turned to Carrie, Han, Margot and Soju. "You all need an education if you're ever going to be worthy of running this business. Nobody gets anything for free. Parks don't make mistakes, and Parks don't rely on outsiders to fix those mistakes. If you're not strong and smart then one day it'll be the law, not me, knocking on your doors. One of us knows that well." He looked at Soju. "Do we need another lesson?"

"No!" Taehwan yelped. "No – I'll be better! I won't get high ever again, I promise!"

The cane dropped from his chin, making both Taehwan and Carrie jump. Han hastily put his hand over her mouth to stop her squealing, but Taehwan and his father's attention had been caught.

"Tell me, Taehwan," the old man sneered. "Do you think Cara Parry will protect you? Is she going to be here forever – is she going to run the business for you?"

Taehwan didn't say anything.

"How did that work out last time?" he continued. "Did Emilia stick around to look after you? Did she think you were worth the time and effort? People get bored of you, Taehwan. You're weak; you need to learn to look after yourself."

He stared desperately over his father's shoulder, tears streaming down his face as his eyes begged Carrie to confirm that he was talking bullshit. She tried to say something but Han was still smothering her mouth.

"No, don't look at her," the old man seized his jaw and turned it away. "You think she's still going to want you if all you ever do is ask for help? She might think she loves you now, but soon enough she's going to realise you're pathetic, just like everyone else. Then will you finally start acting like a man?"

Han's palm was wet with Carrie's spit. Mr Park was just playing with him now; this had nothing to do with shooting Jeb Logan or brawling with Ripley's men. He was tired and hurt and his father seemed to have some strange hold over him that made him believe everything he said. If this was Soju's way of knocking him back down a peg, he had succeeded.

"I'm sorry," Taehwan whimpered. "What do you want me to do?"

"I want you," Park raised the cane. "To learn! Your! Lesson!"

He whipped it through the air with each word, never touching him but making him flinch with fear. The old man regarded him with revulsion then turned to Han.

"Take him to the room."

"NO!" Taehwan pleaded in panic. "No, I'll do anything! Don't lock me up! Mr Park! Dad! Please!"

He turned his back on him and walked away.

"DAD!!!"

Han nodded to the security team and they began to wrestle him from the taps he clung to. This wasn't one of his cocaine-fuelled tantrums – he was terrified. It took a blow to the head from the lead officer to get him to finally let go, the man holding him up by his collar to hiss into his face – "Obey your father" – before they dragged him kicking and screaming from the bar.

"Leave him alone!" Carrie wriggled away from Margot as Han left to accompany them. "Taehwan!"

Han caught her easily, locking her arms to her sides with the strength of his hands.

"You're not pathetic!" she yelled after him. "He's a fucking dickhead! Don't listen to him!"

"Do you have no brain at all?" Han glared. "Do you think you'll help him by getting yourself killed?"

"So I should just stand here and watch everyone be a fucking shit?" she spat. She was too angry for anything to scare her right now. "You're the one letting your thugs bash him around – is that fucking helping!?"

"Yes," he snarled in her ear. "It is. Because now I'm going to go and have a nice, calm chat and get things under control. You don't know how this family works and you've made trouble ever since you arrived. Once this is over, you should consider leaving. For my brother's sake you won't be harmed."

"I'm not-"

"You three," Han threw her at Margot and Soju. "Go to the yellow room. And stay there."

Carrie didn't have much choice but to obey. She had no idea what was going on, where Taehwan was or why he had been so scared, but she had to hope that Han was fixing it. The three of them sat, not saying anything, Margot's face tense and concerned and Soju's indifferent. Carrie wasn't sure which one was more disturbing.

"You're too good for this family," Margot broke the silence. "Han's right; you should get out while you can."

"I can't," Carried replied.

For many reasons, it was true.

"Then you're a fool," she said sadly. "You're both fools and I pity you."

Carrie didn't answer. Margot sighed.

"Well if you're really here to stay, you're going to have to start listening to me. I don't want you to get yourself killed."

"Thanks," Carrie gave her half a smile. "I used to think you didn't even like me."

"Well I can't pretend to understand you," Margot returned the expression. "Money, power, a better life – those are things to die for. But the love of a person, which is bound to go stagnant… there's no logic to it."

"Why do you all hate him so much?" Carrie asked dejectedly.

"This isn't about Taehwan," Margot clarified. "No person at all is worth risking your life for."

Carrie shuffled uncomfortably. "To be honest, I'm sort of getting used to risking my life."

"Perhaps you are a Park after all."

Carrie wiped her eyes. She hadn't even realised they were watering.

"I didn't used to like you," Margot admitted. She dropped her gaze. "You two have always been a certain way together, but

Taeyoon and I are practical people. We don't really do love; it always seemed childish." She took a breath and looked back to Carrie. "Perhaps I was jealous."

"I…" Carrie stammered.

"Don't pity me," she commanded. "I have everything I've ever wanted. You're the one who's going to get hurt."

"I'll try not to," Carrie attempted to be light-hearted.

Margot smiled sympathetically. "He's lucky to have you. Luckier than he deserves."

Carrie watched her face return to its usual superior elegance. The practical woman, who didn't permit herself to show emotions and thus appeared so ordered and controlled – was she looking at herself, before she had been interrupted by the lure of Paradise? Was that her own future; content in her success but never truly happy? No, she told herself firmly. Margot would have been fine if she had remained a lawyer. She had made a mistake when she strayed from her career – a mistake that Carrie would learn from. Margot Stuetz-Lee lacked purpose. Carolyn Hart did not.

"Oops," Soju interrupted her thoughts, making a show of clapping his hand to his mouth. "I left some things, in that room."

"What room?" Margot asked icily.

"Wanwan's room," a cruel smile danced in his eyes. "What a silly mistake."

"Things?" Carrie asked, her pulse quickening.

Something wasn't right. Whatever 'mistake' Soju had made had been one hundred percent deliberate.

"You disgust me," Margot glared at him and got to her feet. "You may fool my husband, but you are still nothing more than a sadistic little boy. Cara, with me."

She swept from the room, a concerned Carrie at her heels.

"What's going on?" she begged.

"I don't care if your junkie boyfriend kills himself," Margot assured her. "But that creature is vile and his father ought to know it."

She increased her pace. Panic rose in Carrie's chest. She still didn't know what was happening, but it was bad. They hurried into the lift, which Margot sent to the penthouse.

"Wait," she stopped Carrie as she made a beeline for Mr Park's office. "Nobody bursts in there, even at the best of times."

Carrie allowed herself to be restrained. They walked briskly up to the door, Margot pausing mid-way to knocking on it. She put a finger to her lips, listening to the voices coming from within.

"Taehwan isn't like Taeyoon," Han was saying darkly. "You keep this up, you'll lose him. Is that what you want; your son to never want to look at you again?"

"He's run amuck for long enough," his father's harsh voice responded. "He has to face the consequences."

"Then so will I."

Carrie heard the scraping of something metal on the table.

"You would defy me?" Mr Park asked in disbelief.

"For the family," Han replied. "Always."

The door handle turned and the two women jumped back. Han emerged, as powerfully calm as ever.

"I told you to stay put," he said.

"Soju left drugs in the room," Margot explained quickly. "You know what Taehwan gets like in there."

Han's composure slipped. He thrust a set of keys forcefully into Carrie's hand.

"One floor down, 5364, room 6C," he barked at her. "Get him out."

Carrie bolted. Margot didn't hurry places. Han didn't snap. It was all wrong. Her heart pounded as she flung herself into the lift and punched in the four digit code, not waiting to see if either of them were accompanying her. She sprinted down the corridor, room 6C seeming a mile away.

266

"Taehwan?" she called, fumbling and dropping the keys as she tried to shove each one into the lock.

"Taehwan!"

The room had been smashed to bits. Curtains hung ripped from the window and stuffing from pillows and duvets was strewn across the floor around the overturned table. Broken bottles and glasses littered the carpet along with scatterings of cocaine and whiskey spills. Taehwan lay sprawled beside the table, collapsed in his own vomit, trying desperately to retrieve powder from the strands of the rug.

"Cara?"

He looked up as the door crashed open and tried to raise himself, but his arms were too shaky to support him, his face smeared with tears and snot and a tinge of blue.

"Oh my God," Carrie rushed forward, knocking her knee on the table leg as she skidded down beside him. "Oh my God, shit."

She heaved him onto her lap.

"Help!" she called to nobody.

"Help me," he croaked. His hair was plastered with sweat and his pupils eclipsed their irises. He had taken way too much. "I can't breathe."

"What did you do?" she cried, hugging his head to her chest. "You stupid – Help! Someone fucking help!"

"I c-" he retched all over her.

"HELP!!!" she screamed.

"Jesus Christ," Margot appeared in the doorway. "I'll call the hospital."

"You stupid, stupid," Carrie cradled his head. "Why did you do that?"

"I can't do it!" he sobbed desperately. "Don't lock me up!"

"You're not locked up," she insisted, tears streaming down her cheeks. "Han gave me the keys. You're fine, you're okay."

Taehwan tried to cling to her but his fingers kept slipping, his whole body shaking uncontrollably.

"It scares me," he whimpered. "Being locked up alone… What I'd turn into… If we got caught…"

He retched again but nothing came.

"You're not alone," she tried to hold him steady as her chest heaved. "I'm here. I'm here – Margot where's the fucking ambulance!?"

"They're on their way," she assured her.

"If I went to jail-" he coughed, panic rising in his dilated eyes.

"I'd come visit," Carrie kissed his hair, hardly able to control her own breathing. "I'd wait for you, I promise."

"No, it wouldn't be me!" he wailed hysterically. "It would change me! I'd be a psycho and you wouldn't love me! I wouldn't love me! I'd be someone else!"

He grimaced, his face twisting in pain. "It hurts!"

"Taehwan…"

She didn't know what to do. She didn't know what to say. All she could do was hold him and feel utterly helpless.

"Please don't leave me alone!" he begged. "I don't want to be like Taeju! Promise me…" He trembled harder. "Please… if I'm going down… just kill me."

"I'm not gonna do that," Carrie's voice cracked. "That's stupid."

"Please," he pleaded. "Promise me… Kill me… Don't let them lock me up."

"Don't make me say that," she cried. "You're being stupid; it's just the drugs, you're gonna be fine."

"Please! Pl-"

The word caught in his throat and he choked, dribbling it down his chin.

"Taehwan?"

His body convulsed, eyes rolling back in their sockets.

"TAEHWAN!!!" she shrieked. "Stop it! Wake up! Okay, okay, I promise, just don't do that!"

Han pushed her out of the way and started doing chest compressions. She hadn't even noticed him arrive.

"The ambulance is coming," Margot promised. "They're private, we pay them a lot of money; they'll be here as soon as they can."

Carrie broke down in her arms. The elegant woman flinched at the vomit and drool coming into contact with her nightdress but resisted the urge to pull away. Carrie just collapsed on her, crying too hard to breathe or speak as Taehwan shuddered on the floor beneath Han's hands. The room spun. There was no Operation Bluebird. There was no Paradise Casino. All she knew was that she didn't want him to die.

The ambulance's sirens still rang in her ears as Carrie tried not to be blinded by the hospital lights. It was too much for her to comprehend. Only yesterday, Taehwan's 'stuff' had had them making love in an alleyway; now it had him in intensive care with a heart attack. It had all happened so quickly, and now the waiting was happening so slowly it seemed the clock was going backwards.

"Thank you," Han said quietly.

"I'm so sorry," she wept. "I should've listened to you. I should've left him alone. It's all my fault."

She had let her guard down and everything had spun out of control. None of this was supposed to have happened. It was a bit of fun while she and David pulled off the perfect covert operation. But Taehwan was sick. The last thing he needed was the emotional upheaval she called fun.

"No," Han told her firmly. "Thank you for not listening to me. Thank you for loving my little brother. You're the best thing that ever happened to him; I've never seen him so happy. I'm the one who's sorry for not trusting you."

"But what if he dies?" her shoulders shook.

Han swallowed hard. "Better to die after months of happiness than be miserable his whole life."

"I don't want him to die," she broke down, sobs wracking her body.

Margot returned with food, but Carrie wasn't hungry. She picked at a wrap, the thought of trying to force it down her throat making her want to throw up. She felt like she was disintegrating with every minute that passed with no news. With her eyes open she saw blank walls and nothingness, when they closed she saw him quivering on the floor. Her face was swollen and her head pounded but she couldn't stop crying.

She didn't care about the case. She didn't care that Taehwan was a dangerous criminal who lost his temper and shot people without a second thought. She just wanted him out here with her so she could tell him he was stupid and selfish and she didn't want to live without him. Everything was a blur. People came and went and she was aware of nothing but Han's constant presence by her side and the fact that nobody was saying anything.

<u>**22 July 2015**</u>

"It's not the first time he's overdosed," Han spoke after a few hours. "It's not your fault. I've always tried my best to protect this family, but I can't protect his head. Even you can't fix him."

"What's wrong with him?" Carrie asked feebly.

"Everything," Han heavily replied. "Taeyoon and I grew up the sons of a successful gangster. We were born for the business; we learned fast how to survive. Taehwan and Taeju grew up in hiding, then as the spoilt children of a millionaire who already had the sons he needed. You try locking a toddler inside and telling him he can't even look out the window without permission. You put a three year old in a crate for a month, then let him out into a world where he can run riot. Lose his mum when he's two, get him another one then kill her too. Put his only friend in prison and return him his worst enemy, and see if all that doesn't leave a mark."

"Emilia didn't abandon him," Carrie murmured. "Did she?"

"Our father mistreated her badly. He had her killed because she was going to leave anyway," Han looked dejectedly at his hands. She had never seen him like this before. "That's why I never told

Taehwan the truth. And because he'd know I was the one who did it. He would never forgive me, and it would break him."

Carrie nodded glumly. "He loves you so much."

"He shouldn't," Han sighed.

They sat in silence again, staring at the floor.

"Did you ever get put in there?" Carrie said after a while.

"No," Han shook his head. "I'm the only one who hasn't. I've always been a good soldier; I look after the family and I don't question it. That's where I've been going wrong." He exhaled wearily. "Taeyoon was the one being groomed for greatness. He spent a lot of time away when we were younger; apparently it taught him discipline, which Taehwan's never had. He hardly even went to school, it was too restrictive for him. Last time he was in that room, he nearly took all the skin off his arms trying to get out."

"Why did you do that to him?" she asked miserably.

"I don't know."

"Mr Park's family?" a doctor emerged from behind the door.

They both shot to their feet.

"He's stable."

Carrie threw her arms around Han and wailed with relief.

This was the reality of the Park empire. Not fast cars or flash parties or private islands; this. There was nothing glamorous about a sick person in a hospital bed. There was nothing glamorous about getting shot at or puked on, or watching a person you loved break apart before your eyes. She had been blinded by what they called the high life, but this was as low as it got. Taehwan's life was nothing more than a mess of vomit, nosebleeds and loneliness hidden behind a veil of crisp bank notes.

And it wasn't just his life. This was what they did to thousands of people; sickness and heartbreak and hospital beds. She had known it before, but never really felt it until now. It wasn't the sort of feeling that could be imagined. Her passion for Lucy's plight – the very thing that had propelled her from the beginning – paled into insignificance when she looked into Taehwan's wretched face.

He seemed so innocent, lying there fast asleep, breath rhythmically whistling in and out of his nostrils in time with the rise and fall of his chest. But he wasn't. He wasn't innocent. Yes, he had reasons to be the way he was, but so did everyone.

Yoonho was like a broken horse; all sense of autonomy beaten out of him since tiny, following the path his father had made for him. Han was almost noble; unconditionally forsaking and removing the rest of the world in order to protect his family. Even Soju had apparently spent his childhood in turmoil and surplus to his father's requirements. Perhaps his desire for ultimate control was, very deep down, intended to make up for his lack of it in younger life. She was sure if she dug hard enough then Mr Park, too, would have some sort of tragic backstory.

Did that mean that every single murderer, rapist and general good-for-nothing should be excused because their own lives hadn't been perfect? Cara would say yes. Because Cara was selfish and Cara wanted nothing more than to wake up next to Taehwan Lee for the rest of her life. If she could find any way at all to convince Carrie that he didn't deserve his fate... then Carrie would willingly believe her.

But Cara wasn't real. Cara would be gone. Carrie wasn't selfish. Carrie didn't love him. Fuck, she wished that was easier to believe. But it was bullshit.

She did love him. She didn't want to, but she did. He knew what his family's business did to people and he willingly chose to ignore it, their approval being more important than people's lives. But how she had felt when she saw him lying on the floor, when his heart stopped, how she still felt now – that had nothing to do with Operation Bluebird. She hadn't been fearing for her job or the effect it may have on her standing in the family; she had been fearing solely for him. She didn't want him to die. She didn't want to lose him. She loved him.

She supposed that made her evil; loving a person like him.

How many others were staring at people in the exact same way, wondering how this could have happened and how they could have saved them? How many of those lives were contaminated by the Parks or their associates? *His* associates. Paradise was a cancer and the only option was to remove the source. All of it.

"Are you okay?" Taehwan squinted at her.

"No," she said quietly. "I hate this."

"Sorry," he looked down guiltily.

"What am I supposed to do?" she asked. "Everything was fine, everything was so pretty, I just forgot how shit this all is. I can't cope with this; I can't watch you nearly die and then sit back and let you all sell the stuff that did it. Taehwan, so many people die, and get hurt, and then you collect the money and we have dinner with it. Why has that never bothered you?"

"I dunno," he mumbled. "I guess it's just one of those things. If we didn't do it someone else would, so why not? At least we're nice about it; we've stamped out some shitbags."

"You think anything about this is nice?"

His eyes widened in alarm and the peaks on the cardiogram increased in frequency. "Are you leaving?"

"No!" she almost screamed, grabbing his face in her hands and looking frantically into his eyes. "No, no, I'm not gonna do that, I love you, please don't die, please don't die, please!"

"Hey," his expression softened with relief. "I'm not gonna die."

She clasped her arms around him, trying to calm her own heartbeat. She was panicking and it was stupid, but she couldn't help it. He had made her. He was her life; there was no Cara without Taehwan and there was no Carrie without Cara.

"Please don't fucking die," she sobbed, her shoulders heaving. "I love you so, so, so much; why don't you know that? It fucking sucks and I wish I didn't cos you're just getting hurt and I can't stop it and I feel like shit. Why did you do that? You go on about how great I am and how you don't ever want me to go, and then *you're* the one who's trying to leave *me*, and I feel like I fucking deserve it!"

"No you don't," his voice cracked too. "I am so sorry. I'm a piece of shit; you deserve so much better, I don't know why the fuck you're still here. I just kept thinking you'd be gone and you wouldn't want me anymore… I dunno why you do."

"Why don't you trust me?" she buried her tearstained face into his neck. He didn't smell so Taehwan-y in disinfected hospital robes. "I'm not just gonna stop wanting you because your dad's a prick or you got stuck in a room; that doesn't make any sense. And you don't need to worry about prison or any of that – I would wait as long as I need to, whether you want me to or not. I'm not just gonna piss off and leave, whatever happens."

"You would have to," he said miserably. "I'd go crazy. I'd be a mess and I'd hurt you and you'd hate me. I'd rather be dead than you hate me."

"I don't think I could ever hate you," she told him truthfully. "Yeah, I hate some things you and your family do, but I couldn't ever hate you."

"I just… I can't explain. I just panic. It's like the biggest, shittest feeling, like everything's just empty and I can't take enough stuff to get rid of it and I can't think about anything except how shit it is and how I'm stuck and I'm not ever gonna be able to get out. I can't even sleep with the window closed, how the fuck would I cope in prison? I'd just explode, or snap, or turn into a fucking psycho like Taeju… I dunno what I'd be – just not me," he took a steadying breath and squeezed her tight. "Dad wouldn't really do that, would he? I'm not clever like Taeju, and I'm not gonna fuck up again – he doesn't need to straighten me out."

"Would you do a deal?" she whispered. "Would you tell stuff about him, if it meant you never had to go to jail?"

"I can't do that," he said in alarm. "He's my dad."

"He's a cunt," she clenched her jaw.

"I'm not a grass," he persisted shakily. "The others would go down too. They're my brothers; I wouldn't do that to them."

"But if it got you off?" she implored. "We could fuck all this and just… do whatever."

"It doesn't work like that though, does it," he gripped her with a trembling hand. "They don't just let you go."

"For shorter though… it could only be for a little bit…"

He shuddered. "Don't talk like that's gonna happen. Please don't let that happen."

"Anything could happen," she gulped. "What if I can't stop it?"

"Just try," he shivered as his heartrate spiked again. "Promise you'll try."

"I'll try!" her throat caught. "I promise."

She couldn't hold back the tears from her eyes as she lied to him.

"I'm so scared," she hid in his chest. "I just want you to be happy and I can't do it."

"I am happy. Seriously, I have never been so fucking happy in my whole life, and that's cos of you," he kissed her hair. "I love you."

"I love you too."

She wondered if Wendy would help. Regardless of his current objections, once the diamond exchange was completed and Operation Bluebird was over, if she had something lined up waiting for him, if he could be saved…

05 August 2015

Carrie stood awkwardly in the doorway of David's room, where he sat on the bed fiddling with a paper plane. It was the first time since Taehwan's solitary confinement that she had managed to talk to him away from the hospital or the Parks' watchful eyes. He looked tired; his face drawn and lifeless. It seemed this whole world was falling apart.

"So an addict's fucked up?" he said unsympathetically. "Revelation."

Carrie swallowed hard. She didn't know what she had expected him to say. That they could write off the countless killings and maimings and overdoses caused by the Park empire and all play happy families? Even her own conscience wouldn't allow that. But it couldn't bear to see Taehwan hurting either. She had nowhere to go. Her heart was turning on itself, tearing itself in two, each side ripping the other to shreds. She wished she'd never taken this stupid job.

"You ever thought to ask about how I'm feeling, having to act like I'm one of them?" he looked up. "All you had to do was dance at a casino. You chose the rest of this."

"Because I'm doing a good job," she said weakly. "And it's fucking killing me."

"I warned you," he told her. "I tried to get you off, Wendy tried to get you off. You and Brian," he tossed the paper aeroplane into the bin. "Just won't listen."

"I didn't want to leave you," she hung her head. "I'm sorry. I got selfish and carried away. You're right; I should've asked. Are you okay?"

"I'm okay," he said roughly.

"No you're not," she replied. "Or you wouldn't have said that."

"No, Carrie, I am," he snapped. "Because I'm being a grown up and I'm taking this case seriously. I could've called Bence my friend, but did you see me crying about it? No, because I can keep my feelings in check and not fall in love with junkie gangster brats."

"I'm not in love with him," she said quietly. More lies. She didn't know if that counted as bullshit or not, when she wished so hard for it to be true. She didn't know anything anymore. "Cara is."

"You *are* Cara," he retorted. "How many times do I have to say that? You didn't grow an extra person. Cara Parry is pretend; she doesn't have separate feelings."

"Exactly!" she clutched at that premise. "This is all pretend! I am taking the case fucking seriously."

"Then what's the problem?" he gave her a hard look.

"I…" she faltered. "I don't know."

-

Ashley threw her arms around her the moment she stepped through the library doors. Carrie appreciated it, but also wished she wouldn't. It was going to make her cry again.

"Are you sure you're alright?" Mary checked. "If you need any more time off then all you have to do is ask."

"Thanks," she said gratefully.

She didn't assure her that she wouldn't need it because she knew that she might. Staying busy was good for her, but she felt uneasy leaving Taehwan alone. She had spent hours turning her eyes square as she scrolled through website after website of sensible NHS advice and terrifying anecdotes, and it was the latter that stuck with her. If his heart failed again, or he freaked out and gave himself a panic attack and she wasn't there…

He insisted he was fine now, but he had been fine before and that hadn't lasted. She wanted to trust him, forget that had ever happened and get back to random plane rides and night-long parties, but after every distraction something would arise to remind her that he was sick and she was a lie.

And David was still asking Brian to pull her out. She couldn't let that happen. When she had kissed Taehwan in the show hall she had committed herself to seeing Operation Bluebird through to the end. It was her job, and she owed him that much.

"Caz?"

She wiped her eyes and realised she had been staring at a row of fantasy novels for at least half an hour.

"The crazy photocopy lady's here," Ashley hesitated. "Shall I take her? Are you sure you don't want to go home?"

"I'm fine," Carrie sniffed. "I can do photocopying."

She paused as she passed the girl. Ashley had looked after her since the very beginning, even before she had auditioned for Paradise Casino. She had been openly delighted to watch her find her feet, had welcomed Taehwan into normal life and even brought chocolates to the hospital – all while having no idea what she was accidentally a part of.

"You're a sweetheart, y'know," Carrie told her. "Thank you so much for existing."

"David's struggling," she informed Wendy as soon as the door was closed and the photocopier whirring. "He won't tell me anything, but Soju's had him doing crazy shit this whole time and I don't think he can cope anymore. He's not himself; I'm worried about him."

Wendy put her hands on her hips in exasperation. "Jesus, you two are a carbon copy of each other. 'I'm worried about Carrie. She can't cope with Jay anymore; we need to get her out': that's what he said. Are you going to ask me to take him off the case too? Shit, Carrie, what is going on here?"

"What did he say?" Carrie winced.

"Nothing much," Wendy replied in frustration. "Just that sleeping with a murderous arsehole for months takes its toll and Brian shouldn't be making you do it anymore." She scrutinised Carrie's eyes; still red and glistening. "Which I'm inclined to agree with."

Well that was something; at least David hadn't been making accusations of her to their boss.

"Brian's not making me do anything," Carrie held her gaze defiantly. "I'm fine."

"You don't look fine to me," she crossed her arms. "Look, Carrie, you have exceeded our expectations times a thousand. You weren't even supposed to still be here, but you've taken initiative and made personal sacrifices and got us some bloody good info. You're already guaranteed a backdated promotion as soon as you return. You've done enough; stop pushing yourself."

"Well what about David?" Carrie drove the topic back away from herself. "He has to cut off peoples' tongues and God knows what else; that's a fuck tonne more scarring than a bit of sex."

"And to be honest with you, I agree with that too," Wendy said severely. "If it were up to me I'd cut our losses, take the information we have and get you both out of there. But I'm not Brian and I don't have the authority to make that call, so if you and Dave could both stop trying to save each other that would be bloody great."

"So you're not gonna take me off?" Carrie asked cautiously.

"Not for lack of trying," Wendy exhaled. "As far as I'm concerned, you're both blatantly cracking and we've got a pretty strong case with what we already have, but Brian won't budge until that goddamn exchange."

"I'm not cracking," Carrie insisted.

"Good," her handler said, clearly not believing her. She didn't blame her; she didn't believe herself either. "Fine, keep up the good work. Just for God's sake, whatever it is David thinks you're doing that's messing with your head, stop it. And I'll say the same to him."

"Wait, Wendy, that isn't it!" she stopped her from opening the door. "I found out things about Emilia… and I need to ask you something."

"I'm listening," Wendy said wearily.

Carrie hesitated, trying and failing to think of a proper way to phrase it.

"What do you think about plea deals?"

"Plea deals?" Wendy asked guardedly. "In what way?"

"How much information would someone have to give to get a reduced sentence?" she gabbled. "And how reduced could it be?"

"Well that depends on what the person did in the first place," Wendy gave her a very funny look. "It's a piece of string question."

"But Brian would take one?" she pressed. "Even for a Park?"

Wendy frowned. "Carrie, what the hell is going on with you?"

"Nothing!" she lied much too defensively. "I just – I'm worried about the dancer girls. They didn't do anything wrong except see things."

Then she thought of a better excuse.

"And Han! Han told me he killed Emilia because Mr Park told him to! But I don't have that on tape cos I don't have a wire, so we'd need him to testify. He doesn't care about himself, but to free one of his brothers – I'm pretty sure he'd do that."

"We have information on the flight," Wendy reminded her. "We have your own testimony. We have passport trackers for Taesuk and Taejong Lee; we know they followed her. We have his friend on that island, we have Durden, we have the china shop lead-"

"But you have no proof that anyone's dead!" Carrie burst. "What, are you gonna charge Han and Mr Park with going on holiday!?"

She could have proof that Emilia was dead. Carrie's thoughts went to the tended ground beneath the olive tree that she still hadn't spoken of. She would tell her, once she had given Han a chance to save Taehwan and tell her himself. Nobody was withholding evidence – just delaying it a bit.

"Shit, Carrie, calm down," Wendy hissed. "Or I'll break your legs and get you out that way. Yes, I'm sure Brian would take a deal for that, but 'freeing' a brother might not be the word for it. He's not gonna be happy if any of them get less than ten years, bare minimum."

"Ten years?" Carrie pleaded. It was justice. He deserved it. He deserved more. "But if it's the only way to get Park for life? Surely he'd be lenient for that. What if Durden and the Dragon are dead ends? Everyone's covered for him before. The old man's squeaky fucking clean except a few dodgy accounts and nobody gets life for money laundering, especially if he just pays people off! You said yourself Han and Taehwan are the least important!"

"Hey, I don't fucking know, alright?" Wendy held up her hands. "Take it up with Brian when you're back; that's not my call."

Carrie breathed heavily, unsure what else to say.

"Jesus, what is up with you?" the handler put her hands back on her hips and shook her head. "You really want to get Park that much you're gonna shout at me for it?"

"Yes," she said firmly.

No. Maybe. She didn't know.

<u>**22 August 2015**</u>

Paradise wasn't Paradise anymore. The glamour had become sickening and overbearing, the seductive blue of the VIP bar garish and blinding. Every face she saw, every person she greeted; she was going to destroy them all. Take out the Parks and the whole ecosystem came tumbling down around them. Bea, Jerome, Lisa, Lali, Jennie – they were innocents. She didn't want to look into their eyes and know what was coming. She didn't want to look into the mirror and see another person that she was going to erase – herself.

It was easier to drink. She could make Carrie go away and Cara could forget and she didn't have to feel like such a liar. She couldn't stand it anymore, allowing Taehwan to think she really was the girl he fell in love with. She couldn't bear the deceit, she wanted it to stop, but she couldn't let David and Wendy remove her, not while a Paradise existed for her to yearn for. She couldn't enjoy this life like she used to but she couldn't leave it either, and she had to be there for Taehwan until the end. She couldn't let them take him without her there to hold his hand. She was the only one who could make him happy and she was determined to do so as much as possible. She would take him every night and tell him she loved him and she herself would breathe for it. When she fucked him the rest of the world was nothing, and when she was drunk she was drunk.

She didn't want to be paying attention to anything else. She didn't want to gather with the others in the yellow room, where Soju presented them with a reem of data that neither Carrie nor Taehwan could hope to understand. It was the first time she had been here since the night of his overdose and the awful colour

283

scheme was making her angry. Soju was a psychopath and she wanted to whip the gun from Taehwan's holster and shoot him in the face. Perhaps when he was arrested she would visit daily just to laugh at him. Perhaps that made her a psychopath too.

"Dad's siphoning money," he announced to the room.

"He can't be," Yoonho shook his head. "There has to be an explanation."

"There isn't," Soju said certainly. "I would have found it by now."

"It is possible for you to be wrong," Han looked at him darkly.

"Not on this," Soju replied. "You heard him – 'nobody gets anything for free'. That includes us. It's all in the accounts; he's been stealing from us for years."

"Yes, *us*," Han said firmly, glaring at him. "We're a family. We don't keep secrets; we work together. *All* of us."

"Like a body, I know," Soju said coolly. "When a body gets cancer, you cut out the organ."

It was chilling how much he seemed to relish that thought.

"Is that what you were doing when you tried to kill your brother?" Margot snapped. "Cutting out an organ?"

"I knew he wouldn't die," he dismissed her. "This is a casino. We play the odds."

Carrie stiffened as she felt Taehwan wither into her shoulder. She squeezed his hand tightly and he squeezed it back. It was Soju's fault, but it was the old man who had done that to him.

"Han," she ventured. "You said you'd do anything for the family, even defy Mr Park."

She meant it in this situation, but she meant it more in her daydream where his information gave Taehwan less time inside. More than ever, turning the family against itself was in her best interests.

Han hesitated. He had told her himself that he regretted never questioning their father.

"Soju," Yoonho exhaled heavily. "What do you suggest we do with this information?"

He smiled callously. "Cut him out. Give me complete access, let me find out the full extent and let me undo every single transaction."

"What happens when he finds out?" Han pointed out.

"You have a security team, don't you?" Soju fixed him with a sinister look. "Paradise is ours. He's a tired old man and he should be allowed to retire properly. He's always looked after us, hasn't he? It's time we returned the favour."

Yoonho nodded. He looked ill.

"This isn't a mutiny," he said. "We're not cutting him out of anything. We leave his shares alone, let him collect dividends as normal – anything above board continues. But he did retire; the empire belongs to us now. I am the CEO, you are the directors and anything he takes without our permission is treason, father or not."

He leant on the table, visibly shaking. This really was hard for him. It was different for Taehwan and Soju, Carrie knew. They feared and admired Mr Park, but he had rarely had any time for them. To Yoonho and Han he had been their mentor, carefully shaping them into whatever he wanted them to be and demanding their undying love and respect. For Yoonho to turn against him – that took guts that Carrie hadn't thought he had.

"Soju," he sighed. "I'll give you access. Do what you have to; you don't need to ask for my permission or my advice. You're the cleverest of all of us."

Everyone stared at him and Margot went to object.

"I'm the CEO," he stopped her. "It's my decision. We're still a family, we work together on this and we don't let anything jeopardise the Ballantine deal. Is that understood? We work together. Soju, no tricks. Jay, get that temper under control."

"Taejong," he turned to Han, his face softening. He wasn't business-Yoonho now, just brother-Taeyoon who desperately needed his support. "You've been his soldier all your life, and I've been his apprentice. We've existed for him for nearly forty years; we deserve our own lives now."

Han gave him a small nod of acknowledgment.

"I won't tell you what to do," Yoonho told him. "Do whatever you think is right. Your instincts have always been cleverer than mine too."

He nodded again.

"Cara, Margot," Yoonho looked at them sternly. "Keep your mouths shut."

Han's black eyes turned solemnly to Soju. "If this is one of your tricks…"

Of course it was one of his tricks. As usual, Soju had exactly what he wanted; Yoonho in his pocket, Han off his back and free reign to play whatever games he desired with their father. Carrie wondered if the eldest Parks would have been quite so pliable if the old man's merciless discipline hadn't almost killed their little brother. More importantly, she wondered if Soju had known that the moment he opened his mouth to bring that discipline down upon him, or the moment he told Ripley that Taehwan had a liking for cocaine.

As much as she hated him though, Carrie didn't object. Mr Park had played enough games with them for their entire lives. He deserved a taste of his own medicine and there was nobody better suited to the task than his sadistic third son.

And she would have the last laugh. While Soju thought he was winning, he was playing right into her and David's hands. Everyone was so busy not trusting Mr Park that they didn't see the two plump cuckoos in the centre of their nest, who would push them all to the ground no matter how much power Soju coaxed from his father and brothers.

Nevertheless, despite all their flaws there was something desperately sad about it; watching the fall of a mighty dynasty. Watching the fall of the man who held her hand.

"Cara," Han called her back as the others left the room.

She reluctantly untangled her fingers from Taehwan's.

"Something's wrong," Han observed.

Carrie gulped. She hadn't noticed the water pooling in her eyes. "Han…"

A lot of things were wrong; things she couldn't bullshit about. But they all fell under one overpowering emotion.

"I'm scared," she confessed. "I've been scared ever since…"

He put his hands on her shoulders, in his best attempt at being comforting.

"Like I said then," he spoke softly. "Thank you for loving my little brother. But you can't fix him. You being scared doesn't help anyone."

He kissed her on the forehead and turned to go.

"Han, wait," he stopped and she threw her arms around him. "Thank you too. Thanks for loving him, thanks for looking after him. He thinks the world of you. Knowing that you give a shit… it means a lot. It really, really, really means a lot."

"Cara," he said sincerely. "You don't have to thank me for anything. I look after my family, and that means you too."

She didn't want to hear him say that.

<u>**33: The Date is Set**</u>

<u>**01 September 2015**</u>

Carrie had practically moved into the casino since Taehwan's release from hospital, and she was acutely aware that David was not happy with her. He told her that everything was fine and they just needed to wait it out, but he had tried to get her taken off the case and he only spoke to Wendy directly these days, giving Carrie absolutely zero access to any information. He just told her he was handling it and she didn't need to worry. She supposed she probably preferred it that way. The less she knew, the less she had to hide.

It was a surprise, therefore, when he called to invite her out to dinner. They hadn't done that for a long, long time. There was something different about his manner; something genuinely positive for the first time since Blue Moon. He talked about light-hearted things, piled food onto her plate and tried to act as if nothing had changed since the times when they whiled away the hours playing Mario Kart and watching *West Side Story* (the only musical that David would tolerate).

But she could tell that there was something bigger than that. He didn't just want to make up with her and joke that he was definitely a Shark because Sharks were suaver than Jets – he was preparing her for something. They walked for no particular reason, finding their way to the illuminated pavement in front of St Pauls where David stopped her, fixing her with a serious look.

"What is it?" she asked. "You've been wanting to tell me something all night."

"The Ballantine deal," he told her with bated breath. "The date is set for the exchange; 13th of September, two weeks from now. The Dragon's forged a paper trail that takes the diamonds from

Russia, through his contacts in China and to one of his guys in London. Yoonho buys Margot a birthday present, giving the Dragon his cut and getting the rest of the money back through Chinatown dividends. Then he keeps a fake and we take the actual stones up to Ballantine and her sister in Scotland, and collect the cash off record. Any sniff of the real trail from Africa stops at Yoonho so Ballantine's safe, and Yoonho has a forgery that he can claim ignorance and blame the Dragon for – Yoonho's safe too. That's what they think anyway."

Carrie stared at him. It was over.

"Does Wendy know?" she breathed.

David nodded. "I'm meeting the main team at the drop-off. Backup will be watching the airfield in case of anything funny."

A thankful smile passed across his mouth.

"You don't have to be Cara much longer."

The relief on David's face flooded into her bones. She collapsed into his arms and he welcomed her. It was over. They were finally getting out of here. The incessant torture would stop and they could forget all about Paradise Casino.

She could look after Taehwan in custody. He could get clean for real this time and he'd be stuck there long enough to forgive her and realise that she really, really did love him. That had never been bullshit. Then when he eventually got out, she would be right there waiting to take him home. Once he had paid for his crimes, she could have him legitimately.

Perhaps that was a frail and impossible hope – a Cara thought that wasn't hers – but it was a hope that she needed and a decision that could be made later.

For now, Operation Bluebird was finally over and Carolyn Hart and David Watts could escape this hell they called Paradise. She wouldn't have to lie anymore. The relief was overwhelming.

Carrie hardly stopped to breathe in the last days before the exchange, making sure to keep herself fully distracted at all times and not allow a single moment where Taehwan was not enjoying himself. There was nothing more precious, more sacred in her mind than the last remaining dregs of his freedom.

He looked so cool, speeding down the country lanes towards the airfield, sunglasses on and fringe blowing in the wind. She didn't know how she had ever thought that he didn't. Her fingers toyed with the hair on the back of his neck and she whooped along with him, playing at racing drivers and forgetting there ever had been or ever would be a time when either of them were unhappy.

"I'm confused," Walter Durden told them upon arrival. "You want the Cessna for yourselves? Not Mr Park?"

"Yeah," Taehwan frowned. "What's wrong with that?"

Carrie echoed his confusion. It wasn't like Taehwan had never taken it before; in fact, he had even carried out a couple of work flights in the months between the gala and that fateful night on Ripley's yacht.

"Mr Park already has it booked out over those days," Durden said uneasily.

"What?" Taehwan scowled. "Why?"

Durden shrugged. "You know he doesn't tell me these things."

That was suspicious, unexpected and displeased Yoonho greatly – Carrie could hear him shouting down the phone. The Cessna was supposed to be taking them and the diamonds up to Scotland soon, and Mr Park was supposed to be retired. Carrie didn't mind so much. It gave them longer to fly the little biplane one last time instead of preparing the turboprop.

She lost herself in the wind that blew her hair into her mouth, laughing at how funny Taehwan looked in goggles and the exhilaration in his eyes as he took them round and round in consecutive loop-the-loops that still made her feel slightly sick. He landed them illegally in somebody else's field so they could kiss in the grass and tuck into a picnic of wine, crackers and expensive cheeses. Carrie encouraged wine, even for him. It wasn't like he had long left to enjoy it. It was only fun, like they always should have been.

"You remember the first time we did this?" she snuggled into his shoulder. "It was like *Pearl Harbor*, plus food."

"I remember you threw up," he teased. "They didn't do that in *Pearl Harbor*."

She laughed. "You did too many loops."

"You ate too much," he gave her a playful shove.

"I thought you were gonna kill me," she said sheepishly.

"If you were anyone else, I would've," he assured her. "I could still kill you."

"You'd miss me," she kissed him softly. "Can we just stay here? I don't wanna go home; I wanna do this forever."

Then she was crying.

"Cara," he looked at her in concern. "Please stop drinking."

"Says you," she joked and hastily wiped her eyes. There wasn't time for crying.

"I know I can't talk," he stroked her face. "And I want you to have fun, but something's wrong when I'm being the sensible one."

Carrie supposed he was right. It was as hard as ever for him to fight his cravings and she certainly wasn't helping, but it was she who woke up panicking in the night and burst into tears at random intervals, to be consoled only by the warmth of his chest and the scent of his neck.

"You don't have to be sensible," she told him. "I'm fine."

"That's bullshit," he looked troubled. "This is my fault. At least admit it; I don't like you thinking you have to pretend to me."

She crumbled into his arms. He wasn't allowed to be troubled. He wasn't allowed to worry about her pretending. She had *always* been pretending. He kissed her hair and held her close as she sobbed too hard to talk. She was allowed to not be fine. With him she could be honest, at least about that. She wept herself into exhaustion, his shirt against her cheek lulling her into a false sense of tranquillity that she was too tired not to embrace wholeheartedly.

He seemed comforted by the fact that she wasn't pretending to be okay anymore and that was consolation in itself. Soon she wouldn't have to lie to him at all. That was something.

"You've got nothing to worry about," he hugged her reassuringly. "I promise."

It was a promise he couldn't keep, but she let herself believe him until she was laying in his arms in bed, her thumb brushing away his tears and her mind returning to the painted name on the side of the plane:

Emilia. He would be finding out what had happened to her soon. Carrie wasn't sure if that was a good thing.

"What do you think Dad's doing with the Cessna?" Taehwan asked.

"I dunno," she replied. Before long, maybe she would.

"I wish Yoonho wasn't so pissed about it," he sniffed. "All this shit about looking into him all the time and letting Taeju do what the fuck he likes… I don't wanna betray my dad. You know Taeju; he could do anything to him."

"Taehwan," Carrie said firmly. "He's a cunt. He doesn't give a shit about you and I hope he rots."

"I know," his chest sunk. "But he's my dad. This is shit."

He had no idea just how much she understood. There were people that she didn't want to betray either. The old man would go down for the rest of his life, and the old man deserved every second he got. Yoonho, Han and Soju would be dampened by prison, but they were smart and resilient. The four of them would get what they had coming and they would survive it. But Taehwan…

Taehwan shot people on impulse and partied away blood money. He let people suffer and die for his extravagant lifestyle and he didn't care. He deserved it too. She seemed to be telling herself that more and more frequently, each time having less and less effect.

"Do you think that sometimes it doesn't matter if you love someone?" she asked quietly. "Sometimes they're just bad, and you have to betray them and do shitty things for the greater good, and you have to be shit yourself to have the guts to do that?"

"Yeah, I guess," he mumbled. "But it fucking sucks."

Yes. It did.

"What is the greater good?" she whispered.

She was sure that she knew. She did know. But at the same time, she wasn't so sure. In this backwards world, good and evil were backwards too.

"I dunno," he half laughed. "I'm no good at thinking about people who aren't me. But I guess that's what it is; whatever's better for the most other people, even if it's shit for you."

She hugged him tighter, more for her own sake than his. Even he was telling her she was doing the right thing, though he didn't know it, and he was the only person she ever wanted to ask. He made her feel better about everything… except the concept of destroying him.

"I'm shit," she choked.

"What?" he frowned. "Why?"

"I just am," she buried her face in his shoulder. "I'm gonna hurt you. I already hurt you. You need better than me."

"Hey," he stroked her hair. "That's bullshit. I love you, and I know you love me, and that's all I need. You're the best person I ever met."

He was stupid and he was wrong – he had to be wrong. He was wrong, and David was wrong, and Ashley and Megan and Han were wrong and she herself was wrong too. Sending a person to prison was not what you did when you loved them, so therefore she couldn't love him. End of.

11 September 2015

With the Cessna unavailable, the two of them had then been planning to travel up to Scotland in the Mustang, but Taehwan was on a horrendous comedown and Carrie was still drunk. Yoonho was close to tearing his hair out, but she had encouraged it. Why not have one last crazy night? It wasn't like there was anything to lose.

They ended up taking to the road in the back of the BMW driven by David with Soju in the passenger side, while Yoonho took Margot in her pretty duck egg blue Silver Cloud and Han transported the diamonds in a van with a selection of his security team. That was fine by them; they could sleep on the journey.

12 September 2015

The party stopped overnight in Carlisle and arrived at their accommodation around midday; a picturesque cottage on the road between Inverness and Aviemore that seemed a little small by the Parks' usual standards but was beautiful nonetheless. They unloaded their luggage and split up to explore the area, taking in villages and wilderness like they were ordinary tourists.

Carrie tried to blank out the world and pretend that she could pause time again as she had on the island – as she had ever since Christmas, ever since she first stepped foot over the threshold of

Paradise Casino. The moors were very tempting. She wondered if she could somehow trap him here with no way to warn his brothers: would the deal still go ahead, the bad guys get caught and Taehwan hide with her in the highlands forever? The answer, of course, was no.

The Parks and Parrys dined together in a rustic inn just outside Inverness before Soju received a phone call and stepped outside halfway through dessert.

"Yoonho," he returned looking more bothered than she had ever seen him before. "We have big problems."

He and his brothers ducked out into the space behind the carpark, leaving an intrigued David, Carrie and Margot to finish and pay for their food then wait apprehensively by the cars. Carrie hovered anxiously by the BMW. Had something gone wrong in London while they were away? Was something up with the deal? Had they somehow discovered that the police were onto them? Was that a decent excuse to take Taehwan and run?

When they eventually returned, Yoonho's face was like thunder and Taehwan looked utterly broken.

"Take the women back to the cottage," the CEO ordered David. "Stay alert. We'll fill you in later."

Carrie hesitated while Margot got obediently into the passenger seat.

"Taehwan," she caught him as he went to follow the others, the three conversing rapidly in Korean. "What's the matter?"

He let her stop him.

"You were right to feel weird about this shit," he told her glumly. "Dad's fucked us. That fake diamond the Dragon made – he switched it out and took the real one. He's been talking to everyone in this fucking deal and he knew everything the whole time. We thought we were being so fucking clever. We were gonna show him we can do shit. He was gonna be proud of us."

"Shit," Carrie breathed.

"Yeah," Taehwan agreed. "Shit. Taeju reckons he's been moving himself out for years. He's been dumping any proof of dodgy shit onto Yoonho and hiding money where even we can't find it; he was always ready to just fuck off and leave. He booked out the Cessna, remember. He kept going on about running the business and sorted out a load of shit with that guy near Blue Moon – and he never bothered meeting Margot like he did with you. I thought he was just trying to fuck with me, but I guess he was testing all of us and I guess we fucking failed. And then he found out Taeju was onto him so he's taking our diamond too, like one last 'fuck you' before he fucks off and dumps us."

His eyes were starting to water. Everyone dumped him. Emilia, Soju, his father, and soon even Carrie herself. It was all he ever wanted – not to be abandoned. Carrie gulped. She didn't want to think about that, and she didn't want him thinking about it either. They should focus on the deal.

"Does Ballantine know?" she asked.

"I dunno," he replied. "We gotta talk to her agent. She's gonna be fucking pissed."

"Jay!" Yoonho barked at him to catch up. "Cara, get back to the fucking cottage."

She felt David's strong hands on her shoulders as he manoeuvred her into the back seat. She let him take her, unable to think of anything else to do. At least if the Cessna was involved then Wendy's guys at the airfield would already be on red alert. She had told David that Wally believed the plane to be in use from tomorrow; they would be ready and waiting to catch him with a stolen blood diamond. This could be a blessing in disguise for Operation Bluebird. And even more reason for Han to give him up and save his brother – for all of them to give him up. Maybe Brian would be so happy he would let Taehwan go free.

No. He wouldn't. Brian would put Taehwan in a cell and he would be broken, and Carrie couldn't do anything about it – shouldn't do anything about it. Taehwan was a bad person, whether she loved him or not.

David tried to catch her alone for a moment once they reached the cottage, but she clung like a leech to Margot's shadow. She didn't want to be a detective tonight. She wanted to be a Parry. She wanted to be a Park.

"Do you think she'll cancel the deal?" she asked as the older woman poured herself a brandy. "Is everything fucked?"

A large part of her hoped that she would.

"I don't know," Margot replied stiffly. "I wouldn't blame her if she did."

"Then what?"

"I don't know," she repeated. "All I know is you and I have nothing to worry about. Taeyoon is weak but he isn't stupid. He'll figure something out and in the meantime he'll keep us safe."

"What do you mean?" Carrie questioned.

"He thinks of things," she told her. "When we found out I was… useless… he disappeared for days. Well, I put on my lawyer hat and prepared for divorce, but it wasn't that. He bought me a villa in California, complete with a live-in housekeeper and untraceable bank account, entirely unrelated to the Parks or the casino.

"It was raining when he returned," she remembered. "He gave me his umbrella and told me that if anything should happen to him, that's where I should go. 'It might take a while,' he said, 'but I'll meet you there.' I've never had any reason to be afraid."

She straightened up, chasing away the fleeting clouds of bittersweet nostalgia that had ever so briefly clouded those serene eyes.

"Of course I'd take you with me, if anything were to happen."

"Don't you ever worry about him?" Carrie said quietly.

"What good would that do?" Margot tutted. "Worrying beyond the point of doing something useful achieves nothing but lines on your face."

She got up and rummaged through a drawer, returning with a small bottle of pills.

"Here," she passed them to Carrie. "These will help you sleep. I know you've been doing a lot of worrying lately. It's okay; they're prescription not recreational."

"Margot," Carrie turned the bottle over in her hand. "Why are you Stuetz-Lee?"

"I told you," she said coarsely. "I've never been afraid. Once upon a time every little girl had a dream. Then it's only sensible to keep a reminder that every little girl grows up. You'll understand that one day."

Carrie didn't want to grow up. She wanted Ballantine to cancel the deal and Brian to hold out for another one. She wanted more time. Cara Lee… the name reminded her of Hollywood.

-

"What happened?"

Carrie shot bolt upright the instant the bedroom door opened and Taehwan returned, the little bottle of sleeping pills untouched on the bedside table.

"Ballantine's pissed," he sunk down next to her. "She'll take the smaller ones but she's gone after that. She changed the meeting place just in case and Han's called for more security to come up tonight. Yoonho says you and Margot can't come anymore. We're screwed. Our biggest fucking deal is screwed."

"I'm still coming," she told him quickly.

She was supposed to be there. She was supposed to be with him.

"No you're not," he said firmly, though his eyes told her he wanted the opposite. "Drew and Yoonho would never let you in the van, and I wouldn't either. Please don't argue. I'm fucked if you get hurt."

"Fuck," Carrie didn't know what to say.

"Yeah," he dropped his head onto her shoulder. "Fuck."

She massaged his scalp with her fingers. This wasn't supposed to be their last night; he was supposed to be happy. If she could do nothing else for him, then at least she could make him happy. They didn't need to think about anything else – everything else was already too late. Tomorrow didn't exist, Mr Park didn't exist and the stupid fucking deal didn't exist. For the last time, the only thing was him.

But she couldn't have him all night and once they stopped the outside world returned. She dissolved into his shoulder, tears streaming down her cheeks before she even had a chance to catch her breath. She clung to him as she sobbed, feeling his heartbeat, his skin, his shoulder blades; everything she would probably never feel again.

"Why are *you* crying?" Taehwan asked in puzzlement.

"I'm scared," she gulped in the scent of his neck. Even now, it was comforting, although it broke her heart.

"I'm scared too," he admitted.

A whimper escaped her throat. She didn't want him to be scared. She wanted him to be happy. She ran her fingers along his jaw, his cheeks, his hair. It was all a dream. A pretty movie. A horror film.

"But it's okay," he squeezed her protectively. "We'll be fine. Yoonho's not an idiot; he'll fix something. All this shit will be gone tomorrow and we can forget about it and go on planes and get pissed. Hey, at least if Dad's gone no-one's ever gonna lock me up. We're really gonna be fine."

She opened her mouth but couldn't talk.

This was her last chance.

Her last chance for what? To get David killed? To stop a stupid diamond exchange and let Ballantine escape, only for Taehwan and his brothers to be caught anyway? Wendy had said and Carrie agreed with her – they already had plenty of evidence. And she didn't *want* them to escape. Cara did. Cara wasn't real.

Cara was bullshit and the law had to be upheld or everything would fall into chaos. Beautiful, beautiful, impossible chaos.

Every bone in her body screamed at her to tell him she loved him, that she had always loved him, that she would wait for him forever even if he hated her, but she knew that if she told him that she would tell him everything and then it would be game over. She couldn't hope for him to just run without warning anyone. He would never betray his brothers; he loved them with every piece of his broken heart.

Her chest tore itself to shreds as she repeated over and over the only thing she could:

"I'm scared."

Carrie wanted to smother the clock and forbid time to ever move again. Taehwan snored so freely, hugging her to his chest, calmed by Margot's pills and completely unaware of the torment that crucified her own sleep. He needed one last night of peace. She needed one last night to look at him. She should never have stayed after Christmas; she should never have taken this stupid job at all. She was naïve and inexperienced and she couldn't cope with the magnitude of what she had to do.

She carefully slipped out from beneath his arm and got out of bed. It was like she had ripped away her soul and left it there with him as she reached for her phone. Wendy's team could go to the wrong drop-off place. They could be overwhelmed by Han's increased security. She could pretend she never knew.

Her fingers numbly typed, warning her of the added defences and reminding her to keep checking the location of David's phone. Perhaps she was firing blanks. Perhaps David had already told her. That was very likely. Perhaps nothing was really her fault. She pressed send and her thumb slipped from the screen as a blackness suffocated her.

It had been a stupid dream. How could any of this have ever worked? He was a gangster. He ruined people's lives, and even if that hadn't been the case, he was an addict and the most destructive person she had ever met. Loving her would drive him crazy and loving him would destroy her. Han was right; she couldn't fix him. Carrie didn't belong in Paradise.

<u>**35: Justice**</u>

<u>**13 September 2015**</u>

She got no sleep that night, just watched him and held him and let her heart spill silently from her eyes until they dried up and there were no tears left.

She felt sick, watching the sun leak through the window from Taehwan's arms like she was a normal person with nothing to hide. She couldn't move as he kissed her and got out of bed, pulled on his clothes and checked his hair. Whatever happened today didn't matter. She had already damned him; she had been damning him since the first day she set eyes on *Dave's Guide to Bullshit*. That was a good thing. She had done a good thing.

"See you later, worryguts," he kissed her lightly. "I love you."

"I love you too," she barely managed to get it out without breaking.

"Go back to sleep," he stroked her cheek. She could hardly feel it. She didn't deserve it. "I'll be back before you even wake up."

No, he wouldn't. He wouldn't be back at all and he needed to get through that door before she started crying and screaming at him to stay, but she couldn't let him go. Just one more minute, one more day, one more lifetime.

"Hey," he gently uncurled her fingers from their grip on his shirt. "If you keep being scared then I'll be scared and then I'll fuck up and punch someone. You want that?"

She laughed but it was empty. Even now, when she was watching him walk away forever, he was the one trying to make her smile.

"Taehwan!" she stopped him as he opened the door.

It was her last chance. Her last chance to be selfish, like he had always told her to be.

"I love you."

She let him go. She had to forget that now.

Operation Bluebird was over.

-

She didn't exist as she shut the window and made her way downstairs. She was a walking case file; a collection of information with no emotions or opinions. She sat down for breakfast with Margot but ate nothing. The older woman spoke as she delicately sipped her tea, but her voice was white noise. The room was shapes that meant nothing. The day that brightened outside the window was nothing but refracted, unperceived, empty light. She was a ghost.

"What was that?" Margot's voice sharpened.

She heard the sound of engines.

In a trance, she stood and crossed to the window, staring blankly at the convoy of black vans that sped past.

"Shit," Margot swore. She had never heard her swear before. "They should never have gone themselves; I tried to tell them. Cara, we have to go." She hurried upstairs, calling down from the landing as she began to hastily throw clothes into a bag. "The villa. We go now, lie low and wait for them there."

"Taehwan," his name numbly escaped her mouth.

"Cara?"

Her body took itself to the coat rack, pulled on somebody else's trench coat and headed for the door.

"Cara!" Margot called in alarm, retreating back down the stairs. "Come with me. Cara!"

She took the keys from the hook and strode out onto the driveway, ignoring Margot's shouts of "You can't help him now!"

She turned her eyes for the briefest moment to look back through the rear-view mirror. Margot was crying.

She changed gears and slammed pedals like her limbs were somebody else's, following the sounds of the police force special operations team. She had no idea where she was going or what she was doing; all she knew was she had to be there to witness the end.

The silver BMW pulled up beside the vehicles blocking the track to and from the warehouse. She spoke robotically to the officers who got out alongside her – "DC Carolyn Hart" – and they didn't stop her. They knew this was all her doing.

She climbed the outside steps to quietly enter the building at the mezzanine level, perfectly positioned for a view of the whole floor, at the centre of which stood the Parks, the Ballantines and their valuer in a circle around their cargo. David hovered by the internal stairs, still holding his cover as part of their defence along with the rest of the security teams that accompanied each party.

They were gangsters, she remembered numbly. They had guns. They deserved it.

It was Soju who first turned to the sound of shouts and heavy footsteps, the others following his gaze.

"Freeze! Hands up!"

The doors burst open and Han reached for his pistol, but Yoonho quickly stopped him.

David ordered the security team to hold fire.

None of them had seen the look he shared with the special ops team leader.

"Nobody panic," Yoonho held up his hands in surrender and beckoned the others to do the same. "This is all a misunderstanding."

Taehwan was panicking. Even from her perch on the mezzanine she could see the fear in his eyes and feel his chest rising with shorter, shallower breaths.

"Taehwan…" Yoonho sensed it too. "No!"

Taehwan bolted.

He sprinted towards the nearest door and was wrestled down by two special operations officers. They were everywhere – at the doors, outside, advancing towards them – there was no chance of escape. But sheer terror made him blind to that and panic enhanced his strength. He broke away from the officers holding him, feet stumbling on the concrete as they reached for him again.

He kicked them away and continued stumbling, but there was nowhere for him to go; backed up against a wall and surrounded. He threw a desperate look at Han, whipped the pistol from his jacket and turned it on himself.

The officer swiped it away, leaving his hand bleeding and empty. He lost control.

"NO!" he screamed. "HAN! DON'T LET THEM TAKE ME!"

He flung himself hysterically at the wall; crazy enough to think he could break it, or crazy enough to hope that it could break him.

She didn't want him to be scared. She wanted him to be happy. He wasn't ever going to be happy again.

"HAN!" he shrieked, blood streaming from his head and his fractured nose. "CARA!!!"

Carrie felt the gun in her hand. She hadn't even realised it was in her pocket.

CRACK.

Taehwan was flung backwards in slow motion as the noise rang in her ears.

"Kill me."

He staggered to his knees, eyes raised to the source of the bullet.

"It scares me…"

He saw her.

"Being locked up alone… What I'd turn into…"

His eyes met hers.

"Better to die after months of happiness than be miserable his whole life."

And he knew.

"Thank you for loving my little brother."

He knew everything.

"But you can't fix him."
It was all there in the wretched look on his face.
"I don't want to be like Taeju…"
The pain. The confusion. The betrayal.
"Promise me…"
He was terrified. He was begging her.
"Please…"
She had promised.
"If I'm going down…"
The hurt in his eyes. The hopelessness. The gratitude.
"Kill me."
She pulled the trigger again.
CRACK.
He wasn't scared anymore.

Time caught up with itself as all hell broke loose. She stared as Han let out a terrible scream and opened fire upon everyone in sight. The special ops team retaliated and were met by his team of loyal marksmen. Soju and Yoonho ducked behind crates and pulled out their own weapons, Ballantine and her sister also taking cover as bullets flew above them. People shouted, people fell and Taehwan bled on the floor.

Suddenly David was snatching the gun from her hand and wrestling her back from the edge as the world continued to explode. She pushed him away and ran. She ran from the warehouse, from the gunfight, from the blood soaking Taehwan's shirt and dribbling from his mouth. She tripped down the stairs outside, got up and kept running, just running. Tears streamed down her face and blocked her vision and she just kept running until her knees gave way and she collapsed in a howling heap on the road. She hadn't been able to hold his hand. She should have been holding his hand. She should have told him everything, she should have died instead of him.

Her head ground into the gravel, broken apart by the images within it. She wanted to be a ghost again. She wanted to disappear.

"Carrie!" David tried to pull her upright. "What did you do!?"

"I had to!" she screamed.

"You killed him!"

"I had to!" she sobbed into the floor.

"What happened to justice?" David wrenched her to her feet. "What happened to locking them up for life? You gave him the easy way out. You started a gunfight!"

"What was I supposed to do?" she wept. "He was getting away and-"

He wasn't getting away. That wasn't the reason.

"And you love him," David finished her sentence.

She wailed at the sky, anguish shattering everything. She loved him. She killed him. It was too much to take.

36: David

<u>**14 September 2015**</u>

"You should both be very proud of yourselves," the newly promoted DCS Brian Hole congratulated them.

Robot Carrie sat in the debriefing room, listening but not hearing.

Operation Bluebird was a huge success. After a battle with police special operations, the brothers were arrested and detained without bail, along with Ballantine and the remnants of their security teams. Mr Park had been apprehended at the airfield, with a pile of dirty cash and Ballantine's diamond. It was perfect – physical possession on an aeroplane primed for a quick getaway was by far the most suspicious situation in which the old man had ever been caught. As for his sons – the red-handed exchange, resisting arrest and the murder of police officers, trails upon trails of laundering accounts and Emilia's bones buried beneath the olive tree; the list of evidence went on.

Brian Hole said they should feel proud. Carrie felt nothing.

"Dave!" somebody called as they made their way down the hallway. David didn't stop. "Dave!"

The man caught him by the shoulder and spun him about. David reacted instinctively, catching the man's stomach with his knee, pinning his arms behind his back and throwing him hard at the wall. Then he pulled back, seemingly horrified with himself. He was jumpy and on edge. He was very un-David.

"What the fuck is going on?" Hole thundered down the corridor, pushing Carrie aside.

"He killed my brother," the man pointed an accusatory finger.

Hole's brow furrowed. "Your brother died in a gunfight."

"He started it," the man continued angrily. "He shot first, the Parks were surrendering."

"We're looking into that," Hole snapped. "And disciplinary action will be taken – discreetly. Now clean up and get back to work."

The man obeyed, casting David the dirtiest look Carrie had ever seen.

"David," the DCS addressed him.

"Yes boss."

He spoke calmly but he was shaking.

"What is going on here?" he asked seriously. "We have half a Spec-Ops team dead or wounded and all accounts say the first shot was from our side. If I don't give their families some sort of closure soon, they'll go to the press and this whole thing will blow up in our faces. We don't want any Park lackies reading your names in the paper. Now, you're a hero in every sense of the word and I don't want to accept your previous confession; give me any name and I'll make it them. Who really shot that first bullet?"

David swallowed hard but answered before Carrie could make out what was happening.

"I did."

Hole sighed sadly. "Then disciplinary action will be taken."

He disappeared back into the debriefing room to make a call.

"Why did you say that?" Carrie asked in shock.

"Because if it was you, that's career suicide," David told her. "You weren't even meant to be there, and don't tell me you thought he was gonna get away. You shot him cos he was a mess and you loved him, and a load of your colleagues died because of it – do you think anyone would ever let you forget that? I told them I was stressed, I snapped and I did it. I can take the backlash for that."

"That isn't fair," Carrie breathed.

"It's okay," he held her shoulders firmly. "Just let me handle this and everything will be okay."

She doubted if anything would ever be okay.

But she obeyed. Robot Carrie was obedient.

She had done the right thing, she told herself for the thousandth time. Whichever perspective she looked at it from, it was the wrong thing, but she had had no choice. People had died because of her, but more would have done so if she had given in to her feelings and let a family of gangsters go free. And the way he had cried that night, the way he made her promise…

Taehwan wouldn't have lasted a moment in a cell, especially knowing that it was her who put him there. It would have killed him; slowly, painfully, madly. To watch that happen and to know she had done it… she would have killed herself too. She had kept her promise. She had done the right thing. She had done her job and she had saved him. But in neither of her lives could she ever forgive herself.

<u>25 September 2015</u>

Carrie tried not to think about Operation Bluebird outside of the rehabilitation therapy room, but it was hard not to catch snippets of rumours and gossip, especially those around acts suspected to be the handiwork of ex-Splitter Drew Parry. Of course publicly DCS Hole denied that Drew had anything to do with the police force and anyone who knew was paid handsomely not to. He said it was for their safety. To his superiors and others in the division, DCS Hole hadn't been told the details of what David was doing to gain the Parks' trust and therefore DCS Hole could not be blamed. He was like Yoonho; they thought if they gave vague but leading instructions and let their fall guys take the risk then they themselves would be invincible – and most of the time they were right. It was David who received the dirty looks and unkind words while Hole lapped up praise and shut down

Wendy's requests for an internal investigation. There wasn't much that any of them could do about it.

The streetlamps and shop windows shone as they were supposed to as Carrie made her way home from the office. There was no rain or fog to warp them into things they weren't, to mess them up and make them think they belonged in a blur together. The stars stayed in the sky and London continued; ordered and unaware of the dimmed lights of Paradise Casino. The world had returned and the world was dead.

She stopped a while to gaze at the traffic lights; perfect circles of red that hung above the stationary cars and buses. The beams of their headlamps, trying so hard to spread and break the confines of marked lanes, were stopped in their tracks.

Her bag was heavy, weighed down by a debit card gorged with the proceeds of a backdated promotion. She didn't want blood money. She should spend it on wine. Wine and pretty lights.

<u>September 2015</u>

Wine and pretty lights, then daytime. Wine and pretty lights, then daytime. That was how she continued.

Carrie didn't want to talk about Operation Bluebird.

David also didn't want to talk about Operation Bluebird.

Cara didn't necessarily want to talk about Operation Bluebird – she wanted to be back living in it, but she couldn't do that without her brother. She didn't need David to be handling things and making it all okay, she needed him to be here. And if he couldn't be here, she needed the only person who could ever hope to make her feel better. But Taehwan wasn't in the daytime. So she needed the wine and the pretty lights.

October 2015

Wine and pretty lights. Then daytime.

November 2015

Wine and pretty lights. Then daytime.

December 2015

Wine and pretty lights. Then daytime.

27 December 2015

"You know what you said about having a person who knows who you really are?" she lowered her head onto David's shoulder. "How it stops you going crazy? I finally know what you mean."

Her brother's new flat was small and even more run down than the house they had lived in in the other world. It was full of beer bottles and dirty laundry and unopened envelopes that looked suspiciously like bills. He was finding the transition back to real life a lot harder than anyone had expected. He was David Watts, the Splitters veteran. But Soju had made the Splitters look tame and suspension during disciplinary proceedings was leaving his mind with too much time to think. The strain of insomnia had sunken his eyes, his chin was rough and unshaven and his t-shirt hung loosely about his neck where he had lost too much weight. He didn't care anymore.

"Hey," he gave her a comforting squeeze. "You're out now. Everyone knows who you are."

"No they don't," Carrie whispered. "They know a nice, hardworking, good cop. They don't know your headcase sister who does what she likes and fuck the consequences. They don't know the murderer."

"Or the girl who still loves Jay Park," David said softly.

"Stop saying that," she snapped, then instantly regretted it. It wasn't David's fault.

"Drew... David," she looked at him wretchedly. "I just need you to be my brother."

David sighed. "You know I'll always look out for you and you'll always be like my little sister, but Bluebird is over now. We have to forget it. You have to be Carrie Hart and I have to be David Watts, or we'll both go insane."

"I don't know who Carrie Hart is," her heart sank. "I need you."

"I'm fucked, Carrie," he rubbed his temples. He looked fucked. He wasn't cool, casual David or slippery salesman Drew; he was just fucked. "I've been fucked for a long time; it's not good for you to need me."

"David, you're a hero," Carrie said in alarm. David may have been fucked for a long time, but he had never admitted to it before. To hear him do so didn't feel right. "You've done all this before, you just need some more time to adjust."

"I messed up," he told her.

"*You* messed up?" she couldn't believe what she was hearing. "It was me who got a load of people shot."

"I was supposed to look after you," he put his head in his hands. "I'm a policeman; I'm supposed to look after people, but I did things, I let you do things – I *encouraged* you to do things."

"Brian Hole encouraged me to do things," she corrected him. "He encouraged you to do things – he's an arsehole... Why do only bad people have the guts to do good things?"

"Doesn't that make me a bad person too?" David asked.

"No," Carrie said firmly. "You're the only good person in this whole mess."

He shook his head. "You don't know the things Soju had me doing – and you don't ever need to know."

Carrie looked glumly at the ground.

"You never shot your boyfriend," she murmured. "Any good person couldn't have done that, or let you take the blame. I'm a heartless bitch."

"Carrie," David looked at her sternly. "What you did was stupid and he didn't deserve it, but it definitely wasn't heartless. Anyone else would've let him rot in jail – I would have. You're not heartless, you just fell in love with a prick."

She didn't reply. She wasn't sure what she hated more; being told she was in love or hearing him referred to as a prick. She was tired of denying it. David was right. He knew it and she knew it; she just didn't want to.

"I don't think I can do this anymore," he said quietly. "I'm just a downer; I'm dragging you back. And it's not your fault, but I look at you and all I can see is Bluebird... I'm guessing you feel the same."

It was true, but to her it was a comfort. She realised with a lurch that to David her presence was a curse.

"Why do you think I took the heat for you?" he asked. "You're doing great, and you're gonna keep doing great. My reputation doesn't matter though – I'm dropping out."

"You're leaving the force?" Carrie gasped in despair.

"The Spec-Ops team's families will be happy," he smiled sadly.

"They can fuck off!" Carrie exclaimed. "This should be me, not you! Y'know what, I'm done with this shit. I'm telling Wendy tomorrow."

"Listen to me," David commanded. "Telling them now won't do anyone any good; it'll just get us both in trouble."

"But why?" she questioned desperately. "This is all my fault, not yours!"

"Because I promised I'd look after you," he answered. "And because if you deny it enough you might forget it was ever true."

"It isn't true," she insisted. She needed to believe that.

He smiled at her with a bittersweet fondness. "Don't bullshit."

28 December 2015

The problem was that she and David had been living different movies, and while his company allowed Carrie to turn the television back on, all David wanted was to smash the screen and throw it out the window. Once upon a time she had honestly believed that Operation Bluebird would be over when Operation Bluebird was over. She could stop any time she wanted. Maybe she still didn't want to.

Carrie wasn't going to work today. She didn't need to be a robot. She didn't need Penny Reichs from Occupational Health trying to help her. She needed to figure out how to cheer David up and not have to lose her brother. She needed to talk to Taehwan, and she couldn't talk to Taehwan when she was sober.

Her phone buzzed as she pushed open the door of the off-license: David. She stuck her card between her teeth to free up a finger and opened the message.

"I'll always love you little sis

I'm sorry

Xx D"

Something was wrong.

Carrie felt sick. She punched in his number again and again but received no answer. She sprinted into the road and wrenched open the door of a taxi as she yelled down the phone at Wendy.

She jumped from the cab without paying, flying up the stairs to David's apartment. Sounds of the television floated through the flaking door – he was home, but he wasn't replying. She pounded on the wood, screaming his name to no response.

The world swum as Wendy arrived to hold her back while the police broke down the door. She hadn't seen it coming. She hadn't been looking both ways. There was no plan, no purpose, no lesson to be learned. Her brother was gone. Just like that.

"Brian Hole did this," Wendy wailed furiously. "He sacrificed you two like fucking animals!"

Carrie didn't care what Brian Hole had done. It was all her fault. She hadn't allowed him to let go. She had started a fight that he took the blame for. She had got him into Paradise Casino in the first place. If it wasn't for her, Drew Parry would still be navigating the London underworld, trying to catch the eye of Yoonho Park. If it wasn't for her, Taehwan Lee would be passed out on the roof with a condom on his face, still determinedly ignorant of his own loneliness. But because of her, David Watts was being wheeled away in a covered stretcher and Taehwan – she didn't even know where Taehwan was. It was unforgivable. She had been selfish and careless and she had killed them both.

"David!" she screamed as the paramedics hurried away to the lift, desperate for someone to deny what she already knew to be true.

Everything was gone. She didn't exist anymore. Operation Bluebird was over. She had done her job, justice was served; there was no need for Carrie Hart. She needed Cara. She needed herself back. She needed David. She needed Taehwan.

She stared into his living room. There was light streaming through the window. There was blood on the carpet. There was nothing left. She screamed. She broke. She ran.

37

"Cara?"

She swigged from her bottle. The drugs had set in nicely and she was hallucinating again. She let it take her. She was back at the casino. Whoever it was behind her, they were Taehwan for the night. He smelled like smoke and desperation; everyone did in this dive. It was enough. When she turned, it was Taehwan's face that stared back at her, reaching down to kiss her as she moved her hips against him. The music was shit but she could still dance.

"Cara!"

And there was Lisa to tell her that she should be working and shouldn't be wasting her time with him. But she loved him.

"It's red wine," she showed him the bottle and drank more herself. "You can always drink the red wine with me."

The shitty music and the cheap alcohol drilled into her brain, the room slipping away as they kissed again.

"Cara!"

Somebody pushed the man back. He wasn't Taehwan. He was just drunk.

"Piss off, you cretin," a strong American accent ordered him away.

She squinted through the disco lights and the grogginess of her own head.

"Lisa? Are you really Lisa?"

"Jesus, Cara, sweetheart, what are you doing here?" the woman seized her in a tight hug.

"Taehwan's here," she wobbled into her. "He went somewhere. Do you want some red wine? It's red."

"Oh sweetie," Lisa stroked the back of her head, still holding her tightly. "He's not here. Come on, let's get you outside; you've had enough."

"It's red wine," she tried to drink more over Lisa's shoulder but just managed to spill a load down her back.

"I know it is, hon," she said softly. "Let's go drink it outside."

"No, I need to wait for Taehwan," she slurred.

"He's outside already," Lisa promised. "Come on."

"Oh," she followed obediently. "Okay."

She looked about as the cold air hit her.

"Taehwan? Where is he? I can't see him."

"Oh honey," there were tears pricking at Lisa's eyes. She wasn't sure why. What was there to cry about? "You're tripping. Jay isn't here."

"You told me he was here!" she started to panic.

Something was wrong. Everything was cold outside. There wasn't enough dancing. There wasn't enough wine.

"Where's my wine? Why did you take my wine? I need my-"

"It's in your hand, sweetie," Lisa caught her as she was about to topple over.

She took another swig, most of it ending up on her chin.

"Where's Taehwan?" she looked wildly about, her heart hammering against her ribs. "He should be here. You're here. He should be here. I need more wine."

She downed the rest of the bottle then threw it to the ground in frustration. She couldn't see him. He had been there just moments ago. The bottle smashed at his feet. He was lying against the wall, head drooping unnaturally to his chest. He was bleeding. It poured in a steady stream from his mouth and soaked through his shirt. He was staring at her. It was her fault.

"Lisa!" she screamed as she tried to fight it back to her subconscious. It wasn't real. It was just a trip. He was alive, he was here, he was somewhere. "Let me go back! He's not outside!

He's in the wine, I can't lose him! I need more wine! Lisa, let me go! Taehwan! TAEHWAN!!!"

Lisa clung onto her as she shrieked in her ear. She couldn't take it. There were memories flashing that she didn't want to remember. It was all gone. That time. Her happiness. Her brother. Her best friend. Han. Margot. Everyone. Herself. It was all gone.

"NO!" she wailed into Lisa's shoulder. Her head was going to burst. She hoped it would. If heaven was Paradise she didn't want to be alive. "No, Lisa, he's not gone, you don't understand. He's in the pretty colours – he's in the red wine. HE'S NOT GONE!"

She broke, screaming at the top of her lungs. Her pulse was throbbing in her temples but she didn't really have a heart. Not anymore. She was a heartless bitch. Someone was a heartless bitch. Was it her? Who was her? Someone who couldn't stop screaming.

28 December 2017

She couldn't remember the journey to Lisa's house or anything that happened when they got there. All she knew was she woke up on a sofa in a worn-out apartment, with a banging headache and the horrible empty feeling of a comedown.

"Morning hon," Lisa said kindly. She was stood at a hob on the other side of the small room, hands on a pan and spatula. "I'm making us a good old greasy breakfast. Jennie, can you get Cara a glass of water?"

She hadn't noticed the other girl was there too. She had grown ghostly pale and scrawny. While she had always been strikingly slim, now she just looked ill. Lisa seemed to have aged ten years in the last two, despite the botox that stuck her forehead in place. She didn't want to think what she herself must look like.

"You okay?" Jennie perched on the sofa arm next to her and handed her a drink. "I know, stupid question. You're shit. We're all shit."

"Where've you been?" Lisa asked from the poor excuse for a kitchen, trying to keep her tone upbeat. "We thought you escaped with Margot."

"I don't know," she didn't try too hard to remember. There was Taehwan, there was her brother, then there was blur.

"The cops are still looking for you," Jennie informed her. "They ask every now and then if you've been round."

She shrank into the sofa. "Don't tell them."

"Of course not, hon," Lisa reassured her.

"What happened?" Jennie asked. "People say cops got to Drew, cut him a deal and the pig sold us out. They had information that only family would know."

She felt sick. She didn't want to talk about him. She didn't want to remember that Drew was David and David wasn't here.

"Leave it," Lisa warned. "No-one can help that now. It's not Cara's fault."

"Is it though?" Jennie scrutinised her with dark curiosity. "Did you know? Were you in on it?"

A sob escaped her mouth and her shoulders shook beneath the blanket. She wanted Taehwan. She needed Taehwan. She didn't do that to him. She loved him.

"Jesus, Jennie, look at her," Lisa snapped. "You think she'd be here if she was in on it? You think any of us would be? Cara, honey, ignore her. She's on the coke every night and it makes her cranky."

"Sorry," Jennie dropped her eyes guiltily. "Really, I'm sorry. I know you wouldn't hurt him."

"You have coke?" she asked weakly. "Or acid? Or wine? I really need some wine."

She didn't want to talk about things being her fault. She didn't want to see Lisa defending her or Jennie apologising. She wanted to see Taehwan.

"Yeah, sure," Jennie started. "It's-"

"Not now, hon," Lisa interrupted.

"Please," she begged. "Red wine was our thing. It makes me feel better."

"Cara, sweetheart," Lisa abandoned the breakfast to come over and pull her head onto her lap. "Jay wouldn't want you to be like this."

"He was always trying to get me drunk," she gave an empty laugh.

"He was try'n'a make you happy, sweetie," Lisa said softly. "This ain't happy."

She didn't deserve to be happy. She deserved to be drunk.

"Where's Lali?" she tried to distract herself. It would have been nice for them all to be together.

"Lali got deported," Jennie said sourly. "She killed a guy. The lawyers got her off for self-defence, but it meant admitting she got in on a dodgy visa."

"What?" she choked. "They found that out?"

Of course David would have reported it; he had no reason not to. He only knew because she told him.

"She went forward herself actually," Jennie chewed her lip. "Thought she could save Yoonho. Obviously she couldn't."

"What happened to him?" she asked, not sure if she wanted to know the answer.

"Yoonho was smart," Lisa told her. "It was the old man the pigs wanted bad, so he gave them everything he knew; reems and reems o' stuff. And you know how he was with business. They could say he knew things and let 'em happen but it was all conjecture, and can't nobody say he ordered any killing. Ten years – he got off light, considering. Clever, clever man."

"And Han?" her throat constricted.

Han had loved Taehwan as much as she did and Han had killed a lot of people. She herself had attested to that.

"Down for life," Lisa said sadly. "Can't be surprised really."

"Soju's still appealing," Jennie interjected. "Cops keep trying to buy us; saying they'll get us some fancy apartment in witness protection if we make up shit against him. I told them the next one who tries that will get a knife in the eye." She pulled a disgusted face.

"That was stupid," Lisa reprimanded her. "You're lucky you got off with a warning."

She wondered numbly if that had anything to do with her. She had always maintained that the dancers were innocents. Not her; the bitch.

<u>**03 January 2018**</u>

Days had no meaning without intoxication. The nightmares brought her closer, Jennie and Lisa's existence brought her closer, but he wasn't there. She didn't want to be in pain. She wanted to be in Paradise.

She waited until the girls were asleep, then threw on her clothes and started rifling through the drawers and cupboards. They had always been darlings to her and she didn't want to be taking their money, but she was weak. Without Taehwan, she barely even existed. She needed the wine and the hallucinations.

Lisa awoke to the sound of her talking in the living room. She was speaking in slurs, but she was speaking to him.

"Cara, honey," she opened the door. "What are you doing?"

She was sitting back against the wall with her eyes closed, chattering happily, but she opened them at the sound of Lisa's voice. Her daydreams faded and she sunk back into the dilapidated room. It was dark and there was nobody there. Only her and Lisa. Despair dragged her down beneath the moulding floorboards.

"I know," she said dully. "He's not here. Taehwan's dead. Drew's dead. Cara's dead."

But that was the problem: Cara wasn't dead. Cara was insane.

She waited for Lisa to go back to bed, then made a run for it. She didn't need money, or shoes or a jacket. Cara was never going to go away, so she would always have nightmares and she would always remember and she would always be broken for the rest of her life.

She leant out over the river, watching the ghost of Ripley's yacht making its way through the darkness. She could see them swimming through the current to Bermondsey Beach, full of life and blissfully unaware of what was coming. She had been drowning ever since. At least she knew one thing; if prison would have made Taehwan feel like this then she had been right to save him.

She moved her numb fingers and tried to feel his between them. She should do what she wanted, he told her. She wanted to follow him. Cara belonged with Taehwan. Taehwan was dead. David was dead. Cara had to be dead too. And if killing Cara Parry killed Carrie Hart too, then so be it.

She kissed him goodbye and fell into the Thames.

38

"Carrie," Penny called as her and Fiona headed to the door of the therapist's home office. "Do you mind if I speak to your sister for a moment?"

"Sure," Carrie shrugged and returned that annoying strand of hair to its place behind her ear. "I'll wait in the car."

She made her way down the corridor, opened and shut the front door then doubled back to eavesdrop.

"How is she really?" Penny was asking. "Has she told you anything at all that happened on the case; anything that might trigger a relapse?"

"Nothing," Fiona confirmed. "I honestly believe her when she says she doesn't remember… most of the time."

"Most of the time?" Penny repeated.

"She has dreams," Fiona admitted. "I think they might be flashbacks of sorts."

"Did she tell you this?" Penny inquired.

"No," she replied. "You know what she's like; doesn't want to inconvenience anyone. I used to hear her sometimes when she was staying with me. Now if I ask her about sleep she avoids the question, so I can only assume they haven't stopped."

Her sister was correct. She did still have dreams, though she could hardly remember them. They were a dance of red and blue and gold to her conscious mind, but she woke from them feeling unbearably guilty or lonely or scared, and on occasion inappropriately horny. They weren't conducive to a practical life, so she kept herself busy and awake as much as possible; when her mind and body were sufficiently exhausted, she had no energy to dream.

That was why she needed Penny Reichs from Occupational Health to sign her off for reinstatement. Volunteering was all well and good, but she was a detective and she needed that state of intense concentration on a case to keep her safe. She had done the right thing and believing that was all she needed; she didn't need to remember details, even in her sleep.

"She is ready to go back," Fiona confirmed. "She hasn't touched a drop since she came to stay with me, and she's absolutely great with George – my son. She's even adopted a cat since she moved out. It's like she hit reset and started a completely new life."

"You do realise blank slates can't last forever," Penny sighed. "I agree with you that work will be good for her and I will recommend that the force give her something in the office, but one day that wall in her head is going to crack. We both have to keep an eye out for any signs at all and be prepared to be there for her, however fine she says she is. She may never tell us what happened, but we have to be ready when whatever it is catches up with her."

"I will be," Fiona promised.

It would last forever, Carrie assured herself. As soon as she stopped having to go to these stupid meetings that tried to remind her of things, she could get on with her life. If she really had felt how David said she did, then she owed it to both of them to continue fighting the cause they had died for. She owed it to David to keep her promise, and never to talk or think about Operation Bluebird again. She could do that.

Except she couldn't.

Because she killed Taehwan Lee. She loved Taehwan Lee.

And nobody could ever know.

HARRY OLD

*

OPERATION BLUEBIRD

*

<u>**Debrief: Han**</u>

<u>**04 January 2016**</u>

Taejong sat with his elbows on the table, chin resting on his hands. To anybody else he might look completely emotionless; a robot waiting to be turned on. It was how he had lived most of his life. He had thought it was the best way to protect them. He had failed.

His father – the man whom Taeyoon had served and he had protected ever since they could talk – had abandoned them all. For all his talk of family, he had never loved any of them. Understandably, Taeyoon had sold him out for less time inside, which meant selling Taejong along with him. He didn't mind the betrayal; he would have given himself willingly to save his brother. Taeju kept fighting, though he wouldn't be surprised if it was more for entertainment than a fear of prison. He had never had the pain thresholds of a normal person. It was like he had given all his suffering to Taehwan.

And now Taehwan was dead, and there had been no better option for him. That was Taejong's biggest failing.

"Han."

He looked up at his visitor. Jerome had been loyal to him ever since they met as teenagers in the gutters of London, and he had kept him spotless; a simple casino security man. They had thought it would be useful to have somebody on the outside in a situation such as this. Currently, Taejong didn't see much point. The family was decimated. There was nobody left to protect.

"Drew Parry's dead," the man informed him. "Apparently suicide. It wasn't us, so I guess that must be true."

He supposed any normal person would be pleased, but he saw no reason to be. Vengefulness helped nobody.

"I don't think he was just a CI," Jerome said solemnly. "He was with the Splitters when they went down, and the things they knew about you; it was too thorough to just be someone saving his own skin from jail."

"You think he was a cop," Taejong observed. He sighed. "I think so too."

It had been his sole purpose to seek out threats like that and remove them from the equation. He hadn't.

"And so his sister-"

"Must have been one too," he finished his sentence.

"I'll find her," Jerome promised. "I'll get to the bottom of this."

Taejong rubbed his temples. "I don't want to know. It wouldn't help anyone."

"But Sir," Jerome hesitated. "She has to pay for what she did."

Taejong exhaled heavily. "Cara became part of my family. I swore I'd look after her."

"Han," the security chief persisted. "If this is true, Cara was never real."

"Yes she was," Taejong mused. "She still is."

Perhaps she had a different name and a different past, but she had loved his brother. Of that one thing he was certain. He thought back on the girl's pretty face. The way she had laughed when he did something stupid, the way she had looked at him when other people were talking, how she went to him when she was scared and how she cried in the hospital like she was dying along with him. She had stood up for him to their father, and to Taejong himself even though Taehwan wasn't there to see it. None of that was an act.

Taejong had missed all of Drew's signals because he had been blinded by the honesty of his sister. It was the perfect ruse and it hadn't even been deliberate.

"So what do you want me to do?" Jerome asked.

Taejong looked thoughtfully at his loyal servant.

"Nobody touches her," he instructed. "That's my final order. Other than that… there's an account in Panama that Yoonho made untraceable. Get a message to Margot; she has access. Work a security job for a man named Fry and he'll give you whatever payment you ask for. You can live a good, clean life and you never have to see me again. Just make sure that nobody touches Cara Parry."

It would be their secret, for Taehwan's sake. Perhaps it was selfish of him, but he wanted to know that there was somebody alive in the world who loved his brother as much as he did. She would be suffering intensely; that was punishment enough.

He took his mother's cross out from under his shirt and kissed it: for her, for Emilia, for his brothers and for Cara.

Perhaps she was undeserving of his sympathy, but perhaps this had all been a long time coming. Even they couldn't outrun the law forever. Even if the old man hadn't sent Taehwan down himself as he had done with Taeju, they all tried too hard and they made mistakes – especially their youngest. Taeju wanted an agent he could control, Taeyoon wanted dancers to confide in and Taehwan wanted somebody to care about him – there would have been other Caras and other Drews. Ones who wouldn't have given his little brother so much happiness for once in his miserable life. Ones who wouldn't have understood him enough to pull the trigger rather than sentencing him to what would have been a living hell.

Taejong knew that no special operations cop had taken that shot. He knew that it had been clear to anyone that Taehwan was not going to escape. Whoever she was, the girl was no killer, but she had done it for him. Because he had begged her to. Because she loved him.

And he had known it, until the end. Taehwan had then and Taejong did now.

For his brother's sake, he would never forget those two things. Even if he was the only person in the world, Taejong Lee would always know.

The biggest thanks to my siblings for starting all this.

Thanks to Jack and Suhwan for coping with my Bluebird-related breakdowns.

Thanks to Ed and Ashley for being my sin consultants.

Thanks to Daehyun for everything.

Existing titles

Not Yet Dead, Nearly

Pigeons

www.harryold.com

Twitter & Instagram: @harrycantadult